A LIE IS BORN
LONDON

Seventeen Years Ago

A black car idled in the drive of a dark Georgian house, the window slightly cracked to allow the sharp November air in and heart-wrenching sobs out. In the car's driver's seat, a young man with limp, dark hair bent over the steering wheel, gripping it tightly as his body wracked with tears. The night outside was silent, save for the man's sobs and the soft patter of midnight rain on the windshield. As he cried, oblivious to anything but his pain, a sharp knock rapped against the window.

The man's head snapped up, red-rimmed eyes peering through the glass.

Standing on the drive, an elderly man in a black rain coat holding a sturdy umbrella waited for the crying man to unroll the window. "Excuse me," he asked loudly. "I'm looking for the man who lives on Blair Street; in the house with the red door."

The man inside the car blinked several times with puffy eyes before finally rolling down the window. "What?" he croaked, voice rough and scratchy as if he'd been screaming at the top of his lungs for days. "What is it? I can't go back inside. I can't. I'm sorry."

"No," said the man with the umbrella. "I am trying to ask if you are the man who lives on Blair Street. In the house with the red door?"

Again, the man inside the car blinked. "Yes," he finally managed. "That's me."

"Good," said the man with the umbrella. "I've been wandering these streets all evening looking for you."

"I'm sorry," replied the man in the car, "but this isn't a good time. If you're trying to sell me something, you best be on your way."

"No, nothing like that," insisted the man with the umbrella. "I've come with a rather special invitation."

"An invitation to what?" The man in the car frowned. He was not the type to receive invitations, special or otherwise.

"For coffee, to start."

"Coffee?" The man reverently shook his head. "I don't think so. Now is not a good time. So, if you'll just back up a step," he tried to shoo the old man away, "I'll be going."

The old man, having none of it, wedged the wooden umbrella handle in the window so it could not be budged. "Please," he began, moving his face inches from the young man's, revealing wrinkles, age spots, haunting pale blue eyes and decades' worth of wear, "just one coffee. That's all I ask."

"Please get back." The man in the car attempted to dislodge the umbrella, but it remained firmly fixed. Annoyed, he turned his grey eyes, the color of sea squalls, on the old man. "The rain is getting all over my dash. Please, go away."

The old man leaned closer, so both were shadowed under the umbrella's black tarp. "It's something of an important proposition, really, one that could very well save your life."

The man in the car paled, swallowing a giant lump in his throat. "What do you mean?" he asked, the words tripping over themselves to escape his dry, chapped lips.

"That was your plan, wasn't it?" the old man arched a wiry, white brow. "To kill yourself. Tonight. That's why you're here – in front of *this* building, wrapping up loose ends and what not?"

The man in the car made a startled grunt deep in his throat and tightened his hands around the steering wheel. "Who are you?" he asked with a hint of concern and a heavy heap of indignity. "Have you been following me?"

"There is plenty of time to explain," replied the old man. "Now how about that cup of coffee?"

For a moment, the man in the car said nothing, staring pointedly at the old man as if deciding whether he had been sent by God to save him. "Alright then," he finally agreed, releasing the steering wheel as if releasing his grip on life. "Just one cup."

The old man smiled, pleased, and stepped back, allowing the younger to exit the car. The door creaked as the young man climbed from the driver's seat, slowly, as if he were the one with rusty old joints.

When the two stood face-to-face, the elder man tipped his head and nodded down the road. "This way." He adjusted the umbrella high above his head and started down the street.

At the end of the block, the old man stopped by a warmly lit diner and when the younger caught up he stepped inside with sly, wrinkled smile, as if he knew something the other did not - as if he'd known all along the young man would follow. "Table for two," he said, raising two fingers to a hostess who greeted them with ginger hair and dark blue eyeliner.

The hostess nodded, grabbing two plastic menus from behind the counter and walking the damp, downtrodden men to an out-of-the-way booth.

After pouring them each a cup of coffee, the hostess departed and the old man reached into his breast pocket to pull out a card, sliding it across the table to the younger man. "Do you know what this is?" he asked, giving it a tap.

The young man scrutinized the card, squinting at it without touching it. It was larger than an average playing card with the image of an average-looking man standing over a table crowded with cups, coins, wands and swords. At the bottom, scrawled in thick black letters, were the words *The Magician*. "It's some sort of playing card," he replied. "With pictures instead of suits."

"Close," the man with the umbrella replied. "It's called a *Tarot* card." He tapped the card again with a bony finger. "Do you know anything about Tarot?"

"No," admitted the younger man, eyes still swollen with earlier tears. He grabbed a handful of napkins from the dispenser and ran the wad under his dripping nose, sniffling. "What's Tarot? What does it have to do with me?"

"This playing card is not just a card but a representation of someone very real. *The Magician,* he is called, one of seventy-eight members of the secret society known as the Order of the Tarot, dating back to the beginning of humanity."

The younger man looked startled and a little worried for the old man's sanity, stirring his coffee and staring purposefully into the watery-brown depths. "I've never heard of anything called the Order of the Tarot. Is it like a club?"

"Heavens no," chuckled the old man. "It's a *secret* society. And it wouldn't be very secret if you've heard of it, now would it?"

"I suppose not," replied the man dryly. "How stupid of me."

"There are seventy-eight members of the Tarot," the old man went on, as if the young man was right on board, "each as different and important as the next." Once again the old man reached into his breast pocket and pulled out another card. He set this on top of the first, still untouched. This card was of a medieval knight in polished silver armor charging on a black stallion toward an enemy with a blazing sword raised high above his head, the scene set against a blood-red sky. "This card, for example, is called the Knight of Swords. This card represents - well, me," he said proudly, placing a hand to his heart.

It was then the young man caught the flash of something green glowing against the old man's left palm, now firmly pressed to his heart. He frowned, studying the old man from behind lowered lashes. "What's that, on your hand?"

The old man glanced down where his hand remained over his heart. "Ah," he smiled softly and slowly lifted his hand to show the younger man. "This is the mark of the Knight of Swords. Each member of the Tarot carries a unique mark, given to them by our master, the Magician. As long as it glows green, my vow is true, and I am linked to the rest of the Tarot. Should it fade to black, it means one of two things: either I am dead, or I have broken my sacred vow, and thus my link to the Tarot."

The young man studied the old man's palm without moving. It was smooth and wrinkled with thousands of lines, some fine and thin, other deep with age; and in the center of his gnarled palm was a dark tattoo of the knight, sword raised as he raced toward battle. The ink, though dark and rich, was not black, but a phosphorous green that seemed to burn against his pale skin. "It glows," was all he managed to mutter, amazed.

"It does," the old man replied. "Drawn by the Scared Wand – by magic."

At the mention of a magic the young man's frown deepened, creasing his brow. "Magic? You have magic?"

"Oh, no, no." The old man waved a theatrical hand. "I'm not magic, the Magician holds the magic. I am just bound to his service by it. As a knight of the Order of the Tarot I conduct the Magician's work, do his bidding, run his errands, if you will."

"The Magician?" the younger man squinted, as if trying to decide if this was some tragic, practical joke and he was being filmed for someone's entertainment.

"He's not a true magician; at least not the kind with rabbits and hats and tricks. The first Magician of the Tarot was the original. The very first magician to ever exist. And he held all the power of our world."

"Well, sure."

Ignoring the young man, the older continued. "Our Magician leads the Order of the Tarot. He is the master of the cards, so to speak, he ties us all together, binds us through our markings. Without him, the Tarot and each of the seventy-eight members would not be bound. His life is precious and his role in our world is pivotal."

"Uh huh." The young man drummed an impatient finger against his coffee mug. "And what kind of work do you do for this Magician, Mr. Knight?"

"Ah," the old man raised a finger, "I do this." He waved a skeletal hand between them, pocked with age spots and bulging blue veins. "I recruit." He shrugged. "Back in the early days I suppose I would have done a lot more knightly things: fought battles, silenced evil, destroyed anyone who wished to take our power. Today it's a simpler job. Mostly I scour the world searching for new members to replace the dying."

"And you are what? Trying to recruit me?"

The old man gave a curt nod.

"I don't understand. Why would anyone want someone like me? I'm a nobody. I push paper for a living. I know nothing about secret societies or magic or anything you'd be interested in. In fact, I am sure you have the wrong person."

The old man frowned, but battled on. "Let me explain a bit more, maybe then you'll understand. As I've said, I am the Knight of Swords. When I was recruited, many, many years ago, I, like all members of the Tarot, was required to take a very serious vow. With this vow I was marked by the Magician." He flashed his green tattoo. "With this mark I was bound to the other members of the Tarot, all seventy-eight. If a member of the Tarot dies, naturally or otherwise, or breaks their vows, their marking blackens and their place within the Order becomes vacant. If this happens, the balance that existed among the carefully chosen seventy-eight members is undone, and our purpose is threatened."

The man from the car raked a hand through his hair, blinking widely, as if to clear the nonsense. "What does that mean? What is your purpose and what does it matter if a place within this Order is empty?"

"Our world is a complex system," replied the so-called Knight of Swords – who didn't look very knightly, as old and wrinkled as he was. "We live in relationship to one another; one man is good, he rides his bike to work, and prays, and recycles. Another is bad; he plots and connives, and murders others while they sleep. We live in relationship to all living things – trees grow, they give us oxygen. Trees grow - we cut them down. We live in relationship to the Earth - it rains, you get wet. It snows, you are cold. It's hot and dry and there is no water for miles – you die of exposure and thirst. The Earth spins, we stay grounded. It stops spinning – we all die."

The younger man listened intently while ripping open a pack of sugar and stirring it into his coffee. "I am a smart man, Mr. Knight. I went to college. I know our world is complex, but I'm not sure what this has to do with me, or you, for that matter."

"It has everything to do with me – and you – and the Tarot."

"But what is this Tarot. What is the *purpose*?"

The old knight leaned back in the vinyl-covered booth, a small smile tilting across his wizened face. "Once I explain the answer to that question, my friend, you cannot un-hear the things I've said."

A brown coffee ring remained on the table as the young man raised the mug to his lips, considering. Eventually, he shrugged. "Believe me when I say, old man, I do not have much to lose."

"So, I understand," the knight replied. "But what I'm about to tell you is rather extraordinary, to say the least."

"I'm listening."

"Very well," the old man tipped his head, leaning forward as if to invite the young man into his inner circle. "The seventy-eight members of the Order of the Tarot are carefully chosen to be perfectly balanced against one another, as they are perfectly balanced within our world and our solar system and the universe. They each relate differently to the Earth's forces and elements and each other. Together, they cement the balance of forces and energy that hold our world together. If you leave here today and buy a deck of Tarot cards, much of what I'm explaining will be visible right there in the cards. Each card has a purpose, a force, energy, and each card interacts with those opposing it. Without one, the deck is not whole and it does not work as it should. The deck of Tarot cards is loosely based on the Order's existence, but the truth is hidden in plain sight. One missing card leads to an incorrect Tarot card reading or an inaccurate game. Translated into our existence - one missing member of the Order of the Tarot leads to the unbalance of opposing forces, and eventually to the destruction of Earth. Through our vows, markings, and relationship to one another, the Tarot keeps the world in balance. It keeps the opposing forces equal so no force is greater than the other."

"I don't understand," the young man scratched his head, his face scrunched in deep thought. "You're telling me these seventy-eight members of the Tarot keep our world balanced because they have each been chosen and marked by a Magician? And these marks, these vows, all connect to one another, and create balance for every opposing force in the universe?"

"Precisely."

"Right. Seems a little farfetched, Mr. Knight, don't you think?"

The old knight smiled wryly, opening his hands in a conceding gesture. "Of course it does. But so do most things in our universe. After all, we are a system of beings living on a spinning rock, floating in the middle of a vast weightless, colorless, ocean, gliding through a plane of space toward...nothing. The sun, the stars, the tides, gravity...it all seemed a little farfetched once, didn't it?"

The younger man tipped his head in agreement. "I suppose. But this…you're talking about magic and markings and secret societies that keep our world from destroying itself."

"What I am talking about is not something you do not already know. For every action there is an equal and opposite reaction – physics 101."

Again, the man from the car nodded. "That is true, but -"

"The Order of the Tarot is nothing more than a physical representation of that law. Every person on this planet holds energy that interacts with the invisible forces around them. You can see it in the way your heart beats – tiny electrical currents running through our bodies keeping us alive." The old knight thumped his marked hand over his heart, *thump, thump, thump, thump*. "And when the right people are placed in relation to one another and bound by the right magic, it creates an intricately woven blanket, each like a knot, holding our precarious cosmic system together. If one knot slips… well, let's just say the world can't survive when one force becomes too strong and there is nothing to oppose it. Eventually that force will destroy everything around it."

"Okay," said the man from the car, setting his cup aside, "say this is all true. Say there is an Order of the Tarot controlling the world's opposing forces by marking seventy-eight people and binding them together with magic – say there are seventy-eight chosen members, to be exact –and each of those members relate to one another to balance everything around them, creating stability for our world. What does that balance mean? What happens if one of the seventy-eight is killed? Or breaks this 'vow', you speak of?"

"Destruction," the old knight offered. "Chaos. The world will be off kilter and eventually, if it is unbalanced for long enough, the world will destroy itself, either through natural disaster or war or disease. Take this for example: you put two eggs on each end of a teeter-totter. Both weight exactly the same and thus the teeter-totter is perfectly balanced, suspended in harmony as long as no other factor invades. One of the eggs breaks – either by its own force or by something else's doing – the teeter-totter is now unbalanced. One end crashes to Earth and the other egg breaks on impact. Our world works much the same. When something is unbalanced it trickles down, like the Butterfly Effect – it may start small, like a fight, which leads to hate, which leads to crime, which leads to unrest, which leads to war. Or the opposite. If there is too much good in this world, it is no better outcome than too much hate. If there is too much good, there is no competition, and with no competition there is no purpose and the economy will weaken, and a weak economy leads to poverty, which in turn leads to starvation and death. The thing to remember is the smallest change can have the biggest impact. A chain-reaction. The world needs balance. Without it, anything can happen. War, natural disaster, famine... it's impossible to predict how one small change will impact the entire world. The Tarot exists to keep the balance perfectly in check. To prevent dissymmetry. Our seventy-eight members represent each and every type of energy force on Earth: good, evil, strong, weak, wealth, poverty, air, water, fire…the list goes on. All those forces are perfectly balanced against one another within the Tarot, and our markings bind us to together, which in turn binds those energy forces to the world. Think of the Tarot as a miniature eco-system. If our energy is balanced within our system, our ancient bond to the Earth balances the greater cosmic system; like a reflection, or a growing wave."

The young man folded his arms across his chest, staring fixatedly at the knight.

"Have you heard of the Philosopher Heraclitus?"

"Cannot say that I have."

"Ah, well. It might help to mention him in all of this. You see Heraclitus was an ancient Greek philosopher. He was also a member of the Order of Tarot. In fact, in his day he was the Magician himself. He preached the Unity of Opposites. He stated that every element was an opposite, or connected to an opposite, and those opposites couldn't exist without one another. Water is cold, so fire is hot. And within those opposites there is always war. The universe is in constant change, but it also remains the same. The Unity of Opposite is present in the universe as both difference and sameness. Heraclitus once said, 'It is wise to agree that all things are one. In differing it agrees with itself, a backward-turning connection, like that of a bow and a lyre. The path up and down is one the same.' You see, a slanted road has the opposite qualities of ascent and descent, yet they are, in fact, one in the same. It is our job as Tarot to ensure all those opposites co-exist and remain balanced against one another. Without one opposite, the other could not exist harmoniously.

"And you truly believe all this?"

"Oh yes," said the old knight, folding his hands neatly on the laminate tabletop. "I have been the Knight of Swords for seventy-three years. My time is running short, and soon someone will replace me, but I have lived a long life, my friend, and I have seen and experienced many things."

"And what, exactly, do you want from me?" the young man raised his red-rimmed eyes, lashes still damp with tears. "I have nothing. I am a broken man. I would fit no mold to uphold any balance within your Order."

"That's not true." The old knight reached across the table and tapped the card of the Magician. "You fit this mold. Perfectly, in fact."

THE BOOK OF ATHIOS
LONDON

Six Months Later

From the corner of a dark room, a baby cooed in a bassinette, reaching toward a man talking animatedly above her.

"Don't you see – ?" the man interrupted himself, pausing to scrub a hand over his stubbled chin. "What should I call you?" After a deep moment of thought, he raised a triumphant finger. "I know – I'll call you Ophelia, after my mother. She was a bit daft and died of pneumonia when I was fifteen, but who the hell isn't daft these days? You'll be clever, though. I'll ensure it."

The baby gurgled, laughing and stretching chubby fingers toward the man.

The man frowned. "Maybe we should start early? It can't hurt. If I'm going to train you to help me, you should know the basics before you can talk. Maybe that way you'll listen. I've been told children are prone to excessive chatter." Smiling softly, the man left the bassinette and crossed the room to a long work bench. Microscopes, hissing beakers, charts and diagrams scattered the table and among the clutter he found a leather-bound book and bottle of milk. Eagerly, he grabbed both items and took them back to the happy, babbling baby. "Ophelia," said the man, giving her the bottle then raising the book. "Do you know what this is?"

The baby grasped the bottle tight and began sucking, making smacking noises with her tiny lips.

"It's the book of Athios." As the man held the heavy book over the baby, light captured the symbol stamped on the front cover: a golden circle with the Greek letter Alpha (α) placed at the center. "And do you know who Athios is?"

The baby grunted in response.

"Athios is the ancient founder of the Order of Science Against Magic. He despised Heraclitus and his Unity of Forces and he made it his life mission to stop Heraclitus and the Tarot from controlling our world with magic."

Again, the baby grunted, this time adding a small burp.

"By the time you're old enough to read, you will have the entirety of this text memorized. Do you know why, Sweet Pea?" The man waited a beat, as if the baby might actually respond. "Because we cannot let dark magic destroy Earth. We cannot rely on something as flimsy as magic and hocus pocus to control something as important as the world's delicate balance. But, don't you worry, little Ophelia, your Uncle Milo will make everything okay. It took me six long months, but I finally found this book – the key. It was given to me by a colleague in the ancient literature department. Can you believe that? All that time at the university and the answer was right under my nose. A scientific solution to this madness! And all I have to do is build it!" Milo hiccupped a laugh, as if amused by his brilliance, and opened the book to the center where a complicated diagram of a clockwork world surrounded in sums and calculations spread across the yellowed page. "Once we build it, and once we discover the secret of how to destroy them from within, the Magician will have no choice but to dissolve his magic cult and let us – no," he shook his head, correcting himself, "let *science* take control." Milo balled his fits tight, a wicked sneer creeping over his face as he tucked the baby goodnight.

THE MAGICIAN
KRAKOW

Present Day

Shadows stretched across the ornate plaster ceiling of the tea shop late into the afternoon while low lit lamps cast amber light over faded floral wallpaper. Among the clutter of mismatched sofas and chairs sat a man who once, long ago, was found sobbing in his car. Now, he was known simply as *The Magician.*

The door to the tea shop opened, chiming a merry string of bells as a young man entered. Alert, the Magician's head snapped up, his gaze fixing on the newcomer. The young man was handsome, no older than twenty, dark, slender and tall like a naval officer - though he held no such title. As the young man approached, he unwound a red scarf from about his neck, lifting his eyes to meet the Magician's. There was a spark of recognition there, but neither man smiled or made any motion of greeting.

"Magician," the young man spoke. It was a lifeless salutation, the way someone might greet an old friend who had once wronged them.

"Jude," the Magician replied, his voice equally unmoving, though it held the hint of something kinder unsaid. Something like, 'It's good to see you'.

With a stiff nod, Jude lowered himself into a high-backed chair, grasping the arms like restraints. The Magician studied him carefully, wondering how to begin.

An elderly waitress appeared, filling Jude's teacup from a steaming pot. "Thank you," he muttered, leaving it untouched.

Across the table the Magician shifted in his seat, tugging at the sleeves of his suit jacket, trying to hide the marks creeping down his wrists. Beneath the fitted fabric, the Magician's skin was nearly completely covered by green tattoos matching the marking of his followers. Up and down his arms, across his chest and wrists and back he was marred by the symbols and signs of the Tarot, each mark connecting him to one of his followers. A few of the tattoos were even black, like that of his old friend the knight, gone dead with their passing. At night, when he stood alone in front of the mirror, the Magician tried his best not to look at those black marks. They were heavy and ugly and reminded him of death. Right now he was trying to ignore the presence of the mark connecting him to Jude, a small tattoo of knight and sword imprinted on his right arm, just above the elbow. The Magician relaxed when the waitress finally moved away, leaving the pair alone again. "I didn't think you'd come," he said to Jude, surprised, yet relieved the young knight had chosen to meet.

Jude tossed him a cold look, one of many meanings, and said, "Of course I came. I took a vow, didn't I? I have the mark to prove it." Jude held out his left hand, palm up, revealing the familiar pulsing green tattoo of a knight on horseback charging with a sword outstretched. It was nearly identical to the one on the Magician's arm and to the old man's who had been Jude's predecessor, though Jude's tattoo was not marred by age.

The Magician remembered the old knight fondly and a great sadness washed over him. He missed his old friend and wanted so bad to be the mentor for Jude the old knight had been to him. "So," said the Magician, brushing away the tattered memories and lifting his cup from the table, "Krakow?"

Jude nodded.

"Why here, of all places?" The Magician's gaze ventured to the window where the tea shop was tucked into a gothic corridor of Krakow's historic Old Town. He knew Jude had been desperate to escape his life as Knight of Swords – though not so far as to forsake his vow – not yet, anyway. But Krakow was hundreds of miles away from anyone who could possibly understand what he was going through.

Jude gave a languid shrug. "Why not? It's as good a place as any. And it's far from Tarot headquarters."

"For one, you don't speak Polish."

"Skąd wiesz?"

The Magician frowned, deepening the faint lines around his tired grey eyes. In the muted light of the shop they appeared hectic and stormy, like the crashing Norwegian Sea off the coast of the Faroe Islands. The Magician knew he'd been tough on the young Knight of Swords, but now, withering with the years, the Magician found repent in his heart and wondered if it was possible to ease before it was too late. As he looked at Jude, once his proudest accomplishment, he felt the sting of sorrow. This boy, turned young man, would never forgive him. And if Jude knew the truth it would surely destroy him. "I didn't want to disrupt you," The Magician said, pulling himself together with practiced ease. "But I'm afraid I've come with bad news."

Jude nodded once, as if to say, 'I know' and waited patiently for the Magician to go on.

The Magician reached into his breast pocket and withdrew a single card. It was similar to the one the old knight had given him that first night, only this one was leafed with gold. He held it for a moment then set it face up. The card was of a beautiful, fair haired woman on a seashell throne, water lapping at the rocks by her feet, staring dreamily into a gold goblet Alone under a cloudless blue sky, her expression was wistful and pensive: the Queen of Cups.

"She's dying?" asked Jude, staring intently without touching the card.

The Magician nodded. "She will not live out the month. The time has come. We must find her replacement."

"Has she predicted who?"

The Magician nodded. He thought of the dying queen: Maggie, a woman that had been with the Order of the Tarot long before he'd been recruited to lead. As Queen of Cups Maggie could see the future and her job was to predict new members when the old passed on. Before he'd travelled to Krakow, the Magician had spoken with the dying queen in her bedroom – curtains heavy, dark, the air thick with incense and sickness. There she had predicted her replacement: a young fortune-teller in Paris, waiting desperately for a new life.

Jude looked at the card again, longer this time, and the Magician knew he was drumming up memories of the dying queen. She had been kind to Jude, warm and loving, like a grandmother, taking him under her wing and protecting him from the darker forces of the Order. Jude had been so young when he'd replaced the old Knight of Swords, no older than three - just a child without a clue, thrust into the regimented life of Tarot before he'd been old enough to understand. That alone made the Magician's heart break. How could he expect Jude to forgive him for forcing this difficult life upon him, when he couldn't even forgive himself?

"Where is she?" asked Jude, concern creasing his brow. "Is she in pain?"

The Magician did not answer immediately, struggling for the right words. He took another sip of tea, letting the cup linger by his lips. "She's at the manor. We're doing what we can, but her time is running short. A week. Maybe two. She must be replaced, or we risk upsetting the balance."

Jude's eyes filled with expressive pain, though he did not shed a tear. "I'm not sure I'm the right knight for the job. Maybe you should ask the others? I haven't recruited in a long time."

The Magician's heart ached for the loneliness Jude must feel. Chosen as the Knight of Swords he was forbidden to love. All members of the Order were required to follow a strict set of rules, defined by their determined roles in order to uphold balance of opposing forces. As the Knight of Swords, Jude's mandate was to remain strong, and steadfast, focused on the job. His was a powerful force in the universe and there was no room left for love – that was his opposition, and it killed him. It also meant he could not love the Queen of Cups as he'd wanted to: like a grandson. And now he'd have to honor the dying queen another way - by finding her replacement. "I realize this is difficult," the Magician continued, "but she asked for you personally. I imagine you wouldn't want to disappoint her after all these years."

Jude challenged the Magician's stare. The hands on the clock above the Magician's head ticked, waiting for someone to make the next move. Several tense moments later, Jude sighed and took the card from the table, tucking it protectively in his breast pocket – exactly as the Magician knew he would. "Where am I going?"

From behind his cup, the Magician smiled, and once again reached into his pocket, this time presenting a train ticket. Silently, he slid it across the table, revealing the hint of green tattoo snaking beneath his shirt cuff.

Jude took the ticket, examining the destination. "Paris?" he asked, sounding vaguely interested.

The Magician gave a small nod and pulled a second item from his pocket: a folded yellow paper.

Jude tucked the ticket away with the card and unfolded the paper. "This is her? The girl Maggie predicted as her replacement?"

The Magician nodded.

"Why her? She looks a little…rough. Are you sure she's right for the job? You're sure she's one of the seventy-eight?"

The Magician raised a wispy brow. "She must be, because Maggie predicated it so, and the Queen of Cups has never been wrong. Not once." With a sharp nod, Jude stood, tucking the paper away. As he turned to leave, the Magician stopped him. "Jude."

It seemed the young knight would ignore him, but then he stopped, turning his face back, though his eyes remained fixed on the floor. "What is it?"

"She had a vision about you, too."

Embers smoldered behind Jude's eyes as he looked back to the Magician. "And?"

"Remember your vow."

The green mark pulsed across Jude's palm in time with the quickening of his heart. "It is impossible to forget." With that Jude turned sharply on his heels and left the tea shop.

After, the Magician sat alone and finished his tea. He paid for both cups, including the one untouched, tipped the waitress generously and left.

THE SCIENTIST
LONDON

Huddled over a cluttered desk, Milo sat before an open notebook filled corner to corner with tiny black scrawl. "It will work," he muttered, squeezing another formula onto the page, so entwined with diagrams and mathematical calculations it smeared. On the wall behind him hung accolades and degrees from Oxford and Columbia and other exceptional universities from around the world, flickering eerily in a humming green light.

"It will work," he repeated as his hand moved quickly over the page. "It will work." Milo stopped his muttering long enough to consult the diagram in Athios' Book. After licking his finger he flipped a few delicate, crumbling pages. In his hurry, Milo knocked the book from its stand, falling to the dusty floor with a heavy *thud.*

"Oh!" He bent to retrieve the precious text, muttering scoldings.

Behind him, the green light shimmered bright, reflecting the glass ceiling of his lab. The light seemed to move, shifting ever so slightly, as if he stood frozen under the sea while the gentle tick and whir of machinery filled the silence, constant and calming, like a ticking grandfather clock.

As Milo stood, a phone rang loud and shrill, bouncing around the lab. He spun and snapped the receiver from the work bench. "Hello?" he answered, in a high, demanding voice.

From the other end, a young woman's voice replied, "Uncle Milo."

"Ophelia." Milo smiled, happy to hear from her. "Where are you?"

"Krakow."

"How is it?"

"Rainy."

"Is the Magician still there?"

"He just left."

"Where?"

"Back to London, I think. He found the Knight of Swords. The missing one."

"The missing one? Ah – yes. I wondered what happened to him. So he's in Krakow?"

"For now. The Magician gave him a train ticket."

"To where?"

"Paris."

"I see." Milo hefted the book of Athios onto the work bench, gingerly putting it back in place. "You'll follow him, then. Find out what he's up to."

"If you think that's best," Ophelia agreed, though she sounded less than enthusiastic.

"I do."

"Then I have a train to catch. I'll see you in a few days."

"Good luck."

After the line went dead, Milo tossed the phone on the work bench and continued his work, chanting softly. "It will work," he said again. "It has to."

A GYPSY IN PARIS
PARIS

Jude disembarked the train with nothing but a small black suitcase tucked under his arm. As he walked, his footsteps echoing across the vast hall of Gare du Nord, watery grey light flooded though the glass ceiling, announcing the gloom had followed him from Krakow.

"Great," he grumbled, pushing through the heavy main doors into a chilly wind that tugged his coat and chased leaves around his ankles. Bothered, he yanked his scarf to his chin and hailed a cab, keeping back from the curb where dirty puddles gathered.

A few moments later, a taxi pulled to a stop and the driver jumped out to help him with his bag. Jude waved him off. "I've got it," he said, slipping into the back seat. It was warm inside the cab, a welcome reprieve from coming winter, and he found himself sinking into the leather, the groan of the heater persuading him to sleep. "Hotel du Louvre," he told the driver, settling in for the ride.

As they pulled from the station, Jude forced himself awake. There was a large sum of money stashed in his suitcase and he doubted the Magician would appreciate him losing it to a cab driver. The car chased traffic down Rue la Fayette, past Parisian apartment blocks, cafés and hotels with gabled roofs, pale stone porticos and beautiful ironwork balconies.

Shortly after, the car pulled up to an impressive stone building with the name *Hotel du Louvre* written in giant white letters above the grand entrance. It was a wide, four-story building with heavy drapery, stylish boutiques, bakeries, and a bistro on the main level. High above, two rows of dollhouse-dormered windows looked over a quaint French street, steps from the famous Musée du Lovure where the Mona Lisa smiled behind the tightest security in the world.

After exiting the car, Jude handed the driver several folded bills far exceeding the fare and turned to enter the lobby. Inside, he registered with a young attendant who eyed him coyly behind lowered lashes. The color in her cheeks rose as he spoke, providing his information and securing two night's stay in the hotel's Pissarro Suite.

"Would you like some help with your bags?" she asked in purring French.

Jude, English born, and having no real knack for foreign languages, shook his head. "No. Thanks," he replied in English. "I'll be out for a while. Can you have dinner in my room when I get back?"

The attendant nodded, her blush deepening. "Of course, Mr. Knight."

Knight was not Jude's surname. In truth, he did not know his surname. He'd been selected by the Tarot at a young age, adopted by the Magician, and took the name Knight for simplicity sake.

"When should we expect you back?" the girl asked brightly.

"An hour," Jude replied with cool detachment. "Would you put this in the safe?" He handed her the suitcase, making sure to meet her eye.

"Right away, Mr. Knight," she hurried to reply, turning to the wall of safety deposit boxes behind the desk. Once the suitcase was secure she brought Jude a small silver key and smiled, letting her fingers slip along his palm in the exchange.

Taking no mind, Jude pocketed the key and turned to go without a word. On the street, while waiting for the lights to turn, he pulled the Magician's paper from his pocket and examined the instructions. They were easy to follow and he headed down Rue de Rivoli along the Tuileries Gardens, all the while wondering why he had agreed to come at all. At least the rain was holding off, leaving the air crisp with the smell of pine and roses. A few blocks along, he entered the park and started toward the heart of the garden, once a supercilious backyard to notorious French royalty.

By city standards it was a big park; a stretch of pathways, flower beds, and public squares dating back to the sixteenth century. The faint babble of the Grand Carré's basin could be heard from a distance, the general din of a crowd rising as the square came into view. Even on the gloomiest days people milled along the paths. There was something about the park, a magic that Jude first experienced long ago, in another time, back when he'd still admired the Magician.

In the shelter of trees, the rain wasn't quite so bad. Flowers were still in bloom and street vendors were selling roasted nuts, water colored paintings and Eiffel Tower trinkets from wheeled carts. There were a few street performers out as well; a traditional French mime with a painted white face, busy taking pictures with a group of young kids, and an accordionist sitting on the ledge of the basin, singing softly as he played a lonely tune, reminding Jude of sad silent films.

As he stood back, searching, it didn't take long to spot the girl. She was seated on the grass, just off the main path under a canopy leaves, protected from drizzle. Spread beneath her was a woven blanket, dark and pattered with gold stars. It was easy to see she was homeless; hair falling in tangles around a heart-shaped face and a waistcoat, once red and white, now pale pink, worn under a blue wool coat, faded so that it looked grey. Dark gloves covered her hands, cut off at the knuckles to expose deft fingers shuffling a deck of cards. Crouched on the blanket, she slid the cards in a semicircle. Jude recognized them immediately. It was no ordinary deck, but a deck of Tarot cards, and even from a distance he could tell they were well-used, pictures faded and edges worn, just like the girl.

Interesting, he thought, approaching.

The girl looked up, meeting Jude's eye before he'd taken ten paces. To her right, a small hand painted sign read, *Rosaline's Psychic Readings*. As he closed the distance, Jude was struck by how much she resembled the card tucked in his breast pocket, although she was much younger than the image of the queen, practically a child. It was clear she tried to hide her unfortunate circumstance, taming her hair with frazzled braids while admonishing her hands with bangles and several gaudy rings.

"Are you Rosaline?" asked Jude, one foot on the path as if he hadn't quite committed to a reading.

The gypsy girl pointed to the sign, rattling bangles around her wrists. "That's what the sign says, doesn't it?" she answered in a faint French accent.

"It does," Jude agreed.

"Do you want a reading or not?" She sounded a little annoyed, as if she'd been sitting in the rain all day and wasn't in the mood for blather.

"Please," Jude agreed, taking a seat on the edge of the blanket.

Silently, the girl gathered the cards and began shuffling, whirring the deck as one. While he waited, Jude studied her, noticing her strange blue eyes, bright and clear, flecked with green and gold like a tiny galaxy trapped within. Again, she spread the cards in a perfect arc, letting the corners show. "Choose one." She nodded.

Jude reached for the card that called to him, the way it always did, and pulled it from the deck. There was no point in looking – he already knew which he had drawn.

The gypsy girl pressed her mouth into a firm, unreadable line. "The Knight of Swords." She raised questioning eyes to meet his. "This is you?" she asked, her voice holding a hint of something deeper, a question within a question. What she really asked was *'Are you truly the Knight of Swords?'*

Jude placed the card on the blanket and tipped his head. "Yes."

Rosaline *hummed* then gathered the cards, splitting the deck in three. "Choose one."

Again, Jude chose without pause; he'd done this many times before though it had been years since he'd last let anyone read his fate.

The girl stacked the deck with Jude's selection and flipped the first card. "The Tower," she said, laying it over the knight.

Jude couldn't help the dark smile angle across face. "You think I'm ruined?"

The girl stared at him with star-studded eyes, and Jude knew the dying Queen of Cups had chosen her replacement well.

"I only read the cards," answered the gypsy. "They say what they want." She pulled the next card from the pile and laid it horizontally across the Tower. The Queen of Cups. "This is your obstacle."

More than you know, thought Jude, expression blank.

There was moment, a spark, where Jude thought she'd seen his soul, but it passed quickly and she continued without comment, laying cards above and below. Most things she predicted he already knew: his longing to overcome, a tormented past, until she flipped the sixth card, one that represented the future coming into being, and it didn't fit.

The Lovers. A card of attraction, love and beauty: a man and a woman standing side-by-side under the spread wings of an angel and starburst. It was impossible. He couldn't love. His vow to that Tarot made it so and the mark on his palm burned in cruel reminder.

The gypsy raised a slender brow, sliding the card in his direction, taunting. "Unexpected?"

With a forced smile, Jude regained control, taking a closer look, examining the card: A couple, not touching – not yet, but leaning toward one another, as if waiting for the moment of impact. Jude's cards had never been wrong, but now, they must. There was no way this prophecy was meant for him. It was an impossibility, one in which he'd come to accept. "It's wrong," he said, matter-of-fact.

The gypsy shrugged, gathering her cards and shuffling them back into the deck. "Think what you like, but the cards are never wrong."

Jude didn't consider himself a patient man, and what little patience he had was used up. "I'm not actually here for the cards. I'm here with an invitation."

The girl shifted her eyes to meet his. "I know."

"Do you?" he asked, surprised.

Just then a gust picked up, so strong it bowed the trees and tossed handfuls of dirt in the air. Jude covered his face as pellets of dirt slapped his cheeks. He squinted through the onslaught, holding himself against the wind. When it finally subsided the square was in shambles, chairs overturned, vendor goods strewn across pathways and leaves floating in the previously pristine basin. An old man with a walking cane chased a tumbling hat and a little boy cried over a lost paper plane wedged in a tree.

Jude untangled himself from the blanket and looked at the gypsy who hadn't so much as blinked. Troubled, he snapped his fingers in her face. "Hey. Are you okay?"

The gypsy did not move, and behind her eyes the universe was undone.

THE GIRL ON THE ROOFTOP
PARIS

High above Paris, on gabled roofs overlooking shuttered windows, bistros and cobbled roads, the sky seemed vast and the city endless. Stretching promenades and tree-lined streets rolled into the distance where windows reflected a powder grey sky. Somewhere far away, music drifted to reach the girl on the rooftop, watching it all.

Ophelia smiled at the view and stepped onto a slender wire stretched between two buildings, placing one foot in front of the other to cross the gap. As she moved, arms spread wide like wings, she raised her chin to meet the rushing wind. She did not look down, not from fear, but because the sight was so captivating she could not look away. Ahead, the two gothic towers of Notre Dame stood stark against the sky and the Eiffel Tower thrust from the ground like a spear.

Below, pedestrians went about their business and Ophelia prayed no one looked up. A tightrope-walking teenager was difficult to understand and the last thing she needed, or wanted, was attention. Carefully, she made her way across the gap, and on a breath of wind she placed her foot squarely on the neighboring roof.

As she scanned the streets for the Knight of Swords, she realized she'd lost him. In a wave of panic, she bolted to the peak, her sneakers slipping over the tin roof as she clambered to grab hold of a chimney stack. Relieved, she spotted him waiting at the nearest corner and let out a breath. She dropped to her knees and slowly slid down the roof. From behind the eves she watched the knight pocket something and step from the curb, his red scarf dancing in the wind, taunting. As he crossed the road, traffic seem to part around him and Ophelia glared, knowing that whoever he was, *whatever* he was, he radiated dark magic; crackling and snapping like sparks in a bonfire.

Determined not to lose sight of him, she jumped, landing on a fire escape and swinging bar-to-bar, accomplished as a circus performer. On the ground, her feet hit pavement, soft like floured dough on a wood board.

Surprised by her sudden appearance, a man sitting on the back stoop of a greasy café gaped. "Did you fall from the roof?" he asked in French.

"Qui," Ophelia replied, sparing him a glance.

"Pourquoi?"

"Pourquoi pas?" she returned and left him staring after her in bewilderment.

The alley emerged on Rue Rivoli and she spotted the knight again, this time disappearing into the Tuileries Garden.

"Oh, no you don't," she grumbled, knowing he could easily get lost in the crowd. Keeping to the shadows, she followed, though it was hardly necessary. She was invisible – well, invisible to the eyes of the Tarot, at least. Mostly, her invisibility from the Tarot made her feel invincible, but sometimes, on particularly lonely days, she felt disappointed, as though the reason they couldn't see her was because she wasn't worthy of being seen. But not today. Today, Ophelia was the hunter stalking the ignorant prey, and that made her entire body thrum with energy.

On the path, Red Scarf turned, walking east toward the Grand Carré. From the shade of trees Ophelia watched him make his way to the far side of a large water basin, approaching a young girl seated on a blanket.

Ophelia moved closer, careful not to draw attention from the girl, edging around the basin and grabbing an abandoned newspaper. For a while, as she peered from behind the classifieds, nothing seemed out of place. Things were going as they usually did: a knight approached a stranger to recruit – offered them a train ticket back to London – and it was done.

The only thing Ophelia did find odd was the Tarot cards. Normally, members of the Tarot didn't waste their time with the playing cards created in their likeness. *Funny things*, *those cards,* she thought. *Who would believe such stupid drivel?* No one could predict the future with a handful of cards, and it was strange for the knight to waste time on something so trivial. Maybe she had read the situation wrong? Maybe the knight wasn't here on the Magician's behalf? After all, this knight, the Knight of Swords, had been missing in action for the past five years. She couldn't even remember the last time she'd laid eyes on him before yesterday. And the gypsy girl seemed too calm, too nonchalant, almost as if she'd expected him to appear. Beyond that, the knight seemed rattled, and that in itself was odd. True, Ophelia didn't know much about this particular knight, but from what she remembered he did not feel and he did not emote and he most definitely never looked *rattled.*

Ophelia's doubt intensified as the gypsy took back the cards. The knight's demeanor changed, rigid. Uneasy, Ophelia stood, dropping the newspaper with the intent of leaving. She had enough to report to Milo, and if she'd misread the situation, so be it, she could make up for it later. But before she could move, the gypsy caught her eye, staring as if in recognition.

Frozen, Ophelia's fists tightened at her sides, ready to fight her way out if need be. Just then a ferocious wind picked up, sending the newspaper around her in a tornado of black and white, trapping her inside.

AN IRREFUTABLE OFFER
PARIS

"Are you all right?" asked Jude, shifting so that he could catch the gypsy if she fainted, which was exactly what she looked like she was about to do.

The gypsy shook her head and waved her hand, cards clutched tight to her chest. "I'm fine."

The color returned to her cheeks though her hair was windblown and strewn in a mane of tangled curls. Jude noticed a patch of dirt on her cheek that could have been new or old and there was something about the way she sat crumpled over the blanket that struck him as horribly sad.

For a moment, he was silent, torn. In a way he felt as if he'd be doing the gypsy a favor by recruiting her to the Order of the Tarot, but he also knew how hard life on the inside could be.

The gypsy, who claimed to be named Rosaline, straightened her blanket then went to fetch her toppled sign. Jude remained where he was, watching as people gathered and up-righted their belongings. Rosaline returned with the sign, now badly dinted where it had struck a tree, and threw it to the ground beside her blanket. "Great," she mumbled, falling to her knees. "Now I have to make a new one."

"Not necessarily," offered Jude. "Like I said, I'm here with a special invitation."

Rosaline lifted her eyes, watching him like an abused dog. "And I said, I know."

Jude raised a brow. "What exactly do you know?"

"I know that you've come to offer me a new life. What kind of life, I'm not entirely sure. My visions can be hazy if the future is not yet set. I think it may have something to do with reading Tarot cards."

"No," said Jude. "Not reading cards."

"That's all I know how to do," Rosaline replied. "I didn't finish school." She didn't sound ashamed – in fact, she sounded a little proud, wearing the unpleasant truth like a badge of honor. In those small words Jude learned a lot about the gypsy: she had sacrificed many things to survive and she was unashamed.

"That's not a problem," Jude assured her.

Rosaline watched him carefully. In her bedraggled coat she seemed to swim, childlike, playing the dress-up fortune teller. She crossed her arms. "Most jobs require school. Why not this one?"

Jude considered how to proceed. This was a delicate moment; the outcome depended on what he said now. Should he overwhelm her or scare her she would walk away. "This isn't exactly a job," replied Jude, "you don't have to work all day, or do hard labor, you just have to keep a vow and you'll be supported for the rest of your life."

A long moment stretched as time seemed to slow. This was the moment, the time when the path diverged, one into darkness and one into light. But which would she choose and which path meant what to her? Jude reached into his pocket and pulled out the Queen of Cups' card, placing it on the blanket by Rosaline's knees.

She picked it up as though it were a dove about to fly away. In her small, gloved hand the card looked oversized, like a toddler with a baking spoon. "The Queen of Cups." She took a breath. "My mother used to call me her little Queen of Cups."

Jude didn't offer an explanation about the card; that would come, in time. "I'm offering you a new life, Rosaline. A better life. If you accept it, anything you want, anything that money can buy will be yours. You'll have expensive clothes and people to wait on your every whim. You'll never sleep on a stone bench or wear charity clothes again." He looked at her hands. At some point she had painted her nails a bright pink but they were chipped now, revealing crescents of dirt beneath. "Name it, and it's yours."

Rosaline made a face, as if it was far too good to be true. "What would be expected of me?"

"Just be yourself. See the future when it's called upon. That's all we require."

"I've seen you coming," she said, eyeing him warily, "but I still don't know if I can trust you."

"You can't know that," Jude admitted, but he reached in his pocket and pulled out a train ticket to London, handing it to her. "But if you want to find out, you'll be on this train."

Rosaline took the ticket and swept her eyes over the Tarot card once more. "I've never been out of Paris, at least not since I was little, before I came to the city."

"There's a first time for everything," said Jude, standing. "You should know -" He broke off, weighing his words carefully. "I promise you a comfortable life, but I do not guarantee a happy one."

A shadow passed over Rosaline's face, but she nodded, accepting his terms.

"Don't worry," Jude assured. "You'll have time to decide once you've learned all you need to know. I'm just not the one to give you answers – at least, not anymore." Jude hesitated then reached into his pocket, pulling out a wad of bills bound with a rubber band. He tossed it onto the blanket where it bounced before settling between folds.

This was not standard practice. In fact, Jude had never given cash to any of his recruits, but there was something about this young girl that tugged at his heart. The least he could do was provide her with the means for a good night sleep and a full belly. "There's a thousand pounds in there. If you want it, take it, and you never have to see me again. If you want more you'll be on that train." He turned to go then stopped, looking back. "I know you're proud but don't pretend you don't need help."

"Aside from the money," she raised her chin, "why should I accept your invitation?" Her voice held a certain amount of challenge – as if she doubted Jude could give a satisfactory answer.

She was right. Jude couldn't answer, at least not well. Some days he didn't know why he continued with Tarot himself. "Because," he paused, considering, thinking of Maggie, "it's your destiny."

The Tarot card seemed to glow in Rosaline's hand. She held it between two fingers, flashing Jude the face side. "Why me?"

Jude teetered on the truth. It was not recommended to share everything about the Tarot up front, but this girl was not like the others. She would predict future recruits as Maggie had, and that meant something. So, with a breath, he answered, "A dying queen chose you to replace her." He nodded at the card in Rosaline's hand. "She saw it in the cards…."

The gypsy frowned, as if trying to solve a riddle that wasn't there.

Jude knelt and took the deck of cards from her hand, spreading them across the star-dusted blanket. Without hesitation he selected a card, seemingly at random, revealing the image of a robed man holding a candle, standing over a table of cups and coins and swords and wands: *The Magician.*

Without explanation, he stood. "I'll be waiting on the platform. When the train leaves, so do I, and so does the offer."

"I might not come," said Rosaline as he turned to leave.

"You will," he replied.

THE GIRL IN THE WINDOW
PARIS

A battered train schedule was crumpled in Ophelia's hand as she stood across the station, wearing a backpack and holding a folded umbrella. She'd been up early, waiting for Red Scarf outside his hotel. Right on cue, he'd appeared sharply at eight and gone straight to the station. Once there it had taken a tricky maneuver to discover his destination, standing behind him in line while reading over his shoulder to see his ticket. She'd even resorted to using magnified reading glasses, just to be sure.

Paris Nord to London St. Pancras.

That had been good. At least she was going home. She hated when the knight's made detours to Shanghai or Madrid or other places she had difficulty navigating.

Now, Red Scarf stood on the platform by the waiting train while Ophelia watched. Like always, the knight couldn't see her. Her charmed necklace kept her hidden. She touched it now, a twisted ball of wire hanging from a chain around her neck: a ninth birthday present from Milo. Without the charm, she would have been caught years ago. But something in the metal kept her safe from the eyes of the Tarot. Her uncle had explained the alloy interacted negatively with the Tarot's magic, acting like a shield. It was a good thing, too. Most of the places Ophelia watched were out in the open, like her vantage point from across the platform. From here she could keep an eye on anyone approaching Red Scarf and be ready to follow when he boarded the train.

From the corner of her eye Ophelia spotted the gypsy pushing her way through the crowd, burdened with a large duffle bag and an old leather suitcase. Red Scarf spotted her a few seconds later and moved to intercept. There was a brief exchange as Red Scarf took the heavy duffle bag, along with his own black suitcase, and started brusquely toward the train with the gypsy girl close behind.

Ophelia hurried across the platform to the correct train car and pushed her way on. The car was packed with commuters; polished loafers and dangerous high-heels cluttered the isle as passengers stored their luggage and settled in. After checking her ticket, Ophelia made her way to her premier seat, shoving and backpack-smacking her way along. As she found her place she caught sight of Jude and the gypsy, relieved to find her seat almost directly across the aisle.

Red Scarf sat with his back to her, the gypsy across the small folded table from him. In the window's reflection Ophelia could see Red Scarf's face, eyes downcast, pouring over a book. There was a familiarity here, even if she didn't know him by name. She had a sense of it with all the Tarot's knights: a curious *knowing.* There was no emotional attachment, nothing about the knights she particularly liked, but after all this time – all these years of following - there was no escaping the sense of being acquainted, like long lost friends.

For a moment, Ophelia worried the gypsy might recognize her from the park, but it wasn't entirely unfeasible they could coincidentally end up on the same train. No matter, it didn't change anything. Her job was to follow Red Scarf and gather information about the Tarot. The gypsy wasn't Tarot, yet….

As the seats around her filled, Ophelia kept close watch of Red Scarf who was writing madly in a notebook. He seemed to be ignoring the gypsy, who looked out the window as the departure chime sounded and the train slowly pulled from the station. The girl, seeming to sense Ophelia's gaze, looked up and frowned.

Ophelia averted her gaze, pretending to fiddle with the umbrella in her lap. Her heartbeat quickened, though she couldn't say why – it wasn't like her to be nervous. She felt as if it were the first time anyone had really noticed her and she couldn't stop herself from raising her eyes to meet the gypsy's gaze once more.

AN EMPTY SEAT
EN ROUTE TO LONDON

"Do you see that girl?" asked Rosaline, whose name Jude knew wasn't really Rosaline, but didn't care enough to ask the truth. Gypsies were weird like that – lying and fibbing and exaggerating. And he had no patience to do anything but play along.

"Hm?" he asked, not looking up from his writing. His account had to be detailed, painfully so, or the Magician would be disappointed and give him that fatherly look that he hated.

"Over there, across the aisle. She's dressed in black."

Reluctantly, Jude looked up from his work. The gypsy was staring over his shoulder, so he turned. "What girl?"

"In black," repeated Rosaline. "Right there."

Jude looked down the train. He spotted several woman, all in their mid-to-late thirties or older, none of which he would classify as a 'girl'. Some were dressed in black, mostly pant suits, some in skirts, and none of particular interest. "Which girl?" he repeated.

Rosaline went silent.

Annoyed, Jude turned back to face her. Still, she stared past him, a look of hardened interest on her face. Again, he turned in the direction she was looking, seeing nothing but an empty seat. "I don't know what you're talking about," he said, but just as he turned, he caught the reflection of a girl in the window. He frowned, puzzled, and blinked, but it was gone as quickly as it had appeared, just the stretch of Paris streets and graffitied tunnels whizzing by.

When he turned back Rosaline was looking at him intensely.

"What's the problem now?" This was possibly his most hated part of the entire process, having to transfer recruits back to the Magician. Depending on where he was in the world it could mean hours of listening to stupid questions, sporadic crying, endless stories, and countless attempts of trying to get to know *him*- which was most definitely not part of his job description. He did not want to know people, or more truthfully, he *could not* get to know people.

"Nothing," the gypsy said and went back to her window.

"Nothing?" Jude narrowed an eye in question. This was the first recruit he'd ever met who eluded his questions. Most were eager to respond, gushing their innermost thoughts. But Rosaline was hiding something, he could feel it, but he wasn't entirely sure he cared enough to find out.

Rosaline looked across the aisle again, and Jude followed her gaze. The seat was still empty, so was the window, although he could see the flash of phantom face in his mind. It had been a pretty face, one of hard angles and a smooth brow. Her hair had been tousled and dark, cut sharp at mid-neck with jagged bangs, which, for a second, had fooled him into thinking she was older. But the glow of her skin and the curve of her cheek told him she couldn't have been older than him, younger probably – still in her late teens.

"It's nothing," Rosaline repeated. "I just thought I saw someone I knew."

Jude let it go. He had no time for hallucinations or psychic babble. There was no denying this girl has some divine gift - that was a requirement for this particular mission to visit this particular girl, and Jude had seen and known enough in his life to believe it - but if she was seeing ghosts, or better yet, if *he* was seeing ghosts, he didn't want to know. He had his job to do and that was that.

After a time Rosaline spoke again. "What's he like?"

Jude looked up from his log book. Mostly, he ignored recruits' questions. They were usually stupid, or ignorant, or things he simply could not answer. This time, however, the question interested him. No one had ever asked him about the Magician – probably because no one had understood enough of what he had said in the first place to know the right questions to ask. He let his pen fall into the spine of his notebook and cleared his throat. "The Magician?" he clarified.

In a jangle of bracelets Rosaline clasped her hands and nodded. Jude noticed she wore the same clothes as the day before, and it looked as if she hadn't touched her hair since the windstorm. Even the smudge of dirt remained on her cheek. What the hell had she done with the money he had given her? He frowned, irritated, but decided not to ask. It wasn't his business. He sat back, watching Paris give way to a colorful countryside of yellowing trees, red roofs and church steeples poking between gentle hills. "He's just the way you'd imagine him to be. Smart, mysterious, aloof and a little pompous."

Rosaline seemed to contemplate Jude's description. After a while she asked, "When we get to London will you stay?"

No, Jude nearly said, but something stopped him. It had been a long time since he'd stepped foot in Tarot's headquarters and even longer since he'd opted to stay for more than a few minutes. There was something about that place, something that pulled him apart. In the outside world he could find ways to keep the emptiness at bay, but inside those gates the wound gaped, seeping and fresh. "We'll see," he said, and wondered what had changed his mind.

Rosaline settled back, apparently done with her questions, and turned to watch the landscape shift into water colored paintings framed by the train window. Once or twice Jude caught her staring through the reflection at the empty seat across the aisle. He did not look back.

THE MAGICIAN'S HOUSE
LONDON

The Order of the Tarot headquarters was exactly as Jude had left it, a massive three story mansion set in twenty acres on the outskirts of London, including vast botanical gardens, a small fishing lake, sprawling apple orchard and a life-sized chess board off the back promenade.

The nagging weariness following him from Paris increased as the town car pulled up to the gates, barbs twisting into a scrolling gold *T*. As the gates parted along with the insignia, the car pulled onto a long paved drive.

"This is a house?" asked Rosaline, nose pressed to the window.

Jude sat back, holding the suitcase in his lap like a shield. He appeared calm, but on the inside he was screaming. "Yes."

Rosaline looked back. "Are you okay?"

"What?"

With bent brows, Rosaline studied him for moment then turned back, leaving the question be. Ahead, the house reared like a great beached whale, white and massive. The car stopped at the foot of a grand stone entrance.

Before the driver could exit Rosaline was out of the car and staring wonderingly up at the magnificent house.

"Can we go in there?" she asked as Jude followed her out, pointing to the labyrinth of shrubs off the left wing.

"No," Jude said sternly, slamming the car door and starting up the stairs.

The driver rounded the vehicle to unload Rosaline's bags from the trunk.

"Leave that," Jude said as she went to grab her suitcase. "Someone will get it."

There was a pause before he heard the thump of the suitcase then her footsteps on the stairs behind him. When he reached the door, Jude turned to wait, already irritated. He watched Rosaline climb the stairs, bangles and beads clattering. "Are you ready?"

The color drained from Rosaline's face as she stood before the two massive doors, but she nodded bravely, jutting her chin.

"Good." With one last breath of free air, Jude led her into the Magician's grand foyer, a two story room of marbled floors and crystal chandeliers. The house was blinding with opulence: plush Parisian rugs, ebony wainscoting, hand crafted Moroccan furniture, heavy silk curtains and stained glass windows.

"Wow." Rosaline cranked her head around to get a look at the frescoed ceiling, painted with breathtaking scenes of the Tarot. To Jude the gypsy seemed out of place in the extravagance, hands clasped and shoulders slumped as if afraid she might bump into something and break it.

Jude, on the other hand, felt a familiar chill, and a familiar *pull.* In an instant the emptiness was whole again - if emptiness could be whole. It was as if the house was the void and he stood in its shadow, the darkness swallowing him like a speck of unwanted light.

"Jude," the Magician greeted, entering the room from the grand staircase.

"Magician." Jude faced the man he once considered a father.

On the stairs, the Magician towered like the great and powerful Wizard of Oz. One hand rested comfortably on the polished banister and from a distance he still looked young – or as young as Jude remembered from his childhood. The Magician had a face that could easily be construed as innocent or sinister, depending on the light. Right now, he looked innocent; his light brown hair slicked back with streaks of grey and dark suit well-trimmed, perfectly fitted to his slender build. “How was your trip?”

Rosaline shifted to stand behind Jude as if he could protect her. *If she only knew*, he thought darkly, *there isn't enough power in this world to protect her if the Magician wanted to hurt her*. But, he wasn't that kind of man – at least not in that sense. For all his show, the Magician took no pride in his work. He was almost haunted by it. It was a thankless, raw, job.

“Fine,” Jude answered stiffly.

“How long will you be staying? Do we have time to talk?”

Jude opened his mouth to refuse, but again, he hesitated. He looked to Rosaline, who watched him, eyes pleading not to leave her alone with this strange, daunting man.

How did that happen? When had he become her protector and what exactly did she think he could protect her from? He'd brought her here, and no one had ever accused him of being a hero. “I can stay,” he replied, surprising himself. “For a bit.”

The Magician shared his reaction, eyes blossoming with hope. “Really? That's – I'm glad.”

Jude inclined his head.

Descending the stairs, the Magician stepped into the foyer and extended a hand to the gypsy, revealing the green marks creeping up his forearm. “Miss Rosaline?”

Rosaline noticed the marks immediately, eyes widening, though she kept her cool remarkably well. Tearing her eyes from the glowing tattoos, she looked up, meeting his intimidating gaze. “Yes,” she greeted in a small voice, reaching to shake his hand.

“You can call me M, if it suits, or Magician if you're feeling formal.”

She nodded, carefully taking back her hand. “Can I ask what I'm doing here?”

"In time," the Magician answered as a woman with long raven hair swept into the room. Despite her age she was beautiful, and even the faint crow's feet around her vibrant emerald eyes seemed lovely. She wore a long robe of pale sky blue, embroidered with golden fleur-de-lis, giving her a majestic air, like a fairy queen or ancient goddess. On her left palm the green mark of a mystic woman wearing a diadem glowed against the silk of her robe.

"Madeline." The Magician smiled warmly at the new comer. "I was about to call for you."

"I heard the car," she answered in a foreign burr. "Jude," she stood before him, eyes dancing, "I was hoping I'd see you before you disappeared on us again."

Jude flinched. "It's good to see you, Priestess." Had it really been two years since he'd last seen her? She looked the same, if a little more grey.

"Will you be staying awhile?" asked Madeline with the grace of a prima ballerina – which she might well have been once.

"For now," Jude replied.

Madeline seemed pleased, her bow-like mouth curving into a gracious smile. "I'll make sure the table it set. I'm so looking forward to having everyone under one roof again."

"Everyone?" The surprise in Jude's voice was audible, bouncing around the foyer an octave higher than normal.

Madeline only smiled. "Come," she said to Rosaline, who had been watching the exchange with curious terror. "I'll show you to your room."

There was a moment of hesitation as Rosaline seemed to decide whether to trust the strange woman. She looked to Jude for an answer.

Again, Jude wondered how he had become her guardian. That had never been his job and he had never wished for it. He waited for the girl to look away, to give up hope of finding solace in *him*, of all people, but she continued to stare. Continued to wait.

Finally, Jude nodded. "It's fine."

Madeline and the Magician exchanged questioning looks.

"Not to worry," Madeline said sweetly, extending an arm to Rosaline. "You'll see Jude at dinner."

Finally, Rosaline took the woman's arm and tossed Jude a nervous look as she left.

When they disappeared through a side door, the Magician turned to Jude with a cheerless smile. "I'm glad you've decided to stay."

Jude nodded, regretting his decision by the minute. Not only was he trapped in this house, he would be trapped here with *everyone.*

"Let's have a drink," the Magician offered, leading Jude off the foyer to his study; a spacious room of dark wood panels, thick rugs and several leather sofas. He faced a large stone fireplace in the shape of a roaring lion, reaching for a crystal decanter of scotch on the mantle. Removing the stopper, the Magician poured them both a glass, handing one to Jude as he took a seat near the empty fire.

"Welcome home." The Magician raised a glass in toast.

Jude returned the gesture with less enthusiasm, taking a seat.

"Was there trouble finding the girl?"

"No." Jude set the scotch aside and unhinged the small suitcase he'd rested against the chair, removing the notebook and handing it to the Magician. "Nothing out of the ordinary, all things considered."

"Ah, yes – well, she does have a magnificent gift."

"She knew I was coming, though she didn't entirely understand the purpose or know anything about the Order. That made things a little easier than usual, though she still seems a little unsure."

"I expected she would see something of our coming. Hardly worth being our new Queen of Cups if her gift wasn't strong."

Jude nodded in agreement – which was rare. In this case though, he understood the Magician's point. Maggie had been a powerful Queen of Cups, the only member of the Order of the Tarot to have the gift of sight. If her replacement wasn't equally as strong, they would suffer as a whole.

"Have you been mindful of your vow?" The Magician asked after a time. The question was casual, but held a significant amount of weight.

Fire burned in Jude's chest. "Is that a serious question?" he demanded coolly. "I have kept my vow every single day of my life, like it or not. What makes you think after all this time – after everything - I'd break it now?"

"Calm yourself, Jude," the Magician mollified. "It was just a question. You seem…distracted. And with you being in Krakow all this time it's hard to know what you've been up to. You know you're the only one who can choose to leave the Tarot. No one can force you."

"I don't want to leave," Jude snapped. "I just need space." He searched the ceiling for reprieve. "You have nothing to worry about."

"She looks to you for comfort."

"She's a frightened kid. There is no attachment. You know that – or you should – you're the one made it so."

The Magician's face took on an ashy pallor, stricken, as if Jude had stabbed him in the back. "That's not entirely fair…."

"No?" Jude raised a brow. "You recruited my before I was old enough to understand what taking my vow as knight would mean."

Straightening his shoulders, the Magician's expression turned fretful and tight. "The Order of the Tarot is not a prison, Jude. It's a family – a home. You may have isolated yourself, but you're still a member of this family so long as you chose to be."

"There are prisons without walls." Jude stared into the scotch as if he could see the bars. He couldn't remember the last time he'd argued with the Magician – probably the last time he'd been in this very room. Most of their interactions were cordial, if not forced, but never heated.

"Do you want out?" the older man asked, as if the argument had reached a crescendo and this was the breaking point. "Is that it? Just say it. Say it and we'll find a replacement and you will be free to live your life however you want."

"Has anyone ever left?" Jude asked, eyes bright with anger. "Has anyone rescinded their vow in the history of the Tarot?"

"I don't know," the Magician replied, his voice aching with sadness. "I must admit I've never known any member of the Tarot to be so at odds with their role as you seem to be. As you know, recruits are chosen to match the role, not the other way around. But I know you cannot continue to live this way for long. Something will break - whether it's you or your vow."

It was not the first time Jude had considered leaving the Tarot, and still is struck him like a punch to the gut. How could he leave? As confused as he was about his place, it was difficult to turn his back on the only life he'd ever known. The Tarot supported him financially, emotionally and in every way a family can support someone. If he left, he would have to start all over, find a way to exist in the real world, and he wasn't sure he knew how.

The Magician took a deep breath, the scotch forgotten as he looked at Jude with fierce, fearful, question.

"No," Jude replied after a moment of silent debate. Then, "No," louder, more assured. "I don't want out. This is my life. It just isn't as easy for me as it seems for everyone else and I don't understand why. I'm supposed to be the Knight of Swords. I'm supposed to hold all those inherent traits. And I know I do – some of them at least. I can be blinded by desire and fail to see consequences. I have a great sense of responsibility and compassion. I am determined, focused, engaged. But at the same time – it's not enough. Serving the Order of the Tarot, recruiting, living for the next great task - it doesn't fill my life with the satisfaction it should."

"It isn't easy for anyone, Jude," the Magician softened his tone, kinder now. "You should come back to the live amongst your family. If you don't wish to return the House of Swords, then stay here at the manor where you're surrounded by people who care for you. Things are clearer here, aren't they? I don't know how you've been dealing with everything alone for so long."

"This isn't home for me, M. Neither is the House of Swords."

The Magician's mouth tightened grimly. "It would be less lonely."

"What do you know about loneliness?" Jude asked, spiteful. "You have Madeline." He didn't know where the anger originated or when he'd turned against the Magician. It had crept up, slow and sure, like a sly serpent slithering into his heart.

"I know more than you seem to give me credit for."

"You're angry with me for being this way," Jude said, frustrated with the Magician, with himself, with the world, everyone. "But you require me to be this way – cold and distant and determined." He pointed at the Magician's elbow where he knew the matching mark of the Knight of Swords was inked into his skin. "You created me."

"I hardly created you, any more than I created the sun or the moon or the stars."

Jude raked his hand through his hair with a scowl. "You know what I mean."

"I don't want you to be *this*," the Magician gestured to Jude's rigidness.

"What's *this*?" Jude mimicked.

"Hateful."

"I'm not hateful," Jude snapped, but he wasn't entirely sure that was true. He certainly hated parts of his life. He wanted to live, creating memories with people that mattered, but as the Knight of Swords it was only, and would only be, just him.

"I think," said the Magician carefully, "you should stay in London for a while. Just until you gain some perspective on what being the Knight of Swords truly means. Without you -"

"I know," said Jude, with a long, tired breath. "Without me the balance would be broken. If my position in the Tarot is unfilled, every opposing force; love, freedom, carelessness, would grow too strong and it would eventually break the balance within the Tarot, and that would replicate in the world and eventually destroy it – tear apart like a blown tire trying to move forward. "

"Precisely," agreed the Magician with a nod. "At least we're getting somewhere."

OPHELIA THE OUTCAST
LONDON

There were a few concrete things Ophelia knew about herself. One was that chocolate gave her headaches. Another was that cats made her sneeze. But the most glaring truth of all was that she was not well-liked.

It was hard a thing to admit. No one strives to be an outcast or admires being difficult, and it wasn't as if she wanted to be that way, she just *was*, like a bad knee or an ugly birthmark. For a long time Ophelia worked hard to overcome her unfortunate unlikable self, smiling and laughing, telling jokes. Sometimes she'd go months before letting her dark side show, but eventually the truth would leak out – like it always did – prompted by something her uncle said, or a scolding from a teacher who didn't understand, and Ophelia would be her unpleasant-self once more. Eventually, it just didn't seem worth the effort to pretend and by her thirteenth birthday Ophelia had resigned herself to life as *Ophelia the Outcast* – or so her primary school classmates had taunted. But all those years of pretending had taught her one valuable life lesson: how to lie.

As she waited for the school bell, a group of boys walked past in the yard. No one spoke, or waved, or smiled, but they did stare. Boys always stared; maybe because she was pretty, but more likely because she was weird. And mute. She had not spoken to a single student since started at this school three years earlier.

Fending off the drizzle, Ophelia tugged the hood up on her rain slicker and ignored the damp, itchy feel of her uniform as she started across the asphalt pad. Ahead, one of the boys looked back. Ophelia dropped her eyes and hooked her thumbs through her backpack straps, pretending to be occupied counting footsteps. Thankfully, the boys went ahead without incident, and Ophelia followed them into the school, her rubber soles squeaking as she made her way down the hall to her classroom.

"Ophelia?"

She looked up as she entered the room to find the teacher appraising her with mild surprise. "You've missed class all week," he said as if he hadn't expected to see her again.

"I know," Ophelia remarked, a little too smartly. But really, he was stating the obvious. Of course she knew she'd been gone – she was there.

He frowned, stepping forward and holding the door open. "You'll have to speak to headmaster before I can allow you back in class."

A murmur of laughter rose from the students already seated. Ophelia ignore it. She wasn't exactly immune, but she wasn't easily wounded, either. It would take a lot more than a few jeers to break her.

"Fine," she said, yanking her bag higher. The same boy from the yard stared intently at her from his nearby desk, watching as she turned. Ophelia shot him a glare, causing him to look away with burning cheeks.

By the time Ophelia reached the headmaster's door she was fuming and struggling to keep it from her face. With a heavy fist, she knocked.

"Come in," a voice replied.

Ophelia took a breath and opened the door, stepping into a typical headmaster's office with wood paneled walls, a large desk and a big window overlooking the school yard. "I'm supposed to see you about missing class," she said, trying to sound innocent – trying to play the lie.

The headmaster looked up from his desk. He was young for his position, early forties, with tired toffee eyes and a scruffy beard. "Ophelia." He said her name as if the very sound were disappointing. "Please, sit."

Sitting was the last thing Ophelia wanted to do, but she entered the office and closed the door before taking a seat in an uncomfortable chair – most likely uncomfortable on purpose.

The headmaster finished his work then set down his pen, folding his hands neatly on the desk. "You missed three days this week."

"Two and a half," Ophelia corrected. She'd missed that morning returning to London, but had made a point to hurry home, change, and get to school. She should get bonus points for effort, though somehow she doubted the headmaster would agree.

His mouth tightened into a dry smile, which was really more of a frown, tweaked down at the edges. "Ophelia, I warned you last month about missing school. I told you one more incident and I'd have to expel you."

"How does that teach me anything?" she countered, genuinely puzzled. "I skip school and I get to miss more school?"

"This is a very good school," the headmaster urged. "Most children would be grateful to be in your shoes. You're lucky you were accepted with your record." Even though his tone remained light, Ophelia could see the judgment in his eyes. If he only knew the truth - that would wipe the look right off his face.

"I think," Ophelia began in a dangerously sweet tone, "it was the large donation my uncle made."

The headmaster's frown intensified. "Regardless," his folded hands tightened, "I just don't understand, Ophelia. Help me here. When you're in school, you're not a bad student.

You're no prodigy but you get decent grades, write good reports, and complete your assignments on time. You'll probably graduate this year, despite the abhorrent amount of time you've missed. You're uncle is a renowned physicist; one of the smartest men of our time. What's going on in your life that's leading you so astray?"

He seemed to be looking for a generic response like divorce or an angst-ridden break-up or drug use. But Ophelia's problem was none of those things. It ran much, much deeper, and it was nothing she could explain. *My uncle has me follow members of a secret society called the Order of the Tarot. It's my job to keep tabs on men called knights and to report back to him with my findings so one day he can destroy them and pass control of the world's balance to science through a complicated clockwork world he is desperately trying to perfect.* Somehow, it didn't sound convincing.

With a sigh the headmaster picked up the phone. "I'm sorry but I have to call your uncle about this."

"Good luck," she mumbled, picking absently at her nails.

The headmaster ignored her, dialing. After a long stretch of endless ringing, he finally hung up. "No one home," he said, flipping through files for another number. "I'll have to try him at the university."

Still, Ophelia said nothing, peeling chipped polish from her nails.

Again, the phone rang. This time someone answered, but by the look on the headmaster's face, the conversation wasn't going as planned. He spoke quietly for a few minutes, nodding and saying things like, "I see," and "Okay," and, "I wasn't informed of that." After ending the call he made a quick note in Ophelia's file and looked up. "Why didn't you tell me your uncle no longer works at the university?"

Ophelia shrugged. "No one asked."

"Where did he go?"

"Nowhere," she answered plainly. "He's unemployed."

"Oh." The headmaster sounded genuinely surprised. For a second Ophelia thought he was going to ask why, but instead he scrawled his signature across a piece of paper and handed it to her.

Ophelia took the paper, scanning the expulsion notice. "Thirty days?" Horrified, her eyes blazed with anger. "That's not fair!" Out of all the kids in school she probably wanted to be there most. In fact, she'd begged her uncle to attend. It wasn't her fault he pulled her out every other week. The truth burned on her lips, but she quickly smothered them with a sulk. No matter what happened, she could never expose her uncle's secret. They would think he was mad. Probably throw him in a hospital ward. Heck, they'd probably throw her in too, for good measure.

"These are the rules, Ophelia. This is your last chance. If you miss any more class after this you'll be removed from this institute, generous contribution or no."

"But –," She crumpled the paper sloppily in her hand, "I'm a good student. You said so yourself. It's not like I fight, or talk-back, or cheat on exams."

"I'm sorry, Ophelia." The headmaster seemed genuinely remorseful, but he remained firm. "Rules are rules. But, if you need someone to talk to the school counselor would be more than happy. Your file says you've been on medication for anxiety?"

To keep from exploding, Ophelia bit the inside of her cheek, breathing sharply through her nose. "How should I know what my file says?"

The headmaster closed his eyes, gathering his composure. "I'm not asking what the file says. I'm asking you if it's true. I'm trying to offer you help. It also says your parents are deceased. Is that true as well?"

A sharp pain cut through her chest. How dare he read her chart as if it explained everything about her? He had no idea. "I don't know," she answered bitterly.

"You don't know?" The headmaster voice was tense with question. "Ophelia, honestly, I'm just trying to help you, but I can't if you don't open up a little."

Defiant, Ophelia squared her shoulders with a murderous scowl. "And I'm telling you the truth. I don't know if they're dead. All I know is they're not around. My uncle never told me what happened."

Pity altered the headmaster's severe expression. "That must be difficult," he offered sincerely. "I think you should set up an appointment to speak to the school counselor. You seem to be dealing with a lot. It might help."

Annoyed, Ophelia stuffed the expulsion letter in her backpack and stood. "Thank you, but I don't need your help." With that, she left, bolting from the school before anyone could see the tears burning in her eyes.

The walk home was cold, but welcome. She wrapped her arms over her chest, sniffling against the chill as she made her way down the tree-lined streets carpeted in damp yellow leaves that clung to her shoes like wet paper. When she reached her uncle's townhouse, tucked between two tall stone buildings, she stomped into the foyer, tossed her bag into the corner, and headed straight for his study, which – unfortunate for her temper – she found empty.

"Typical," she grunted, crossing the room to slam the crumpled expulsion letter on the coffee table. With a sigh, she collapsed into the sofa, tired and shivering. While she waited, she toyed with her uncle's antique solar system. It was an ornate thing of gears, wheels, spindles and knobs, all done in dull brass. The gears clicked as she moved the earth, elevated on a slender rod around a polished gold sun at the center. As it moved the other planets followed, rotating round and round. Glyphs were carved into the plate, early mathematical calculations and runes. She ran a finger over the symbols, wondering what they meant.

"Ophelia," her Uncle Milo said from the door, startling her. "What are you doing home early?" He held a cup of tea in his hand, casting a glance as he walked to his desk.

Milo was a brilliant scientist renowned within the scientific community for his advancements in theoretical physics. Despite his oversized brain, he was a relatively small man with fast-graying hair and round wire spectacles. As a man, he was neither cold nor warm but somewhere in-between – lukewarm - someone who seemed not to care much either way. Though he had taken her in as a child, kept a roof over her head and opened a trust fund in her name, which meant he must have been inherently good, if not loving.

Snatching the letter from the table, she held it up, flapping it like a flag. "I got expelled."

"Again?" he asked with faint interest, taking a seat.

Most teenagers would be thrilled with Milo's minimal level of concern, but it angered Ophelia. It made her feel horribly sad and alone, which often manifested as the anxiety attacks the headmaster pointed out from her file. She could feel the sparks of an attack coming on now, burning at the base of her lungs like wildfire, and did her best to stifle the flames with deep gulps of air. "Yes, again," she replied sharply, tossing the letter in the fire. He wouldn't care to read it anyway. It was better off burning. "The headmaster called. You never answered."

Milo set down his tea and began picking through papers scattered across his desk. "I was busy."

"Of course."

If he heard the snide undercurrent in her voice, he ignored it and Ophelia knew there was nothing more to say. There was no use convincing her uncle to care. He'd wanted her to be homeschooled and always made it clear spying for him came first.

For years Milo had been on the verge of a breakthrough, needing Ophelia to do the leg work. School, he felt, could jeopardize everything he'd worked for and it was not something he was willing to risk.

"Forget about school," she dismissed the topic, which was exactly what Milo wanted. "There's something else I want to talk about."

"Hm?" her uncle said without looking up.

"Why is he back?" She'd told Milo about Red Scarf's mysterious return. Milo hadn't been concerned, but it bothered her – persisting like bad cold. Where had the knight been these past few years and why was he back?

Her uncle gave a reproachful look. "Does it matter?"

Ophelia shrugged. "I don't know. A little. I'm curious."

Milo closed the book on his desk, giving her the full force of his intelligent stare. "It doesn't matter who they are, Ophelia. It matters what they do. The point is he's back now. So you'll follow him, gather what I need to know, and report back. Maybe he's the key to finally breaking the Tarot's control on the world's forces."

For years Ophelia had been gathering information on the knights – learning their habits, their ins and outs, but so far she'd learned nothing about how to break their vows. The knights were unbreakable - or at least they seemed so. Red Scarf, on the other hand, was different since she hadn't seen him in years. Maybe he was the weakest link? Maybe that's why he'd disappeared? She didn't know much, if anything, about him. He'd vanished five years ago when Ophelia was only twelve and just starting her illustrious career in surveillance. What information she'd gathered in the months before he'd left had been vague – more snippets than fact. And then one day, just like that, he was gone, evaporated like a ghost in fog. The Magician no longer visited him and he did not stop by Tarot headquarters – at least not that she knew of. For years she wondered what became of the dashing dark haired boy with big, expressive eyes, but eventually the curiosity faded, and she'd almost forgotten about him. That was until a few days ago when she'd followed the Magician from his manor to Krakow and nearly fell off her chair when the Knight of Swords swept into the room, as if he'd been there, hiding in that tea house all along.

Uncle Milo continued, "You left him at the manor?"

Ophelia nodded. She'd followed the Knight of Swords inside the town car to the gate, but that was as far as she dared go. For a while she'd lingered outside the iron bars, but after nearly an hour she realized he likely wasn't leaving and she had to get back to school.

"Good. You can go back. I want you to find out what he's doing there and if he's planning on staying for good."

"You want me to sneak onto headquarter grounds?"

"Precisely."

"Isn't that a bit dangerous?"

"You said yourself you wanted to find out why he's back. Now is your chance. If he's back for good you have years worth of missing data to gather." Milo pulled out a scientific chart, so large it spread over the entirety of the desk. "I'm close to figuring this out," Milo tapped the Book of Athios, which rarely left his side. "Just a few more calculations and I should have it –

but if we can't find a way to break the Tarot, it's all for nothing. I can't take control of the world's balance if the Tarot is still in control."

Ophelia resisted the urge to roll her eyes. Milo's dramatic monologues were a common occurrence, which she'd grown weary of before she was old enough to talk. "Fine. I'll go," she replied, weighing the decision and deciding it wasn't worth the argument.

"Good," Milo flashed his best smile. "The time is growing ever near."

A RARE APPEARANCE
LONDON

Once in a blue moon Tarot headquarters was transformed from a dusty old English manor of oddities and secret passageways to one alive with laughter, color and life. These were the blue moons Jude tried hardest to avoid. He stood back, arms crossed over his chest, half hidden in the shadows of a grand hall of soaring mirrored ceilings, chandeliers and a wall of glass overlooking a dark garden terrace.

An impressive table, nearly as long as the room, was piled high with steaming, delectable dishes, its surrounding seventy-eight chairs slowly filling, though most of the Magician's dinner guests still mingled about the room.

The Magician stood at the center of pandemonium with Madeline, the High Priestess, on his arm. He held a glass of champagne in a slender crystal flute, talking animatedly with two men. Jude already knew the guests, at least by name if not personally, for he had spent most of his life surrounded by the Magician's followers.

The dinner guests looked to be manufactured straight from Rosaline's Tarot cards. A young man in a jester hat juggled silver balls, his hat ringing with tiny bells: the Fool. An elderly man in a long blue robe, the hood pulled low over his face, holding a staff and lit lantern, guiding the way: the Hermit. A woman dressed brightly in orange and red, a sunburst crown upon her head: the Sun. And her counterpart, a young man dressed in fur with the hood of a wolf's head: the Moon. There was the Empress in her robe of patterned pomegranates and crown of stars, Death in black, and countless others who made up the Magician's whimsical Tarot court.

Jude, although one of them, had refused his knight's uniform crested with the symbol of Swords, instead arriving in a modern, tailored suit.

"Who are these people?" Rosaline appeared at his elbow. She looked innocent in the crowd, dressed in a gown of flowing green chiffon, her hair brushed in soft curls, although somehow, Jude noticed, she still managed to look a bit rumpled.

"Don't they look familiar?" he asked. Normally the recruits were clueless, too unfamiliar with the concept of Tarot to understand what stood before them. But Rosaline was different. She had knowledge of the cards and how each created balance to the deck. She also had the gift of sight, which meant she probably knew more than he guessed.

She tilted her head, examining the crowd as if they were a strange menagerie. "They seem familiar," she began, "they look like my Tarot cards. Is this a costume party?"

Jude smiled, pleased, and took irrational credit for her perception. "Sort of," he replied. "Come on." He stepped away from the wall toward the heart of the room. "I'll show you your seat."

Rosaline trailed close behind, nearly tripping over Jude's heels. "Where did they come from?" she asked, appraising the juggling Fool with bright, astonished eyes.

"Some live here in the manor, others come from four distinct corners of the world," replied Jude. "The Himalayas of Nepal, Erta Ale in the heart of Afar badlands, the Białowieża Forest of Belarus, and the Faroe islands in the Norwegian Sea."

"I've never heard of those places," Rosaline admitted, sounding a little ashamed.

Jude inclined his head. The places he spoke of were remote, on purpose.

Heads turned as the pair approached. Beautiful women with curious smiles, men holding brandy snifters and deeply questioning looks; they all stared, wanting to know, where had Jude gone and why had he returned?

Pretending he walked alone in an empty room, Jude ignored their not-so-inconspicuous stares. He'd always been the target of gossip among this crowd, only now he was present to hear it.

"They're staring at you," said Rosaline, whispering from the side of her mouth.

Jude remained indifferent. "I can see that."

"Why?"

"Because," he stopped beside an empty chair, "they want to know where I've been for the past five years."

"You left?"

"Yes." Jude motioned for her to sit.

Rosaline remained standing, a look of concern flashing across her face. "Why?"

He returned the look with his own impatient one. "That's none of your business. Now sit." Again, he motioned, snapping his fingers at the chair. The chair, which was really a throne, was carved from white stone with sea scallop engravings. At the base crashing waves, leaping trout and starfish ensnared the legs, fusing it in place.

"Where did you go?" Rosaline pressed, apparently not easily dissuaded.

Jude gave an incensed sigh. "Anywhere that wasn't here. Satisfied?"

"Not really," Rosaline grumbled, but she sat anyway. "Why did you come back?" she asked over her shoulder.

Jude placed a hand on the top of the throne, thinking of Maggie. "Someone special asked for a favor."

"The Magician?"

"No."

"The dying Queen of Cups?" Rosaline's voice softened making her sound older and wiser than the little girl he accused her of being.

Jude considered for a moment then answered, "Yes." He meant to stop there, but for some reason kept talking. "This was her chair." He patted the throne Rosaline sat upon gingerly. "Well, really it still is. Until she dies and the new queen takes her place."

Rosaline placed a hand on the worn arm, running a cleanly scrubbed palm across the smooth surface. Jude pictured Maggie in the chair, old, wrinkled and full of life. He had gone to see her before dinner. She'd been fragile. White hair, skin and bone under a pile of heavy blankets The Magician had brought in a doctor to slow her death, but it was still there, lurking in the shadows. Jude could smell it, heavy like old perfume, burning as a half-remembered nightmare. Death was coming for her and it was only a matter of time.

Maggie had held out a gnarled hand, searching for his in the fading light. Jude took the withered thing in his and squeezed tight. With every raspy gasp his heart broke. "You came," she said. "I knew you would. I saw it in my dreams."

"Of course I came. Did you tell him where to find me?"

"Yes," she croaked.

Of course. But Jude had already guessed as much. The Magician had mostly left him alone since their last argument. He knew it would have taken some effort to track him down in Krakow. But Maggie's death changed things. This was *his* Maggie; the woman who had been like a grandmother in those early years. And the Magician had known Jude would never turn down her last request.

"Will you stay?" she asked.

He smiled, eyes filling with years of unshed tears as he brushed a strand of straw-like hair from her fevered forehead. Regret balled in his throat. So much wasted time. He hadn't visited in years and he couldn't possibly make up for it with so little time left. And so Jude did the only thing he could do, and stayed, all afternoon and into late evening, until Maggie had fallen into a deep sleep and the High Priestess fetched him for the dinner party.

"She won't last long," Madeline had said on the way out. "Just long enough for the gypsy girl to complete the tasks and take her vow."

"Maggie has seen the girl succeed?"

Madeline clasped her hands, leading him down the hall. "I'm sure you know she sees many futures. In some the girl succeeds. In others she fails. And in a few…well, that doesn't matter now. All that's certain is that Maggie will soon die and someone will need to take her place to ensure the balance within the Tarot remains."

Ice hardened around Jude's heart. He did not want Maggie to die and he certainly didn't want to talk about her as though she were replaceable.

"You should say your goodbyes," Madeline said, not without kindness.

Jude nodded but deep down all he could think was *how can I begin to say goodbye when I only just said hello*?

Now, Rosaline looked at him from where she sat in Maggie's chair, waiting for him to say something. Before he could, a man with white-blond hair wearing a garish fish-shaped amulet approached.

"Tristan," Jude greeted him, recognizing the man immediately. It had been several years since he'd last seen the King of Cups, but he still looked the same with his handsome face, baby-blue eyes and unmistakable snowy hair.

Tristan's grin nearly stretched ear-to-ear. "Jude!" he boomed, raising both hands in overzealous welcome. "Is that you?"

Jude wanted to run. He'd spent years running from his past and wasn't quite prepared to face it now. "I assure you," he replied wryly, "it's me."

"God, I haven't seen you in what? Ten years?"

"Five," corrected Jude, wondering if he really looked that much older. Sure, he'd been a little skinny back then, maybe even a little bit short, but the reflection in the mirror still looked the same. Or was he just too blind to notice?

"Well, it's good to see you." Tristan clasped Jude's hand in his. "Will you be staying for the evening? I know how much everyone would love for you to join us."

"For dinner, yes," Jude replied. "I've just brought Rosaline from Paris to meet the Magician." Jude placed a hand on Rosaline's shoulder, directing her attention to Tristan. "Maggie has selected her as our next Queen of Cups."

Tristan dipped his head in a graceful bow. "Ah, yes." He took Rosaline's hand in his and delicately brushed her knuckles with his lips. Instantly, Rosaline looked on guard, watching him with narrowed, fearful eyes. "I am Tristan, King of Cups."

The fear turned to trepidation, swimming in the pools of her eyes. "Nice to meet you."

"Tristan sees over the Cups with the help of Maggie." Jude explained, though the explanation was weak, at best, and Rosaline remained stiff as an over-stuffed scarecrow propped on a rod. But it was the best he could do. There were things he could not explain and a lot of things he simply didn't want to. "I have to take my seat," he said, stepping back. "I'll find you after dinner, Rosaline."

"Can't you sit here?" Rosaline looked to the empty seat on her right.

"That's taken," he answered, "by a friend of mine. Don't worry. You'll be fine."

The color nearly vanished from her face. Only the fake rouge on the apples of her cheeks remained, vibrant against her pale skin. "If you say so." She turned and faced her empty plate, head bent over the silverware in the same way she did her cards.

Jude felt a pang of guilt, though there was nothing he could do about it now, and after a reluctant moment, he left. On his way across the room he spotted the friend in question. "Nicolai," he said, intercepting the Knight of Cups. His oath brother was three years his junior, both tall and broad with perfectly swept golden hair and charming good looks - everything Jude felt he wasn't.

Nicolai stopped, one brow jutted in surprise. "What are you doing here? I thought you were in Krakow?" he asked in heavily Czech accented English.

The twist of mourning tightened in Jude's stomach. Funny how it started before a loved one was even gone if you knew it was coming, grieving the future you would never get to share. "Maggie."

Nicolai nodded. "I'm sorry."

"It's fine," he managed.

Nicolai gave him a cheerless smile. "Well, I'm glad you're here. I haven't seen you in weeks."

Jude forged a smile. "One big happy family under one big roof."

Nicolai's mouth bent down at the corner. "We'll talk later. I'll find you."

"Sure." He let his friend slip by and then called after him, "Be nice to her. She's just a kid."

"I'm just a kid," Nicolai reminded him with a wink.

Jude watched as Nicolai introduced himself to a stricken-looking Rosaline and then continued his trek around the table. By now all the dinner guests had found their places. He rounded the table past Madeline who gave him an encouraging smile – though he wished she wouldn't – and hurried on. On the far side he found his place with the House of Swords, seated together.

The Swords, one of the four suits of the Tarot, were considered his family, of sorts, because they belonged together in the deck, though he felt the same warmth toward them as he did toward a stray cat. And he was sure the feeling was mutual.

Paxton, the Page of Swords, was the only exception. He greeted Jude with a bucktoothed smile, nearly knocking back his chair in his hurry to stand. "Jude! I had no idea you were coming. I haven't seen you since… since the Magician sent me to find you in...," Paxton paused, wrinkling his brow in contemplation, "where was that?"

"Brussels."

"Brussels!" he cheered. "That was so long ago. My god, you're taller."

"Am I?" Jude shook the page's hand. "It's good to see you, Pax."

Paxton pulled out Jude's chair next to a willowy woman with sleek blond hair and a severe expression. She was stunning in the way hoarfrost can be, both cold and beautiful with blazing blue eyes and glistening, iridescent skin. She wore a gown of velvet red, trimmed with fur, and a low cut neck revealing overly-voluptuous breasts.

It wasn't hard to see why Jude had fallen in love with her as a young man. Adalain, the Queen of Swords, was still painfully beautiful. But like all Swords she had a sharp edge. She no longer seemed the majestic creature he once knew - the person he had longed to marry, before he understood why he never could.

"Jude," Adalain greeted in a cool burr, the sound soothing as rain on hot skin. Jude resisted the urge to close his eyes. He could not let her get to him. "How are you?"

"Adalain," he replied, taking the seat beside her. "It's been a long time."

"Three years?" she asked, arching a perfectly shaped brow.

"Something like that," Jude answered, knowing damn well she remembered the last time they'd spoken. At fifteen she'd tried to seduce him and he'd been young and foolish enough to believe she loved him. *Love.* How could he have been so stupid? The Queen of Swords did not love. She possessed. And she had wanted to possess him, like a toy. He'd been too young to understand not everyone in the Order of the Tarot was good. Some were cruel and calculating and cold, as was needed to complete a perfect balance of opposing forces. And it had nearly cost him his vow.

Now he understood it as her nature, her mandate, to be cruel to men, just as it was his to be honorable and headstrong. He couldn't blame her for what she was – for without her, without any one of them - the Tarot, and the world, would fall. They needed her. The Magician needed her. And for that Jude had never forgiven him. Though deep down, if he was truly honest, his resentment had nothing to do with the Magician and everything to do with himself. He was ashamed of how badly he had failed, for the Knight of Swords should never have fallen for the queen's seduction. He should never have felt compelled to love her. He should have been as he was born to be, and if Jude was truly meant to be the Knight of Swords, why did he find it so difficult?

The night he left, the Magician had said, "I see the way you look at her, Jude. The Knight of Swords cannot love. You are not like Nicolai or even Kieran, the gentler of the knighthood. You are strong like Sol. You must dedicate yourself to being a knight, not a lover or husband or even a friend. The Knight of Swords is devoted beyond belief. He is an iron spike at the center of a wooden wheel. This is your *vow*. And if you cannot keep it in the presence of Adalain, I suggest you find somewhere you can."

He hadn't meant run away, of course. But that's what Jude had done – and in five years he had never once looked back, until now.

If Adalain could feel the tension between them now, she pretended otherwise, engaging the elder King of Swords in conversation.

A tap of silverware on crystal turned the dinner guests' attention to the far end of the table where the Magician stood. "My dear followers!" he begun, opening his arms wide. "You have been invited here to greet our newest recruit." He smiled, though it looked tired and strained, even from a distance. "Rosaline," the Magician raised his glass toward the gypsy trying to make herself small between Tristan and Nicolai. "Please stand and say a few words."

INTRODUCTIONS
LONDON

The din of the dinner party fell away, leaving Rosaline with one clear thought: *It's him.*

The boy smiled, taking his seat next to her.

How was this possible? How could he be here? She stared at him, unblinking, deciding if it could be real. Perhaps she'd fallen into a dream.

"I'm Nicolai," he greeted, his voice holding the faintest hint of recognition, as if he thought he might know her, but was unsure from where, "Knight of Cups."

Rosaline had seen his face a thousand times over a thousand lifetimes in her dreams. This was the face she had scratched into her notebook on the darkest days, daydreamed of when she had lost all hope. He was her knight in shining armor, come to save her, and despite never knowing him, she missed him, and now he was here, like a loved one back from the dead...Nicolai.

Nicolai. She felt his name on her lips, cherishing the sound, but before she could speak it the tapping of a glass stole his attention away.

For a moment she watched him, so captivated by the familiarity of his movements, his every feature, she could not look away; the faint scar across his cheek, the shape of his jaw, and lashes dipped in gold.

At the sound of her name, she turned. In her shock, she had missed the Magician's speech and suddenly all eyes were on her.

"Stand and say a few words," he said, champagne flute tipped in her direction.

Horrifyingly, her voice lodged in the same place her heart had climbed.

"It's okay," Nicolai looked at her with beautiful, blue eyes, "just introduce yourself."

It took a second for the words to process, lost in the sea of his eyes. They were bright with flecks indigo and hues of sky and when he smiled the corners crinkled, fixing on Rosaline with amusement. Something about him was radiating, an inner glow that diffused all dark. Where she was heavy, he was light, and his voice seemed to dance across her skin.

"Are you going to say something?" he asked as if he'd been waiting all his life to hear her speak.

"I'm sorry?"

His smile widened. "Are you going to speak to the guests?"

The question detoured around her heart before sparking in her brain. Appalled, she lurched to her feet, greeted by dozens of staring eyes. No one aside from Nicolai looked pleased. "Hello." Her voice was small, barely venturing across the table. Apprehensive, she twisted the dinner napkin in her hands, desperate for words that wouldn't come. She had never been good at speaking, especially in public. All Rosaline could think was how inadequate she felt compared to Nicolai, who even in her dreams had been a knight while she had been a peasant.

Now she tried to gather her courage. The Queen of Cups had chosen her for a reason. She was meant to be here. She had a gift. When her father drank, she'd seen her future in the stars and carried on. When her mother was arrested, she had read it in the cards that all would be well. Sometimes, she heard the dead, and every now and again she saw them. And when she'd dreamt of Jude, the Knight of Swords, she knew one day he would come and offer her a better life. And yet, the tangibility of this moment, of Nicolai, the dinner guests, and the Magician, was something entirely different. It was as if someone had told her she would one day learn to fly, and then, just like that, she had, and it was incredible and overwhelming and so extraordinary she couldn't believe it.

Across the table Jude met her gaze with a nod. The gesture was simple but kind and it gave her the courage to speak. The words were late, much too late to be eloquent, but then again, Rosaline had never been perfect. "My name is Rosaline," she went on, giving the name she used on the streets. "I'm a gypsy… from Paris." She swallowed, wondering what these people wanted to hear. What was she supposed to say? "I read cards for tourists in the Tuileries Gardens."

A general murmur spread through the crowd. Interest? Mocking? It was hard to tell.

The murmur faded to a buzz that felt like one of her readings. She was ignorant, sure, but not stupid. As she looked around the room it didn't take a genius to recognize that every person here, including Jude and Nicolai, seemed to represent a person from the seventy-eight card Tarot deck. But why? Was the Magician some lunatic with a living collection? Or was it more complicated than that? Something in the back of her mind said it was.

The murmur died and dinner guests waited for her to either speak or sit. Rosaline sat, smoothing her gown and dropping her eyes to the table. A lull followed, but slowly conversation resumed, marking the end to her horrible speech. Embarrassed, Rosaline folded and refolded the napkin in her lap, avoiding Nicolai's gaze. She felt like a cast away, adrift in a stormy sea, alone in a boat slowly taking on water. A moment of painful silence passed before she had the courage to raise her eyes. Beside her, Nicolai gently touched her arm. "Have we met?" he asked softly, as if they stood on opposite ends of a great divide.

Rosaline blinked. How could she possibly explain? "Before tonight?"

Nicolai nodded as if he knew he sounded ridiculous.

Again, Rosaline searched for words, but before she could reply several waiters entered the room with bottles of champagne.

"Wonderful!" Tristan, the King of Cups, exclaimed from her other side. "The Magician sure knows how to host a feast!"

In the second it took her to smile politely in return, Nicolai was pulled into a conversation on his right, and the moment passed. As she listened to him speak, even his voice was familiar, like a long-forgotten melody. When the conversation ended, he turned and offered her a bread basket. "Bread?" he asked, giving the basket a gentle shake.

To disguise her trembling hands, Rosaline took the entire basket and clutched it to her chest.

Nicolai's mouth twitched. "You must be hungry."

"Famished," she replied, taking a biscuit and passing the basket along. "So," she began, terrified yet desperate to hold his attention, "what exactly does the Knight of Cups do for a living?"

"Well," Nicolai bit into his mini loaf, "We don't really do anything for a living. We just exist, I guess. As long as your part of the Tarot, the Order takes care of your needs. In fact we're discouraged from working, or being too involved with the outside world, for fear it might interfere with our vows. Within the Tarot I'm part of the Knighthood. You already know Jude, the Knight of Swords. And Sol, over there, is Knight of Coins," he nodded to a dark brooding man in the corner, "and Kieran on the end is Knight of Wands." He waved at a young boy with tousled auburn hair and perfect white teeth. "We're required to do the Magician's dirty work. Running errands, protecting the secret of the Tarot, finding new recruits…."

"Like me?"

"Yes." He nodded. "Like you."

"So why can't the Magician do it himself?"

"He already has a lot to manage."

"Like what?"

"Like everything. He is the tie that keeps our vows together. It's a lot to take on. He is covered in our markings – the weight of that alone is immense to bear."

"Markings?"

Nicolai lifted his left palm as if he were an Indian chief. There, in the center of his palm, was a dark green mark in the shape of a medieval knight in full armor wearing a winged helmet and holding a goblet on horseback. If the tattoo wasn't strange enough, it seemed to be glowing.

"You're glowing," Rosaline articulated, slightly concerned for his health.

Nicolai laughed. "Yes, it is glowing. That's a good thing, believe it or not. It means my vow is intact and strong."

"How does it work?"

Nicolai smiled. "Magic."

Rosaline had heard a lot of strange things over the past two days, so this, though bizarre, did not surprise her. "You're not going to tell me more, are you?"

"No," he answered kindly. "I'm sorry. That's the Magician's job."

Behind them, a waiter appeared, and Rosaline moved aside to allow him to fill her champagne flute. Unintentionally, her shoulder brushed Nicolai's and the contact sent and unexpected jolt through her bones, nearly knocking the glass from the table.

Nicolai felt it too, jerking back. Wide-eyed, he stared at her as if she'd done it on purpose, brows drawn with intense question.

"Sorry," she breathed.

After a moment he shook his head. "It's fine."

Silence filtered between them and his eyes swam with questions she longed to answer. Only, she couldn't. Not yet. Not here. Instead, she looked away, finding Jude locked in conversation with a striking blond woman. At first glance the pair looked cordial, conversation stiff but pleasant. And then Rosaline noticed the woman's hand clamped on Jude's arm, long nails pressed into his sleeve as if holding him down.

"Who is that women?" Rosaline asked Nicolai, a frown pulling across her face.

Nicolai followed her gaze. "Adalain," he answered, voice chilly with distain. "The Queen of Swords. Or the Ice Queen, as I like to call her. Sharp as a whip and cunning as a fox with a chip the size of an iceberg on her shoulder."

"What does she want with Jude?" The aggravation on Jude's face was plain, and Rosaline felt a swell of loyalty toward the recluse knight. He had been her savior, of sorts, and she didn't like the idea of someone upsetting him.

Nicolai fought a laugh. "I imagine she wants *him*." At Rosaline's confused look he continued, "Adalain is - complicated. She hates men, and loves them. And now that Jude's back…well he certainly isn't a kid anymore."

Rosaline's frown intensified. Why would someone like Adalain taunt someone like Jude? "He doesn't seem to care for her."

This time Nicolai did laugh. "Jude cannot *care* for anyone."

SPY GAMES
LONDON

The gap between fence posts wasn't large enough for Ophelia to squeeze through. She stood outside with one hand wrapped around a coffee cup and the other around a freezing iron bar. "Well," she said, trying again to wedge between, but no matter how she shimmied or shook, she could not get her flat-chested self through the bars.

In the end, she gave her coffee the honor of going first, kneeling to place it between the bars on the frosty grass beyond. Once the coffee was safe she stood, watching the steam curl and evaporate into chilly night air. "Don't you dare get cold," she ordered the coffee, backing away to make a run at it.

Sneakers thundering, she jumped, reaching the fence and scrambling like a squirrel up a tree. The spear-heads were sharp, so she twisted to get her foot between the gaps before skewering herself. And just like that she was airborne, landing with a soft *thud* on the other side, only slightly winded.

Calmly, Ophelia retrieved her coffee and took a sip while stalking toward the house lit at the end of a long drive. It was not her first trip to Tarot headquarters. It wasn't even her first trip to the mansion in the middle of the night. But it was her first time *inside* the fence. As she tiptoed carefully over leaves and crunching gravel, she felt a strange off-ness, like being somewhere you knew you were not supposed to be, like the mall after closing or school grounds after dark.

As she walked Ophelia encountered the familiar sights she had grown accustomed to seeing through the fence: a fantastical fountain of a jester, bushes groomed in the shape of kings and queens. A part of her wanted to stop and admire the scenery, but she heard Milo's lecturing voice in her head and ducked low to sneak along the sculpted shrubs toward the impressive stone house. Several feet from the door she stopped and crouched between trees.

Soft sounds flitted through the night, cricket calls and a soft rustling breeze, but the house remained still. Ignoring the growing sense of unease, she kept on, staying low. Above her, the mansion's windows peered like soulless black eyes, judging her. *Trespasser!* they whispered. *Dirty, rotten, trespasser!* Ophelia shot the windows a cold look and pressed against the house, her back to cold stone. For a few minutes she stood motionless, straining to hear beyond the silence. When she was satisfied no alarms had been triggered she grudgingly abandoned her coffee and hoisted herself over the rail onto the flagstone terrace.

The soles of her sneakers padded softly over stone as she crept around back where she found the house lit by garden floodlights. She glanced at her watch: past midnight. Everyone in the house would be asleep. She yanked her sleeve over the watch, annoyed Milo had her chasing ghosts while he was snug inside his lab, tinkering behind closed doors.

At the edge of the terrace she came upon a wide stone patio backing onto a small fishing lake that shone under the full moon. The terrace doors were closed but lit from within, bringing her up short. She stopped, surprised to hear the din of chatter and clatter of dishes from inside.

The commotion was unexpected, but not extraordinary. She knew the Magician often threw parties; though she had never been this close to seeing one. Silently, she edged toward the doors, anxious excitement bubbling in her stomach.

"What are you up to Magician?" Ophelia peered inside the window, careful not to be seen.

The room beyond was opulent, more so than any ballroom she'd seen in London's most lavish hotels. A long table was decorated with silver candlesticks, crystal bowls and vases of beautiful flowers. Around the room men and women of the Tarot mingled and drank, looking like cut-outs from a children's story.

Enamored, Ophelia didn't notice the Knight of Swords approach the terrace doors from the crowd. As he reached for the knob, she stole back with a gasp, just in time to avoid being smacked in the face. He stepped outside, the swinging door narrowly missing her body as she twisted away.

"Who's there?" Red Scarf asked, pausing as if he'd heard her.

Ophelia's excitement boiled into fear, fusing her joints. Instinctively, her hand shot to the invisibility charm around her neck – the wire necklace Milo created to keep her hidden from the Tarot. Her eyes darted to the garden, wondering if she could make it. *No*. She had to remain calm, not draw attention. The invisibility charm was good, but she didn't know if it was fool proof. She would wait and slip away when he went back inside.

The Knight of Swords turned toward her, staring into darkness. Thundering seconds ticked by as blood rushed in her ears and her lungs burned, full of air. Eventually, he let door fall shut and took another step onto the terrace.

Edging away, Ophelia let out her breath in a huff. She was steps from slipping into the garden plot when Red Scarf walked into a pool of light. Only, he wasn't wearing his red scarf tonight. Tonight he was dressed in a fitted suit, and looking rather dapper, she had to admit. His dark hair was combed back and shirt unbuttoned as if he'd recently yanked off his tie, but as cutting as he was, she couldn't miss the turmoil behind his eyes, both sad and angry.

Calm down. Ophelia tried to relax her breathing. *He can't see you.*

Unaware of being watched, Red Scarf surveyed the terrace, seemed to give up his search and went to lean against the rail overlooking the lake. He ran a hand through his hair with a heavy exhale, as if releasing a great weight.

"Jude?" A voice spoke from the house and Ophelia turned to see the gypsy standing in the doorway. "Are you okay?"

Horrified panic seized Ophelia. She may be invisible to Red Scarf, but the gypsy girl wasn't Tarot – not yet - and she had certainly seen her on the train.

Jude looked back. "Yes," he answered flatly. "Go back inside, Rosaline."

The gypsy ignored him, stepping out onto the terrace. "Did that woman at the table say something to upset you?"

Jude laughed, though it held no heart. "That *woman* doesn't have to say anything to upset me."

"Is there anything I can do?"

Jude turned, mouth pulled in a stiff smile. "No," he replied. "Thank you. Go back inside. Finish your dinner."

"I'm not hungry." The gypsy took another step, eyes wandering across the yard.

Ophelia caught her opportune moment to make a run for it. She turned and the deafening crunch of a dry leaf underfoot stopped her dead.

"What was that?" The gypsy jerked around in the direction Ophelia stood frozen and wide-eyed.

There was a long stretched of silence followed by Jude's voice, "Probably a mouse. Come on, it's cold out here."

"You go," Rosaline answered. "I need some air."

"Suit yourself. Don't stay too long. The Magician will be looking for you."

"Okay."

The door shut as Red Scarf left and Ophelia cracked an eye. She nearly screamed, stumbling back. The gypsy stood inches from her face with a condemning stare.

"Who are you?" the gypsy demanded, calm but accusing.

Ophelia put another step between them, clutching her chest. "You scared the hell out of me."

"Why are you following me?"

"You?" Ophelia nearly laughed. "I'm not following *you*."

The girl seemed to consider that, though the reproving look on her face remained unchanged. "You're not a ghost, are you?"

Ophelia frowned as if she hadn't quite heard right. "What? No. I'm -" she scrambled for a lie, "just getting some fresh air."

The gypsy's eyes narrowed, unconvinced. "From the party?"

"Yes," Ophelia moved back, placing one hand on the terrace rail. "Quite stifling in there, don't you agree?"

The gypsy did not budge. Instead, she crossed her arms over her chest, rattling gold bangles around her slender wrists. "Why can't he see you?" The question was straightforward but spoken in a detached way.

"Red Scarf?"

Looking over her shoulder the gypsy found Red Scarf seated at the table beyond the glass. He still looked unhappy, distracted, and only partially engaged in conversation. "Yes," the girl turned back to face Ophelia, "him."

"I have no idea," Ophelia announced, using the momentary distraction to swing her leg over the balustrade and jump. "You'd have to ask him." Her voice trailed as she leaped into the garden below.

The gypsy was fast, but not fast enough. She got her hand around Ophelia's shoulder but her grip wasn't strong enough and the material of Ophelia's jacket slipped through her fingers.

Something snapped at Ophelia's neck as she hit the dirt with a thud, but there was no time to stop and look back. Panting, she tore through the trees like a bull through the streets of Pamplona, branches scratching her face and roots attempting to trip her, but finally she reached the gate and hurdled herself over the fence, practically falling into the street.

Still no alarm, she thought, listening as she climbed back to her feet. It wasn't until she'd flagged down a cab and was on her way home that she realized what the gypsy had done. Her invisibility charm was gone.

A LESSON IN TAROT
LONDON

"Now is a good time for me to explain what you're doing here." The Magician sat across from Rosaline on his private jet. The plane was already airborne, flying away from London at breakneck speed, leaving a world of ants and matchboxes behind. Through the small window, Rosaline could see the river Thames winding through London, and off into the distance a bright mid-day sun streamed golden light across brown fields and scattered English villages.

The Magician produced the same card Jude had shown Rosaline in Paris and placed in on a small table between them: the Queen of Cups. "You know this woman?"

Rosaline wasn't sure what he meant. "I know the card," she answered.

The Magician shook his head, looking disappointed. "No. Do you know this *woman*?"

For a moment Rosaline stared at him, waiting for clarification. When he offered none, she shrugged. "I know what the card means in a reading. The Queen of Cups is nurturing and compassionate. She is emotionally connected with others. She is fair and honest, loving and warm. Often, she is someone who heals, or counsels or in some cases sees the future. In general, she has incredibly strong intuition and can read energy."

The Magician nodded approvingly. "Well, that's a start."

"To what?"

He tapped the card. "On how to become her."

Rosaline's delicate brow furrowed, confused. "Why would I want to *become* her?" She stared at the card. Of course, the queen was beautiful. She looked happy too, but in a sad way, as though she was happy despite something instead of happy because of something.

The Magician mirrored that smile. "Because the balance of the world's forces depends on it."

The declaration was dramatic and Rosaline wanted to roll her eyes, but instead she gave him a puzzled look. "What do you mean?"

"How to begin?" The Magician waved a flippant hand. "You know of the cards? Of the balance each card brings to a complete deck?" He seemed to be waiting for an answer, so Rosaline nodded. "There are good cards and bad cards, happy cards and sad cards, adventurous cards and domestic cards. Cards of earth, air, fire and water. Wealthy cards and cards of poverty. Cards of sense and logic and longing and loss. Cards of life and death."

"Yes," she agreed. She'd known all this since she was old enough to talk. Her mother had first shown her the Tarot cards as a small child, often doing readings for those in nearby villages. She could still smell the varnish of the box in which they came and her mother's perfume as she leaned close, explaining the meaning of each delicately painted card.

"Without one card," the Magician raised a finger, "the deck is no longer whole. It is no longer balanced."

A part of Rosaline wanted to hurry the Magician along. These were basic facts of reading Tarot. You needed a complete deck for the reading to be accurate. But she held her tongue and waited for him to finish.

"Think of it like a machine, where each card is a gear that keeps it moving. If one card breaks, or disappears, the machine no longer works. Sure, the machine is still there, and it might chug along, but it is missing a part to function as it should. The Tarot is like that machine. If one card is missing, the deck no longer works and eventually, if you leave it long enough, it will break."

Rosaline blinked. "So the Queen of Cups is a gear?"

The Magician's mouth twisted in a frown, but he nodded. "Yes."

Rosaline had never been big on analogies, but she thought of one now. "So, every wheel has a lynch pin, right? Something holding it together. Are you the pin? If you break, does the whole machine fall apart?"

A smile flickered and faded from the Magician's lips. "Well. Yes. I suppose it would," he answered, his voice deep and grave. "Very good, Rosaline."

Pleased, she wanted to smile, but the seriousness in his tone kept her stoic. Instead, she took a breath and asked, "And what does this have to do with me? What do Tarot cards have to do with anything? They're just cards, and I'm a person. How do I become a card?"

"You cannot become a card," the Magician answered, almost scolding. "That's foolish. In fact you cannot become anything other than what you already are."

That confused Rosaline even more. If she couldn't become anything more than what she already was, then how was she to become Queen of Cups?

The Magician looked at her, peering deep as if he could see something behind her eyes. "Do you know the history of Tarot, Rosaline?"

Rosaline chewed her lip, thinking. She knew quite a bit about Tarot- every meaning of every card both upright and reverse, as well as the story behind each. Unfortunately, gypsies were notorious liars, often fabricating the truth or embellishing tales. Anything she had ever been taught was questionable and she didn't want to risk a repeat scolding. Just in case, she phrased her answer like a question, "They started as playing cards in Italy, sometime during the fifteenth century?"

"Wrong."

Her cheeks burned. She looked at her feet, mortified. *Stupid, lying gypsies.*

The Magician settled back as the plane climbed through a thin layer of clouds and the rumbling engines quieted to their cruising altitude. "What very few know is that the Order of the Tarot began at the beginning of time and continues to exist today. There are seventy-eight fundamental categories of forces in this world, ranging from emotions to elements: love, life, death, gold, silver, wood, strength, courage, intelligence, air, ice, ignorance, wealth... the list goes on. And each category is represented by a member of Tarot, broken into four great houses: Coins, Cups, Wands and Swords. Each House corresponds to the Earth's four elements: earth, water, fire and air."

The Magician poured himself a glass of sparkling water, wetting his tongue before going on. "Somehow, in fifteenth century Italy, the idea of Tarot ended up on a deck of playing cards called *Tarot de Mantegna,* based on bits of fact and fiction. Today, the cards are seen only as a silly way to predict the future, but I can promise you Rosaline, behind every story there is an ounce of truth – and in this case, there is a whole world of it. The Order of the Tarot was established to uphold the world's delicate balance of opposing forces. Without it, without each member, each opposing force, the world would not function as it should. Too much hate leads to too much war. Too much love to poverty. It works with the elements too. If a member of the House of Coins disappears then the other elements of air, fire and water are unbalance which is reflected in the world, leading to volcanic eruptions, hurricanes, even violent earthquakes. There are an infinite amount of outcomes and it is the Tarot's job to ensure we uphold the balance as best we can. Without us, the world would be in constant chaos, ripped and pulled apart at the mercy of unpredictability. Eventually it would be destroyed."

Most people would have laughed at the Magician's words, or fainted, or cried or tried to run away, but Rosaline was used to the bizarre, even if she admitted this was pushing it. In any case, she couldn't exactly run, being on a plane, so she tapped a finger against her chin and said, "You're telling me the Tarot is not just a deck of cards, but a real system established to control the world's balance of forces?"

"Quite," the magician replied, sounding pleased with her adeptness.

"And how do they control it?"

"Through magic," the Magician explained, revealing tarot markings on his wrists. "We are bound to the earth by magic, and to each other."

"So," Rosaline said calmly, "you play the Magician? And it's your job to – what – exactly?"

"Oh no," the Magician looked stricken. "This isn't some part. I was *foreseen* by the dying Queen of Cups to be the next Magician, just as you have been chosen to replace her. I was chosen to lead the Order of the Tarot. I did not ask for it. It's my responsibly to run the headquarters, provide sanctuary, and most importantly bind all the members together." Again, the Magician displayed his markings, pulling up his sleeve to reveal more green tattoos scrawled over his skin. "Has anyone showed you the marking of their Vow? Jude perhaps?"

The marks seemed to cover every inch of the Magician's flesh, almost like a second skin. "Nicolai," Rosaline said, "the Knight of Cups. He showed me the mark on his hand."

"Ah, yes." The Magician bent forward and pulled up his pant leg, revealing the identical mark to that of Nicolai's inked across the front of his ankle. "You can see I am running out of room."

Rosaline squirmed in agreement.

"These markings represent each vow my followers must take to secure their place within the Tarot. They are made by the Sacred Wand, cut from the first tree on earth. As long as the marks burn green, their vow is strong and unbroken. Each mark is linked to mine, and thus to each other. Our markings create a system of balanced forces. What happens within the Tarot is mirrored in the world."

In her years on the streets Rosaline had perfected the art of reading faces. She stared into the Magician's now, watching for ticks or flicks or noticeable changes in color. "Why should I believe you?" she asked. "How do I know the Tarot is real and not just some cult with fancy green ink?"

With a slight bow of his head the Magician smiled politely. "All I can do is try to show you."

Rosaline's nature kept her grounded, and skeptical, but she'd grown up understanding there was more to the physical world than what appeared. She had seen things, heard things, and experienced things to make her believe. She understood that the fabric of time was not linear or one dimensional. She felt emotion and energy and saw quite clearly that everything in the world interconnected, weaving people and elements and atoms together like a quilt. *It is possible,* she decided, *everyone has energy and if those energies align and intertwine and oppose it could, theoretically, affect the world's balance.* And if anything, she was curious.

"So where are we going?" she asked.

"To begin," the Magician dipped his head, "Belarus. To the ancient forest of Białowieża."

"Why there?"

"Because," he smiled triumphantly, "it is home to the House of Coins."

A LONLEY LIFE
LONDON

Alone in her room, Ophelia stuffed her backpack full things she would need: a wad of cash, bank cards, passport, homework, clothes and her mobile phone - which rang as she finished packing.

"Yes?" she answered, knowing it was Milo since no one, save the phone company, knew the number.

"It's Uncle Milo."

"I know."

"I just wanted to say goodbye."

"That's fine," she mumbled, though it wasn't. She'd been growing increasingly annoyed over the past two days. Milo hadn't emerged from the lab since her return and was already sending her back to Krakow to follow Red Scarf– who she now knew as Jude, the Knight of Swords.

It was strange to know his name. The knights of Tarot had always been just that – knights: the nameless mercenaries of the Magician. It was the gypsy who had spoke Jude's name on the terrace, and now Ophelia felt connected to him somehow, which was strange since he didn't know of her existence.

"What time is your train?" asked Milo, sounding parental but not all that interested.

Ophelia checked her watch. "Two."

"Right. What hotel will you be staying at?"

"The Fortuna, near Old Town."

"Good. I'll call you tonight then."

"Fine," Ophelia replied, her temper short. For a second she thought of telling him about the stolen necklace, but bit her tongue. She didn't have the courage to admit she'd been so careless or that she'd been so close to being caught.

There was a brief lapse of silence while both Milo and Ophelia struggled for something more to say. "Remember your reports," Milo said finally. "The sooner I have the information I need on the resurrected Knight of Swords, the sooner you can come home."

"I will." Ophelia hitched her bag over her shoulder and headed for her bedroom door.

"Good," replied Milo. "Be safe."

Ophelia hung up, shoving the phone in her bag and heading downstairs. As she left the townhouse she tossed a look at the lab where Milo conducted his work, annoyed he hadn't bothered to climb the two stories to her bedroom to say goodbye. Quickly, she turned away and jogged down the steps to the waiting taxi where she threw her bag inside and climbed in.

"Where to?" the driver asked, glancing in the rearview mirror.

Ophelia lifted her chin. "Away from here."

GHOSTS
KRAKOW

Back in the city he'd grown to love, Jude walked through Main Square on his way home. Evening draped the renaissance Cloth Hall in blue velvet and high above carved theatrical masks stared down on him with wide, all-seeing eyes.

Though dark, it wasn't yet late and the plaza swarmed with tourists admiring the magic of Krakow at night. Happiness spilled from open windows, greeting Jude like a long lost friend. As always, he felt a pang of sadness at the sound, but he also felt more at peace than he had in days. Leaving London had been the right decision. He couldn't wait for the gypsy girl – his part of the job was done - and there was no way he could stay with Adalain purposely driving him mad. Only a cruel woman would find pleasure in his pain. Then again, cruelty was as much a part of the Tarot as kindness.

Shoving his hands into his coat pockets, Jude looked up to check the time on Town Hall Tower - a brick steeple with a dark-faced clock. Ahead, Saint Mary's Basilica loomed, her silver spire jabbing a satin sky, rising well above surrounding medieval buildings. He headed toward it in pursuit of his favorite dive, a little pub in the basement of a fifteenth century armory.

The Old Armory Pub, as it was called, had a misfit charm Jude appreciated; ancient, gritty, rundown, and authentically Krakow. It still had bits of shield and rusted chainmail tacked on exposed stone walls. The floors were grimy, ceilings low and reinforced with wood beams blackened by age, and it was always dreary enough to convince even the most hardened tourist of its birthright.

The din of the square faded as Jude headed down a narrow side street and took a sharp left along a winding alley. Tourists might shy away from streets like this, but not Jude. He considered himself a local and walked with ease along the gutter.

Despite being cold enough to see breath, the night was clear and the moon shone bright, shimmering across paving stones. Jude followed the path, walking to a door indistinguishable from those on either side. Without knocking he pushed inside, ducking so he wouldn't hit his head on the low-beamed stairwell.

"Oi! Jude!" a burly bartender greeted as he carefully tackled the sloping stairs. When Jude reached the final step the bartender grinned with a cigarette hanging from his mouth. "Long time I no see, eh?" His English was heavily accented with Polish, but clear, if not a little broken.

"Tak," Jude agreed in Polish, taking his favorite seat near a blackened stone fireplace. It was lit, crackling and snappily merrily, spewing heat from behind an ornate iron grate. After unwinding his scarf and pulling off his gloves, Jude held his hands to the fire and settled back in the worn armchair.

"What you have?" the bartender, an ex-army commander named Ludwik, asked.

Jude raised a finger. "Piwo."

Ludwik nodded and turned to a row of silver taps along the bar, filling a pint glass with liquid gold.

The Old Armory Pub was quiet this time of night, most of the tourists moved on to restaurants with quainter charm, but a few locals sat around playing cards, drinking and laughing loudly.

Ludwik came around, handing Jude his pint. "Dzięki," thanked Jude, taking the spot-stained glass.

With a grunt Jude guessed meant, 'you're welcome,' Ludwik returned to his post behind the bar where an old TV noisily broadcasted news. Jude watched for a while and was halfway through his pint when the pub door groaned open. As everyone did when with new arrivals, Jude turned to look.

From the darkness a women's boots appeared atop the stairs. They stopped short of the final step and she ducked under the overhang, a pretty face appearing to peer tentatively into the gloom. Another step and she was inside, facing several gawking Polish men. She ignored them, crossing the room with searching eyes. After a quick scan, her gaze landed directly on Jude and froze.

Light from a nearby lamp fell across her face and Jude was surprised to find he recognized her from somewhere. But from where?

Immediately, the girl looked away, heading for the bar.

"Co mogę podać?" Ludwik asked, casting her look between glances at the TV.

"English?" she asked.

Jude perked up, convinced he must know her now.

"Ya," Ludwik answered. "What you want?"

"Water?"

Lukwik gave her a look that said 'Who drinks water in a pub?' but nodded and went to fetch a glass. While she waited, the girl looked back at Jude. He was still staring like a fool.

A silent exchanged passed between them, each assessing the other in a way too calculated to be considered flirting. When Ludwik returned she turned and took the glass. "Thank you," she said, retreating to a table in the shadows.

Jude's stare followed her across the room. Even the way she moved was familiar, as if he'd seen this girl, even walked with this girl, a thousand times before. It was maddening, like waking from a coma to discover he'd forgotten her.

After a time Jude got to his feet and took his pint to the bar, leaning close to speak to Ludwik. "Have you seen that girl before?" he asked in hushed Polish, jerking his head toward her.

Ludwik spared the girl a second look. "Nie."

"I think I might have…."

Ludwik winked. "Piękny."

Ignoring Ludwik's lewd tone, Jude stood. "I'll be back," he said, taking his pint and heading for the girl. As he walked, her eyes burned holes through his shirt. For a moment he considered turning back, but he had come too far already. "Hello," he greeted politely. "This is a strange question, but have we met before?"

It was hard to see in the shadows, but the curve of her face lifted toward him. "No," she said firmly.

"Are you sure? You're English. Maybe in London -"

"No," the girl repeated. Her body language was coiled and uncomfortable and instantly Jude felt horrible. Maybe she was scared of him? The thought left a bitter taste in his mouth, but he couldn't blame her. Growing up as the Knight of Swords did not shape him into a particularly charismatic young man. If anything, he was sharp and standoffish.

Even as Jude backed away, trying to give her space, the girl looked as if she wanted to bolt. "Sorry. I just thought…."

"I don't know you," the girl insisted, voice rising with panic.

A thought struck him. Maybe it wasn't him she feared at all? Maybe she was hiding from someone else? That would explain her appearance in the pub. "Is everything all right? You look…upset."

Unexpectedly the girl shot to her feet, causing her chair to smash against the wall.

Jude started. "What?" He stumbled back a step. "Hold on. I didn't mean -" But she was already darting for the door.

"Trouble?" Ludwik asked, a concerned frown folding his bushy brows in one.

The girl sprinted up and out without looking back.

Jude exchanged stunned looks with Ludwik. "Iść," said the bear-sized bartender, waving a hand. "Go after her."

"Put it on my tab," replied Jude, dashing up the stairs in pursuit.

Outside, the street was dark, night fully settled over the city. Stars were bright overhead, leading a narrow swath of sky between buildings. Jude saw the girl running ahead and went after her. "Wait!" he called. "Wait a second. I just want to make sure you're okay!"

The girl did not stop. She was fast, moving with the agility of a professional sprinter. Jude followed her back to Main Square, all the while calling for her to stop. A part of him thought he should give up – clearly she wanted to get away - but another part worried something worse was wrong and as a knight it went against his moral code to turn away.

Nimbly, the girl jumped curbs and darted around tourists and for a moment Jude lost her in the crowd. Finally, he caught sight of her again, streaking toward Town Hall Tower.

"Would you wait up?" he yelled, hurrying after. "I just want to talk to you!"

Several bystanders watched the chase with drawn expressions, as if they considered intervening.

"Go away!" the girl shouted over her shoulder, and then, as bizarre as it was, started climbing the tower.

"What the hell are you doing?" Jude tried to grab her foot, but she scrambled out of reach. "Get down! Are you insane? You're going to kill yourself."

If she heard him, she pretended otherwise, and kept climbing. Her arms stretched and pulled, feet finding crevices in the brick, working toward the observation deck above. If it had been any other situation Jude might have been impressed, but in the moment he was terrified and utterly baffled by her motives. "Shit," he muttered, darting around the building in search of a door. When he finally found one it was locked. "Great!" He thundered a fist against the wood, hoping someone might answer. When that yielded no result, he ran back around.

For a second his heart skipped, thinking he'd lost her. But then, there she was, still climbing. Nearly halfway up, the girl looked back. "Are you out of your bloody mind?" Jude called, panic expanding in his chest. "I'm calling the police."

The strange girl continued to ignore him and on a ledge no wider than a book's width, she stopped. "Leave me alone!"

"Get down!"

When she made no move to obey, Jude cursed under his breath. This was not how he envisioned his evening going. It his mind it had ended intoxicated, falling into bed with no recollection of how he'd got there. "I'm giving you five minutes to get back down here before I call the police."

Clinging to the building, dressed all in black, the girl looked like a dark angel, deadly and fierce. Moonlight glinted off her skin, grazing sharp features, and in that moment Jude remembered the girl on the train.

The reflection, he realized, choking on shock.

Even from a distance he could see the familiar challenge in her eyes and the realization pushed him back a step. This girl wasn't afraid of him, she'd been *following* him, and now she was trying to get away. "Who are you?" he croaked. Try as he might he couldn't formulate a theory. Who would want to follow him? And *why*?

The girl turned back and continued climbing. Jude watched, dumbstruck, unsure what to do. Something in his chest tightened, restricting air. He thought about running, but what good would that do?

Answers. He needed answers.

As she reached for the next hold, a wind picked up, gusty and strong, tossing dust and swirling leaves around the square. Something heavy fell from above, crashing to the ground in a shatter. Jude jumped, heart hitching, and when he looked up the girl screamed, losing her footing and falling in slow motion back to earth.

Jude had two choices: watch her fall or try and break it.

At the last second he threw himself in her path. What felt like a bag of cement slammed against him with a heavy *thud.* Air whooshed from his lungs, leaving him gasping. Everything hurt and the girl's unconscious body sprawled over him like a fallen tree. For a heartbeat, Jude panicked, thinking she was dead, but then her head lolled to the side and he felt the whisper of her breath on his neck.

Hissing in pain, Jude crawled from beneath her as onlookers scrambled to their aid.

"What happened?" a young American asked, helping Jude to his feet.

Stars shot behind his eyes, every muscle in his body protesting. "She tripped," he answered, dropping to one knee. "I caught her."

Two women helped the dazed girl to her feet. She looked sleepy-eyed and out of it, but groaned. One of the women asked for an ambulance in Polish.

"Nie," Jude shook his head, reaching for the girl and taking her in his arms. "I'll call a taxi." When the woman refused to let go he repeated the words in Polish "Taksówka. Dzięki"

The woman nodded and backed off.

After a minute, the American left with the two women, leaving Jude alone with the mystery girl. She was unsteady, but on her feet. "Come," he said quietly, pulling her close so not to attract attention. "You're going to tell me who the hell you are and what you want from me."

The girl whimpered in return.

A FAMILIAR FACE
KRAKOW

The last thing Ophelia remembered was falling in an endless motion. When she finally awoke she found herself in an unfamiliar room, awash in warm light. For a moment she thought it could be her hotel, but the bed was too soft and the ceiling too low. The roof was gabled and a small dormered window opened to the noisy street below, allowing a sharp breeze to cut through the room.

Disorientated and deliriously comfortable, she stretched and blinked in sleepy content.

"Look who's finally decided to rejoin us."

At the sound of a man's voice, Ophelia lurched, jolting upright and regretting it as a throbbing pain drove a stake through her skull. Shakily, she put a hand to her head and squinted across the room. Through weak light she could see the outline of someone seated in a chair. "What?" she croaked, her voice dry and scratchy, as if she'd been out for days. "Where am I?"

The shadow rose, stepping into better light. "You're in my flat."

Her breath caught, recognizing Jude`s face. There was something overwhelming about him up close, tall and enduring, as if he'd been cut from the hardest, most striking stone and nothing could break him. "Jude," she whispered, moving back until she bumped against the headboard.

His expression went from one of general perplexity to rigid question. "How do you know my name?"

Damn. She hadn't meant to say it aloud, it just escaped in surprise. Now there was no playing dumb and getting caught had never been part of her training, Milo always claimed it impossible. And yet, here she was, with Red Scarf looking directly at her. In fact, his red scarf was draped over a chair only a few feet away. The whole thing seemed oddly surreal. The scarf itself was a symbol of her life – always taunting and making chase - now she could almost touch it.

"Are you mute now?" Jude asked, jaw flexing with impatience.

Ophelia held his gaze, a difficult thing to do while curled on his bed. "Am I being kidnapped?"

His expression darkened and the tension grew thick. "Maybe. I haven't decided yet. It depends."

"On what?" Her voice held a hint of reservation, though she wasn't scared exactly, more apprehensive. Jude wasn't a stranger– even if she was to him. Though he'd been gone for years, she had known him before, following him since she was old enough to track. In that time he'd done nothing to make her nervous. In fact, out of all the knights Jude seemed the most intelligent and levelheaded. There was a cool confidence about him the others did not possess. He didn't have the charismatic charm of the ruddy haired Knight of Wands or the stoic grace of the raven haired Knight of Coins, but he had something else, something much more alluring. Like always, Jude appeared still as a frozen river, but beneath the ice she knew his soul ran deep and his thoughts swift.

Jude straightened, studying her with a steely glare. "It depends on who you are and why you're following me."

For a crazed moment Ophelia considered telling the truth. A part of her wanted to release the burden, but Milo's angered face blazed across her mind. She couldn't risk his years of endless work. She may not agree as passionately as her uncle that the Tarot needed to be stopped, but she'd been raised believing science was the only solution to solving the problem of maintaining the world's delicate balance of forces. And that meant making sure Milo succeeded in his plans. "I'm afraid I can't tell you."

Jude lifted a brow, though he didn't look very stunned. "And why not?" he asked, grinding teeth.

Ophelia knew she had to stall and gain some time to think. She pulled her knees close. "Do you have water? I can't talk with a dry throat."

"Water?" Jude echoed, looking both baffled and annoyed. "Yeah, I have water. Stay there." He pointed then disappeared into a small kitchen off the living area. The sound of clattering dishes and a running tap drifted from the next room.

Alone, Ophelia studied the apartment. It was small, but comfortable, cluttered with bookshelves against cracked plaster walls and a beat-up acoustic guitar leaning against a battered armchair. Several black and white posters of old bands were tacked to the walls - none of which she recognized. On the wall above the door she spotted a tacked Tarot Card: the Knight of Swords charging on a horse, sword extended. And below that she noted the bolted door. "Great," she grumbled. She'd never get the latch undone in time.

Jude returned, water in hand. "Here," he said, stabbing the glass at her. "Drink. Then talk."

Warily, she accepted, taking a long sip.

Calmly, he returned to the table and sat, leaning forward on one arm, and wordlessly opened his hand as if to say, 'go on.'

"What do you want to know?" she asked, peering restlessly into the glass.

"Why were you following me?"

That wasn't easy to explain and creating a plausible lie would take time. She had to stall. "Because I had no choice," she said.

A flicker of surprise passed over Jude's face. He straightened, eyes narrowed in suspicion. "Had no choice?"

There was dull ache persisting above Ophelia's left eye and she desperately wanted pain-killers and sleep. Funny, she could no longer remember the fall. Her last solid memory was of the dingy basement pub and trying to outrun Jude. Rubbing the spot gingerly, she answered, "It's complicated."

Jude sat back, the chair squeaking beanth his weight. From behind lowered lids he eyed her with mistrust. "What *can* you tell me?"

Ophelia shrugged, trying to look innocent. "Not much."

Jude's frown intensified. "All I want to know is why."

The two locked eyes, challenging the other to crack first. "Fine, I'll tell you," Ophelia agreed after a moment, "but my head is killing me. I need aspirin before I do."

"Aspirin?" Jude asked in the same annoyed tone.

She nodded.

After a suspicious, drawn out glare, he stood. "Wait here."

Again, Ophelia was left alone, but this time she didn't wait for Jude's return. As the kitchen cupboard squeaked open, she turned and bolted, clambering out the open window. As she went, her knee knocked over a lamp, sending it clattering to the floor and alerting Jude's attention.

"Hey!" he called, but she was already gone.

Outside, a narrow stone ledge ran the length of the building and Ophelia managed to wedge her toes firmly before finding a handhold in the rain trough. Quickly, she shimmied out of reach, headed toward the inner corner where it was easiest to reach the roof.

Surprisingly, Jude was halfway out the window in pursuit. "Where the hell do you think you're going?" he shouted, climbing onto the ledge after her.

A nervous flutter plucked Ophelia's heart as she scrambled onto the sharply slanted roof. The roof tiles were rough, old clay covered with years of dirt and grime, but they had good grip and she was able to claw back to her feet. Behind her, Jude scaled the wall with ease and Ophelia paused to admire his surprising elegance. It wasn't just anyone who could fearlessly climb a building.

Turning her back on him, Ophelia grabbed hold of a stout brick chimney and started toward a neighboring apartment block. It was about this time she realized how badly she'd been injured in the fall. Something was wrong with her knee and it clicked as she ran, shooting pain up her thigh. Admittedly, she had done many stupid things in life, but this might take the cake. A ripping pain twisted her right ankle and she realized it was probably sprained, if not fractured, and as if on cue her knee gave out. As she fell, she screamed, her head cracking the tiles as she collided with the roof in an explosion of pain.

The city lights blurred as Ophelia slid down the angled roof, grappling for grip that wasn't there. At the edge, her feet went over, and the scream sharpened an octave, as if it might stop the world from sliding out. For a dizzying second she caught sight of the street, black as night and hard as stone. With a terrified gasp, she braced for impact and was unexpectedly jerked back. Had her shirt caught? Her hands? No. They were pin-wheeling uselessly at her sides.

The scream in her throat cut off. She looked up, searching wildly to find Jude's hand tangled in back of her shirt. Amazingly, he was leaning over the edge, face red with strain as he worked to keep her from falling to her death. Desperate, Ophelia's only thought was survival. She couldn't die here – not like this. It was too ironic.

"Please don't drop me," she begged, not something she would normally do, not even if she'd been kidnapped or tortured. But for some reason, with her life literally hanging by a thread, she clung to it – to him. "Please."

Jude's arm shook with the exertion, his teeth bared in effort. "I won't, but you have to climb."

Breathe, Ophelia reminded herself. If she could trust him – which she had no other choice – she could survive this. With a shaky breath, she reached up, grabbing hold of a rusted bolt driven into the stone exterior. Next, she found purchased where mortar had worn away from the brick and with Jude's help scrambled clumsily back to safety.

Gasping, she rolled onto her back, sucking air. "Thank you," she rasped.

There was no reply from Jude who sprawled next to her, staring at the sky, chest heaving in starts and falls.

Eventually, Ophelia pushed herself to her elbows, every inch of her trembling. She looked down at Jude. His dark lashes brushed pale cheeks, tinged crimson by cold and effort. "I'll give you five minutes to run," he said plainly.

It took a moment for the words to register, but once they did, she needed no time to act. Ophelia didn't know why he let her go – maybe because she'd risked her life for freedom – but it didn't matter. Quickly, she got to her feet, facing a large gap between buildings. The only way across was by steel cable. Her body thrummed as she stepped carefully onto the thick wire, feet sliding easily, one in front of the other with her arms spread wide for balance. The wind gusted, which made it hard to keep her footing, and several times she wobbled. Each time she heard Jude's sharp intake of breath at her back, but she ignored it, deadly focused.

When at last she reached the adjacent roof, she paused. With her back pressed to the opposing wall, Ophelia closed her eyes, giving silent thanks. When she opened them she found Jude staring at her from across the way. He was crouched on the balls of his feet, watching with intense passion.

A weighty silence hung between them, sharp and crisp as winter's night.

With a strange sense of regret, Ophelia tore her gaze away and left, climbing over the roof and down the exterior to run the length of Old Town back to the Fortuna Hotel.

In the safety of her room, she bolted the door, sliding into an achy puddle on the floor. What had she done? How had things gone so terribly wrong? She reached for the knot of twisted metal at her throat, forgetting it was gone. When her hand found nothing, she closed her eyes, furious at herself. It was *her* fault. She'd entered the pub thinking she'd still be invisible to Jude, forgetting the gypsy had taken her charm.

She shivered. It appeared the Knight of Swords had finally taken notice.

THE PATH TO FOLLOW
BIAŁOWIEŻA FOREST, BELARUS

In the heart of a dense wood, the Magician wacked his way through the bush with his walking cane. For most a forest is not a great sight, especially for Rosaline who spent part of her childhood in the backwoods of Romania, but there was something about this wood in particular that had her captivated, as if the very air pulsed with energy and the trees sung with magic.

"What is this place?" she asked the Magician, following him over fallen logs covered in thick earthen moss.

"This," said the Magician, "is the Białowieża Forest, one of the oldest primeval forests in the world. It is ancient, old as time itself, and the birthplace of the Order of the Tarot. It is home to the House of Coins whose element, as you might imagine, is *earth*." The Magician inhaled the smell the soil as if it were ecstasy. "This way," he said, starting down a seemingly indistinguishable path. "This forest is home to the Coins," he rattled on as he walked, "but you may have noticed the Major Arcana, or the Trump cards as they are called in the deck, live back at Tarot headquarters. The High Priestess, the Fool, Death, the Tower, the Hanged Man; all twenty-two of us live under the same roof as the ruling members. The four remaining Houses, or suits, that make up the remaining fifty-seven members of the Order of the Tarot live in separate corners of the world, each in a place that reflects their elemental bond. It's where they flourish, where their forces are the strongest. And you shall have the chance to visit them all on your journey."

Rosaline thought of her Tarot cards tucked into the battered suitcase she'd dragged from Paris, left behind at the manor. The Major Arcana were trumps cards with the strongest meaning and greatest force. Her mother had taught her to think of them as ruling cards, laying influence over the others suits and setting the tone of a reading. "And you live in the manor with the Major Arcana?" she asked. "As their leader?"

"Yes," he replied, "although I don't consider myself a leader so much as an organizer or a link."

Rosaline nodded as they continued through the trees, ducking and swatting their way along. "But what exactly are we doing here? I thought you wanted me to be the Queen of Cups, not Coins?"

The Magician carefully picked his way over tree roots and stumps. For a man pressing sixty, he was deftly agile. "First, you must meet the King and Queen of each House."

"I see," said Rosaline, though she still felt lost.

The Magician glanced back, catching the uncertainty in her voice. "Before you can become Queen of Cups you must earn the respect of the four Houses. To do this you must journey to each House and pass a predetermined task."

Like a quest, thought Rosaline, dread creeping slowly up her spine. Quests did not always end well for the hero and she didn't like the sound of the word *task*. She had never been smart or overly athletic. What happened if she failed? Would she be sent back to Paris? A swell of panic hitched her breath. "What kind of task?" she managed bravely. "Like a game?"

The Magician gave her a long look, continuing his steady pace. "In order for this to work, my girl, you must stop thinking of the Tarot as cards. We are not cards – this is not a game. The Tarot is very real."

"Okay," allowed Rosaline. "But what does the Tarot do exactly? Other than standing around being themselves?"

"Not much," admitted the Magician. "The kings and queens oversee their Houses, keeping each member inline. The Pages run messages to the manor, and sometimes on rare occasions, for me. The Knights have similar roles, although they are sworn to protect the Tarot at all costs. They also do our recruiting. The Queen of Cups though," the Magician held up a finger, "well, she is special. She is our oracle. For as long as the Order of the Tarot has existed the Queen of Cups has seen the future. She sees our new members, and predicts the death of old. Without her, we would be lost."

Rosaline swallowed, she had never been good with pressure. She tried her best to shove the discomfort aside and asked another question to keep her mind occupied. "What about Jude, the knight who found me, he mentioned he lived in Krakow. Is that where the House of Swords is?"

"Krakow? Well, no." The Magician shook his head sadly. "Jude is an exception. He chooses to live alone, away from his House and other members of the Tarot."

This puzzled Rosaline. She couldn't imagine why anyone would want to live a life of exclusion and isolation. She'd experienced enough of that on the streets of Paris to know it was no life to live. "Why?"

A muscle tightened in the Magician's jaw and Rosaline thought he would not answer, but eventually he replied, "Jude turned his back on the Order for many reasons. The one thing you must understand is that accepting a role within the Tarot does not guarantee an easy life. The responsibility is heavy. Each member has their part to play, and each role is different. Although he has not yet left us completely, it may only be a matter of time before Jude renounces his vow and we must replace our Knight of Swords. Who can say?" Sorrow wavered behind the Magician's rainy, grey eyes, "But for now he is still an important member of the Tarot. There are not many things in life that I do not understand, but Jude happens to be one of them. He is a complicated young man."

Rosaline wholeheartedly agreed, but she couldn't fathom why Jude was so miserable. She imagined herself here in the forest, living among trees and rivers, and found it easy to be happy. No more sleeping under bridges or stairwells or breaking into abandoned buildings to find shelter for the night. It sounded just like the fairytale she'd always imagined. "Well, I like it here."

The darkness lifted from the Magician's eyes and he smiled. "There is much more to see, child."

Rosaline nodded, her excitement growing. If the House of Cups was even half as lovely as the Coins' forest, she knew she would be happy forever. "What else do I have to do in order to become Queen? Besides the tasks, I mean."

"Nothing, really," the Magician replied happily. "You must accept who you are and swear an oath to honor it. You already possess the force of our Queen of Cups. You just have to cherish it. Other than that, the Order will provide for you, give you shelter and food and anything else you need. Your only obligation is to uphold your vow."

"And what if I can't do that?" she asked, needing to understand. What if she wasn't the person they thought she was? Or better yet, what if she ended up being someone she wasn't? "Could I leave?"

Above, the trees were thick and leafy, casting shadows over the narrow, winding path. "The Tarot is not a prison," the Magician replied. "You can leave whenever you wish. But if our current queen dies before we find someone equally suited for the role, the wheel will break. The world will suffer and everyone in it. In order to maintain balance over the world's opposing forces, every card, every member of the Tarot, must be filled."

"But that doesn't explain what will happen," insisted Rosaline. "What *happens* to the world if I say no?"

"War," the Magician shrugged. "A hurricane, a pandemic maybe, it's hard to say. It's different every time and only gets better once the balance resumes. If we don't mend the break quickly, it could lead to total destruction."

"But how can an unbalanced Tarot deck create war? It's just one card."

The Magician gave her a sturdy look. "Because, my dear, think of it this way: The Tarot deck is balanced, but take away a good card – say the Six of Coins - whose role it is to give charitably, and suddenly there is less good in the deck. It becomes unbalanced. Now there is too much bad, or evil, or hate, depending on how you look at it. And where there is too much hate follows war. Same goes with the elements. If you remove a card like the Cups, that corresponds to the element of water, then the there are more cards of fire, which can make the earth hot and dry and burdened with drought. It is a delicate balance, a card that seems so insignificant, becomes increasingly significant when it is removed."

Rosaline nodded, seeing things clearer, but still unsatisfied. "And what if I take the oath and break it? What if it turns out I can't be the Queen?"

"You cannot betray who are already are," the Magician remarked, and he was right. There was nothing Rosaline could do about her gift of sight. As a child she'd never wanted it, but all the crying and head shaking could not dislodge the unwanted images from her mind. "But if you go against your character, or if you become hateful or cynical or deceiving, you will break your oath and the balance will be undone."

A thought struck her, recalling the cards once again. "Is that why Jude is the way he is? The Knight of Swords can't care for others, can he? He is a fighter but it is not in his card to love. He is supposed to be too blinded by the job."

The Magician's mouth set into a grim line. "Jude has never been a perfect fit. He struggles to maintain his oath. When they are chosen as young as he it is never easy. People grow, they change, and he grew into someone he doesn't necessarily want to be. There are many things about Jude that reflect the Knight of Swords; inherent traits. He is intelligent, a born fighter, he will do what is asked of him, charge at full force to get it done, but it has never been all of him…that's all I can say."

A new understanding filled Rosaline. "And what if I change my mind later? What if I want to leave like Jude?"

"Jude does not want to leave," the Magician insisted and for a moment Rosaline regretted asking. He led her further into the woods, following a path surrounded in fallen logs, thick ferns and lush undergrowth. Even the air smelled different now, heavy with evergreen, rich earth and sap.

"Jude doesn't know what he wants," the Magician continued after some time, calmer now. "The Order of the Tarot is not a life sentence; it is a way of life – one which Jude has only ever known. If you take the vow as queen, you must take it seriously, but if, at some point, you decide this is not the life you want, you are welcome to return to the streets of Paris and forget us. All I ask is that you give me time to find a replacement before you break your vow. If there is no one to take your place when you leave, the balance will break all the same."

It seemed fair to Rosaline. There wasn't much she was giving in exchange. She knew enough about her card, the Queen of Cups, to know she was allowed to live and be happy and thrive, unlike Jude. She felt no sadness, or bitterness, or heartache over leaving Paris behind, or her mother - who she had long ago accepted she might never see again. There would be dinner parties and lavish gowns and crowns in her future. No more rats or cold nights or hunger. Without a shard of a doubt, Rosaline looked to the Magician and nodded. "You don't have to worry, Magician. I will be your Queen of Cups."

"Good," replied the Magician, in a voice suggesting he already knew this would be her answer. "You can prove it by passing your first task."

THE KNIGHTHOOD
PARIS

Paris at twilight was Jude's one true addiction. As the sun sank behind the Eiffel Tower, pale gold light streamed along the Seine, glittering across the surface and backlit by a sky turned blood-orange.

Jude watched the sunset, leaning in the doorway of a closed patisserie. He knew the girl was somewhere close. He could feel her. In fact, he'd felt her presence since leaving Krakow and as bizarre as it seemed, it had become a comfort. For so long he had felt alone, but now the dull ache of loneliness relented, if only a little, replaced by the curious consolation of someone always being there, just out of sight.

As the sky faded from fire to dusky rose as if a curtain had been drawn across the heavens, stars began to appear, sparking to life. Now, the Eiffel Tower lit up, dancing with a thousand shimmering lights. In all his years and all his visits to Paris, Jude could still feel the magic of those lights. He remembered something the Magician had said once long ago, touring the city for the first time.

"Do you feel that, boy?" he had asked, the lure of Paris alight in his eyes.

Jude and the Magician had stood on the Pont d'lena, halfway between Paris' Left Bank and Right, staring wide-eyed at the lattice iron tower. Jude could never say what it was about the gargantuan structure that made it beautiful, the iron itself was cold and lifeless. Maybe it was the greenery surrounding it, or the people admiring it, or just the impact it had on everything else, like a raven in a field of doves - so out of place in the rightist way, it was mesmerizing.

"Feel what?" Jude had asked, his head tilted back so far he nearly fell over so he could take in the tower's height.

"The air," the Magician answered with a sense of wonder. "It sparks." He illustrated, wiggling his fingers until it seemed like the air crackled with magic.

Jude looked from the tower to his mentor, tucking his hands in his pockets. It was a clear summer day and the city was lush and green. The air smelled of roasted caramel and candy floss while a stunning carousel of galloping white horses slowly turned before him, marching to the sound of circus flutes and bells. He thought, just for a moment, if he could climb onto one of those horses the magic of Paris would surely carry him away.

"Yes," he answered, so caught in wonder he could barely speak. The enchanted city with its grand mirrored palaces, immense gothic cathedrals and ancient stone monuments spoke to him in a way the House of Swords never had.

That first day in Paris Jude had fallen in love. Years later it seemed bittersweet. The city, *his* city, was still the same, and he still loved it more than he had ever loved anything in his life. And that was rather heartbreaking. For a time after he'd left the House of Swords, Jude had lived in Paris, fitting in well with starving artists and tattered musicians. But the loneliness howled strongest here; a constant reminder of just how little he had in life. For as beautiful and magical as Paris was, it did not, could not, love him back.

Despite all that, it was good to walk these streets again and Jude's sprits soared.

"Paris at night," a voice said from the dark. "Could there be a more beautiful sight?"

Jude turned, meeting the glint of Nicolai's eyes in twilight. He smiled, despite himself. It wasn't often he saw his oath-brother these days, not since he had made the choice to live away from the Tarot. "I was worried you wouldn't get my message in time."

Nicolai stepped into the light of a nearby streetlamp. "I got it, but I can't stay long. I have somewhere to be."

"What does the Magician have you jumping to do now?"

Nicolai smiled and pulled up the collar of his jacket "A job you wouldn't want."

Jude grunted in response.

Nicolai let the subject drop. "So where are we going this fine Parisian evening?"

"The Hotel du Louvre," Jude replied and stepped onto the road. Nicolai followed and together the pair turned down Port Debilly, headed along the Seine.

"Why there?"

"Because it's public and open. Nowhere to hide."

"Nowhere to hide from *who*?" asked Nicolai, shooting Jude a dark look.

"I'll tell you when we meet up with the others."

Jude knew Nicolai wouldn't press for more. His oath-brother knew Jude too well for that. True to assumption, Nicolai slid him a sideways glance but offered a new question in place of the other, "Then why Paris?"

"It was central to the Houses," Jude replied, not mentioning he was testing the girl to see if she would follow him abroad.

Nicolai did not look convinced, but he nodded and kept on.

The walk to the hotel was short, with Jude checking over his shoulder every few minutes and Nicolai following his paranoid glances with puzzled looks of his own. "Who the hell are you looking for?" he finally asked.

"Hm?" Again, Jude checked for the girl. There was no doubt she was there; the silent heaviness that came with being watched from a distance lingered, but wherever she was, she remained well hidden.

They rounded the corner to the hotel entrance. "You keep looking around like you're waiting for someone to jump you."

"Not here," Jude answered, pushing into the hotel lobby.

Nicolai made a disgruntled sound and followed. Inside, the hotel was busy with dinner guests and tourists checking in. Without a word Jude headed for the lounge, separated from the lobby by heavy red curtains tied back with twisted gold-spun cord. The tables were polished mahogany, oval-shaped and low, surrounded by leather chairs. In the middle, two young men waited - the older sipping from a glass and the other staring into space.

Immediately, Jude recognized the dark haired man as Sol, the Knight of Coins; the eldest of the Order's Knighthood. He was in his late twenties, though recruited very young, and possessed a haunting grace that was the epitome of what Jude thought a knight of Tarot should be: tall, sturdy, with dark sweeping hair and piercing onyx eyes cut sharp as black ice.

Beside Sol sat Kieran, the Knight of Wands, closest to Jude in age. He also looked the part, though more traditionally handsome, like Nicolai, with copper hair, blazing green eyes, and a dashing smile. In fact, Jude had always thought himself the only one not to fit the part. He wasn't overly tall or broad shouldered, his hair wasn't long and flowing and he certainly didn't have the chiseled features of Nicolai or the blinding smile of Kieran.

Jude was like any other nineteen-nearing-twenty-year-old, still somewhat scrawny from his last growth spurt, although he'd been working hard to put on muscle, with an ordinary face and unremarkable blue eyes, dark like the ocean. Although he'd never admit it aloud, Jude always felt the Magician had made a mistake when he'd recruited him to be the Knight of Swords. Once, when he was quite young, Jude had asked the Magician if it was possible to make such an error. The Magician had simply answered, 'No', and Jude had never asked again. For if it was true, and the Magician had made a mistake, he wasn't sure he wanted to know. If he didn't belong here, where did he belong? He couldn't see himself among regular people and their regular problems, not now – not after everything he knew. But no one else in the Knighthood seemed so out of place. Just him, alone.

"Jude." Kieran raised a hand in greeting. Sol turned but kept his expression blank, as always. If it wasn't about business, Sol had nothing to say. He dedicated his life to being the Knight of Coins and nothing would sway his drive – not love, not family, not freedom, nothing.

For a long time Jude had admired the older knight's resolve; he didn't struggle with acceptance or fight to maintain control, he seemed to be exactly who he was supposed to be. He was not a risk and he most certainly didn't need to be reminded of his vow. But recently Jude had changed his opinion. Now, whenever he saw his oath-brother, the only thing he felt was pity. Neither Jude nor Sol was permitted to love, but at least – Jude thought – *he* was capable of it.

Nicolai and Kieran, on the other hand, were free to love nearly anyone they desired. It was part of them to love and be loved, they didn't hold everyone at a distance, putting their work first like Jude and Sol.

As Jude took a seat across from Kieran and Nicolai pulled out a chair, Sol locked eyes with his oath-brother. "What's this about, Sword?" he asked, having a habit of calling each of the knights by their House.

"Let me order a drink." Jude signaled for a waitress while simultaneously searching the room for signs of the mysterious girl.

"What's wrong?" Kieran asked. "You seem agitated."

Jude gave a dry laugh, returning his attention to his oath-brothers. "You could say that."

"Get on with it, then. What's so important you called us here?" Sol's tone was sharp, accusing.

There was underlying meaning in the older knight's words, but Jude tried his best to pretend otherwise. "I think I'm being followed," he announced, keeping his voice earnest.

For a moment no one spoke. Kieran and Nicolai exchanged a look while Sol leaned back in his chair, appraising Jude with cool, dark eyes. "Followed?" he asked, one brow lifted in doubtful question. "By who?"

"I have no idea," answered Jude honestly.

Sol folded his arms across his chest. "Explain," he said sharply, true to his short-tempered nature.

The last thing Jude wanted was to come off crazy - he was sure his oath-brothers already thought he was. "I don't understand either," he began, shooting another glance around the lobby. If she was here, she was well hidden. The hotel was well-lit and open with little place to hide. But he was sure she hadn't given up and gone home, either. "I caught a girl following me in Krakow. I think she followed me all the way from London. But she got away before I could question her."

"Hold on," Nicolai raised a hand. "You caught someone? And then she escaped? God, Jude. That sounds a lot like kidnapping…." He leaned forward, intent on Jude, with a small worry line creased between his brows.

"I didn't *kidnap* anyone," Jude insisted. He was mildly irritated that Nicolai could even think so. "I told you, she followed me. Something is really off. I need your help to figure out who she is and what she wants."

"It's probably just some girl who's fallen madly in love with you, Jude." Kieran gave his oath-brother a long look. "I'm sure it's nothing...I thought you had a girl in Krakow that you – well, you know. You sure it's not her? Maybe she's jealous and stalking you. Girls do things like that."

Jude met Kieran's eyes with fierce intensity. How could he think he'd involve his oath-brothers in something so stupid? "It's nothing like that. I swear."

"Jude isn't nearly charming enough for that," Nicolai added.

It was true, so Jude didn't bother denying it. There was nothing charming about him.

"Who do you think this person is?" asked Sol, the only one who seemed to be taking the matter seriously. "And why do you think she's following you?"

"I have no idea," Jude insisted, glad someone was paying attention. These three men were supposed to trust and honor him until his death and right now he certainly did not feel trusted or honored. He bit back what he wanted to say and instead replied, "That's why I need you– to help me solve it without getting the Magician involved. I don't know for sure, but I think she might know something about us."

A heavy silence passed over the table, each knight contemplating the one question they had to ask: *how much does she know?*

Sol spoke first, "Maybe she's not following you. Maybe you just think she is. Could it be a coincidence?"

Jude wished he could say yes, but there was too much evidence against it. "No." He shook his head. "For one she climbed a building to get away from me – several, actually. Second, she followed me to Paris."

"Here?" Nicolai's voice caught on surprise. He twisted in his chair, looking around the lobby. Sol and Kieran did the same, although less obviously.

"She's not in the hotel. But she's here in Paris. I know she is."

Sol slid his gaze back to Jude, tapping a rhythmic finger against his glass. "How do you know she's here? Did you see her?"

No. Not exactly, was the truthful response, but if Jude said as much Sol would drop the matter until he had proof, and there was a nagging feeling in the pit of Jude's stomach telling him he didn't have time to waste. "She was at the train station when I left, then again outside the hotel this morning. And across the street from the café I was at this afternoon. She's here."

Slowly, Sol sat forward, his dark eyes lingering on shadows about the room. "This doesn't make sense. Why would anyone want to follow you? And how could they know anything about *us*?"

"There's more…," Jude went on, "I think she was at the manor the night of the dinner party."

"Headquarters?" Nicolai questioned, stunned. He shook his head. "There's no way…."

"You saw her there?" interrupted Sol.

"No," Jude tried to explain, but he wasn't exactly sure how. "I *felt* her there, although I didn't realize it at the time. But I think Rosaline, the new recruit, did. I think she may have seen her. Spoke to her…."

"Did she say so?" Nicolai asked.

"Not in so many words."

"Well, did you ask her?"

"I didn't think I had a reason to ask. I didn't know the girl existed." Jude snapped, growing tired. "Which is why I need you to go and ask Rosaline now."

"This is getting absurd," Sol cut in, his brows drawn tight and menacing.

"Why don't you ask her yourself?" Nicolai suggested.

The question was rhetorical since Nicolai knew very well Jude would not step foot near the Tarot again so soon. "If I showed up the Magician would know something was wrong. I need you to ask her; she likes you, she'll talk to you."

The tips of Nicolai's ears reddened.

"Just ask her." Jude rubbed his eyes, feeling a headache coming on. "There's something about Rosaline. She sees things no one else can. It's the only lead I have."

Nicolai seemed to consider Jude's request a moment, then finally nodded. "Okay, fine. I'll ask her when I see her next."

"And I'll see what I can learn," added Sol, downing the last of his drink.

"That's all I ask," replied Jude. He had no idea what Sol could possibly uncover, but he trusted the older knight and knew he was good at his job, if nothing else. "I just don't want her hurt." He wasn't sure why he added the last part. Sol wasn't the type to hurt a woman – even ones that spied. But there was something about the girl he couldn't explain and he couldn't stand the idea of her being tortured for information.

Sol gave him a look from over the brim of his glass. "Why would I hurt her?"

Jude lifted one shoulder and let it drop. "I don't know. Just – don't."

Sol stared at him for a long time as though trying to read his thoughts. "I won't."

Jude nodded, his gaze faltering.

The older knight straightened, his mark blazing brilliant green against the glass still gripped in his hand. "Just remember your vow, Sword."

THE ART OF SCIENCE
LONDON

Ophelia tossed her bag into the corner of the foyer and looked up. "Hello?" she called, searching the empty banister above. When no one answered, she turned to her uncle's study, finding the door ajar.

Strange, she thought, waiting for someone to appear.

What Ophelia really wanted was a warm cup of tea and her bed, but the door beckoned, pulling her closer. It was late. Milo should have been home, and even though she dreaded telling him what had happened in Krakow, she knew he needed to know. It was why she'd come all this way after being unable to reach him by phone.

"Uncle Milo?" she called again, her feet creaking across the wood floor.

Tiny hairs on her arms stood as she stepped over the threshold into the study, greeted by a crackling fire and an empty room. From the state of the desk, cluttered with papers and pens and dirty dishes, it looked as if Milo hadn't been gone long.

"Uncle Milo?" she called once more, this time louder, letting her voice travel along the tiled ceiling.

Still, there was nothing.

For a long while she stood, feeling the house. Something wasn't right. It itched in the back of her throat. Then an acidic stench reached her nose. At first she thought it was smoke from the fire, but it was stronger than the burn of fresh cut wood, with a sharpness that stung her eyes. She spun to face her uncle's lab - a door tucked between two towering bookshelves. Seeping from beneath, Ophelia spotted a faint stream of smoke creeping along the floor.

"Uncle Milo!" she screamed. Instantly, she was across the room, pounding a fist against the door, but it wouldn't budge and no one answered on the other side. For several hopeless minutes she tried to kick her way in and shake the knob loose, all to no avail.

Conceding, she raced back to the hall, her mind a tornado of thoughts. Should she call the fire department? Evacuate? Rescue the small box of memories hidden under her bed? But all of that seemed trivial compared to the devastating need to save her uncle. She ripped open the hall closet, yanking coats and umbrellas aside to find a small fire extinguisher. It was wedged between an old cricket bat and a pair of riding boots she hadn't touched in years. Her hands trembled as she pulled it free and stumbled back to the study.

The room was slowly filling with smoke, the acrid smell burning her eyes and throat, making it difficult to see as she fumbled across the study. Back at the lab door, she used the extinguisher to smash the doorknob. Within a few swift strikes, the knob clattered to the floor and Ophelia was able to force the door open, kicking it with the heel of her boot. As the door burst in, a blast of choking smoke nearly knocked her back. Instinctively, Ophelia covered her mouth with her arm, dragging gulps of polluted air into her lungs. "Uncle Milo!" she screamed, squinting through thick smoke. It was so dense she couldn't see, not even the source of the fire, but then she spotted the low burning ball of flame engulfing a nearby table.

Coughing, Ophelia managed to pull the pin on the extinguisher while shuffling closer to the blaze. The air grew hot and thin, sweat beaded down her forehead and smoke charred her lungs. A few feet from the blaze, Ophelia pulled the trigger and a stream of heavy white foam burst from the nozzle. For a heart pounding minute Ophelia thought it wouldn't be enough. The fire continued to lick the foam, long blazing fingers stretching for anything that would burn.

And then it was out, and all that remained was a room full of smoke and watery puddle of foam at her feet.

"Uncle Milo!" Ophelia cried, turning blindly in the haze. She could see only shapes and streaks of dancing light from halogen bulbs burning high above. Still clutching the extinguisher, she stumbled to the window, using the butt to smash it out. Glass shattered musically to the floor as cool wet air drank the smoke and carried it away.

Ophelia sucked in drags of fresh air through rounded lips, trying to clear the poison fog from her head. When at last the smoke began to dissipate, she let the extinguisher fall to the ground and went in search of Milo.

Despite the heat of the blaze, the lab was relatively unharmed, minus the unfortunate table. Ophelia waved a hand in front of her face, coughing as she tried to clear a path through the smog. At last she found him, huddled in a heap near the door. He was unconscious, a balled lab coat crumpled in his hand and a small fire extinguisher abandoned by his feet.

Crashing to her knees, Ophelia placed two fingers against his throat, trembling in panic. Through the smoke, she could see the faint rise and fall of Milo's chest and feel the faint flutter of a pulse beat beneath her fingertips. "Thank god," she whispered. He was alive, but not in good shape. She needed to get him somewhere safe to breathe.

She looked around, searching for something to carry him from the room. Milo wasn't a big man, but he wasn't exactly a twig, either. In the end, Ophelia was forced to roll him onto a lab coat and drag him from the room like a slab of cargo, huffing and puffing the entire way.

Once free from the smoke, she dropped the coat and went about opening windows to air out the study. When she returned to her uncle's side, she knelt, smoothing his sweat-slicked forehead. "Uncle Milo." She touched his burning cheek. "Wake up."

He began to stir, his brow creasing as if in pain, coughing and moaning as his head thrashed side-to-side. "What happened?" he croaked, his voice raw.

"There was a fire," Ophelia whispered, hoping to keep him calm.

Milo closed his eyes, letting his head loll. "How bad? My lab…"

"The lab is fine," she answered. "The house is still standing."

Milo relaxed, shoulders slumping. "Water."

Ophelia climbed to her feet, reluctant to leave his side, and found a pitcher on the desk. She poured him a glass and returned. "Here." She held the glass to his lips as he struggled to sit. "Should I call for help?"

"No," Milo shook his head, taking the glass in a shaky hand. "I can't have anyone inside the lab. They'll see my work and the book of Athios. They'll destroy everything the Order of Science Against Magic has achieved."

Ophelia frowned. "Well, maybe I should take you to the hospital. I can call a cab."

"No," he clutched her hand, squeezing harder than she would have thought possible in his state, "no hospitals. I'm fine."

"But -" Ophelia looked him over, noticing the vivid streaks of soot on his once pristine lab coat. "All that smoke…."

"I'm fine," he wheezed, struggling onto the couch.

Ophelia helped him then took a seat, keeping one hand on his shoulder. There was no benefit in arguing. She would just have to keep a close eye on him and call an ambulance should he lose consciousness. "Can I get you anything else?" she asked, taking back the empty glass. By now most of the smoke had cleared from the study but the horrid smell of burning chemicals lingered, seeping into the walls. They would have to call a restoration company to get the smell out, and even then Ophelia doubted it would ever smell pleasant again.

Milo shook his head. "I feel better now. I just needed some air." He paused, his face suddenly stricken. "Did you check the Omniworld?"

"No," she admitted. "There was a lot of smoke. I couldn't see."

Milo's hand tightened on her wrist in panicked desperation. "Check! Now!"

"Okay," she replied a little sharply. "Calm down and wait here." She rose and crossed the room to the lab. It reeked of charred oxygen and scorched metal, sharp on her tongue. Swirling gray smoke filled the room while bands of moonlight streaked from the glass-domed ceiling above and the breeze from the broken window tossed papers about like weightless white birds.

An outsider would see the room as it was – a lab like any other, fitted with tables and beakers and microscopes and computers. But Milo's lab held something other did not. At the center of the room stood a mountainous structure, partially covered in a tattered burlap sheet. Ophelia made her way carefully across the room to the base of the structure. One corner of the sheet had come loose from its twine tie and hung limply. She grabbed a fistful, yanking it free and letting it fall in a flutter of dust, covering the floor like a moth-eaten blanket.

Before her, huge and awe-inspiring, loomed a globe with the inner workings of a turn of the century clock. It was so tall it nearly scraped the ceiling and through gaps in the beautifully crafted land masses, gears and cogs ticked and whirred as the gargantuan structure slowly turned. The exterior was polished bronze, some parts new and others tarnished and worn, looking as if it had been built a hundred years earlier before batteries and electricity could power such a thing. Between moving continents, where oceans should have been, Ophelia could see newer gears, shiny and oiled among the old, creaky, and slow. And behind it all, barely visible at the core, was a glowing glass orb the size of basketball.

Ophelia took a step closer, mesmerized by the light at the center: green flame, white light, and sparks of orange, coiling slowly like a spiral galaxy.

"The Omniworld," she said in a detached sort of way, enamored and frightened by the globe every time she set eyes on it. It was a gigantic structure, blueprints outlined by the Book of Athios; a machine supposedly capable of maintaining the world's balance of opposing forces once the Tarot was destroyed. She had no idea if it would ever work – a part of her didn't think so -but Milo was so adamant, so passionate about his Ominworld, there was no reasoning with him.

"Thank God," Milo wheezed from the doorway, one hand pressed to the frame, the other clutching his stomach as if his insides were about to spill out.

Startled, Ophelia took two soldiering steps to reach him. "Milo. You shouldn't be on your feet. Sit back down!"

He ignored her, stared at the mechanical world with adoration on his wrinkled face, shuffling into the room until the light of the Omniworld reflected an eerie green in the depths of his pale grey eyes. He placed a hand gently on the globe, letting it run beneath his fingers. "I am so close, Ophelia. I can feel it. Can't you?"

Ophelia said nothing, watching Milo watch the globe. In truth, she could feel nothing but the sense of dread that had been slowly rising in her chest for months as Milo's machine edged closer and closer to completion.

"The chemical balance of the core is still too weak, but I'm close. Very close. Soon."

"Maybe we don't need the Omniworld at all, Uncle Milo," Ophelia offered, trying to placate him. "The world doesn't seem that *unstable* to me."

"That's only because of the Tarot!" he shouted, startling her. "It's their magic that keeps the world stable. But we can't let them! We have to stop them! They steal innocent human souls. Twist their minds until they see nothing but lies and deceit!"

"Are you feeling okay?" Ophelia stepped forward, reaching to touch his forehead. Maybe the smoke had given him a fever? He seemed erratic – even more so than usual.

Milo jerked his head away, eyes sharp with impatience. "I'm fine." He glared. "You think I'm crazy, don't you? I raised you from a baby. You've seen the Tarot with your own eyes! How could you doubt me? How could you doubt the Order of Science Against Magic and the Book of Athios?"

Ophelia glanced at the book propped on the counter, unharmed, thankfully, for she didn't know what Milo would do had it been damaged. It was practically his soul. She wasn't entirely sure what she believed. She knew the Tarot existed, that was true, but she had never seen them sacrifice souls or do anything else Milo was convinced they did to maintain power. "I'm not sure what I believe," she admitted, trying to phrase her disbelief gently. This was Milo, after all - the man who had raised her. He was also a world-renown physicist, or at least he had been, once. She had a hard time believing he would waste time on something that had no merit whatsoever. It was unlike him to be wrong. But then again he hadn't been very forthcoming about being fired from the university months ago. Could his growing obsession have something to do with it? Could his mind be unraveling? She'd heard somewhere geniuses were far more likely to go insane.

"Would I lie to you?" he asked.

"No," she answered without hesitation, knowing it was true. Her uncle may be many things, but he was not a liar. Not like her.

"The Tarot are bad people, Ophelia. Evil. And they'll steal your soul too, if you let them." He stepped closer, blinking wildly. "They use old magic, dangerous and powerful, left over from the beginning of time. And the only way to overcome it is through science."

The power in his voice unnerved her. She swallowed, trying to hide her discomfort.

Milo drew himself up. "The time has come. We must break them now."

She did not like desperation in his voice; it rattled and wheezed, making him sound like a murderer about to make his first kill. "And how do we do that?"

"By breaking a vow. If we do that, we can weaken them, and then it's only a matter of time until the Tarot's control unravels. That's when we step in. The Omniworld will take control of the forces, which will relieve every last Tarot from their role. The answer lies in one of the four knights. Two are no good. There is nothing you or I could do to break their vows to the Order. The other two have potential to be broken, but only one is vulnerable enough for us to work with."

"Which one?" Ophelia asked, dread heightening.

"Our reappeared knight," Milo answered with a gleaming smile shining wicked in the Omniworld's strange light. "The Knight of Swords. He is the Magician's weakest link. If we can break his vow, we can break the Tarot."

"And how do we that Uncle Milo? Ask him nicely? He isn't going to lie down and let us rip the vow from his heart."

"Ah. But we *will* rip it from his heart," Milo replied cruelly. "He is the Knight of Swords, forbidden to love. If you can make him fall in love with you, his vow will break and the Tarot will be destroyed."

That was the last thing Ophelia expected to hear. She gaped, stunned. "In love? With me?"

Milo began pacing the perimeter of the Omniworld, all the while watching the throbbing green core. "Yes."

Ophelia remained where she was, watching her uncle wearily as he traversed the globe. "How can I possibly get him to fall in love with me? I'm not exactly charming."

"You're beautiful," Milo answered, and although it was spoken with kindness, there was a scientific quality to his voice that left Ophelia feeling empty and used. "And charismatic and persuasive."

None of Milo's words made any difference. Jude suspected she was a spy. He would never fall in love with her. But if she admitted she'd been caught to Milo and refused it would break his heart. This Omniworld was his entire life. If she let him down, he would be destroyed, and she didn't have the heart to deny him his one true desire, no matter how lunatic it seemed. Besides, what did it matter to her? What was she losing in the end?

"Will you do it?" Mio asked in a voice that was almost pleading.

"There is no other way?" she asked, knowing the answer but fearing it all the same.

"No," Milo answered. "You must break him. You must make him love you."

LIES AND CHOCOLATE
KRAKOW

Darkness shrouded Krakow like the black lace of a widow's veil. Jude made his way home from the grocery store, both hands weighed down with heavy bags. Usually, he avoided crowded Main Square, but tonight was a true fall night, the air crisp with the distant smell of bonfire on a sharp breeze and most of the tourists would be indoors, huddled inside pubs and wine bars, warming their hands near a fire and chasing the cold away with brandy and Polish vodka.

Jude's own hands were frozen and he silently wished he was beside one of those fires, drinking his depression away. He smiled as he passed windows, wanting to go in, but knowing the milk would sour unless he got it home. As he passed under the Cloth Hall's dark shadow, a figure appeared. Or really, it had been there all along, standing alone in the middle of the empty square as if waiting for him.

Jude slowed as he approached, feeling a familiar tingle along his spine. Closer now, he recognized the face and his heart stopped, though somehow he convinced his feet to keep moving, one after another toward the girl.

She waited patiently, unmoving, wearing a heavy wool coat with both hands tucked in the pockets. Her hair was free and tousled under a gray knit cap and he could see the smooth planes of her cheeks, highlighted by iridescent moonlight. Cautiously, he eyed her and she did the same, sharp and alert as a delicate tendril of breath curled from her slightly parted lips.

"Still following me, I see," he greeted her like an old friend, though he couldn't say why. There was a strange connection here, as if he'd known this mysterious girl for years. The curve of her cheek, the shine of her eyes, the gentle smirk upon her lips – it should have been foreign, but it wasn't.

Since his rendezvous with the Knighthood in Paris the girl had ceased her stalking, and he'd felt oddly sad to see her go. It was how he imagined someone might feel after losing a loved one. For a while the departed soul might linger, watching over, but then, just like that, the soul would move on, leaving the living to face their grief.

"I'm not following you now," the girl answered, matter-of-fact. "I'm standing right here."

Jude tipped his head in agreement. "It's freezing out here," he said, taking a small step toward her. She did not back away. "You want to go inside?"

The girl's eyes flickered to the nearest pub, windows filled with rowdy after-dinner patrons. "Okay," she agreed, turning to the door.

"Wait," Jude called. "Not there. Follow me."

The girl stopped, eyeing him with one beautifully arched brow. She said nothing, but shrugged and followed.

Bags in hand, Jude crossed the square to a small chocolatier nestled in a dark corner. Its windows were lead paned and lit with tawny light from hanging Tiffany lamps. In the display, pewter trays were stacked with chocolates, white and dark and strawberry drizzle with truffles wrapped in colorful tissue paper and fudge cut into thick delicious squares. Candies filled crystal bowls and caramels spilled over the table like coins around taffy stretched in deliciously colorful ribbons. Above the door a sign read, *Bernarda Czekolada.*

"Why here?" the girl asked, pausing to read the sign. "It looks empty."

"Exactly," Jude said, pushing inside.

A bell chimed as they entered and an old man in a white frock looked up from arranging chocolates in a box. Jude raised a hand in greeting and the old man did the same, his craggy face brightening.

"I'm not sure I want our conversation overhead," the girl whispered behind Jude.

Jude continued toward a small bistro table in the front window. "Trust me," he answered, "this is the best place in the city to have a discreet conversation."

"And why is that?" the girl questioned accusingly, one hand placed on her narrow hip.

Jude tossed her a charismatic smile and slipped into a chair. "Because Bernard is as deaf as a tree." He unwound the red scarf from his neck and pointed to the counter where a sign read, *Hello, my name is Bernard. Welcome to my chocolate shoppe. I am deaf, so please point to what you'd like! Thank you!* And below, the same in Polish.

Seemingly satisfied, the girl cautiously lowered herself into the seat opposite him, as if expecting it might explode.

Resisting the urge to grin, Jude signaled Bernard in a quick series of hand gestures. The chocolatier smiled and nodded, turning his back to face a hissing espresso machine.

"You can speak sign language?" The girl sounded both impressed and slightly annoyed, which pleased Jude.

He sat back, the grin desperate to break free at the corner of his mouth. "A little. I love this place, so I learned enough to order."

"And you ordered?"

"Hot Belgian cocoa, drizzled with milk chocolate, finished with homemade whipped cream, cinnamon and nutmeg."

She gave a stiff nod, apparently having no complaint.

For a while they were silent, the girl looking out the window and Jude looking at her. At last, he spoke. "Are you going to tell me what you're doing here?"

The girl's coal black eyes snapped to his. They were startling, deep and dark as infinite sulfur pools. From her stare Jude could tell she was unafraid, something he rarely saw in girls his age. "Isn't it obvious?" she asked, her voice languid and rich as melted chocolate.

"I imagine you want to talk, though you don't seem to be doing much of it."

"True." She smiled, softening her sharp features.

The smile itself was neither genuine nor fake, but something in-between. That suited Jude just fine. He'd practically invented that careful, calculated smile and he recognized the distance it created. As sweet and kind as this girl pretended, there was something deeper hiding just under the surface and it did not have him fooled.

"Well?"

She studied him and brushed the bangs from her face in an impossibly smooth gesture. "I followed you because I saw what you did in Paris. You helped that gypsy and took her away from the city."

Whatever Jude had been expecting, this wasn't it. "Rosaline?" he asked, the name slipping out in surprise.

The girl tilted her head as if to say, 'sure'.

"I don't understand."

"I don't expect you to understand."

Jude leaned forward, lowering his voice despite it being unnecessary. "I hate to be rude, but if you want me to continue this conversation you're going to have to do a better job of explaining yourself. What exactly do you want from me? Why did you follow me from Paris?"

"I'm sorry," the girl replied, though she sounded anything but. "It's hard to explain. But I really do need your help."

"My help? Why -"

Bernard interrupted, appearing with two oversized mugs of steaming hot cocoa. Jude thanked him with a few rushed signs and pushed one mug toward the girl.

After Bernard retreated, she resumed her explanation, "I was in the park when you helped that homeless girl," she said, wrapping her hands about the mug.

There was something falsely tender about the way she moved, as if she were trying to seem demure. It might have worked on someone else, but Jude had been raised outside the world's social conventions in the House of Swords. He'd also spent his outcast years studying people from afar. He knew subtleties that gave insincerities away, like the tightness of her fingers around the cup, the intensity in her stare, and the stiffness in her shoulders. Whatever she wanted Jude to believe, it wouldn't work. He could see through her lies like they were made of glass. Regardless, her need to pretend intrigued him.

"I heard you tell that gypsy you were a knight. Then you rescued her. You took her from Paris to London. You gave her sanctuary in that big mansion. She trusted you. I could tell."

Momentarily, Jude lost his control, letting his façade slip. He had no words. How could he possibly explain how wrong this girl was without revealing the Tarot?

The girl waited for him to respond but when he came up short she went on, "What you did for her was - incredible. I've seen that girl around. She had nowhere to go. And you helped her. You showed up out of the blue and told her you could give her a new life and you did."

Gears whirred and ticked furiously inside Jude's mind, yet he could form no response. "I see," was all he managed, one hand resting on his untouched cocoa. "I'm afraid you're missing some crucial details."

The girl gave him a long questioning look, reminding him of the models he saw around Krakow - tall and willowy and intimidating. "Will you tell me one thing?" she asked in a voice much kinder than her expression revealed.

Jude knew he would regret it, but he nodded.

"Did you or did you not help her? Did you save her from the streets?"

How did he lie without sounding like a complete ass? "I'm not sure what you mean by help, but yes, I took her off the streets."

"Somewhere safe?"

That was a loaded question. Was Order headquarters really safe? It wasn't dangerous in the literal sense, but it had darkness and evil just like any other place. "She is safer where she is now than she was in Paris."

The girl nodded, seeming to make up her mind. "I need you to help me like you helped her."

Jude's brows shot up, nearly bowled off his chair. What was her game? She had no idea what his 'helping' meant. He couldn't help this girl the way he helped Rosaline even if he wanted to. Despite that, he was curious enough to play along. "Why do you need help? Did you run away from home or something?" She was too squeaky clean to be homeless. Her nails were neatly trimmed and free of dirt, her hair brushed, clothes washed and she smelled good too.

The girl looked insulted, brooding over her cocoa. "I don't have a family to run away from."

No family. Interesting. "So what then?" he asked.

She dropped her eyes to the table. "My father was an art dealer. And by that I mean he dealt stolen art." After a pause she lifted her eyes, unashamed but withdrawn, as if she were telling a tale instead of her life story.

That was all it took to convince Jude of her lies, though he reasoned it wasn't his place to judge. Maybe she was in trouble and had good reason to keep secrets?

She went on, "He died six weeks ago. Left me everything. Only some of his clients weren't happy with his will. They believe his inheritance belongs to them."

Curious. "So you have gangsters after you?" he clarified with an amused grunt.

The girl gave him an exasperated look, as if he should know the story without her having to explain. "I have criminals after me, not gangsters."

Jude sat back, looking her over. It was nearly impossible to read her. He knew something was off, but he couldn't say what, and despite it, he still felt drawn to her, like a puzzle he wanted to solve. "What makes you think you're being followed?"

She laughed as if it were the dumbest question ever asked. "I know because they kidnapped me the day after the lawyers meeting. They threw me in a basement, threatened to kill me if I didn't give them access to my bank account. I gave them bad information and escaped. After that I fled for Paris and I've been hiding out ever since, jumping from city to city and never staying in the same place long. But they can track me; through the bank, I think. I try to pay with cash, but eventually I have to withdraw money and they know."

Jude's first instinct was to laugh. "Are you serious?"

She pressed her lips into a scowl.

This girl was desperate, for what he wasn't sure, but if even half of what she said was true it was enough to get his attention. "Is that why you followed me here?"

"I had to go somewhere," she replied. "When you said you were a knight I thought maybe you worked for an organization protecting women against violence. Or that you were some sort of vigilante. Either way it sounded exactly like what I needed – a knight."

That rattled him. No - more than that. It terrified him. He might be a knight of the Order but he sure as hell was no one's savior. "Look, I wish I could help you, but I'm not that kind of knight."

The girl's face darkened and it was clear she wouldn't let the matter drop so easy. "But you helped that girl."

"I did," Jude admitted. "But you don't understand. You need to go to the police. You've got things seriously messed up."

"I tried the police." She was calm but direct, leaving no room for misunderstanding. Tears brimmed in the corners of her eyes as she blinked, ready to fall.

God, he hated when girls cried. If she let one tear drop that would be it – he would have to help her. "What did they say?"

The girl lifted one shoulder in a pathetic shrug. "There is nothing they can do until I prove the law was broken. I don't know who these men are. As far as the law is concerned they don't exist. My father's business wasn't exactly legitimate, which makes things complicated. The best they could do was file a restraining order. Only, I wouldn't know who to restrain and I don't think they are the type who would particularly care about a piece of paper, if you get my meaning."

Jude certainly did. He pictured nineteen thirties American gangsters in pinstriped suites carrying Tommy guns though the streets of Paris. "Listen -" he began then stopped. "I'm sorry, I didn't catch your name?"

The girl hesitated, seemed to consider, and answered, "Ophelia."

Of everything she'd said Jude knew this, at least, was true. People could lie about a lot of things, but names were a tough – too personal to hide. "I'm Jude." She nodded, waiting for him to continue. "Ophelia, my life doesn't leave room for helping strangers. It's complicated. I can't have *friends*."

She made a face, which made him feel stupid - as if he'd suggested they head back to his place and get it on. "I don't want to be *friends*," she countered. "I have friends. What I want is for you to help me like you helped that girl in Paris. If you don't I'll be dead in a week. I can't run forever. They will find me. And when they do they'll kill me."

Was she really guilting him into helping her? "Don't you have anyone else you can ask? A relative?"

"Not really," she answered. "They know everything about me. They know everyone I know. They'll kill them too. I have to find somewhere to hide where they'll never know to look."

"Do these people know you're in Krakow?"

She shook her head. "I don't think so. The last place I withdrew money was Paris. I followed you back there thinking I might get the courage to ask for help. I wanted to get a better idea of who you were, you know, make sure you weren't some psycho. But they tracked me to Paris and I ran back to London. And then I got scared and I came back here to beg for your help." She hitched a small breath. "Jude," she began again, making a point to speak his name. Her tactic worked. His name on her lips sent a jolt through him. "I'm asking you, as a knight, for help."

"I don't know what you want me to say," he muttered, feeling his resolve crack. "How can I help you?" His stomach twisted in familiar warning, telling him things were getting dangerously close to feelings. Compassion? Pity? He wasn't sure what, but it was something. He didn't form relationships, aside from Nicolai, and although he considered the knight his friend, they weren't close like that. More like brothers with an unspoken bond. If he helped this girl it could lead to feelings and feelings led to broken vows. He didn't know what to do. He could get up, leave, and hope she'd be okay. Or he could agree to help her and risk his vow….

Ophelia looked at him, her head slightly tilted, every movement conveying desperation. "I just need somewhere to go if they come for me," she said. "I need a safe house. And maybe someone to talk to. Someone I can trust if things go wrong."

"What makes you think you can trust me?"

"I've been following you for a long time," she reminded him.

"Right." He tossed her a look that said he didn't approve of being stalked, but she stared back with cool, drinking eyes, unfazed.

Could he do it? Could he help her and not develop a connection? Every logical part of his brain screamed no, he could not, but he was so desperate for contact he found a way to twist the logic until it leaned the other way. He couldn't just leave her. No matter his mandate, he was still the Knight of Swords, and knights were sworn to protect. The Magician would understand, surely.

"Okay," he agreed after a time. "I can do that, but no more." Ophelia's face changed, blossoming into a smile so beautiful it made Jude's chest hurt. *My god,* he thought, *what have I done?*

THE CAROUSEL
BIAŁOWIEŻA FOREST, BELARUS

Two rutted roads diverged deep in the woods. There were no signs or posts or indicators to mark the way, just an ancient oak standing sentinel at the divide.

"Which way?" asked Rosaline, coming to a stop. She looked one way, then the next, assessing each option. Both paths were heavily treed with branches boughed over a worn footpath, creating a leafy canopy where sunlight flitted, catching particles and brightening patches of undergrowth. Down the left path, stars cut from silver foil and bright red apples hung on twine from trees, as if someone had imagined falling stars and apple trees and failed to quite grasp the concept. The path on the right was equally strange, trees stung with little white lights and a colorful flag-banner swinging branch to branch, leading as far down the eye could see.

"We wait," the Magician answered, looking down the apple-lined path.

"For what?"

"For your guide."

Rosaline followed the Magician's gaze, listening hard for someone approaching, but the woods were dense and quiet and all she heard was the sound of a distant stream, the odd croak of a cricket, and the rustle of critters. It all seemed so impossibly vast, as if the entire world must be covered in trees.

"Who is my guide?" she asked the Magician, curious. "Aren't you coming with me?"

"With you?" The Magician sounded genuinely surprised. "I'm afraid not. My place is back at Headquarters."

"I see." Rosaline wasn't sure how she felt about that. She had been expecting the Magician to guide her to every House, and the idea of being left alone frightened her. It wasn't the same as being alone on the streets of Paris, but similar – as if she were suddenly given control of a destiny she didn't understand.

"Not to worry," the Magician assured her with a wan smile, "you have an excellent guide. One who knows these woods well."

She nodded, looking away to hide her disappointment.

"There he is now." The Magician's face brightened, turning to face the road.

Rosaline's head swiveled in the same direction, but she saw only an empty path disappearing into the trees. "I don't see anyone."

"He's coming," the Magician assured her. "I can feel him."

To this, Rosaline frowned, feeling no different than she had moments before, but as always the Magician was right, and moments later a man appeared, trotting slowly toward them on a white horse.

A laugh bubbled from her lips.

The Magician frowned, casting a concerned glance. "What's the matter?"

"It's just," Rosaline waved at the horseman, "a prince…on horseback?"

The Magician's frown intensified. "I'm afraid I don't understand."

"Prince charming, in the woods. Riding a white stallion? Coming to save his damsel in distress?"

"Are you in distress?" The Magician asked, taking a fretful step forward.

"No," Rosaline bit her lip, feeling stupid. Apparently, he did not understand irony. "Nothing like that. It's just a fairytale, that's all." Like the fairytales she'd grown up reading in her mother's books, leather-bound, with thick parchment that smelled of pine and spice. She still remembered pulling them down from the bedroom closet in the caravan, standing on tiptoes to reach the shelf. They had filled her with hope and dreams she would never have known otherwise. There was no such thing as princesses or fairy godmothers where she was born.

"Well," the Magician went on, "Nicolai is not a prince. He's a knight. You must recall? You met him at the manor the other night."

"Nicolai?" Rosaline paled. "The Knight of Cups?"

"Yes," the Magician replied, looking at her as if she were slightly mad. "He will be your guide."

Star-struck, Rosaline turned and watched the handsome knight approach. He was even more breathtaking than she remembered, fair hair dusted with light, eyes sparkling, sitting tall in the saddle of a stunning white mare. He may be a knight, but he certainly looked like a prince.

"Magician," Nicolai greeted as the mare slowed to a stop, smiling brightly. "Sorry I'm late."

"Not to worry," the Magician waved off his concern and turned to Rosaline, his robe trailing a circle in the underbrush. "Can you ride?"

"A horse?" she clarified.

He nodded.

"I'm a gypsy." Rosaline raised her chin. "I learned to ride before I could walk."

The Magician nodded in approval, turning his attention back to Nicolai. "Take care of her, then. I'll leave things in your capable hands."

Nicolai bowed his head graciously.

The Magician paused. "Did you see Jude while you were away?"

The smile on Nicolai's face faded. "I did," he replied gravely and Rosaline got the distinct impression there were things taking place behind closed curtains.

"How is he?" A sadness in the Magician's voice cut through the trees.

"He is…troubled, sir," Nicolai replied.

The Magician gave a solemn nod. "Rosaline," he said softly. "I will see you at your final task."

Task. There it was again. No matter how casually he spoke the word it held a ring of finality, as if a mountain, a sea, and land of fire stood between her and happiness. She nodded, though she wished he would stay. It seemed an impossible journey without his guidance.

Bidding farewell, the Magician turned and started back through the woods, batting branches with his walking stick. Silently, Rosaline watched him go, until the deep green of his cloak blended with the trees and all that remained was the distant crunch of his footsteps. Rosaline turned back to Nicolai, catching a glint in his eyes. God he was perfect. How could he not see how stuck she was by him? Embarrassed, she looked away, scuffing her foot in the dirt.

"Are you ready?" he asked, holding out a hand.

Rosaline eyed it nervously, trying to quell the butterflies in her stomach. There was no way she could get on a horse with her stomach in knots. What if she threw up on him? "Where are we going?" she asked softly.

"Come," he said, waving her to him. "I'm taking you to meet the King and Queen of Coins. They will present you with your first task."

Task. *Task. Task. Task.* With a deep breath she raised her eyes to meet his. They were smiling, a vivid violet, alight with laughter and fixed on her. Her cheeks burned under his stare and his smile broadened as if warmed by her reaction.

"I promise I'll take good care of you," he said sincerely. "Come on. Take my hand."

With a breath, she placed her newly scrubbed hand in his, letting his fingers closed around hers, strong, as he lifted her into the saddle before him.

"You might want to hold on," he suggested once settled.

Rosaline nodded and gripped the saddle tight.

As Nicolai took the reins he let his arm brush against hers, tiny hairs tickling her skin as he turned the horse toward the path strung with lights. There were many instances in Rosaline's short life where she'd been nervous - stormy nights in the park, the soup kitchen, hiding in a dumpster after stealing - but none of those things made her feel quite like this, all mushy inside, like her guts had turned to mash.

"Are you comfortable?" he asked, urging the horse down the path.

Rosaline swallowed, feeling the warmth of him against her back. "I'm fine," she breathed, though she was anything but.

As the horse moved deeper, the woods grew dark, beginning to feel less like a forest and more like a cave. The canopy twisted thick and tight, blocking all light, trees standing abreast, towering like oak soldiers as they journeyed deeper.

"Why are there lights?" Rosaline asked.

"To light the way," Nicolai answered.

That seemed like a vague response, but she let it go when she caught sight of the first jar. "Fireflies," she said, pointing to the light on the path. Inside a glass jar a single orange firefly flitted. Ahead, more and more jars joined, until the entire path was flanked by firefly lanterns, making the forest glow like candlelight. She breathed a deep sigh, never having seen anything so beautiful.

"Pretty, isn't it?" said Nicolai.

"Mmhmm," Rosaline agreed.

"Can I show you something else?" he asked, and his voice was hesitant, as though afraid she might refuse. "It will take us out of the way a bit."

"Of course," she replied, turning to look at him.

He smiled down at her, one corner of his mouth pulling in a quiet smile. "I thought of it when you gave your speech at the manor." As he led the horse off the main path, the sound of distant music reached Rosaline's ears in a melancholy flutter of flutes and clarinets. She perked up, listening. "Where is the music coming from?"

"You'll see," the knight said with laughter.

The music grew louder, in lulls and peaks, like a melody from a music box. When at last the trees parted Rosaline gasped, clapping her hand over her mouth. There, in the middle of the woods, stood a replica of the Eiffel Tower's famous carousel - the carousel she had spent days watching from afar and wishing she could ride. Sometimes she even imagined the white horses would take her away.

The carousel was enchanting, just as she remembered, with water-colored images of Paris hand-painted along the crown, two tiers of perfect galloping white horses, and hundreds of lit bulbs following every beautiful curve. It moved in a graceful loop, round and round, marching to eternal music.

"It's the carousel."

Nicolai brought the horse to a stop. "Do you like it?"

"Why is it -? What is it doing here?" she asked in wonder.

"Jude loved it so much as a child the Magician built it for him. When we were kids he used to cry because he wanted to ride it all the time. So, one day, the Magician surprised him.

It's a little strange, off in the woods, but it wouldn't do well on a mountain or in a dessert where the other Houses are. When you mentioned your life in Paris I thought of the carousel. I thought it might make you feel more at home. "

Rosaline didn't know what to say. No one had ever done anything so generous for her.

"Do you want to ride?"

"Can we?" She looked from Nicolai to the carousel. If he hadn't offered she wouldn't have asked, but the longing in her eyes was clear. Rosaline had never ridden the Eiffel Tower carousel, but she'd watched it every day that first year on the streets. Sometimes, watching the other families made her feel a little less alone, and every once in a while someone would buy her ice-cream or cotton candy if she stood close enough and waited patiently. And although she considered herself too old to ride now, the sadness of never experiencing the joy had left a small but undeniable hole in her heart that was screaming to be filled.

"Of course." Nicolai beamed. He climbed down and grabbed her around the waist, lifting her to the ground like a weightless child.

Just like a real knight, she thought, wondering what he would save her from.

He smiled, catching her eye, and his stare lingered a beat longer than necessary. As they crossed the clearing, Rosaline imagined the carousel wasn't alone in a wood, but center stage at a carnival, surrounded by children waiting impatiently for their turn. It was how she always pictured her first ride.

"Up you go," said Nicolai, helping her onto the platform.

A tingle of excitement ran along her fingers, yearning to touch the horses, so lifelike she nearly expected them to blink.

"Which do you want?" asked Nicolai, joining her.

Rosaline looked around, choosing one on the lower level. "This one," she said, reaching the pearly white horse with colorful saddle, golden mane, and shining black eyes. It reminded her of home. Home before her mother had taken her from the gypsy band, back when she'd helped her father train horses in the fields, bareback and wild.

"Good choice," said Nicolai with a smile as he climbed onto the next horse. He looked silly, like an adult playing dress up just for her entertainment. The thought made her smile uncontrollably. "There it is," he said, his face breaking into a wide grin. "I've been wondering if you were capable of smiling."

"Of course I am," she said, dropping the smile and looking away. "I just haven't had much to smile about."

"We can change that," Nicolai replied, and there was something in the way he spoke that made her heart race.

Hiding her face, Rosaline let her hair fall forward and rested her hand on the horse's wooden head, feeling the vibration of clicking gears and popping widgets, working to raise the beast up and down the shiny pole. Carefully, Rosaline climbed on and held tight, looking through a curtain of hair to watch Nicolai's face. For some reason it mattered that he was enjoying the carousel, too.

"Fun, isn't it?" He smiled and she nodded.

Ahead, the horses pranced and the forest blurred, fast enough to feel as if they were flying. She closed her eyes, listening to the music dance around the woods. And for the first time in a long time, she was happy.

MAGIC AND MEN
LONDON

Milo stood on his tip-toes, examining the Omniworld's core. The clockwork world slowly rotated around the glowing green orb, casting ever-changing shadows about the darkened lab. Beyond the glass domed roof stars burned behind a thin veil of cloud and Ophelia watched them from where she sat on a work bench, spinning an abandoned gear in her hand.

"Why is it so important to destroy the Magician?" she asked, glancing at the Omniworld with a growing sense of unease – as if the machine had stole her most valued possession. And maybe, in a way, it had.

"It's not about destroying the Magician," her uncle answered, focused on the task at hand. "It's about science."

"Beating magic," Ophelia contested.

This time Milo stopped long enough to give her a chiding look before returning to his tinkering. "Honestly, Ophelia, it's like you don't listen at all. Magic is…is unpredictable, unstable. Very little about it is understood. There is no conclusive evidence of long-term effects or calculable outcomes. It's all random and messy. Magic is nothing but untamed energy being manipulated by a man who should be pulling rabbits out of his hat, not trying to maintain the world's precarious balance of forces. He should leave it up to tested methods, ones that have been theorized through meticulous experiments and demonstrated with successful results. Something as important as the world's stability should be left up to experts with concrete tactics, not thrown to the wind hoping magic will save the day. Really, you should understand this. Wouldn't you feel safer knowing the world was being held together by science not hocus pocus?"

"I'd feel better knowing the world didn't need to be held together at all." She dropped the gear and came to stand beside her uncle, looking into the pulsing green core. "You keep talking about the world like it's a broken light bulb strapped together with duct tape. What makes you so sure it needs to be fixed, anyway? Why can't you just leave the Magician and the Tarot be? They seem to be doing a fine job."

Milo was shaking his head before she'd finished speaking. "The world is an intricate machine unto itself. It has been proven by scientists as far back as the Ancient Egyptians. You can see it in their work, their carvings and tablets and drawings in the Great Pyramids. There are repeating patterns in nature, the alignment of stars, the rotation of our planet. Don't you find it strange that after all these years searching for other inhabitable planets, we're the only one? It's because it takes balance – the perfect balance of temperature, distance from the sun, molecular structure, eco-system, atmosphere, and that's just the tangible quantifiable qualities. What about all those we cannot measure? There has to be certain kinds of people in this world to make it run the way it does. There has to be smart people and hardworking people and spiritual people and aggressors; warriors, lovers, nurturers. The world requires all of us, and every kind of us. And all those people give off energy and forces that make up the world just as much as the ocean and earth and sky. It all connects, don't you see?" He paused to interlock his fingers, pulling at them to create a circle. "It is a weave, a complicated sophisticated weave that is delicate, ever-changing and constantly at risk of unraveling. Without something to hold it together it will pull apart."

"Then why destroy the Magician? If he is holding it all together…."

"Because it's a temporary solution and not a reliable one." Milo was using his frustrated tone, the one that suggested he was no longer in the mood for explanations.

Ophelia moved on. "So why did you call me back? The Omniworld is obviously not ready." She waved an impatient hand at the massive globe. "You interrupted my progress with Jude."

"What progress?" Milo abruptly stopped working, craning his neck to look at her with interest.

"What does it matter? I'm doing what you want. I'm making him like me. I'm doing this for you -"

"Oh, no," Milo corrected sternly, "you're doing this for science!"

"Science…." Ophelia echoed. She wanted to groan, but managed to smother it in her throat. What did she care about science? Or magic, for that matter. It had nothing to do with her. There was only one reason she did any of this and it was to gain her uncle's acceptance – to finally be considered his equal. After so many years of being nothing more than a lab assistant, she wanted to prove she could be integral to his work. Useful. Needed. "Why couldn't you have just called?" she complained, turning back to retrieve the cup of tea she'd left on the workbench. "It's a two hour flight."

"Call?" Milo made a noise in his throat that suggested this was the most absurd idea he'd ever heard. "This information is far too sensitive for a phone call. The Magician could be listening." He sounded rather hysterical and quite convincing. "I want a report every week. In person," he added as an afterthought. "It's important."

Ophelia heaved a sigh. The argument – if it could be called such – was over. "What about your progress?"

"Progress?" Milo squawked. "Oh, the core. Yes. Well…yes."

"Is it working?"

"Working? No. Not quite. Almost…another week maybe?"

Ophelia eyed the core, garish green with orange sparks, blue gas, and pink mist all swirling together in an unearthly brilliance. It didn't scare her exactly, but it unnerved her to know what it was capable of – or at least what Milo claimed. Despite her unorthodox upbringing she was still somewhat skeptical when it came to matters of the extraordinary. "Well," she said, leaning against the table with her feet crossed at the ankles. "If that's all for the night, I'm off to bed. Apparently, I have an early morning flight back to Krakow I need to be on."

Milo tore his attention from the globe long enough to smile in complete ignorance. "Okay, good night then."

Ophelia left her uncle in the lab, grumbling all the way to her bedroom. It was a small room with a narrow twin bed and a tall wonky bookshelf cluttered with old literature. A dormered window overlooked the street below and provided a small reading nook. She climbed inside, pulling her knees to close with a tired sigh. When had things changed? When had Milo stopped being the brilliant uncle she admired and become this mad scientist? The line was so thin. The changes so subtle she hadn't realized until now. As she stared into the night sky she wondered, not for the first time, what exactly she had gotten herself into.

WINTER
KRAKOW

It was hot in the flat, wedged between the rafters of a century old building. In the winter the pipes creaked and moaned and all the steam from below pumped through Jude's walls whether he liked it or not. It was so hot he rarely touched the thermostat, the heat simply emitted through the plaster, drenching him in sweat.

He tugged off his sticky shirt, discarding it on a battered arm chair before picking up his guitar. It was old, found at a flea market with frayed strap and worn varnish, but he loved the sound. It was the sound only old instruments could play: rich and full of past lives. Jude sat on the edge of the bed, the springs squeaking beneath him, and pulled the guitar into his lap. The first few notes were sharp until he plucked the strings and tuned the pegs, persuading the guitar to listen.

Always Jude had loved music, though he had never been a songwriter. The lyrics always came out whiny. Beyond that, he couldn't sing worth a damn, so instead he played familiar tunes; humming snippets of songs he liked when no one was around to listen.

Alone in his flat he did so now, quietly humming as he strummed a simple song. He was lucky not to have neighbors except the one below, who was nearing a hundred and hadn't heard a thing since World War Two. Because of this, he was free to play with reckless abandon, but found he never had the nerve. He had been raised to hide his emotions and playing passionately made him feel out of control. On some level Jude knew if he started, he would never be able to stop.

Lost in thought, he continued to strum, falling into the haunting melody of an ill-fated love song. He still remembered the musician who wrote it, playing on a dark stage with a single spotlight. The song had been about his fiancé who'd died on their wedding day. It was not a happy song, yet it suited Jude well. He liked the bitter-sweetness of it, long and drawn out and painful, yet oddly hopeful. He'd only heard it that once but it had stuck.

Beyond the frosted window, snow dusted Krakow in crystalline sugar, while inside a thick candle cast flickering light over yellowed walls. The window to Jude's back was open, a gentle breeze tickling his neck, carrying car noise and distant shouts. He was halfway through the second verse when he heard the window creak. It was faint, barely audible over the guitar, but Jude knew someone was there. He tensed, but kept playing as if he hadn't heard a sound, one knee pulled onto the bed, rumpling the quilt.

"I know that song."

Jude let the music fall away. "Really?" he asked.

"Yes. It's a sad song."

Jude turned. She was sitting in the window box, one leg folded under her, the other foot dangling to the floor. Her face was turned toward him, thoughtful, with one fist tucked under her chin while the melting snow on her sneakers dripped a small puddle on the floor.

"How did you get up here?" Jude asked, setting aside the guitar. He wasn't angry, not even surprised – he had stopped being surprised when it came to Ophelia days ago. Now he was just curious.

"I climbed," she replied, as if it were obvious.

"You could have used the door."

"I could have," she agreed. "But I didn't want to intrude if you were busy."

Jude fought a grin. He'd never met anyone quite like this girl, pretending to be so innocent, yet so complex...almost like the two halves didn't fit. "Instead you climbed four storeys to sneak in my window and check?"

"Something like that." She kicked her other leg out, facing the room with her back to the window. "I saw you were alone. I wanted to hear you play."

No one had ever heard him play. He wasn't sure if this counted, but it bothered him all the same. He stood and fetched his shirt, pulling it on. "Are you coming in?" he asked over his shoulder, "or are you going to sit in the window all night?"

"I'm coming in," she announced, as if it needed to be said. After climbing inside she pulled the window closed, bolting the latch. "It's cold outside."

"It's hot in here."

"Yeah," Ophelia agreed.

They stood facing each other, a weighty silence between them. Jude had never been alone with a girl before, at least not like this, in such an intimate way. Of course he'd been with a few women, not many, mostly just Karazyna, a Polish girl that lived in the building. But they were fleeting encounters and they all meant nothing. Karazyna would usually light a cigarette and tell him some broken story about her life, as if it were an excuse for showing up at his door. Then she would leave, disappearing for weeks before showing up again when she got lonely or drunk. For longest time that had suited Jude just fine. Only lately it left him feeling hollow and dead and he'd taken to ignoring the door whenever she came knocking.

Eventually, Jude could no longer stand the intensity of Ophelia's stare. "Is everything okay?" he asked.

"It's fine," she said in her usual voice – sweet and layered with complicated things. "I was just – lonely."

He had heard those words from Karazyna's lips a hundred times, and yet they had never held this credence. Something about it cut deep, his heart skipping and lurching in unfamiliar rhythm. "You disappeared," he said. "I thought maybe you'd left the city and gone back to London."

"I did." Ophelia found a guitar pick on the windowsill and began caressing it between her fingers leaving Jude's head filled with inappropriate thoughts. "I'm back now."

"Your back?" He felt stupid for repeating her, but all originality escaped him at the moment.

Ophelia brushed jagged bangs from her eyes. Bathed in candlelight, backlit by the moon, she looked menacingly beautiful and dangerous – nothing like the innocent girl she pretended to be. In this light her secrets were revealed.

She put down the pick and took a step forward. "I guess so." She hesitated. "Do you want me to go?"

Jude broke her gaze and stared at the floor, trying to decide what he wanted. Every fibre of his being told him she should leave, but there was no doubt in his mind, or his heart, that he wanted her to stay.

"No," he said firmly, meeting her eye again. "You can stay."

A fleeting look of triumph passed over her face. To others it might have looked smug, but Jude saw beyond it to the truth: *relief.* She looked at the guitar abandoned on the bed. "You're good. Did someone teach you to play?"

"No." He didn't mean to be blunt, but too late now. He crossed the room and reclaimed the guitar, tucking it behind the bed out of sight. "I taught myself." There was more to the story. Truthfully, the Magician had taught him, but that was hard to talk about. It was difficult to remember his foster-father as anything more than what his name suggested.

"I'm sorry," Ophelia replied, her voice soft and honest in a way he hadn't heard before. Her response didn't fit, but he understood. She'd heard the pain in his voice.

For the first time he looked at her – really looked at her - trying to see past the wall she had built. Maybe that's why he felt drawn to her, because he saw himself in her reflection; someone strong but broken by too many secrets.

For a moment Jude said nothing. He could feel the familiar tug in his gut, warning him not to get too close. There was something forming here, something perilous. "Can I get you something?" he asked, breaking the spell. "Water? Coffee?"

"Wine?" she suggested.

"Sure." He headed for the kitchen. "I think I have an old bottle in the fridge, if you don't mind watered down rubbish."

"Watered down rubbish would be great," she answered and he could hear the echo of laughter in her voice – foreign and intoxicating. "Who doesn't love a glass of watered down rubbish?"

"In Krakow?" he joked. "No one."

In the kitchen, which wasn't so much a kitchen but a single burner, fridge and sink, Jude found wine and two semi-clean glasses that would pass for useable. He pulled the cork from the bottle, hoping it was still moderately drinkable and went back.

In the other room, Ophelia sat on Jude's bed, boots discarded and jacket hung on the back of a chair. He hesitated when he saw her and she leaned back on her hands, watching him with sharp, steely eyes. "What?" she asked, as if she'd done something wrong, and Jude got the distinct impression she'd spent most of her life on the defensive.

"Nothing," he said, clearing his throat. "Never mind. Here." He crossed the room and handed her one of the glasses.

"Thank you," she said, taking a sip. "That's good."

Jude laughed, backing away and putting distance between them. "Sure," he said, noting one more lie from her lips and taking a seat at the table across the room.

Ophelia seemed to relax, her shoulders dropping and eyes softening. "Why do you live here?" she asked, cradling the glass to her chest.

Jude frowned, confused. Why wouldn't he live here? What was wrong with it? Suddenly, he was self-conscious. He wasn't the cleanest of freaks, but he thought he kept the place relatively tidy. Besides, there was only so much scrubbing he could do for these tired old walls. "What do you mean?"

"I saw you in Paris. You stayed in a nice hotel. So you can't be poor."

Jude swallowed a mouthful of wine. It tasted like truth serum. "I have access to money if I need it," he admitted. "But I like the simple life."

Ophelia nodded, seeming to understand.

In that moment Jude realized how strange it was to be sitting in his tiny flat with a girl he barely knew, protecting her from some enemy that may or may not exist and pretending to believe her.

"I like it here," she added, so long after the initial conversation Jude almost forgot what had been said.

"Thanks," he replied, not believing her for a second. His place was *fine,* but it certainly wasn't somewhere people *liked.* He took another sip, discovering his glass was empty. *How did that happen?* He thought about pouring another but decided against it.

"It's cozy," she continued. "A home away from home."

Screw it. More wine. Jude grabbed the bottle from the table, filling his empty glass. He was about to offer Ophelia a refill when he noticed her wine untouched and quickly shoved the bottle aside. "It is what it is."

Ophelia scooted back until she leaned against the headboard, which made him even more uncomfortable. "What's that, on your hand?" she asked, nodding.

Just looked down, unsure, and caught the glow of green against the glass. "Oh, it's just a stupid tattoo." He hid his hand instead of showing it, tucking it away from sight. It was the first time he'd been careless enough to let anyone see the mark of his vow. He was usually so good at keeping his palm turned inward and away from curious eyes.

"It's green."

"Yeah. Special ink," was all Jude said, trying to make it clear it wasn't something he was willing to discuss.

Ophelia seemed to take the hint, and looked away. "What's that picture of?" she asked, changing the subject and nodding to the Knight of Swords framed above his door. He had hung it there as a reminder of his vow, so it would be the last thing he saw before leaving the house. "It's a knight, isn't it?"

"Yes." Another long drink. He had to admit he wasn't a talented conversationalist.

"A real live knight," she teased, but there was something in her voice he couldn't place. A taunt?

Jude wanted to say something witty, but by the time he'd thought of anything good Ophelia had closed her eyes and let the conversation die. For a long time he did nothing, hoping she'd open them again, but when her breathing steadied he knew she was asleep. He also knew he should wake her, but he couldn't find the courage to cross the room and shake her shoulder. Leaving her sleeping somehow required less nerve, so he finished two more glasses of wine, retrieved Ophelia's tipping glass from her hand and covered her with a blanket for the night.

THE COIN BOX
BIAŁOWIEŻA FOREST, BELARUS

The castle in the woods blended seamlessly with the surrounding oaks being a single stone spindle with thatched roof and thick earthen walls. If it wasn't for the tower's height Rosaline might not have noticed it at all, threaded between towering trees, but as they emerged into a small clearing, she spotted a puff of smoke from a chimney and blinked with surprised.

In the clearing, Rosaline and Nicolai were greeted by a man and woman standing patiently in front of the tower door. Like the tower itself, they looked part of the backdrop, as if they'd sprouted from the earth to grow where they stood, awash in green and grey and brown. Both she recognized from the Magician's dinner party, but had yet to be introduced. The woman was pretty, in her early forties, with dark auburn hair and faint creases around rich chocolate-brown eyes. The man was similar in coloring, tall and stately, broad shouldered with a proud rise to his chin.

"Welcome," the woman said warmly. "I am Matilda, Queen of Coins."

"And I am Cazmul," introduced the man. "King of Coins." His attention was on Nicolai, who brought the white mare to a stop. "It's good to see you again, Knight of Cups. We've been eager to meet your charge."

"This is Rosaline," said Nicolai, dismounting and turning to help Rosaline from the saddle.

Glad for solid ground, she let him lift her to the forest floor, yet found she was oddly sad to leave the road behind. It had taken all day to reach the castle and in that time she had become accustomed to the steady movement of the horse and the comforting feel of Nicolai at her back.

There were many things in life Rosaline did not understand, but she knew she felt safe in his arms.

"Nice to meet you." Rosaline stooped her head, keeping her hands tucked at her sides, unsure of what to do with them. It was her first official meeting with royalty, and she had never been told what to do. She figured a curtsey was appropriate, but no one had ever taught her how.

The queen's mouth bent up at the corner, amused. "We're so glad you've come," she said sweetly and Rosaline whisper thanks in return.

Neither Matilda nor Cazmul looked exactly as Rosaline's Tarot cards, but they held striking similarities; both dark - Matilda with a nurturing, intelligent eyes and Cazmul, sturdy and dependable.

As Rosaline studied them a soft smile played on Matilda's pink lips, while Cazmul stood stiff, unbreakable. "Please come in," the queen invited. "We've prepared tea for your arrival."

Gently, Nicolai pressed his hand to the small of Rosaline's back, guiding her forward. Heat flashed across her cheeks at his touch. "Are you all right?" he whispered, catching her hesitation.

Quickly she nodded and started for the tower.

Nicolai dropped his arm, but followed close enough their shoulders brushed.

Ahead, the royals led them across a narrow bridge spanning a small moat to the tower door. As the group passed over the threshold Rosaline held her breath, anxious. She didn't know what to expect. She had never entered a castle before – even one as ramshackle as this. The closest thing she'd ever seen was the Louvre in Paris, remembering it had once been a palace before it came to be a museum. Even then, she'd never been inside. It cost money to walk the halls of a building so grand, and Rosaline had always been dirt poor.

Inside the forest castle, Rosaline was disappointed to find it more or less a ruin; dark and heavy with the smell of earth. Sunlight broke through cracks in the stone where thick vines had forced inside, winding about the banisters and furniture, so the entirety of the tower looked forsaken to the forest. Despite that, it was homey somehow; lived-in with a crackling fire, plush chairs and chests overflowing with gold coins. High above, rustling birds nestled in the rafters and the ceiling was all but decimated by an ancient oak growing through the thatch. Around the room candles burned waterfalls of wax, draping the room in syrupy light.

"What do you think?" Nicolai asked in her ear.

"It's – like a storybook," she replied, as they followed the king and queen inside. "Rustic."

"Yes," he agreed. "It is a little."

"Is your home like this?"

"The House of Cups?"

She nodded, trying to imagine what it would be like. If she remembered correctly, Jude had mentioned a mountain, an island, and a dessert for the other locations of the Tarot Houses, but she couldn't quite imagine anything impressive enough.

"It's beautiful. Waterfalls and rivers and sea as far as the eye can see."

He had her captivated; making her ache for a home she didn't even know. "It sounds breathtaking."

He flashed a charming smile as they stopped in the tower's receiving hall.

In the center of the stone room a circular table sat atop a thick Indian rug set with bright flowers and fine bone china. Pastries and cakes and colorful Parisian macaroons spilled from pewter trays and silver serving plates.

Stepping carefully over the vines along the floor, Rosaline made her way to the table and stood awkwardly, thinking it was impolite to sit before the host. Together, the king and queen seated themselves in high-backed thrones. The queen's elaborate chair was cut from a beautiful blue-white stone, depicting a scene of birds and small animals scattered around pears and figs. The king's throne was more menacing, carved from ebony with two giant bulls' heads swiveled to glare upon those who stood before him.

"Join us," the queen motioned them to sit.

As Rosaline and Nicolai took their seats, three others moved from the shadows to join them. First was an elegant woman in a long gold robe and braided honey hair. The second was an elderly man with murky white eyes hunched over a walking stick. And finally, a young man in green tights and a cap, carrying leather bound book and ridiculous feather pen.

"These are a few chosen members of the Coins' Court," the queen explained, nodding to each newcomer. "The Nine of Coins," she introduced the elegant woman in gold, "and our Wiseman, the Ten of Coins." The old man tipped a wrinkled head in Rosaline's direction. "And of course, Owen," she said of the boy, "the Page of Coins. He will record our meeting for the Magician as well as guide you to your first task."

It was the first time the queen had mentioned the task, in fact Rosaline had almost forgotten the reason for being here, so caught up in it all, but now the fear returned, tightening around her throat. Would the task be dangerous? Would she be asked to risk her life? And more importantly, would she be willing to oblige?

"Are you all right, dear?" the queen asked, noticing the green tinge of Rosaline's skin.

Rosaline hurried to nod. "I'm fine. Just – anxious."

The king barked a laugh. "That's the spirit."

On her left, Nicolai's brow knit in with concern, though he said nothing and kept his attention on the king.

Even the Page seemed nervous, which didn't help. He looked a few years younger than Rosaline with the same coloring as the king and queen and she wondered if he could possibly be their son. Did the Tarot have children? And if they did were they included in the cards? But then she noticed his blue eyes and the distinct hook of his nose, suggesting he wasn't related at all.

"Can I get you something to cool your face?" the page asked, sounding genuinely worried. "You look a little red."

If she wasn't red before, Rosaline sure was now. "No." She forced a smile. "Really, I'm fine."

"Please," said the queen, "have something to eat." With a pale, delicate hand, the queen poured Rosaline a cup of tea and the room filled with the scent of apples and spice mingling with earth and freshly cut wood. "Did you know we grow everything right here in the forest?" Matilda waved a hand at a basket of strawberries and muffins on the table.

"All this?"

The queen nodded. "Of course. We are the element of earth. It is our responsibility to provide food for the other Houses of Tarot. We each do our part to keep the balance."

Fascinated, Rosaline leaned close, wondering if she would ever be as gracious and refined as the Queen of Cups. *Not if you fail the tasks,* something reminded her, but she shoved the thought aside. "And what do the other Houses do? Do you all have a purpose?"

"Some more than others!" the king boomed. "The forest is by far the most important."

Queen Matilda shot her husband an incensed look, clicking her tongue. "Don't fill the girl's head with nonsense, Cazmul. Each land plays their part equally. The Fire Lands of the

Wands give coal and diamond, the great mountain of the Swords, granite, and the Island of the Cups provides fish and ocean pearls. Without one, we would all fall."

Another cog in the wheel, thought Rosaline, realizing how complex the system really was. If she spent the rest of her life in the Order of the Tarot, she doubted she'd ever fully understand.

"Some say water is the blood of life," Nicolai declared with a dramatic edge to his tone.

The queen nodded courteously, placing a raspberry truffle on her plate. "I suppose *some* would say that." Nicolai laughed, though the queen looked mildly displeased as she sat back and sipped her tea. "Would you like to hear about the tasks, Rosaline?"

"Yes, thank you." Rosaline straightened in her chair, eager.

Matilda cut her truffle with a golden knife probably worth more than Rosaline's family caravan. "It's simple, really," she began, "Each of the four Tarot Houses will present you with a task: Coins, Swords, Wands and finally, Cups. If you pass the task, you will earn the respect of the House and thus a vote. Since there are four Houses, and majority rules, you cannot fail more than one challenge. If you do, you must return to your ordinary life. If you pass, you will take your vow as Queen of Cups and live happily ever after within the Tarot and you will never want for anything again. Understand?"

It seemed simple – yet unimaginably difficult. "Are they dangerous?" asked Rosaline, fighting the nerves in her voice. "Can I get hurt? Could I die?"

The queen trilled a laugh. "The Coins would never do such a thing. We are the House of skill and cunning." She took a bite of her truffle and gave an exaggerated groan of pleasure.

It seemed awfully trivial to be enjoying a truffle at a time like this and Rosaline wondered how anyone could be so distracted by food. Her own stomach grumbled, but she had no desire to eat as long as her insides felt like squirming maggots.

Around the table, the court members joined the queen, cutting cakes, sipping tea, and sharing squares of chocolate. Only Rosaline and Nicolai remained hungry.

"So," the queen went on, dabbing her mouth with a starch-white napkin. "Rumor has it you're an orphan? And homeless. How tragic."A general murmur of agreement spread across the table at the queen's words. "I do hope you pass."

Despite the sincerity in the queen's voice, shame flared across Rosaline's cheeks. She bit her lip, angry and embarrassed, although she couldn't say why. She had never been humiliated by her life before now. If anything, she'd been proud. Only, then she didn't care what others thought. Here, there was Nicolai to consider. Being a homeless, orphaned gypsy would not put her high in his regard. He would probably assume she was stupid and that she wore charity clothes and ate out of dumpsters when things got bad – which she did.

Dropping her gaze, Rosaline balled her fists, trying to hide the scar she'd received from a sharp piece of glass at the bottom of a trash bin. In truth, no one would even notice the faint white line across her palm, but to her it was always a bleak reminder of her worth. Maybe she'd been foolish to hope for all this? Even if she managed to become Queen of Cups she could never erase her past. It would follow her like an oil slick across the ocean, unto death.

Beside her, Nicolai flinched. "The Cups are looking forward to welcoming Rosaline. It will be nice to have someone humble for a change. The company of the privileged can grow old fast. "

There was a drawn out pause as the king and queen contemplated Nicolai's reply. It sounded like an insult, but even Rosaline couldn't be sure with such honey in his voice.

After a moment, the queen cleared her throat. "Of course." She seemed to realize her mistake. "I'm sorry. How insensitive. Please, let's enjoy our tea before it grows cold."

It was all Rosaline could do to lift her eyes and nod, silently licking her wounded pride. She couldn't look at Nicolai for fear of what his eyes might hold. Pity? Disgust? All she wanted now was to move on. "If you don't mind, your majesty, could I complete the task now?"

The queen's eyes lit with surprise. "Now?"

"Rosaline," Nicolai protested. "We just got here. You should eat and rest...."

"No," she shook her head, determined. "Forgive me, but I would like to get it over with."

The king and queen exchanged curious glances, but eventually Matilda conceded with a nod. "Of course. It's your task, after all. Owen, would you please fetch the box?" Her voice, though kind, was strong, and it echoed through the tower with authority.

Owen stood and retrieved a large wooden box from the mantle. He brought it over quickly, bowing as he presented it to the queen. Matilda took it gently in her hands, holding it as if containing Cinderella's glass slipper. "This is the Coin Box," she announced, setting it next to a tray of éclairs. "Inside you will find everything you need to complete the Coins' task. You must finish it alone and in the time allowed."

From the queen's side, Rosaline regarded the box, wishing she could see through the wood. "What are the rules?"

"You will find instructions inside." Delicately, the queen opened the lid, facing it so only she could see the contents. After a moment she shut it and raised an intricate silver hourglass. "You will have one hour once this glass is turned." Carefully, she set the hourglass aside, sand undisturbed. With a tilt of her head the queen slid the box across the table to Rosaline, gently shoving the tea pot and several dishes aside. "Take this box and you have officially accepted your first task."

With a nervous nod, Rosaline cradled the box to her chest as if it contained her fluttering heart.

The queen nudged her plate away and motioned for the page. "Owen, please show Rosaline to the study."

It had been a long time since Rosaline experienced the anxiety of failing, but she'd never forgotten. Like learning to ride a horse under her father's scrutinizing stare or not being good enough for her mother to stay by her side. It was still the same, even if it was a little different, like her insides were bunched up and swollen with fear.

"This way," said Owen, nodding to a spiral staircase near the back of the tower.

Careful not to drop the Coin Box, Rosaline tucked it under her arm and pushed from the table. Feeling Nicolai's eyes on her, she cast him a quick look. There was something overwhelming about the way he was staring at her, as if he didn't want to let her go.

"Good luck," he said, breathy, as if he were holding back.

The thought of leaving was suddenly difficult. What if he disappeared while she was gone? How could she risk losing him after finding him? "You'll be here when I get back?" she asked.

A smile pulled at the corner of his mouth. "I would never leave." The look in his eyes was vast, all consuming, and for a spark of a second Rosaline swore he knew, swore he understood. But the moment passed and Nicolai was once again a knight, not friend.

Silently, Rosaline prayed for the strength to overcome, knowing this task was also for him. If she failed, he could never be her knight to love. With one last bow to the king and queen, Rosaline followed the page deeper into the tower.

As she mounted the stairs, she glanced back, catching Nicolai's eye one last time.

"Don't be nervous," said Owen as they climbed.

Easy for you to say, she wanted to reply, but instead swallowed hard and nodded weakly.

They continued up several flights before Owen stopped at a plain wood door off a small landing. "In there," he said. "There's a desk. Work quickly. You won't have much time to waste."

Gripping the Coin Box, Rosaline stepped forward. It was difficult to balance the box and turn the door knob, but somehow she managed and stepped inside. The study was small but comfortable with narrow window, stone fireplace and a large oak desk. Several portraits of past Kings and Queens of Coins covered the curved tower wall like a patchwork tapestry. Desperately, she wanted to stop and admire the paintings - watch the colors change in the light and trace the shadows with her hands - but the Coin Box grew heavy in reminder.

"You can get seated," Owen instructed from the door.

Obediently, Rosaline crossed the room and took a seat behind the desk. The chair was comfortable, padded and backed, although she felt small and childish, dwarfed by its size. Carefully, she set the box on the desk and scooter closer, chair legs scrapping an ungodly sound across the floor.

Owen cringed.

"Sorry." She rested a hand on the Coin Box. "Can I open it?"

"As soon as I close the door," he replied. "Are you ready?"

Rosaline was not ready, but she doubted she ever would, and she certainly couldn't expect him to stand there all day. With a shaky breath she nodded.

"Alright then, good luck," said Owen as he shut the door.

When she was alone, Rosaline stared at the wall, terrified of what came next. It took several minutes before she gathered the courage to flip the latch and open the box. Inside, she found a matching silver hourglass to the one Queen Matilda had produced, and as she flipped it, the sand shone like bits of crushed diamond, winking and smiling and cheering her on. Rosaline set it on the desk with a *thud.*

Her time had begun.

ONE DAY
KRAKOW

Halfway between sleep and consciousness, Ophelia tossed in bed, throwing an arm over her face to block the ungodly light. On some level she knew she was hot, sweltering, and kicked off the sheets. With her face pressed to the pillow, an intoxicating smell pulled her from sleep. It was sweet, yet earthy, and so invigorating she nearly groaned. Not until she opened her eyes did she realize the scent belonged to Jude, clinging to her pillow as if he lay next to her.

Instantly, she was alert, drawing the covers to her chest and searching Jude's flat with wild panicked eyes. Mercifully, it was empty and the knight was nowhere in sight.

"Hello?" she asked, tentative, praying he was truly gone. When no response came she let out a captured breath. How had she let herself fall asleep in his bed? How could she be so stupid? As she sat up her hand brushed a piece of paper on the pillow. The note read:

Gone for coffee. Be back soon

J.

Ophelia fell back, tortured, trying to convince herself to leave before Jude returned, but unable to move. There was something she couldn't shake about the Knight of Swords. He held so many contradictions: sad but strong, hard but kind, loyal but lonely. How did all the pieces fit together? How did he make one perfectly cohesive person? It seemed impossible, yet right. She had never met anyone quite like him and since the previous night it had somehow become difficult to separate her mission from reality.

A knock sounded at the door, soft, almost hesitant, yanking her from thought.

Ophelia froze, eyes wide as she lay tangled in Jude's sheets.

"Jude?" a woman's voice floated from the hall. It was heavily accented in Polish, sweet and alluring, which immediately had Ophelia on edge. "Are you in there? I thought we could grab coffee."

Ophelia's heart thunked in her chest. She kicked off the sheets and padded down the hall to the door, blood rushing in her ears. As she yanked it open, Ophelia came face-to-face with a tall, slender blonde, older by a few years, wearing faded ripped jeans and a pull-over sweater. Her eyes were big, doe-like, and her bleached blond hair was greasy, as if she hadn't showered in days.

"Can I help you?" Ophelia positioned herself in the doorway, leaving no gaps for the stranger to slip through.

The girl blinked. "Who are you?" she demanded, clearly surprised to see someone else in Jude's flat.

Was this Jude's girlfriend? He had never mentioned one, and it clearly went against his vow, but that didn't make it impossible. "I'm just a friend," Ophelia explained, voice prickly. "He let me sleep here last night."

"Sleep here?" The girl crossed her arms over her chest and dropped a hip. "Jude doesn't have *friends*. And he certainly doesn't let people *sleep here*."

That confused Ophelia. If Jude didn't have friends who the hell was this girl? "Can I take a message?"

The girl huffed. "Tell him I stopped by."

There was a familiarity here Ophelia didn't like. The girl seemed to *know* Jude, showing up at his door unannounced. Questions burned like hot coals; how long had Jude known her? Did they share secrets and smiles she had never seen? Like a wicked punch to the gut, Ophelia realized she was jealous. *She* wanted to know Jude this way. She wanted to show up and be invited inside. She didn't want to sneak through windows or stalk. She wanted Jude to want her like he apparently wanted this blonde. Only, Ophelia had no idea how to be mysterious and alluring and haunting. And she knew she could never be likeable – not unless she was lying. Through grinding teeth she managed to ask, "Who should I stay stopped by?"

"He knows who I am," the girl insisted with a scowl.

"Well," Ophelia's patience was nearly run dry, "I don't."

The girl's eyes narrowed in knifing slits. "Karazyna," she spoke in a shout, and Ophelia knew that even if she hadn't been jealous, she still wouldn't have liked this girl, all sharp angles and ropy hair and ratty face.

"I'll tell him you were here."

Karazyna didn't move, a seething glare fixed on the door as Ophelia shut it.

Alone again, Ophelia leaned against the wall, trying to quell the rush of emotion. *Jealousy.* She had never felt it before, at least never this strong. Even now it left a bitter taste in her mouth, like metal and hot blood. Anger boiled in her veins, knowing she could never compete with someone like Karazyna. Where she was shadow, crumbling ash through spread fingers, Karazyna was smouldering fire, crackling and burning bright.

There was movement coming from the hall and Ophelia turned, yanking the door open, ready to smother Karazyna's glorious flames in her ash.

Jude stumbled back in surprise, key in hand.

"Jude," Ophelia stammered in surprise.

"Were you leaving?" He lifted a tray of coffee, bundled in his scarf, nose red with cold. "I thought we could talk."

"I wasn't going anywhere." Ophelia blanched. "I – just wanted to help you with the tray." She took it from his hand, knowing she should tell him about Katarzyn, but unable to force the words from her lips. What was she doing? *Just spit it out*…but she couldn't and the words remained clamped behind her teeth.

"Thanks," Jude replied, sounding mildly baffled but grateful. He uncoiled the scarf from his neck and followed Ophelia into the living area where she set the tray on the table and he shrugged out of his coat, hanging it on the bedpost. "I didn't know what you liked so it's black. I have milk and sugar in the kitchen."

"Black is fine." In truth, Ophelia didn't like coffee at all. *One more lie to the tally*, she thought, wondering why it bothered her. She lied about everything to everyone. She lied about her uncle, about the errands she ran for him, about why she missed school…the list went on and on and on, endlessly. Only, the lies to Jude felt heavier somehow, like they rested on her shoulders.

He took a seat on the edge of the bed, ramrod straight. "It's from the café down the street. The make the best bagels, but I didn't know if you liked bagels."

Ophelia hid a smile, taking one of the coffees from the tray. "I like bagels," she said. "Plain. Sometimes blueberry." It felt good to say something true.

"I like blueberry," Jude agreed. "With jam."

"With jam," Ophelia concurred. She twisted the second coffee from the cardboard tray and handed it to him. "I'm sorry about falling asleep." She stood before him, unsure of whether to sit, stand or pace.

He shrugged. "It's fine."

Ophelia looked down at her coffee, toying with the plastic tab on the lid to keep her hands occupied. "Well, thanks. I appreciate it."

"No problem." He popped the lid on his paper cup and took a long sip, steam curling about his face. "Do you want breakfast?"

"Breakfast?"

"Yeah."

"I don't know." Ophelia flicked the plastic tab repeatedly. "I thought you didn't want to be friends?"

Jude raised a brow, as if surprised, or at least caught off guard. "You spent the night in my bed. I think it's a little late for that."

She figured that was probably true and nodded, trying to hide a smile. "So. Did *you* sleep in the bed?" The idea of him lying next to her all night was a bit horrifying. Maybe she snored? Or talked in her sleep? She could feel the heat rushing to her cheeks and hoped he wouldn't notice.

"No. I slept in the chair." He nodded to the old armchair in the corner with tattered arms and lumpy seat.

"Sorry," Ophelia apologized, and meant it, which was a rare thing. "I hope it wasn't so bad."

"No." He was looking at her as if she were a portrait that required years of study to be truly appreciated; beautiful, yet complicated. She wasn't sure how that made her feel, but she suddenly had the strongest urge to kiss him.

From somewhere deep within the room began to tremble, so faint Ophelia wasn't sure she felt it at all. Then Jude noticed it too, cocking his head to stare behind her. And just as quickly, the shaking quieted, fading away. "Did you feel that?" she asked, frowning at the walls.

Jude stared at the cracks in the plaster, a worried expression creasing his brow. "Yes." He remained perfectly still, as if movement would cause the shaking to resume.

"Are there earthquakes here?" Ophelia asked. She was good at geography, but couldn't recall anything about fault lines in Eastern Europe.

Jude shrugged. "I have no idea. Maybe it was a delivery truck on the road."

Ophelia went back to sipping her coffee, watching Jude, trying to read his expression. He looked spooked and glanced down at his left hand. She swore the color in his face drained a little. "Are you okay?"

Jude blinked back to attention, closing his fingers around the green mark etched on his palm. "Yeah," he said slowly, as if he wasn't quite sure. "I'm fine. Let's get out of here."

Ophelia gathered her coat while Jude put on his boots and together they left the apartment. Outside, the day was cold, fall racing toward winter with icicles in its grip.

"Was it just you and your Dad?" Jude asked as they crossed the street, hands tucked in the deep pockets of his coat.

"No," Ophelia lied. And the lie took on a life of its own. Maybe because she felt the need to elaborate her story – a good lie had substance - or because she liked the make-believe family living in her head. Whatever the reason, she kept talking. "My mother was a seamstress." She pictured a woman in black, head bent over needle and thread in a dimly lit room. "Her name was Helena and she had a shop on Willow Street, just down from my school. Sometimes she'd let me stay late and watch, help with stitching and buttons. She died when I was young. Car accident."

Jude gave her a sympathetic glance, eyes shining with unspoken understanding. "Sorry. That's tough."

Ophelia nodded. She expected to feel remorse or guilt for accepting his underserved compassion, but she didn't. Perhaps it was because she thought she deserved it anyway. Her parents really had died, or so she assumed. Just because she didn't know their names or what they had done didn't mean they weren't real. They had been true once....

"Here," Jude said, unwinding his red scarf and wrapping it about her neck. "It's freezing out here."

Ophelia smiled, burying her nose in the wool. It was ironic. She had been chasing the scarf for days, and now, it was hers. She glanced at Jude from the corner of her eye, noticing a change. He was more relaxed, less knight and more man. "How about you? Do you have any family?"

The ease stiffened, only slightly, but enough for Ophelia to notice. "No."

And Ophelia let it go. She understood not wanting to talk about family. She also knew enough to know that, just like her, Jude's upbringing had been anything but content.

"There's the best restaurant down here," said Jude, changing the subject and pointing down a narrow side street that looked more like somewhere Jack the Ripper would stalk than the location of Krakow's best restaurant. "They serve amazing borscht."

Ophelia made a face.

Jude caught the look and laughed. "Trust me. It's good."

"Okay," she tucked the scarf into the neck of her coat, "I trust you. But if not, you owe me."

"Owe you what?"

She stopped, tapping an animated finger on her chin.

Jude walked a few paces then turned back. "Well?" He looked boyish, eager, as if waiting for her to run after him screaming, 'you're it!'

"You owe me another morning like this," she said at last. If almost everything she'd ever said to him was a lie at least this was the truth. She had never in her life had a morning so perfect.

He laughed softly and smiled. It was a quiet smile, one Ophelia had never seen before. She'd seen his fake, cold smiles and faraway, cheerless ones, but she had never seen one quite like this. It was warm and open and it made her heart skip. Had Karazyna ever seen this smile? She didn't want to think so.

"For you?" Jude asked. "Anytime."

Despite the cold, heat rushed to Ophelia's heart, making it drum. She was captured in his stare and for a second swore he was about to kiss her. They stood frozen, eyes locked, the world revolving around them. *Do it,* she silently demanded, willing him to step closer, *do it, kiss me.* But the moment passed and he looked away with a waning smile.

"Come on," he said. "Let's get out of the cold."

The disappointment was heavy, and as she moved to trudge through it, Ophelia caught a shadow overhead. She stopped, eyes snapping to the rooftop, but whatever the shadow had been, vanished, leaving nothing but a patch of bright blue sky behind.

"You coming?" Jude asked, stopping to look back.

"Yeah," Ophelia replied, tearing her eyes from the roof.

It could have been a trick of the eye, or a bird, or a plane, but she knew better. She'd spent half her life spying, so there was no doubt in her mind someone had been there watching her. A shiver that had nothing to do with the cold ran along her arms and the question echoed, trailing down the long, lonely corridor: *who* and *why*?

SIMPLE MATH
BIAŁOWIEŻA FOREST, BELARUS

At first, the Coin Box was puzzling. Rosaline squinted and rubbed the small gold pieces inside, trying to decipher their worth. When that did no good, she dug through the remainder of the box until she found a leather ledger buried at the bottom. Flipping through it, she discovered the previous pages had been ripped out, leaving a jagged edge like torn paper wings.

Rosaline ran her finger along the stumps, wondering why they'd been removed and what had been there she wasn't meant to see. On the inside cover she found instructions neatly written with calligraphic pen. It took three reads before she fully understood, and the instructions read as follows:

You are the Mayor of CopperVille. As Mayor it is up to you to distribute the town's yearly profit of one hundred gold coins accordingly. There are eight people of CopperVille whose occupations qualify them for additional funding from the Mayor's Office. Without additional support, these people would no longer be able to support themselves, and would be forced to abandon CopperVille for another town. The more funding a person receives, the better their services to CopperVille and its citizens. As Mayor you must use your best judgment to determine how many of the one hundred gold coins each of the eight qualified people will receive in order to keep the town and its citizens healthy, happy, prosperous and safe.

The eight people eligible to receive coins are: teacher, preacher, farmer, carpenter, miner, actor, peacekeeper, and doctor. At the end of your allocations, be prepared to defend your decision to the town council. If you cannot convincingly defend your actions, the council may choose to remove you from the position as Mayor. If you are removed as Mayor of CopperVille, you will fail the Task of Coins.

When Rosaline finished reading, she sat back, frowning and fighting frustrated tears. It seemed like a complicated game, something her father might have taught her as a child, but her mother had taken her from the gypsy band before she was old enough to learn and she had never been good with numbers. In all honesty Rosaline could barely add and subtract. She was lucky she could read. Over the past few years she'd picked up some money handling skills from Tarot readings, but otherwise she had a primary school education.

The sand in the hour glass was already slipping steadily through the funnel, gathering in a small pyramid at the bottom of the glass. With a shaky hand, Rosaline flipped the ledger to the first available page, crisp and untouched. She found a pen in the desk and unsteadily scrolled the eight titles down the length of the page: *teacher, preacher, farmer, carpenter, miner, actor, peacekeeper, and doctor.* That was a start, at least she'd written something down. After which, she was stuck. How much did each deserve? Surely the town didn't need an actor – what good would that do them? An actor wouldn't keep them warm, or well fed, or safe from harm. But why was it on the list if she wasn't meant to allocate anything at all? The instructions had said the people would leave the town if she gave them nothing, and if so, could she risk the actor leaving altogether? What was he worth to the town's happiness?

Eventually, Rosaline began sorting the coins into equal piles, where she discovered an unequal distribution. Each pile would need twelve and a half coins to be even, but the coins were full, leaving no room to divide and meaning at least four people would earn twelve coins while the rest earned thirteen - which wasn't even at all.

As time slipped by Rosaline grew more and more discouraged. After ten minutes, she gathered enough sense to start marking allocations as best she could, but no matter how she worked the numbers she felt sure she did it wrong. The numbers swam in her head like swift moving fish and soon it was a mess of coins and totals smeared in her childish hand as the sand in the hour glass slipped away - her future going with it.

"You can do this," she told herself, gripping the pen awkwardly. "It's just numbers. Just count."

She was forced back to the beginning, scrubbing each column clean. After some serious thought, she figured dividing the categories into percentages based on her perceived importance was the logical solution, but after far too much deliberation, she realized it was too complicated for her skill level, and was forced to abandon that approach as well.

"How do I do this?" she asked the portraits watching, mocking. Aggravated, her eyes filled with angry tears and for the first time in a long time she wanted her mother. In a fit of childish rage, Rosaline knocked the box from the table, scattering coins across the floor. They fell in a shower of metal, clinking and rolling in every direction. "Oh no!" She dropped hard to her knees, gathering runaway coins in trembling hands. "Idiot," she chided, tears hitting the floor like rain.

It took precious time to recover the coins, and when at last she had them back in the box the hour glass was nearly out. In the end she had to act quickly and simplify, dividing the total coins by the number of categories then adding and subtracting to and from categories she believed to be more or less important. It wasn't exact, she knew, and it wasn't the ideal solution, but it was the best she could manage. Her tally ended like this:

Teacher: 10

Preacher: 8

Farmer: 16

Carpenter: 12

Miner: 15

Actor: 8

Peacekeeper: 15

Doctor: 16

When the last grain of sand fell she breathed a heavy sigh of relief. At least she's tried, and after a quick double-check, she verified the numbers summed correctly.

"Time's up." Owen the page reappeared on cue, poking his head inside the room.

Rosaline stared at the numbers one last time, praying they made sense. She was still clutching the pen in her ink-stained hand when Owen cleared his throat.

"How did you do?"

"Okay," she answered. She wished she could have sounded more confident, but there was no hiding her work. It was there for everyone to see, plain as ink.

Owen smiled again, only this time he pressed his lips together. "I'll take the ledger down to the king and queen. After their review, you will have your chance to defend your decisions."

She swallowed. Why did it have to sound like a trial for murder?

Owen hesitated as if waiting for her permission to proceed. When she didn't speak he crossed the room and took the ledger from the table, closing it as he did so. It was a simple act, but she knew he had done it to respect her privacy, and for that she was grateful.

"I'm sure you did fine," he said, before turning and leaving the room.

When the door closed for the second time Rosaline did not stand to admire the portraits as she had planned, or to look out the window and get some air. Instead, she sat frozen, breathing rapidly, eyes fixed on the back of the door wondering what would happen if she failed.

I can fail one task, she reminded herself. The queen had said so. *If I fail this task, I can still pass the others. I can still become Queen of Cups*. It was that thought that kept her from breaking down completely. The thought she didn't allow herself to think was obvious: *the other tasks may be just as hard*. If she could barely complete this one, what made her think she had a shot at the others?

In a blink, she was back on the streets of Paris, wandering through the rain, alone and shivering. It was days like that she hated most because she had nothing to occupy her time and nowhere to go to keep warm. She would walk for miles through the city, her stomach grumbling and toes freezing inside her worn boots. She especially hated seeing families comfortable and happy inside their homes. It wasn't like she was spying on purpose, but sometimes she couldn't help it. Outside would be dark and miserable, but inside it would be warm and bright and it was impossible not to notice. When that happened she was jealous and angry and sad and she would cry, only it wouldn't matter because the rain would wash away her tears as quickly as they fell.

In the tower study, Rosaline closed her eyes, praying she would never see Paris again. This was her chance at a new life and if she lost it now she didn't know what she would do.
It felt like hours dragged while Rosaline's hands grew clammy and her throat dry. And then, just when she thought she might scream from needing to know, Owen returned.

"Miss Rosaline?" The page pushed open the door, stepping inside.

Rosaline jumped to her feet in a screech of chair legs. "Yes?"

"The king and queen are ready for you. Would you like to join us downstairs?"

With her heart beating against her chest Rosaline managed a curt nod.

"Good," said Owen. He turned before Rosaline could examine his face, but she swore she saw a flash of pity behind his unassuming eyes.

Or maybe he doesn't know, she reasoned, following him from the room. *Please, please say he doesn't know.*

When they reached the castle floor, Nicolai stood near the door, watching her intently with an encouraging smile on his handsome face. The way his eyes shone made her pulse race and suddenly things seemed vastly worse. What if the king and queen announced her failure in front of him? Then he would know the truth, that she was both homeless *and* stupid.

"Rosaline," the Queen of Coins called, sounding regal and foreboding from her throne. The table and tea had been cleared, leaving only the dark, eternal thrones in the center of the room. "Come closer, child."

Rosaline did as she was instructed, leaving Nicolai at her back to stand before the royals.

"How do you think you did?" the queen asked when Rosaline faced her.

No intelligent thought came to mind, but she couldn't very well tell the truth – it had gone horribly; as horrible as expected, maybe worse. "As well as I could manage," she answered at last, holding her head high. She might be homeless and stupid, but she was proud, and she would defend her position until death.

"We've reviewed the ledger," the king announced from his ebony throne. "Your approach was…interesting."

Rosaline's heart dropped into her stomach. *Interesting,* was never a good word. It was almost always followed by 'but'.

Matilda held the ledger aloft. "It took us quite some time to discuss your allocations, and I will be honest it wasn't easy. There were arguments both in your favor and against."

Rosaline bit her lip, tasting the sharp tang of blood.

"It is now your chance to defend your decisions," said the king. "Please, enlighten us."

Rosaline struggled to find her voice, buried deep under despair and fear. The king's expression grew disgruntled and even the queen's kind smile tightened, impatient. "I- " Rosaline began, discovering her voice frail and trembling and she hated herself for it. "I divided it as equally as I could to start," she explained, trying to forget Nicolai, for if she thought too much about him, her nerves would surely choke her. "But I know things cannot always be equal, for if everyone was exactly the same no one would prosper and the town as a whole would suffer. I knew food was important. If people can't eat they can't live, and what is the point of having entertainment and doctors and school if they aren't alive? So, I gave the farmer the most coins. I knew that every one of the eight positions was needed in CopperVille, even the actor, who was there to make people happy. You can be as healthy and well-fed as you can be, but if you're bored, the world is a lot less worth living in."

At this, both the king and queen nodded, and Rosaline swore she heard Nicolai murmur approvingly at her back.

Minutely more confident, Rosaline went on, "I didn't want the distribution of wealth to be too vast. I thought half was reasonable. An actor, though important to the village's happiness, is not directly essential to survival. So, I figured the entertainment an actor could provide is worth about half the value of having food to survive. From there I based the rest of the roles around those assumptions. Without a doctor or access to medical care, the villagers could sill die, even with food, so I marked the doctor as the same level of importance with the farmer, and gave them both sixteen coins. Having a source of income is pretty important too, without it the town would not have profits for the next year, so the miner was nearly as essential as the farmer and the doctor. He got fifteen coins. The carpenter was similar, though probably not as important since I assumed there was existing places to live. But if a storm swept through or new citizens moved into town, they would need shelter to live, so having someone available to provide shelter seemed crucial." Rosaline felt the most unsure about this argument. Truthfully, she'd allocated the carpenter a fair amount of coins simply because she'd wished she'd had someone to build her a house when she'd been on the streets. It was significant to her, though she wasn't sure how to explain it without sounding childish.

"Teachers are needed too," she continued, "though not directly related to survival, so I ranked that a bit lower. Education is a luxury, not a necessity; though quality of life will be better with it." She didn't mention the fact that it would have helped her a lot in this situation, which was another reason she'd kept it higher than other categories. "I already explained why I ranked the actor last, but I decided the preacher was of equal value, though not more so. Having something to believe in and connect to is important for most, but not all, and though it relates to quality of life and happiness, it doesn't directly influence survival." She finished with a breath.

There was a long moment of silence as the king and queen considered her. "Thank you, Rosaline," Matilda finally said, bowing her head. "If you'll excuse us for a moment, we need to discuss in private."

Rosaline nodded, letting Owen lead her across the room to Nicolai.

"That was good," Nicolai said, smiling when she reached his side.

Rosaline felt stupid, but nodded thanks anyway.

He seemed to sense her disquiet and stood silent, not bothering to create mindless chit-chat or distracting conversation.

Several long minutes ticked by before the king spoke again. "Please return, Rosaline."

Nicolai gave her a long, meaningful look. *Be strong,* it seemed to say. *You are brave enough to be queen.*

Rosaline wasn't sure if she'd read the look right, but she hopped so.

As she returned to greet her fate, the king spoke first. "Your approach was rather rudimentary," he said and Rosaline's heart plummeted to her feet. "There was little calculation in your method," he explained, "and as you know, as Coins, our House takes a very mathematic approach to solving all problems. Most that perform the Coins' task use a weighted system to calculate the distribution, using percentages and odds. Their defense is usually quite long-winded, heavily detailed, providing insight into calculations and deductive reasoning."

Rosaline nodded, admitting defeat. She knew she lacked the skills necessary to complete the task right, but there was nothing left to say. At least Nicolai stood behind her so she didn't have to see the disappointment on his face.

"But you also showed great heart," the queen added. "It's basic, but in the most honest form. A simple evaluation of life. And in its simplicity, it is rather beautiful."

The queen's words were unexpected. Had Rosaline heard correctly? Or was the queen simply letting her down easy with a parting compliment?

Behind her, Nicolai shifted position and she realized he was just as anxious to hear the verdict.

"So for that alone," the queen went on, "we have decided to pass you."

Pass? Rosaline blinked. "I passed?" she asked, dumfounded.

"Yes," answered the king, "though you should understand it was a very close fail. Your genuine belief in your decisions is what saved you, not the answers themselves."

Who cared how she passed, whether by a hair or a mile, as long as she did! She wanted to cry, from joy, from relief, from happiness, but no tears came. Not yet. It wasn't time to cry. Instead, a smile broke across Rosaline's face, so wide it hurt her cheeks.

And then Nicolai was there, pulling her into a hug. "Congratulations," he said warmly. "You passed the first task."

Rosaline let him hold her and buried her face in his chest, glad he was there. So many times she'd celebrated things alone. And now, for the one thing that really mattered, she had someone to share it with, someone who was proud of her.

"Thank you," she said. She couldn't remember the last time she'd felt this happy - or if she'd ever felt this happy.

"You're on your way to a new life." Nicolai cupped the side of her face. "Everything is about to change."

At his words Rosaline's heart soared.

KNIGHT OF WANDS
KRAKOW

A heavy-fisted knock thundered against the door, yanking Jude from sleep. He groaned and rolled over, stuffing a pillow over his head.

The knock grew louder, more impatient, until it was no longer a knock but a rumble of fists on wood.

Jude was about to shout for the assailant to leave when he realized it could be Ophelia. Maybe she was in trouble? "I'm coming," he mumbled, shoving the quilt from bed and stumbling toward the door. "Who is it?"

"Just open up," returned a voice from the other side.

Not Ophelia.

Jude's excitement vanished as he pulled the door open, expression set in a deeply irritated scowl. There, standing in dingy apartment hall, was Kieran, Knight of Wands - his auburn hair windblown and face flushed with cold. "Kieran," Jude greeted in surprise. "What are you doing here?"

"What do you think I'm doing here?" The young knight shouldered his way inside, not bothering for an invitation. "It's like an oven in here. How do you sleep?" He headed for the window, throwing it open and inhaling a lungful of cool winter air.

"It's the pipes," Jude rubbed the sleep from his eyes.

Kieran didn't seem to care. He took a quick walk around the room, which was more of a rotation. "It looks like you haven't left your apartment in weeks."

Jude leaned against the wall and crossed his arms over his chest, yawning. "I've been busy."

"Busy *alone*?"

The way he said 'alone' struck Jude as oddly decisive. He straightened. "What are you doing here Kieran? It can't be to check up on my housekeeping."

"No, I'm afraid not."

"Then what?" Jude's patience with the Magician was wearing thin and it was starting to show. He was sick of the man prying into his life without actually being present. "What does the old man want now?"

Kieran frowned. The younger knight knew the Magician's tricks just as well as Jude. "Let's get out of here," he said, evading the question and heading for the door. "I need a drink."

"Fine," Jude agreed. He was aggravated but not enough to refuse his oath-brother. It wasn't Kieran's fault, after all, and after a quick search of the flat, Jude found his boots under the bed and pulled on his coat, using a hat to hide his bed-head. On the way out he grabbed his red scarf, pleasantly surprised to find it still smelled of Ophelia: vanilla and flowers and feminine in a way he could never understand. Girls always smelled good - too good - and Ophelia smelled better than most.

Outside, the world was white and cold, people bundled in wool, looking like walking sacks of laundry. Jude tugged his scarf close, hoping he could prevent the wind from carrying off Ophelia's scent.

"Which way?" Kieran asked, looking down a narrow street lined with soot stained buildings puffing smoke from precariously leaning chimneys.

"Down here." Jude started along a weaving alley emerging beside the Visula River, bloated with ice and moving sluggish in the cold. The sound of the river faded into street noise as the pair turned away, passing Wawel Castle propped on a small craggy hill. They skirted the castle and down a street crowded with cafes, pubs and souvenir shops, forcing Jude to shove his way through the tourists to the side-street where the Old Armory pub squatted. He herded Kieran through the creaky door and down the steps into the dungeonesque establishment, greeted by the smell of smoke and fried grease.

Ludwik nodded from behind the bar. "Jude. Dzien dobry."

"Dzien Dobry," Jude offered in reply. "Piwo, prosze." He held up two fingers and went to his regular table, dropping into the worn armchair by the fire.

Kieran took a seat across from him. "Are you going to tell me what's going on?"

Jude shot him a baffled look, only partially forged. "How would I know? You're the one who showed up at my door."

"I know," Kieran muttered. "But I know you know why."

Jude did know. Or, at least, he thought he did. It was about Ophelia. He had no idea how the Magician already knew - he barely knew himself - but it was not the first time the old man had sent someone to remind him of his vow before he'd realized he was at risk of breaking it. The one sign he had noticed was the faint dulling of his mark on his left palm. The vibrant green had seemed to fade over the past few days, settling in a muted shimmer. But he wasn't about to tell Kieran so, and did his best to hide it. "I have a vague idea," Jude confessed.

Ludwik appeared, placing two pint glasses on a wobbly table between them. "Enjoy," he rumbled as the table dipped and golden-brown liquid sloshed over the brim. The gruff bartender spared a glance at the mess, tossed Jude a filthy rag, and retreated.

While Jude sopped up the spill, Kieran eyed him with suspicion. "Is this about that girl in your building? Karazyna? Are you risking your vow for some local broad?"

Annoyed, Jude focused his attention on mopping the table, afraid Kieran would see it in his eyes. He wasn't sure how the knight had learned of his escapades, Nicolai most likely, but either way it disturbed him anyone could think Karazyna worth breaking a vow over. "No," Jude said firmly, tossing the rag aside and sitting back with his pint. "This has nothing to do with her."

Whether Kieran believed him, it was clear he had come to make a point and wouldn't easily be put off. "You're on dangerous ground, Jude. Do you have any idea what could happen if you break your vow before renouncing it?"

"No," Jude admitted and challenged the younger knight to enlighten him, "do you?"

Kieran wavered, doubt clouding his eyes.

"The Magician doesn't exactly trust us with his divine knowledge, does he?"

"Well, I know whatever it is, it's bad," Kieran insisted. "And not just for you. For *everyone.*" He clipped the last word, drawing attention to the importance he assumed Jude missed. "Don't you remember why you joined the Order of the Tarot?"

"No," Jude answered resolutely, "I don't remember. My judgment was impaired by being a child. I wasn't old enough to make important life decisions. *He* should have known that."

"*He* was like your father," Kieran countered. He was angry now, hands white-knuckled around the glass. A lot could be said about the Magician, but owning no loyalty was not one.

"You don't know anything about this, Kieran. Stay out of my business, would you?"

"Your business is my business! We're oath-brothers. We're knights of the Order. And if you break your vow, we all suffer." Kieran's voice rose well above discreet, attracting the attention of the pub's patrons.

Ludwik glanced at Jude from the bar, raising a brow that asked, *do you want me to throw this clown out?*

Jude jerked his head, implying, *no,* he could handle it.

Unaware, Kieran continued his rant, "The Magician offered you a blessed life and you're throwing it away for some *girl*?"

She's not just some girl, Jude wanted to protest, but he held his tongue, knowing it wouldn't help. The Magician did not care who Ophelia was. All he cared for was maintaining the balance and destroying whatever threatened it. "I know what I'm doing, Kieran."

"Do you?" The way he asked it, imploring, not accusing, made Jude pause.

Did he really know what he was doing? Had he considered what his actions meant? Until recently he had never met anyone worth renouncing the Tarot for, but now… he wasn't sure. There was something about Ophelia that made him doubt everything he knew. But she was also a liar. He didn't know her, not really, and the girl he thought he knew might not be real at all. How could he give up his life for a phantom?

"If you want to leave the Order, you better say so," Kieran added after a while. "You better tell the Magician and forsake your vow before it's too late. Before something bad happens. Don't risk everyone for your happiness."

That stung. Jude chewed on the insult. "Does my happiness not matter?"

"No," Kieran replied with little remorse. "The Tarot is about sacrifice, Jude. I thought you knew that. If you keep acting the way you are you will destroy us and in the end everyone will lose, including the girl you're throwing it all away for. Think about that, won't you? Do you want her to lose everything because you wanted to have it all?"

"Have it all?" Jude bit off a laugh. "I have nothing."

"You have everything." Kieran remained calm, but rigid. Jude could tell his oath-brother was livid but trying to get his point across without shouting. "But you turn your back on it at every turn. Come back to living amongst Tarot where you belong and maybe you'll see. Stop resisting like a scorned child and maybe you can learn to be happy with what you have, instead of what you don't."

Wise words, thought Jude, but he wasn't convinced. He'd given up a lot in this life, things Kieran could never understand. He was not the Knight of Swords. "And what do I have?" Jude asked, interested to hear Kieran's take.

"You have a simple life. You will never go cold or hungry or be poor. Yet you choose to live the way you do – you choose to be miserable, Jude."

Jude sat back. He shouldn't be surprised, the Knight of Wands was supposed to be passionate. Maybe that's why the Magician had chosen him – if anyone could drum up inspiration to rejoin life among the Order it would be Kieran. And truthfully, Jude agreed with most of what the knight said. He *was* being selfish, but it didn't make the choice easier: to sacrifice his own happiness for the sake of many, or renounce his vow and turn his back on everything he'd ever known? "It's not easy," he said after a long pause. "We may both be knights, Kieran, but we don't walk the same path."

"I never said we did."

"Then why are you asking me to decide right now? I need more time. It's not easy to give up the Tarot. It's all I've ever known and it's hard to walk away."

"I know," Kieran agreed, sounding sincere and distraught at the idea of Jude leaving. "But you can't be two people, Jude. You have to choose whether you want to be the Knight of Swords or someone else. And you have to do it before it's too late."

Jude thought that was funny. There wasn't supposed to be another version of himself. He was supposed to be the Knight of Swords through and through, no doubts and no apprehension. "I will choose," he insisted. "Just not today."

"Fine," Kieran looked stiff, as if he were holding back. "But you should know the Magician will come for you next. And Jude -"

"Yes?"

"I think if he could renounce you himself, he would."

A dull ache throbbed in Jude's chest, deep and unrelenting like a partially healed wound to the heart. All his life he'd thought it impossible to disappoint the Magician. Now it seemed impossible to avoid.

A HEARTBEAT
KRAKOW

It was dark inside the flat, though a swath of moonlight danced along the floor. Ophelia climbed through the window and followed the shimmering band inside, stepping over furniture and abandoned articles of clothing. As her eyes adjusted, she spotted Jude asleep in bed, and for a moment considered turning around and leaving. It was stupid to be here. So why had she come?

For a moment she stood watching him, iridescent light falling across the planes of his face, peaceful in sleep. "Jude," she whispered, dropping quietly to his side.

He stirred and but did not wake.

Gently, she placed a hand on his chest. "Jude," she whispered again. His skin was warm against her cold palm and beneath it she could feel the faint flutter of his heart. As she sat motionless, something deep within her stirred, longing to hear the sound, and like a stone, she sank, lowering her head until it rested on his chest. Paper wings beat against her ear, hopeful and constant, forcing a faint smile on her lips.

Jude's hand pressed against the back of her head and she looked up. "Ophelia?" he whispered, as if it might be a dream.

She nodded.

"You're back."

For some reason she felt like crying, so relieved, yet so torn with guilt. It was choking, all consuming, and she couldn't fight it. Tears brimmed and fell, tracking down her cheeks onto Jude's bare chest.

He lifted his head from the pillow, moving his hand to rest on the side of her face. "Are you crying?"

She didn't speak.

He stared in silence, eventually sliding over and pushing the covers back. Without considering the consequences or what it might mean, she climbed in, curling into the crook of his body and burying her face into a pillow that smelled of him. Once settled, he covered her with the blanket, wrapped his arm around her, and pulled her close.

For a long time Ophelia could not stop the tears from falling, but if Jude heard, he never said. He just let her cry. And if she knew nothing else, she knew this: he was kind and he was gentle and he understood what it meant to be alone.

The room trembled in warning, so soft she thought it must be in her head.

Leave, the walls said. *Leave him be. Let him keep his vow and his heart.*

But she couldn't move and she couldn't let him be. She squeezed her eyes tight until the shaking subsided.

Jude's forehead rested along the curve of her neck, his breath soft, tickling small hairs and making her shudder. And as she lay there in his arms she thought that if her lies had been true - if someone had been after her - she would want Jude as her protector.

The guilt gnawed.

Her thoughts ventured to the last place she wanted them to go. The trip home had been brief, but it had also changed everything.

***

Milo's townhouse was dark, curtains drawn and lights snuffed. Before trying the door, Ophelia looked around, feeling the restless chill of someone watching. She was sure of it now, but she still didn't know why, and the stalker was careful not to be seen.

The silence howled, yet no one appeared and the shadows remained still. Eventually, Ophelia went back to the door, but it was locked. *Strange*. Milo never locked the door. Something felt wrong, her bones ached in warning, and for a moment she stood facing the door, head bowed, waiting, listening… but nothing happened.

After a while she climbed down the steps and found the fat plastic toad crouched in the front flower plot. The figurine's stomach was hollow and concealed a spare key. She rattled it into her hand and returned to the door, unlocking it with a sinister *click.*

"Uncle Milo?" she called, stepping into the foyer.

The front entrance was black and cavernous. After ditching her backpack, Ophelia found the light and flicked it on. The room brightened as usual, familiar and warm with an expensive glow. The rush of fear made her spin and bolt the door, pressing her hand to the cool wood while trying to catch her runaway breath.

When no one kicked the door down, she backed away and headed for Milo's study. Inside, the lab door was closed, but she noticed the Omniworld's eerie green light shining through the gap. When she reached the door, she expected to find it locked, but it opened easily under her hand. "Uncle Milo," she said, peering into the room. For some reason her heart was pounding, as if her body sensed something her mind could not.

In the lab, the giant clockwork globe rotated on its base, moving effortlessly, without the creaks and groans she'd grown accustomed to hearing. The core was burning bright, so bright Ophelia had to shield her eyes from the glare.

"Ophelia?"

Ophelia dropped her hand. Her uncle appeared from the dark, face ghoulish in the ethereal light. She gasped, gripping the doorknob in surprise. Milo's hair had gone completely white. He was thin too; face gaunt and ashen as though he hadn't eaten in days.

"You don't look good," she told him, taking a cautious step into the room. "When did you last sleep?"

Milo rubbed his red-rimmed eyes. He blinked. "Sleep? I'm not sure. What day is it? No. Never mind. It doesn't matter. When did you get here?"

Ophelia frowned, unsettled. "Just now. I just walked in the door." She hesitated then added, "It was locked."

"Oh." Milo shook his head as if he had a lot of cobwebs to clear.

"I tried calling. You haven't been answering the phone."

Milo screwed his face in thought, as if the question were complicated and required a significant amount of concentration to answer. "I've been busy."

"I can see that," Ophelia replied, using a delicate tone. She glanced at the globe with increasing agitation. "Where's the housekeeper? Hasn't she been cooking for you?"

Milo turned away, headed for the workbench. "What? Oh. I had to let her go."

"Let her go?" Ophelia was stunned. Milo's housekeeper had been in the family for years, longer than she had been alive. "But…why? What did she do?"

"She was nosy," he answered coldly.

Dread pooled in Ophelia's stomach. What had happened here? What was wrong with him? Something wasn't right….

Milo kept his head bowed, breathing heavy, eyes fixed on the table.

"Are you okay?" she asked, walking toward him, one hand extended.

"I'm fine," Milo replied, though he sounded far away, lost in another place and another time. "I've been working. It's not easy being a brilliant scientist, you know."

"I imagine," she replied as if speaking to a child on the brink of a tantrum. She'd never seen Milo this disturbed. Was the stress of the Omniworld finally breaking him? "Is it done yet?" she asked, hoping he could rest at last. "Does the Omniworld work?"

Milo looked up, expression changing in such a way it frightened her – he was *grinning*. "Yes," he hissed. "It finally works."

Ophelia's stomach churned. She looked back to the globe, eyes averted from the core. It was a terrifying machine, powerful and awe inspiring. It reminded her of something she might see at a museum and it left her feeling oddly insignificant and important all at once. "What does that mean?" her voice trembled, though she wasn't sure why.

"It's time." The glow of the Omniworld cast wicked shadows across Milo's sunken face. "We're ready." He clenched his fist, as if imagining a tiny Magician in the palm of his hand. "And you must cast the first blow."

Ophelia swallowed, thinking of Jude.

***

Tormented, Ophelia lay awake for a long time beside Jude, unaware of the enemy in his bed.

SKYWARD
KATHMANDU, NEPAL

From the primeval forest of Białowieża, Nicolai took Rosaline a day's journey northeast to the city of Minsk where they boarded the Magician's private jet for the Himalayan Mountains of Nepal. In the early morning hours the plane landed in Kathmandu, a poor, vibrant city carved from the bowels of the monstrous mountains, built of temples and monuments, polluted by noise and devoured by modern power lines, toppling apartment blocks, and blaring advertising.

In the crowded city center, Nicolai paid a Nepalese owner of a rundown Ford pick-up several thousand rupees to drive them an hour northwest into the sub-tropical foothills of Mount Manaslu. As Rosaline and Nicolai bumped around in the back of the truck, they drove deep into a sacred valley of farmland and rolling hills as growing snowcapped mountains marked their slow progress.

At the end of a rubble road the driver lurched to a stop outside the tiny village of Arket Bazar, where he shouted in Nepalese until Rosaline and Nicolai exited with their bags and he sped off, leaving them alone on the side of a dirt road.

"What now?" Rosaline asked, anxiety pealing her voice as she stared wide-eyed at the alien surroundings.

"This way," Nicolai instructed with a sly smile, heading down a steep grassy incline to a wooden shed at the base of a small trail. Rosaline followed closely, nervous and treading on heavy feet. When Nicolai reached the shed he pulled a long key in the shape of a sword from around his neck and fit it into the padlock of the heavily chained door.

"What's in there?" she asked, taking several shuffling steps back.

"Don't worry," Nicolai assured with a gentle laugh. "It's nothing dangerous." With a grunt, he pulled open the door, kicking up a small cloud of dust. Rosaline coughed and ducked her head, taking another step in reverse. "You okay?" Nicolai asked.

She gave a stiff nod, her lips pursed, staring fixedly at the door.

Nicolai paused, one hand resting on the rusted handle. "I'll take care of you, Rosaline, I promise. You're safe with me."

Rosaline studied the seriousness of his expression: knit brows, intense eyes – a soundless promise. This time when she nodded, she meant it, and relaxed.

Seemingly satisfied, Nicolai turned back to the shed and disappeared inside the gaping, black hole.

"Nicolai?" Rosaline called after a few minutes, fear clinging to her words. A rumble caused her to start and she nearly tripped over her feet trying to back away. "Nicolai!" she shouted, voice ringing like alarm bells. "Nicolai!"

The rumbling grew louder, filling the shed and seeping into the valley where it bounced around rocks and up into trees. From the darkness a beast emerged, spitting exhaust and making the ground tremble. Rosaline blinked, frowning as Nicolai smiled at her from the roaring motorcycle. He put his feet on the ground and silenced the engine. "This will get us up the mountain trail," he said, beaming.

"You want me to get on that thing?" Rosaline pointed at the rusty old machine that looked as if it belonged in a junk yard, not on a treacherous mountain road.

"It's tougher than it looks. Have to dissuade thieves. Trust me, it's got a powerful engine." Nicolai patted the machine with a loving hand. "It's carried me up and down many times."

"Somehow I can't imagine the Magician scooting up a mountain on that thing."

Nicolai's smile widened. "He usually helicopters."

"Helicopter?"

"Yes, but you and I are going to take the scenic route."

"Why?"

"Because," said Nicolai, "it's your first trip up the mountain. It's tradition."

"Great," Rosaline replied dryly.

"Hop on." Nicolai tossed her a helmet and scooted forward, making room at the back of the bike.

Cautiously, Rosaline approached, securing the helmet over her hair and swinging her leg over the seat behind Nicolai.

"Hold tight," he warned, starting the engine.

Beneath her, the motorcycle groaned and spewed exhaust. She tightened her grip around Nicolai's midsection, closing her eyes and squeezing for dear life.

"A little looser," said Nicolai in a pinched voice.

"Sorry," Rosaline mumbled and relaxed as best she could.

As Nicolai kicked off, the bike barreled up the incline, onto the road, and away in a cloud of rolling dirt. For a while they seemed to coast along the foothills, weaving through the backcountry roads, woods, and along fields, creeping slowly closer to the snowy peaks in the distance. Then, as if the great mountains had quietly snuck up, they were surrounding by nothing but rock and jagged horizon, leaving the trees behind.

Eventually, Nicolai turned off the main road – if you could call it a road – down a steeper, rockier trail, with a warning sign nailed to a post reading, *'Danger. Private Property. All trespassers will be shot,'* in multiple languages.

"Are you sure this is the right way?" asked Rosaline, twisting to get a second glance at the sign before it vanished in the distance.

He tossed her an amused look over his shoulder. "I'm sure."

As the bike climbed higher, the warm Nepal air cooled significantly, and Rosaline was forced to duck her head behind Nicolai's back, hiding from icy wind. Ahead, an enormous mountain punched forth in great granite folds, the snowy peak jutting into a sapphire sky rimmed with gusty white clouds, as if a giant had swirled them about the summit like a halo.

"It's incredible." Rosaline peered from behind Nicolai, straining to see the rising cliffs and crags. Growing up in a forest with lakes and meadows she had never seen a mountain, and was utterly spellbound by the magnitude of the hulking rock mass.

"Blade Mountain," said Nicolai. "The little sister to Sprit Mountain, Manaslu, and home to the House of Swords."

"Up there?"

"Way up there."

Rosaline bent back her head, searching for a glimpse of the Swords' House in the sky as Nicolai propelled the bike over the crunch of rock and gravel. On either side the earth dropped away, vanishing into a great gorge, brown and grey and desolate as the wind picked up, whistling loud and lonely with nothing to break the mournful cry.

"Did the Magician create the House of Swords?"

Nicolai veered the bike up the twisty, hazardous road, making Rosaline's heart thump with every turn. "No," he said, speaking loudly over the hum of the engine and the screaming wind. "The House of Swords has always been here. It's one with the mountain."

"So the Magician didn't create the Order of the Tarot?"

"No," Nicolai replied. "It's always been here, since the beginning of time. You didn't think our Magician was the first, did you?"

Rosaline thought about it. "No. I guess not. But I thought maybe the Magician lived forever."

"We all die," Nicolai answered, matter-of-fact. "Being part of the Tarot does not make you immortal. If it did, the dying queen wouldn't be dying. You wouldn't be here, and you and I would never have met."

"We would have," Rosaline replied without thinking. She said it so casually, so simply, because deep in her heart she knew it was true. In this lifetime, past, and many to come she knew, and would know, Nicolai.

"What do you mean?" Nicolai's voice was deep, as if holding a secret he was hesitant to share.

Heat rushed to Rosaline's cheeks. She'd been stupid to speak so openly, now how would she explain? Nicolai would never understand. He did not have her gift of sight. *Stupid, crazy, gypsy.* "Never mind."

The motorcycle cut sharply toward the cliff's edge and Nicolai pulled back, urging the metal beast against the mountain wall. On instinct, Rosaline gave a small gasp and tightened her hold. "Sorry," said Nicolai, "the road is rutted. It pulls the bike from time to time."

"I see that," Rosaline replied weakly, locking her fingers tight around him.

"Please," he said. "Finish what you were saying. I want to know."

The way he spoke, as if he already knew, was the only reason Rosaline found her voice to go on. "Do you know the Queen of Cups?"

"She is my Queen," Nicolai answered, implying that, yes, of course he knew her.

"You know she has the gift of sight?" In Rosaline's visions she had seen her past lives and knew many had been more difficult than this. But always, like two distant rivers, she and Nicolai would flow from opposite ends of the world to meet, just as they were now on this mountain path.

"I do." Nicolai risked a quick glance in her direction and she had never wanted to reach out and touch someone so badly.

"Then you understand that I *know* things. I see things."

For a moment Nicolai fell silent, the howling wind filling the void. "What is it you know?"

Rosaline hesitated, but she had come too far to turn back. "That we were meant to meet, and this is not the first time we have."

Several long moments stretched and when at last Nicolai did speak, he chose his words carefully. "You knew we would meet? You've always known this?"

"Not always," Rosaline admitted, glad he could not see her face, "but after we met, I did." She wanted to tell him more, about their lives together, both lovely and tragic and whole, but she would die if he rejected her. How could she go on then? How could she possibly complete the Tarot's tasks knowing Nicolai did not want her?

Without a word, Nicolai cut the throttle and pulled the bike slowly to a stop, sideling it up against the mountain.

"What are you doing?" Rosaline asked. Suddenly afraid, she twisted, wide-eyed, staring into the gorge dotted with scrawny trees and a distant stony creek.

Nicolai dismounted, pulling Rosaline with him. Stunned and confused, she feared he was going to throw her over and fought back, balling her fist and slamming it into his chest. "Let go! I'm sorry! I didn't mean -"

"I'm not going to hurt you!" He gave her a hard shake then released her on the trail, breathing heavily. "I just wanted to look at you."

Trapped against the mountain, Rosaline steadied her gaze, still blurred with adrenalin. Nicolai's face was broken, questioning, as if he wanted to understand but couldn't quite comprehend. "I didn't mean to upset you," she said quietly, trying to ignore the sheer drop five feet away. "I can't help what I see in my visions. It just is…."

"Is it true?" he demanded, though it was not an angry demand. "You've known me before? How is that possible?"

Rosaline considered lying. Maybe he wasn't ready for something so profound? But she was no liar, and she couldn't pretend, the truth would be written all over her face. "I don't know," she admitted. "I don't choose what I see… I don't know how to explain it. I just know I know you."

For a moment Rosaline thought Nicolai was going to walk away, start the bike, and leave her on the mountainside, disgusted, but then he ran a shaky hand through his sunlit hair, as if overwhelmed and struggling to gain control. Rosaline was about to ask if he was okay when he suddenly turned, grabbed her, and kissed her roughly, shoving her back against the mountain.

A boulder bit her back but she barely felt it, stunned by Nicolai's lips pressed tight against hers. The kiss was short, sweet but hard, jarring her teeth so she gasped when he pulled away.

Even in the mountain's shadow she could tell Nicolai's face was flushed. "I knew something was different the moment I laid eyes on you," he breathed. "I knew it was you. I wasn't sure at first, but on the carousel, I knew. "

"You knew?" she whispered. "Knew what?"

"That it was *you.* I don't know how I knew, but I did. Flashes of memories that weren't mine, and your face – *I knew you.* Your eyes, your laugh, your smile…."

A faint wrinkle fell across Rosalie's brow. She did not understand. How he could possibly know? But then, how could he possibly not? It was so glaring, so obvious, so *right.*

"I knew you long before you showed up at the Magician's," he said. "I don't know how I know, but I do. It's in your voice. It's in your eyes. And I have this overwhelming feeling I should be kissing you, holding you, and that it's not the first time I've done those things. I *know* you." He said the last few words as a plea - a plea for validation, because if she didn't it would break his heart.

Rosaline took a breath, filling her lungs with cool mountain air. "I know you too," she answered, trying to sound brave and wise, though she was truly neither.

"Is this possible?"

"I don't know," she replied honestly. All her life she'd dreamed of Nicolai, but she'd never dared believe him real – until now.

Despite the marvel in his voice, Nicolai looked stricken, his hand resting on her arm as if afraid to let go. "We have to keep going," he said, pulling back. "The Queen of Swords is expecting us. We can't keep her waiting and we're already behind."

Rosaline didn't want to go. She wanted to stand on the mountain with Nicolai forever, but he helped her back onto the bike. This time when she wrapped her arms around him, he placed a hand over hers and things felt different, she was no longer alone. If she could just pass the Tarot's task they could live happily ever after, just like the fairytales from her mother's books. Only a little further. Only a little longer and her life would be complete.

They resumed the long trek up the mountain and neither spoke, Rosaline afraid of what Nicolai might say if she pressed and Nicolai seemingly lost in thought. Sometime later, long after the sun had crossed the sky, Rosaline caught a glint between the peaks. She squinted, and eventually it came into view: an ice-castle jutting from the mountain, each tower an icy blade. "Is that -?" she asked in awe.

"The Skyward Castle, House of Swords." Nicolai nodded. "Seventy-eight blades of ice. One for each member of the Tarot."

"It's beautiful."

"In its own way," Nicolai agreed, though his voice held a certain amount of indignation.

The bike continued higher into the sky, treading across the perilous path until the wind blew sharp and snow dusted the trail, chasing circles around them.

"Night is coming," said Rosaline, looking to the indigo sky.

"Soon," agreed Nicolai. "Don't worry, it's not much further. Just over the next few peaks."

And finally, over the next ridge, the Skyward Castle appeared, icicles stabbing a night sky void of stars. It was odd, but somehow Rosaline knew she'd seen this empty sky before – in a dream, no doubt – and it was comforting to know she'd been meant to be here under this strange sky with Nicolai.

As the path began to widen, cutting deeper into the mountain, Nicolai bent his head toward Rosaline's and whispered, "The queen can't know."

Rosaline frowned. She knew what he meant but she didn't understand why. "Okay," she agreed, though her heart sank. Was he ashamed of her? Or was it his vow as a knight?

Nicolai tightened his fingers on hers and smiled, comforting, and it made Rosaline feel better.

Just ahead, the castle soared, wedged between two mountain peaks, surrounded in a bowl of ice and snow. Rosaline looked back, wondering if she could see the city of Kathmandu from such dizzying height, but there was only rock and snow and darkness behind.

When she turned back a figure was approaching from the castle, dressed in robes of soft white fur. A hood with wolf ears was pulled low over the stranger's face, casting it in shadow, but Rosaline knew it was the Queen of Swords.

On a gust of icy wind, the queen swept closer, trailing a path in the snow. Rosaline's heart clinched at the sight and she knew the next task would not be so easily won.

A CLOCK IS TICKING
LONDON

Alone in his study, the Magician stood naked from the waist up, staring out the window overlooking his estate. Crisscrossed over his back, around ribs, and down his arms, were hundreds of Tarot markings, most of which throbbing green in the frail light of the room, making him glow as if he'd been dipped in phosphorescent ink. Just above his left elbow, one of the markings had grown noticeably dark - Knight of Swords, battle-ready and charging on a great horse. Though it still held a tinge of green, the tattoo was clearly on its way to black, which, the Magician knew meant one of two things: the Knight of Sword was dying or close to breaking his vow.

The yard beyond the window was drenched in multiple shades of black, fat snowflakes falling from a muted grey sky dusting the grass. At the Magician's back, a tambour clock ticked.

Tick. Tick. Tick.

There was a tremble. A deep earthly quake that started somewhere far below his feet and travelled deep within his bones. He closed his eyes. It had been a long time since he felt the earth shudder this way. To most it was nothing, hardly worth notice, and if they noticed, it was easy to dismiss. But this was no ordinary tremble. It was a shift; a warning from the world: *Be careful - the balance of forces is shifting and something or someone has made it so.*

Like a dreaded phone call, finally, it had come, and the Magician knew who was to blame.

A knock sounded soft and questioning at the door.

"Come in," the Magician said, turning to greet the visitor.

Gracefully, the High Priestess swept into the room, head high and shoulders back. "Magician," she spoke his title tenderly, as if it were his name.

The gesture touched his aching heart. In all his years, the Magician had never revealed his given name, not even to Madeline. Most probably assumed it lost, gone with the winds of time, but he had never forgotten, and in his dreams he was still known by his birthright.

"Madeline." The Magician turned with a smile, always glad to see her. She wore a silver diadem upon a head of black locks streaked with grey. How had he missed that? Of course, Madeline had been going grey for years, but when exactly did it start to show? One day his love had been youthful and the next…she was not. She was still beautiful, she would always be beautiful, but she would not live forever. And neither would he. What would happen when they were gone? Who would replace them? Who would pick up the burden and carry it to the ends of the Earth? He knew who he'd wanted for the job, but it seemed that dream had died tonight. Jude would not succeed him.

Allowing a member of the Order to take the place of another had never been done before, but it must be possible if the person was right for the job, especially in Jude's case. The Magician had always known the boy wasn't completely right as Knight - but when he'd found him alone and orphaned he could not turn his back. He had to do something. So, against his better judgment, he had trained Jude to be a member of the Tarot instead of finding Maggie's suggested recruit to fill the part. Only two other people in the world knew of his terrible secret, Madeline and Maggie – the dying Queen of Cups.

Jude had grown up thinking he was chosen like the rest. At first the Magician thought he'd done the right thing, but as Jude grew older he realized it had been a dire mistake. Jude blamed himself for his failure, unable to understand the struggle since being the Knight of Swords was supposed to be easy. Of course there was a part of Jude that reflected the knight, but a greater part of him was someone else entirely. Ever since the incident with Adalain the

Magician knew his decision had been wrong, but he could not take it back. He could not, would not, ask Jude to renounce his vow unless the boy chose to do it himself. It was inconceivable to punish Jude for an error that was never his.

For years the Magician had tried to make Jude into the Knight of Swords, and after battling and failing, it finally hit him: if Jude could not fit a knight's role, maybe he could fit a Magician's? He certainly had the audacity, the determination and the heart. He knew it, because he recognized the traits in himself. And even if the Magician could not marry, he could still love, the proof of that was right here with Madeline, which was something he knew Jude wanted very much.

Selfish, the Magician cursed himself for the mess he'd caused. *How could I have been so selfish? I thought I was doing the right thing, but in the end I destroyed him, and I took away his chance at happiness.*

"Are you all right?" asked Madeline in a soothing voice. "You seem distracted."

"Did you feel it?" the Magician asked, one hand clasped tight behind his back, the other holding a glass of wine.

Madeline nodded, touching his elbow and glancing at the blackening mark on the Magician's skin. "He has broken his vow?"

"Not yet. Not entirely. But close."

"Is there no hope for him?"

"I sent Kieran to speak with him, but it doesn't look good. He does not realize the repercussions and I cannot make him understand."

"You need to try," she urged. "You need to tell him your plans. Maybe then, if he knows, he could endure just a little while longer?"

"Is my life any better than the Knight of Swords?" he wondered aloud, rubbing tired eyes.

Madeline smiled and moved her hand to touch his cheek. "You love me, no? Doesn't that answer your question?"

"I was lucky to fall in love with someone who understood."

"You mean," Madeline corrected, "that you were lucky I fell in love with you."

The Magician's eyes smiled even if his mouth remained hard. "Yes, of course." He kissed her softly on the forehead. "But even if Jude were to become the Magician, it would not be easy to find someone like you. Someone who understands. Someone who would not threaten the balance."

"It may be difficult but it is not impossible."

The Magician swirled his wine, staring deep into the blood-red depths. "I fear it is too late. I believe he is already falling in love."

"Then maybe this girl could understand. You don't know what people are capable of when they're in love. You don't know what she'd be willing to do for Jude."

"No," agreed the Magician. "I don't."

"Then you need to go. You need to find Jude and tell him your plans before it's too late - before he breaks his vow." She reached out, touching his cheek with a sad smile. "You've always been like a father to him. He deserved to say goodbye."

The ache in the Magician's heart expanded, spreading deep.

Sensing his pain, Madeline stepped closer, comforting him with a touch. She looked at him with wide, heart-broken eyes. "My love, Jude deserved to know you're dying."

SLOW BURN
KRAKOW

Ophelia stood under the cascade of hot water and closed her eyes, willing herself to normalcy. Of course, her life had never been *normal,* but since meeting Jude she'd begun to feel out of control. Always it had been *her* following *him,* stalking and calling the shots, but now the Knight of Swords consumed her every thought, dominated every action, and it was scary and exhilarating and confusing, all at once.

Things couldn't go on this way. She had to make a choice between Milo, who had raised her, and Jude, who she barely knew. It seemed obvious. She should pick her uncle. She should do what he'd asked, because that's what family did, without question and without complaint. But in the end it came down to doing what was right, for once. And it wasn't right to lie to Jude. It wasn't right to destroy his life. She couldn't do it. Not now that she knew him – not now that she saw his pain and he held her heart. So, she decided, she would leave and he would be safe and he would never hate her because he would never know the truth. It was cowardly, but Ophelia had never been brave. So, earlier she had sent him a message, telling him she was leaving and not to look for her. It hurt to write the words on paper. It hurt more to cast the note away. She could still see farewell on the page….

A heavy-fisted knock startled her from her thoughts, nearly causing her to slip on the slick tile. She froze, shampoo seeping in her eyes, stinging.

The stalker. It was him. She knew it. He'd finally found her….

When the pounding came again, louder, reverberating through the room, Ophelia turned off the water and grabbed a towel from the rack. Had she remembered to bolt the door? Slowly, she crept into the hall, knowing it couldn't be Jude. She had never told him where she was staying and he'd never asked. Even the messenger had been given strict instruction not to speak. In fact, she'd never told anyone but Milo and he would never leave the Omniworld.

Horrible, gruesome, thoughts flashed through her mind. Was this how her life would end - in a Krakow hotel at the hands of an intruder? As she inched toward the door she could almost hear the dry, craggy voice narrating the last moments of her life.

"Ophelia!" A voice came from the other side. "I know you're in there."

She stopped, one hand pressed to the door, the other protectively grasping the towel. She knew that voice, and it was no stalker. Hastily, she unlocked the bolt and pulled the door open.

Jude stood in the hall, expression dark as Ophelia's broken heart.

"How did you find me?" she demanded, surprised.

He held up her note, giving it a wave. "You wrote this on the back of a room service slip. It has your hotel and room number right on it."

Every inch of Ophelia's exposed skin reddened. "That was a mistake."

"Was it?" he asked, sounding a lot like the first time they'd met, suspicious and cold.

"Of course it was," she replied, but doubt wormed its way into her voice. Had she meant to write on the slip?

"You're leaving?" Jude crumpled the paper and let it fall to the floor.

Ophelia felt like that ball of paper: fragile and tossed aside. "Yes," she answered, inhaling the word.

"Can I come in?"

No, she told herself. *No, he cannot come in. If you let him in you will not let him go*. But aloud she said, "Okay," and stepped back.

Jude hesitated, as if he'd expected her to refuse, and then slid past her, shutting the door. As he faced her, Ophelia opened her mouth to speak, to apologize, to try and explain without having to explain at all, but no words emerged. She looked at the rug, her toes, anywhere but Jude's face. What had she done? What had she really destroyed? It certainly wasn't his vow.

"Why are you leaving?"

Ophelia considered how to reply without adding more lies to the pile. "I don't have a choice."

"Is it because of me?"

She bit her lip, clamping down. "Yes."

"Because you don't care about me?"

Ophelia looked up, finding his arms crossed over his chest, leaning away from her. The simple body language stung. "That's not why."

He worked his jaw, as if trying to understand. "Then why?"

"I can't say."

"Then tell me the truth about something, for once, Ophelia. Is this real?" He motioned between them, momentarily filling the divide.

It was hard to meet his stare, so dark and blue and endless like the night sky beginning to lighten after a long winter's night. A part of her wanted to keep lying, it would make things easier, but she had lied so much already and it had started to stack, heavy like bricks – one for each lie told. "It's real for me," she said quietly.

And then he stepped into her, wrapping his arms around her so tight her body pressed firm against his. The air vanished from her lungs and finally his lips were on hers, fierce and wanting. Against her back, his hand twisted in the towel, the other flat against her damp skin.

Heat flashed along flesh full of emotion she'd never known. Giving in, she wrapped her arms around his neck, pulling him closer, deepening the kiss. His shirt was soft, jeans rough on her thighs, and as he ran a hand along her back it ignited sparks. One hand tangled in her hair, never breaking the kiss that lingered and ached.

"Will you stay?" he breathed after pulling away just enough to brush the hair from her face.

"I don't know if I can," she answered truthfully, trying to control her heart from hammering away with her life.

Jude's expression fell and he tried to back away. "Then I should go."

Ophelia clamped her arms around him, shaking her head. "No. Don't."

"Then what do you want?" he pleaded.

"I lied to you."

"I know."

"Don't you care?"

"Of course I care."

Now her chest hurt, scared of what he might say and how it might change things. "But you want me to stay anyway?"

Jude's eyes remained dark, but hopeful. "More than I've ever wanted anything."

Never had Ophelia felt anyone *knew* her, and yet oddly the person who knew her the least seemed to know her the best. "I was pretending to be someone I'm not."

"I know that too," he said softly, "You can tell me who you are tomorrow." He touched her face.

She hitched a breath and kissed him again, knowing it was true. Knowing he had seen her all along. "I know you too," she whispered against his lips, tightening her hold, vowing to never let go again.

HEIGHTS
SKYWARD CASTLE, BLADE MOUNTAIN, NEPAL

A dazzling light cut through the ice, fractured in a million directions. Rosaline lay on a bed of furs, mesmerized by the rainbow prisms trapped in the ice. Eventually, her stomach drove her from bed and she rose to dress in the heavy fur robe Adalain had laid out.

After dressing and splashing freezing water on her face, Rosaline left the room in search of breakfast, entering a long ice-hall that seemed to disappear in light. As she passed a doorway, she paused, feeling a familiar pull. She had never been inside the castle before last night, yet she recognized this door as it if were her own bedroom. Above the doorway, etched in ice, was a symbol of a knight's helm and crossing sword.

Jude's room, Rosaline realized, struck with curiosity. Unable to resist, she carefully pulled aside the fur curtain and stepped inside. The room was small, similar to the one in which she'd woke, with a single bed and sturdy wardrobe. Old movie posters and a few superhero comics were the only sign it had once belonged to a child, and even though it was tidy, the space held a sense of abandonment, as if the occupant had died and the owners had left it untouched as a vigil, frozen in time.

It made Rosaline sad, though she couldn't say why. It was as if Jude had been chased from this place and all that remained was his ghost. No, that wasn't quite right. It was more like this had never been his home and he had never been welcome here. The castle did not suit Jude as it did Adalain and the other Swords, built for colder hearts. And for the first time she understood why he had left.

With a final look, Rosaline let the curtain fall with a soft *swish*, shutting Jude's childhood inside. Back in the hall, she followed the curving ice-wall to the central staircase where the ceiling soared out of sight, decorated with beautiful icicle chandeliers, sharp as diamond.

Careful not to slip, she descended the icy stairs, gripping the rail tight to keep her footing. For several minutes she wandered the endless ice-halls of the castle, poking her head in one empty room and another until finally she came upon a great hall where rows tables and benches filled a cathedral-like room. A few Swords were scattered about, talking and eating their morning meal, including the page, Paxton, who Rosaline remembered from the Magician's dinner party.

He smiled, waving her over.

Rosaline recalled the ginger haired Page as friendly, if not a little goofy, and after a quick scan to determine Nicolai was nowhere to be found, she headed in the young man's direction.

"Good morning." Paxton smiled brightly. "How did you sleep? I hope it wasn't too cold."

Rosaline smiled in return, slipping into the seat across from him. "I slept well, thank you. The castle is breathtaking."

"Isn't it?" he replied with a grin, shoveling eggs into his wide mouth. He was a funny looking boy with a kind face and an eager manner. "Takes a bit of getting used to, but once you learn to dress warm, it really grows on you."

Rosaline nodded politely, thinking that although the castle was beautiful, it was far too cold to call home. "Have you been here long?" she asked, taking a fresh baked roll from a tray and smothering it with butter and jam.

"Seven years," Paxton replied. "Not so long as most of the Tarot members."

"Seems long."

"Not when you consider how old the Tarot seem to live. The last Page of Swords lived to be a hundred and two. Maggie, the dying Queen of Cups, is nearing that herself."

Rosaline lifted a brow, surprised. She had never met the dying queen, and though she knew the woman was elderly, she hadn't guessed by that much. She was about to ask who the eldest living Tarot member was when Nicolai appeared at the base of the staircase. They locked eyes from across the room and held the gaze for several heart-stopping moments. Eventually, he broke it off and came over. Anyone in the room could have easily have mistaken him for the King of Swords with his enduring stature and handsome features. Even his eyes spoke wisdom, dark and mossy, like the forest they'd left behind, vibrant against the white of the room.

"Good morning, Rosaline, Paxton," he said when he reached the table.

There was something Rosaline didn't like about his voice this morning. It sounded heavy and burdened with something she couldn't place. What had changed over night? His every movement conveyed anguish: the way his hands clenched and unclenched - even his jaw, tight, the muscles popping and flexing.

Paxton looked between them, clearly catching onto the tension. "I'll leave you to eat," he said, hurrying to gather his plate. "I have to go find the queen before the task begins. Enjoy your breakfast and I'll be back soon."

Rosaline looked grimly at her food as the page stood and left.

After he'd gone, Nicolai cleared his throat. "How are you?" he asked, throwing his fur cloak aside to take Paxton's vacated seat. He picked up an abandoned fork and gripped it tight, though he made no move to eat.

Rosaline stared at the fork, watching the way Nicolai's hand trembled as if his anxiety was being transmitted through the silver. He seemed to notice and dropped it, forcing a smile. "Fine," she finally answered as an anxious pit widened in her stomach. "Are you all right? You seem upset."

"I'm great," he replied with a look that betrayed him. "Why wouldn't I be? We made it here. You passed the first task. All it good in the world. What about you? Are you ready?"

Rosaline eyed him with puzzled suspicion, trying to pinpoint a reason for his erratic behavior. This wasn't the Nicolai she knew from the day before. That Nicolai had been calm as a summer stream, all confidence and ease. "As I'll ever be," she eventually replied, letting her true sentiments whither in silence.

"You'll be fine." The smile plastered to Nicolai's face looked as if it had been painted there by a puppeteer, fake and distorted and not at all his.

Rosaline wanted so badly to reach out and touch him, pull him back from whatever brink he teetered on, but it was as if he'd built a wall of ice overnight, too tall to reach and to thick to break through. "Thank you," she managed, though she suddenly felt hopeless. If Nicolai no longer wanted her, she wasn't sure she could succeed alone.

Nicolai nodded and started on a bowl of cereal, reclaiming the forgotten fork, which he was promptly forced to trade for a clean spoon when the milk strained through the prongs.

"Are you sure you're okay?" Rosaline asked again, puzzling at the fork and spoon.

Nicolai filled his mouth, chomping, as if it would fill the void growing between them. "Yeah. Of course."

"Okay," she replied, letting the subject drop. It was clear whatever he was hiding he did not want to share, and Rosaline would not force him to tell. She was still a stranger to this world and to him.

The two started on their breakfasts in silence. For a while it was just the sound of their clinking utensils and grinding teeth, but then suddenly Nicolai leaned close and whispered, "You know, you're stronger than people give you credit for, Rosaline. No matter what, you'll do great."

Rosaline held his gaze, searching for deeper meaning. It was there somewhere, his eyes sparked with it, but without accompanying words she could not understand. "What do you mean?" she asked, leaning closer.

"I just mean – I just mean, no matter, if you become queen or not, you are beautiful, and smart, and capable, and you will find a way to survive."

Rosaline's mouth filled with acid. Was he trying to tell her something? Did he think she would fail? "Should I be worried? Do you think I'll fail?"

"No." Nicolai jerked back as if he'd been smacked. "No. I didn't mean it like that. I was just trying – to be encouraging."

Funny way of showing it, thought Rosaline, chewing her lip and choosing to keep her thoughts silent. "Okay," she said instead. "Well, thank you."

"I've been meaning to ask you something," he said, hurrying to resume his meal.

"About what?"

"Jude."

Rosaline tilted her head with a questioning frown. She couldn't imagine what she would know about Jude Nicolai did not. They two knights were best friends and she barely knew either.

"He thinks you may have seen a girl at the Magician's party. Someone who might have been following him."

Though surprised to hear it, the question didn't shock Rosaline. She had been waiting for the girl to come up in conversation eventually, though she'd thought it would come from Jude. "The girl," she replied evenly.

Nicolai gave a slow, worried, nod.

"I know who you mean. At first I thought she was a ghost."

A wrinkle formed between Nicolai's brows. "Do you see ghosts?" he asked as if caught off guard by the notion.

Rosaline considered. "Not usually," she replied. Truthfully, Rosaline had seen plenty of ghosts in her short life. They had even spoken to her on more than one occasion, but that seemed like a conversation for another day.

Nicolai's expression relaxed. "So who was she then?"

It was not the first time Rosaline had asked herself that question, though she had come no closer to answering it. "I don't know," she said honestly. "I thought maybe she belonged to the Magician."

"No," Nicolai confirmed, "she's not with the Tarot."

"She had a necklace," Rosaline remembered. "It came off in my hand."

"A necklace?"

"A strange necklace," she explained. "Not pretty. It was a mess of wires all coiled in a ball. I don't know why anyone would wear something like that."

"Wires?" Nicolai sounded as if he didn't believe her – which struck Rosaline as odd since they were sitting inside an ice castle on top of a mountain.

"Wires," Rosaline repeated firmly.

"Where is it now? Do you have it?"

"It's back at Headquarters, I think. I left it in the pocket of my gown."

"Do you think it was magic?"

Rosaline frowned, trying to remember how the necklace felt in her hand. Magic had always been a funny thing to her, and she didn't believe in it like Nicolai. To her it was more like energy, every changing. "No," she said at last. "It wasn't magic. It felt like a deadweight. Like an anchor," she added. "It felt like the opposite of magic."

"What's the opposite of Magic?"

Rosaline shrugged. "I don't know...." She looked to the floor, wondering, and then looked up as a thought struck her. "Science?"

"Science?" Nicolai ran a hand through his hair. "Strange."

"I think she followed us from Paris on the train," Rosaline said, hopping it would help.

Nicolai nodded. "Jude saw her."

"He saw her? I didn't think he could," she said, more to herself. "Do you think she's dangerous?" Fear tugged at Rosaline's heart. The girl might not have looked threatening, but Rosaline had felt something in her – not evil exactly, but something dark, like hollow lies and malicious intent.

Nicolai tried his best at a reassuring smile. It looked genuine, but there was a sliver of doubt Rosaline could have spotted from the moon. "Jude is the Knight of Swords," he began, "he can take care of himself. Besides, she's just a girl. I'm sure he'll be fine."

As she struggled to sort out the mystery of the phantom girl, Paxton returned to the hall, putting a sudden end to the conversation.

"The king and queen are ready for you," he said, speaking with a new air of importance.

"So soon?" Rosaline felt the blood drain from her face and pool in her stomach.

"Yes. The weather is perfect at the moment and that can change quickly in the mountains. We cannot wait if we wish to stay on schedule for the Magician."

Weather? Now, that was alarming. What could the Sword's task have to do with weather? They were the House of bravery and loyalty. Though she supposed their earthly element was air. Solemnly, Rosaline nodded and stood.

Paxton stepped back and motioned his head toward the exit. "This way."

For a heartbreaking second Rosaline thought Nicolai would not follow, but then he shoved his bowl away and stood, waiting for her to go ahead. Paxton led them silently out of the hall and through the castle's twisting corridors to a winding stairwell that seemed to stretch endlessly into the tallest spire.

At the base Rosaline stretched her head back to look up, shielding her eyes from the glare of sunlight streaming from high above. "Up there?" she asked, having never wished so badly for an elevator in all her life.

"I'm afraid so," Paxton replied, starting up the steps. "It's not so bad once you get going. Just hang onto the rope." He shook the rope bolted to the wall. "It's sturdy."

"I'll be right behind you," said Nicolai.

With a sigh, she hiked up her fur robe and began the long climb. The stairs seemed never ending and Rosaline tackled stair after stair until she was out of breath and huffing. Nicolai was quick on her heels, urging her forward.

"Just a little further," he said and Rosaline noticed the evenness of his breath compared to her labored gasps.

Halfway, she fell against the wall, letting the ice sooth her sweaty skin. "It's so high," she said in a voice thin and tired. Her thighs shook, screaming for her to quit, and she remembered the last time she'd felt this exhausted: running through the backwoods with her mother, evading her father after a particularly bad night of drinking. Her chest had burned, eyes watered and limbs quaked as mud splashed her legs and twigs clawed nasty scratches over her face. She'd been a child but even now the terror remained fresh; the sense of a shadow at her back, claws stretching toward her, waiting to tear her down if she stopped running. If she quit.

Nicolai grabbed her hand and pulled, stepping around her to keep her moving. "You can't stop now," he said, jerking her up another step. "You deserve this, Rosaline. You're so close. You can't quit before you've even began."

Reluctantly, Rosaline picked up the hem of her robe and followed, concentrating on one slippery step at a time. She breathed, swallowed, and kept on. She had to do this. She had to reach the top and she had to pass this task.

Just when she thought she couldn't take another step the stairs punched through the roof like a fist through ice, forcing Rosaline to shield her eyes from the glare of sunlight.

"You made it," Nicolai said cheerfully in her ear, and it was the first time since they arrived at the ice castle he sounded like himself.

She smiled at him then turned to look around. They were standing on the roof between the castle's two tallest peaks, snow and ice surrounding them, glistening blinding-white under a punishing sun.

"This way." Paxton touched her shoulder, guiding her away from the ledge onto the roof.

As Rosaline moved to follow the page, it was hard not to think of the height. One slip, one wrong step, and she would plummet, speared on ice and crushed by snow. Nicolai seemed to sense her discomfort and came to stand between her and the edge, blocking the view. He smiled dutifully, but somehow the warmth had vanished once more. She wanted so badly to ask what was wrong, but now didn't seem like the time. Instead, she smiled back and looked toward the page, trudging a path in the snow ahead.

The wind whipped, trying for hold and she wished Nicolai would grab her hand, tell her it would be okay, but she remembered his words, *"The queen can't know,"* and she balled her fists instead.

Ahead, teetering on the edge of the world, the King and Queen of Swords sat on two giant thrones with nothing by sky at their backs. They were still as statues, firm as the granite mountain at their feet, watching the trio approach with stony expressions.

Queen Adalian was as breathtaking as always, her blond hair pulled over one shoulder in a gentle braid, dressed in the same robes of white fur. Her eared hood was drawn back, revealing flushed cheeks and bright eyes that blazed blue against the sky.

Beside her, several feet shorter, the King of Swords sat with a scowl. He was older than the queen, much older, and Rosaline couldn't recall meeting him at the dinner party, though he must have been present. His hair was grey and thinning, wrinkles heavy and stomach bloated with age. He wore a brown fur cape clasped at his throat by a silver sword-shaped pendent. "Welcome," he greeted in a voice as rough and old as time. "I am Ronan, King of Swords."

Rosaline bowed her head and lowered her gaze, unable to meet their stares directly. These royals were nothing like the Coins with their kind eyes and fair nature. These royals were hard, focused, and sure – as all Swords should be. When she looked up Adalain was smiling a chilly smile, cunning and shrewd.

"We've met." the queen inclined her head. "Are you ready for the Swords' task?"

The mountain air grew thin and thinner until Rosaline felt as if she were going to faint, but somehow she managed a nod.

"Good. No time to waste, there are clouds on the horizon."

Rosaline followed the queen's stare, noticing a dark swirl of clouds over the next mountain peak. She did not like the look of them and wouldn't want to be standing outside when they reached the castle.

As if on cue, the queen drew a silver blindfold from her sleeve, sliding it theatrically through her fingers. "Come closer, child," she said in a voice full as a bow being gently drawn across a violin.

Rosaline took three small steps toward the queen as Adalain rose gracefully from her throne and stepped down to meet her on the dais. "Just a small thing, aren't you?" the queen cooed, tying the blindfold securely around Rosaline's head. "Such pretty hair."

Rosaline kept quiet as the queen tugged the blindfold tight.

"Can you see?" She rested cold hands on Rosaline's shoulders.

"No," Rosaline replied, blind and without a speck of light to guide her. Deep inside she began to tremble, lost in a world of shadows. Again the claws were there, reaching for her back, and she wanted to turn and scream. Instead, she clamped her teeth down on her cheek and stood firm.

"Your second task is one of courage," the queen's voice rang clear across sky, louder than necessary.

"And trust," added the king from somewhere behind her.

"What do I have to do?" Rosaline found her voice, suddenly aware of the short distance between her and the cliff's edge. Her skin prickled with fear, sensing the possible nearness of her death.

Adalain released her shoulders and grabbed her roughly around the wrist, pinching freezing skin. "Come with me," she said, leading Rosaline through the snow.

A few times Rosaline tripped on the hem of her robe, nearly falling if it wasn't for the queen's vice-like grip on her arm. It was a terrible thing to trust someone as cold as Adalain with her life and Rosaline's heart pounded violently in her chest with each step. But as much as death scared her, returning to the streets of Paris scared her more. So, she followed, cautiously at first with little shuffling steps, and then easier when she realized Adalain was not going to push her over the edge and she if she could fly.

"Stop here." The queen yanked her to a stop, releasing her. "You're standing on a ledge," she said in a voice so calming the meaning was nearly lost. "Do you understand?"

The wind was sharp on Rosaline's skin, a thousand tiny needles, numbing her fear. "I understand," she answered, mirroring the queen's composure, even if she did not feel it on the inside.

"One step forward and you will fall."

Rosaline's toes burned, itching to step back.

"The ledge you stand upon is less than a foot wide. It twists and turns, spanning twenty feet, a sheer drop on either side. You must navigate the path blindfolded to reach safety on the opposite ledge."

Was this woman mad? How could she cross a narrow bridge blindfolded? She wished Nicolai would speak, tell her it was a lie, but a sharp breeze cut from below and Rosaline knew it was the truth – and she was alone.

"What do you want me to do?" she managed, terrified of the answer.

"Cross it," the queen replied without compassion.

"But -?" Rosaline's breath wedged in her throat, seized by fear. Behind the blindfold her eyes were wide, searching for something, a shade of grey, a shape, but there was nothing – just black and howling wind. "How is that possible? I can't see. I'll fall."

"Swords are no cowards," answered the queen, as if it explained everything and more. "Paxton is waiting for you on the other side. You must trust him to guide you to safety. Remember, this challenge is about bravery."

Rosaline wanted to ask if it was about stupidity as well, but she thought better of it.

"Ready?"

No. Never. "Now?"

"Now." Rosaline felt the queen move away. "Begin."

"Step forward. Straight ahead," she heard Paxton call. He sounded unsure and shaky. How was she supposed to trust someone who wasn't confident? This was her life on the line! Not just some stupid game.

Angry, she shouted in return. "Straight ahead?"

"Yes," replied Paxton, distant, like he stood on the other side of the world.

Rosaline demanded her brain to pick up her foot and reluctantly it agreed, sliding forward a few desperate inches.

"No! No. A tiny bit to your left."

At the sound of Paxton's shouts, Rosaline froze, foot fixed and heart in her throat. "Left?" she asked, hearing the quaver in her voice.

"Left," Paxton confirmed. "Just a smidge."

"A smidge!" What the hell was a smidge?

"Yes."

Rosaline adjusted her placement, trembling foot hovering in the air. "Here?"

"Right there."

She lowered her foot, squeezing her eyes tight, terrified she would find nothing but empty air. Thankfully, her foot connected with solid ground and a relieved breath escaped her tightly pressed lips. She felt weak. So weak she feared she might faint and willed herself to stay conscious.

"Again," Paxton called.

Again Rosaline stepped, only this time she reached the edge and her toes curled around the lip, hugging oblivion. She sucked in a sharp breath, too terrified to step back and too terrified to move forward. The moment stretched like taffy, long and contorted, twisting as it pulled apart. What did she do now? Somewhere in the muddled distance she could hear Paxton calling, but there was no space left in her brain to understand, all her energy was fixed on breathing and remaining perfectly still should she flinch and fall to her death.

What now, what now, what now?

"You're fine! You can do this." A second voice reached her ears. It took a second for Rosaline's mind to catch up, but when it did she realized it was Nicolai, calling from the ridge behind her.

"I can't!"

"Yes you can!" Nicolai insisted, raising his voice, battling for prevalence. "Just listen to me."

It only took a second for Rosaline to decide to go on for she knew he would never let her fall.

"Step again, slowly. Put your right foot down centered with your left."

She did, and her toes did not slip.

"Again," he said. "Now just a slight turn to the right. Good. Now left. Now there's a sharp turn here, you need to listen to me carefully."

Rosaline did as she was told, following Nicolai's every instruction. His was voice clear and sure and it did not quaver like Paxton's. If he was afraid, he did not show it, and his confidence drove her on, step by terrifying step, until the worst was behind her.

"You're almost there," Nicolai said and Rosaline could hear the smile in his voice. "One more step. Just one more and you're there."

And she was. One final step and both feet were on solid ground.

There was a long pause while she waited for the queen to speak. "You can remove the blindfold," she finally announced, sounding somewhat disappointed.

Rosaline did as she was told and nearly lost her stomach at the dizzying sight. The queen had not exaggerated, and there had been no safety net below the gorge. She stood beside Paxton on an ice shelf connected to the castle by a slender rock bridge, slippery and sheer. Below, razor sharp peaks and granite cliffs poked from beneath snow drifts. Shaking, Rosaline backed away from the edge and pressed against the mountain wall. Wave after wave of nausea hit her as she clutched the blindfold to her chest and the wind tried to tug it from her grasp.

"Well," the queen stood at the opposite end of the divide, watching her with hardened eyes, "that was a bit unorthodox." She tossed a deeply questioning look at Nicolai, eyes narrowed and mouth pulled in a grim line. "But I have no choice but to conclude you've passed this task. The Swords will stand behind you if you ascend."

Rosaline dropped to her knees, slowly, but hard, one hand pressed against the wall for support. After several deep breaths, she lifted her head and asked, "How do I get back?"

A sadistic gleam twinkled in the queen's eyes. "You walk."

CANDLELIGHT
KRAKOW

Ophelia woke in panic to the glow of candlelight. The room was curtained with shadow, heavy like death. Next to her Jude lay asleep, his breathing steady, and she relaxed. For a moment she couldn't place what had woken her, then the phone rang, shrill, and she snatched it from the stand, desperate to silence the receiver before Jude woke.

"Hello?" she whispered, turning her face into the pillow, hoping to muffle the sound.

"Ophelia?" Milo's voice came from the other end, rushed with alarm.

"Why are you calling?" She glanced at the clock burning blue in the dark, squinting until the numbers cleared, reading quarter after two.

"I've been waiting. Are we ready? Did he break his vow?"

Jude stirred in the bed, rolling over in sleep. Ophelia's heart drummed, clunking around her chest in erratic rhythm. This wasn't how she wanted him to discover the truth: with her whispering on the phone in the middle of the night. "I can't talk now. I'm busy."

"This is important," Milo persisted. "Please, Ophelia."

Shame flared across her skin, red as a rash as she cast a look at Jude, serene in sleep. He didn't deserve this. Any of it. What had she done? "I'll call you back," she said urgently. "Give me ten minutes. Don't call here again."

There was a long pause on the other end. "Okay," Milo eventually agreed, though his tone was troubled.

Ophelia couldn't worry about that now. She hung up and slipped from bed, careful not to disturb Jude. Quietly she dressed, pulling boots over pajama bottoms while hopping toward the door. She paused when she reached it, one hand on the knob. The door was heavy and creaky and would wake Jude the second she tried to escape. *The window.* She turned, air tickling her shoulder, to discover a gauzy curtain breathing in the wind. *Thank you*, she whispered and crossed the room on silent footsteps.

With the lightest touch, Ophelia drew the curtain aside and extended her leg over the sill. Outside, the night was crisp, cold prickling her skin as she crawled onto the ledge, grappling for purchase. When she found a foothold she eased her way out, balancing precariously until she got hold of the drainpipe. The hotel was only two stories high, barely worth a sweat, and Ophelia used the wall to brace before jumping, landing on the balls of her feet with a soft *oof*. The impact jarred her ankles, but she'd experienced worse, and she managed to shake off the pain and stand without any serious injury.

The street behind the hotel was poorly lit and smelled of garbage -not somewhere she particularly wanted to linger - so she headed round the side and jumped a fence onto the main street. The road was abandoned, sleepy, and Ophelia discovered Krakow vastly changed at night. It seemed ancient, even by European standards, the trees gritty and old, whispering secrets of a troubled past. Every step along the cobbles spoke of tortured souls ripped by war, and older still, to medieval bloodshed and gothic rule. There was a haunting beauty about the city that shone brightest and night, bathed in moonlight and shimmering stars. Snow crunched underfoot and Ophelia's breath lay before her, leading the way.

Shivering, she tucked her hands over her chest and walked quickly. A block from the hotel she turned toward the nearest pub where she knew a pay phone waited at the corner. Mid-stride, she stopped. There were no cars, the streets long-since deserted, but the wind howled silent warning and the stillness was heavy, as if something in the shadows waited for her with baited breath.

A twig cracked.

Ophelia's head snapped around, staring into a black alley. For a moment she didn't move, hands clenched tight, ready to fight if needed. Her only option was to run. But how far could she get and where would she go?

And then a thought struck her. Why should she run? Who was she running from? Maybe it was about time to find out….

INFINITY
ERTA ALE, AFAR DEPRESSION, ETHIOPIA

If Rosaline believed the Skyward Castle was the most amazing thing she'd ever seen, it was short lived. The scorched lands surrounding the volcano of Erta Ale was something out of a science fiction film: red earth, dust, and permeating heat. Steam rose in shimmering bands, wavering on an endless rose-colored horizon while pockets of molten rock hissed and cracked beneath the earth, visible through fissures in the crust.

Nicolai's borrowed camel treaded lightly over the desolate land, cognoscente of her cargo as black ash dusted her legs and a trail marked their progress in the soot.

"Is that it?" Rosaline croaked, her throat dry and irritated. She desperately needed water and was near tears to see a building looming against the horizon of uninhabitable earth. In the distance, perched on a sandstone outcrop, a massive clay fortress rose from the desert. It thundered from the wasteland, uninviting, with twisted iron gates, broad sentry towers, and crenellations sharp as dragon's teeth.

Nicolai ran a soothing hand along the camel's neck. "The Sand Castle," he said to Rosaline. "Home to the House of Wands."

From a distance, the castle really did look like sand, built by the hands of a very angry child. As the camel clopped closer, they passed along a steep thoroughfare paved with slick black stones, pounded together in tight zigzag formation. On either side the arid earth fell away as the great gate of the Sand Castle reared ahead. It was tall, enormously so, as if built for war, and Rosaline wondered what it was meant to keep out. Or in.

Nicolai pulled the camel to a stop outside the gate. Through the iron bars Rosaline's could see a large stone courtyard, scattered with sand and whistling wind. No sentries came to greet them, giving Rosaline the distinct impression of being very much alone on a vast, uninhabited planet.

As they waited, an eerie feeling settled over her like fog. There was something dark about this place, soaked in fire and magic. She could feel pulsing, radiating from the earth, deep and ebbing like lava flow.

"Where is everyone?" she asked, her gaze fixed on the gate, wondering how they would get inside where there must be water, shade, and relief.

"They're here," said Nicolai, doing his best to keep the camel calm. The generally docile beast was growing agitated, throwing her head and stamping the ground while smacking her lips.

"Do you feel that?" Rosaline whispered, tightening her hold on Nicolai. The magic was in the air and all around, tightening around her chest like vines. Wide-eyed, she scanned the battlements, scouring for the source.

"Yes," answered Nicolai, though if he truly felt as she did, he did not elaborate.

Then, as if solidifying from smoke, a black cat appeared, slinking through the gate to stand at the camel's feet. The camel jerked away and barked, trying to throw her riders. Rosaline clenched her eyes and held on. The bleating cry was awful, gut wrenching, and it rolled across the endless desert as the camel's front hooves clapped the stones, ringing like a thunderbolt. Nicolai slid from the saddle; murmuring comforting words to the camel, attempting to bring the animal back from the brink of insanity.

As Nicolai whispered, the camel calmed, shifting from foot-to-foot, eyes bulging with alarm. Gracefully, Nicolai turned from the camel and knelt before the cat, bowing his head and extending a hand toward the feline's bared teeth, as if it were a king. It hissed, claws drawn and ears back, ready to strike.

"Watch out," Rosaline warned. "It's going to bite you."

"I know," replied Nicolai, stretching his hand an extra inch.

Rosaline frowned but kept quiet, watching the exchange with interest.

The cat struck with a hiss, gouging four long scratches along the back of Nicolai's hand. He winced but did not move, blood seeping from the wound and onto the stone at his feet.

"Nicolai," Rosaline tried to climb down but he motioned for her to stay put.

"Don't move."

She captured a breath, one hand pressed to the camel's back, the other at her throat.

The cat bowed his head and began licking the wound, smearing blood across Nicolai's hand.

Rosaline grimaced, crinkling her nose. "Is that cat –," she struggled to say the words, "drinking your blood?"

Nicolai did not reply.

Gross, she thought, unable to keep the disgust from her face.

The cat raised its head, yellow eyes glowing molten gold. There was something astonishing about those eyes - too intelligent and too bright to belong to an animal. Seemingly satisfied, the cat turned and strutted proudly toward the gate. Only when it disappeared did Nicolai rise. As he did the gate boomed and clicked, opening in a drone of gears.

He turned back and mounted the camel, adjusting the scarf wrapped around his head. "The cat is the Sand Castle's guardian," he explained, clicking his tongue and persuading the camel forward.

"He's creepy," Rosaline replied and Nicolai laughed.

Beyond the gate, the courtyard windows were dark, doors closed, and ramparts abandoned with no flicker of candlelight or shadows to suggest the building was occupied, by cats or otherwise.

"Everyone is gone," said Rosaline anxiously. What if she couldn't complete the last tasks before the old Queen of Cups died? Would the Tarot fall? Would she still have a chance to earn her place?

"Just wait," said Nicolai, stopping the camel in the middle of the courtyard.

Black crows settled on the battlements, their wings flapping, fallen feathers gliding slowly to the ground. Rosaline watched them with despair, thinking they looked a lot like carrion crows desperate for her flesh. At least the cat had sense enough to disappear.

"Easy there." Nicolai patted the camel's head. "Everything's fine."

The camel didn't look convinced and neither was Rosaline.

Somewhere deep in the fortress a door opened and closed, banging heavy on iron hinges. Rosaline flinched, gripping Nicolai's arm. He squeezed her hand reassuringly and held his ground. Finally, two figures appeared from the inner courtyard, walking slowly toward them. They both wore blazing red robs and circlets of gold flame, holding staffs of glowing bronze in the image of leafy tree branches. The pair was young, one female and one male, early forties, both with fiery hair and sun kissed skin.

"Welcome," said the woman, opening her arms in greeting, "to the Sand Castle, House of Wands."

Nicolai dismounted and helped Rosaline down, handing the camel's reigns to a young boy who appeared at his side. "Gretchen," Nicolai greeted the woman warmly. "Rosaline, meet the Queen of Wands."

There was something powerful about this queen, even more so than Adalain who scared Rosaline. This queen was strong but in a different way, less jaded and more self-assured. She seemed to breathe magic. It swirled around her, slinking about her arms and disappearing in her hair like smoke.

The queen embraced Nicolai then turned to the king. He was handsome, with a scruffy, copper beard and friendly amber eyes. "Nicolai," he inclined his head, "it's good to see you again. I see you've brought us a guest."

Nicolai nodded, motioning Rosaline forward. "Rosaline, meet Gustav. King of Wands, ruler of the Fire Lands."

Rosaline stepped closer and bobbed her head. "Good to meet you." As she raised her eyes to the king, Gustav smiled and Rosaline knew she had never seen anyone so regal in her life. His hair hung in auburn waves down to his shoulders, broad and relaxed, embodying a king in every fiber of his being. Even the way he held his staff seemed significant: level, so he appeared tall and sturdy as an ancient oak from the Białowieża Forest.

In the same fashion, Gretchen appeared more queen-like than Matilda or Adalain put together, with genuine warmth behind her clever brown eyes that seemed to snap and crack with fire-light. As the introductions finished, the black cat reappeared at her feet, liquid gold eyes watching Rosaline as if she were a snack. "Ignore him," the queen's eyes flicked to the feline, "he's not kind to strangers."

Rosaline gave a nod, taking a mental note.

"Artemis is friendlier," the king added and Rosaline spotted the green salamander perched on his shoulder, so small she would have missed it had the king not pointed the creature out.

Infinity, thought Rosaline. She recognized the sign of the salamander. When the reptile bit his tail it was never-ending like the circle of life. The perfect partner to fire.

"Please, come inside." The queen touched Nicolai's elbow, steering him toward the castle doors. "We have food and drink and beds for you to rest."

Gustav extended an arm to Rosaline and she accepted. As they walked toward the inner courtyard, Rosaline spotted the cat slinking through the queen's legs, watching her with a sneer.

Good luck, it seemed to say, *you'll need it.*

HIDE AND SEEK
KRAKOW

It was little more than a flash of silver eyes in the dark, but Ophelia knew he was there. Without looking back, without thinking, she followed the stranger into shadow, down a narrow alley and into a hidden courtyard. A frozen pond framed by skeletal trees and a low stone bench stood center, surrounded by decrepit apartment buildings, sorrowful in the stillness of ice. Above, the sky was clear and inky, painted with stars and a moon floating heavy in an ocean of oil.

For a moment, Ophelia thought she was alone – having lost her prey in the chase. By the pond, she tried to catch her breath and noticed the windows surrounding the courtyard were all broken, long-since abandoned. Dreadful realization washed over her in horror-soaked waves - she had walked into a trap and she had let herself be cornered.

Have you learned nothing? She scolded, turning on her heels. But then, like a sigh, he appeared, solidifying between her and the exit. She wondered if this was how Jude had felt the day she'd confronted him in Main Square? Probably not. She was small and this man was big, that much was clear before he'd even stepped into the moonlight. When he did, Ophelia bit back a gasp. "Who are you?" she demanded, triumphant in keeping her voice flat.

The man did not speak. Slowly, he walked on. By his shadow she could tell he was tall, over six feet, with dark hair and features. Late twenties, she guessed, with a gait that made her heart race. "Don't come any closer," she warned, thrusting a hand out to freeze him in place.

Surprisingly, he obeyed, stopping a few feet from her outstretched hand. Now she could see his eyes, sharp as steel and brutal.

"I'm warning you," she said, louder now, "there's no point in attacking me. You'll never catch me."

A slow smile spread across the man's face, though it couldn't be mistaken for kind. "You think?"

"What do you want? Why are you following me?" Stall, she needed to stall as she took inventory: a drainpipe bolted to a nearby brick wall, window ledges, and a tree. Not much to work with.

"I thought it was about time someone followed you for a change," he said in a slithering voice.

A chill hummed along Ophelia's spine. Who was this man? How did he know her? "Who are you?" she asked again, firmer now.

Once again he surprised her by answering, "My name is Sol."

Sol. That was familiar, but from where? "I don't know anyone named Sol."

The man took a step forward and Ophelia took an equal step back. His smile widened. "Perhaps you know me by another name?"

"What other name?" *What other name?* She couldn't remember, but it was there on the tip of her tongue....

"The Knight of Coins, perhaps?" He raised a hand, revealing a glowing green mark on his left palm: a knight, tall in his armor, holding a large coin.

Whatever she had been expecting – this wasn't it.

Sol. Jude's oath-brother. How stupid could she be? She knew him now; the eldest of the knighthood – and the fiercest, with no mercy in his black heart.

He caught the flash of recognition in her eyes. "Ah. So you *do* know me?"

"Yes," Ophelia croaked, knowing it was useless to plead ignorance, "I know you."

"At least we're not playing games. That will make this easier."

"Make what easier?" She backed up an inch, steadily putting distance between them. "What do you want from me?"

"Better question," said Sol. "What do you want from Jude?"

Jude. Her throat tightened. *Oh, no, he's going to tell Jude.* "Nothing."

"Nothing?" Sol questioned, mocking. "Tell me, does he know of your uncle? Of his grand plans for the Tarot?" Sol hissed the last word, exposing teeth in such a way it made Ophelia's stomach roil.

"What do you know?" she asked, losing the calm in her voice.

"Enough to know you're playing Jude like a sad violin." The knight was taunting, toying.

"I'm not -" she began but stopped short, knowing whether she wanted to admit it, Sol was right. She had manipulated Jude. It didn't matter that she cared for him. Every second she didn't tell him the truth she was playing him. "It's not exactly like that. It's - complicated."

"More lies? More twists, more turns? I must say, this is some vicious game you're playing, Ophelia."

The sound of her name on Sol's lips was revolting. She swallowed back the bile. "It's not a game."

"A game of hide and seek. A game of wits. A game of deceit. No matter the rules, it's clear who will lose. You want to destroy the Tarot and you've decided Jude is the weakest link. But why? Why would you want to destroy the one thing holding this miserable world together? You don't strike me as a tyrant. So I'd like to know."

"I'm not a tyrant," Ophelia replied, jaw clenched and hands balled at her sides. "I thought you knew everything?"

"I know enough."

"Then why haven't you told the Magician yet?"

Sol arched a brow. "What makes you think I haven't?"

Ophelia lifted her chin, defiant. She may be many things: coward, liar, pawn, but she was not weak and she would not go down without a fight. "If he knew, he would be here with you. He would never let Jude break his vow."

The dark knight shrugged. "Maybe he doesn't believe Jude can be broken? Or maybe he believes fate should take its turn...." Sol cocked his head in a maniacal way. "But you should know all this - you've been following us for years, learning our secrets, studying our behavior. The perfect little spy, collecting data for your uncle, letting him calculate and theorize and formulate a plan to take control for himself."

"He doesn't want control," Ophelia argued, angry that anyone would dare attack Milo and his genius. "He wants to help."

"And I thought you had more sense than that. Guess I was wrong."

Ophelia narrowed her eyes. "What is that supposed to mean?"

"It means you're sadly mistaken if you think your uncle wants anything other than power."

A flicker of doubt wormed its way inside Ophelia's mind. Could he be right? Could Milo really be out for power? He was brilliant. A man of unimaginable potential. He'd discovered theorems and written theories that left even the most talented physicists scratching their heads in awe. There was no way he would sink to the lowest urge of human nature to control. Afraid the knight might be right, but unable to admit it, she stood rigid in disquiet. "You don't have to believe me, but I tried to make it right. I care about Jude."

"Don't you get it?" Sol's expression darkened. "That is the problem."

Ophelia couldn't – wouldn't - accept she had doomed the one person who cared about her without wanting something in exchange. "Get out of here." She lifted her eyes, filled with loathing and pain-filled tears. "Stay away from me."

Sol took a step closer. "We both know I can't do that."

This, she realized, would not end well. She would not be going home to Jude. She may not be going home at all. "I'll scream. Stay where you are."

"Scream all you want." Sol took another step, closing the gap.

There was no way out with the knight standing directly in her path. She scanned her escape routes: the drain pipe, trees, windows. The knight would catch her before she reached the drain pipe and the trees were far at her back. Milo had never trained her to fight, but she was fast on her feet. Surely, if she couldn't run, she could get in one lucky punch, enough to distract him? Maybe go for the eyes.

"No one will hear you," Sol continued in a slippery voice.

"I told you the truth. What else do you want?" Ophelia demanded. She backed up a step, treading toward the pond.

He laughed, cold and calculating, as if he'd waited all his life for this moment. Finally, his true purpose was unfolding: protecting the Tarot at all costs, as a knight should. "I want nothing from you. I'm going to make sure you can't hurt Jude. I'm going to make sure you leave the Tarot alone."

She caught his meaning clear enough. There was no room for leniency. The Knight of Coins had always been the toughest knight, the most dedicated to the job. Why would she expect anything less? He would do what he must to protect the Order of the Tarot – including murder.

Somehow, someway, she would find a way to explain things to Jude, but right now she had to get out alive. Ophelia whirled, hard packed snow slick underfoot as tree shadows stretched across the ground like skeletal, reaching, fingers. She slipped and bumped into the ledge of the pond just as Sol's hands clamped around her throat. A scream ripped from her lungs like a shard of glass, ripping across the winter sky. Sol wrestled her to the ground, using his weight to twist her off balance. Tangled, they fell and Ophelia used the momentum to pull him backward, crashing through the pond's thin layer of ice and shattering the silence.

Icy water hit her like a slap, biting and tearing exposed flesh. The pond was only a few feet deep but the cold drilled bone deep, enough to knock her stupid. She thrashed, trapped in wet clothes and numb limbs, struggling to gain purchase, but there was only water.

I can't believe this, she thought hysterically, lungs burning for lack of air, *I am going to drown in a foot of water*. And for a few seconds, it appeared she would. And then, at last, her foot found bottom and she pushed off, breaking the surface.

Cold cut flesh, and on some level she could hear herself screaming, but she didn't know if it was aloud or in her head. In the same instant an arm tightened around her waist, jerking her from the water. "No!" she shrieked, kicking and twisting, trying to get free. "No!" she was splayed on the ground face down, cold stone burning her cheek. Water pooled around her, seeping between stones as she coughed, and coughed again, until water leaked from her nose and mouth.

Something pressed against her back as the last of her energy waned, blackening into spotty emptiness. With one last attempt she twisted around, trying to squirm free. "Leave me alone!" She clawed empty air.

"Ophelia!"

It took a second for the voice to register, and it wasn't Sol's. Astonished, she blinked to find Jude kneeling beside her, bundled in his scarf, hair mussed from sleep and expression drawn. He pulled off his coat, wrapping it tightly around her. "Are you okay? What happened?"

"Jude?" She was forced to whisper, her throat raw from screaming. Wet hair clung to her face in freezing dreadlocks, the cold chattering her teeth. "Where did you come from?"

Deep concern imprinted across his brow. "I woke up and you were gone. I came looking for you and heard you scream."

Thank god.

She reached for him and he helped her sit, trying to warm her hands between his. "What happened?" he asked again, his tone questioning and noticeably distressed. "Are you hurt?"

"I'm fine," she gasped, eyes darting, searching for Sol, but the other knight had vanished. Behind Jude the pond was a mess of broken ice and sloshing water. "Did you see...?" she trailed off, unsure what to say. She needed time to think. But more importantly she needed to get warm.

"See what?" asked Jude, worry hampering his voice. "What happened?"

Ophelia shook her head. "Nothing."

With a grim look, Jude helped her stand. "I guess we'll add this to your list of truths to be told?"

Ophelia gave a watery smile. "I think you better."

"Okay, then," he said, rubbing his hands up and down her arms. "We'll go to my place, its closer."

She nodded as he hooked his arm about her waist. Before leaving the courtyard Ophelia looked back, scanning the dark for the missing knight, but the only remaining was his warning.

SEEDS OF MAGIC
ERTA ALE, AFAR DEPRESSION, ETHIOPIA

The Queen of Wands stood in the middle of a lush garden where tropical vines scaled stone walls and flowers turned their faces toward a plum colored sky: a strange sight in the middle of a land that looked as if it couldn't support a cactus.

"You asked for me?" Rosaline stepped from a narrow doorway into the small courtyard garden.

The Queen turned, light catching fire in her hair, and smiled warmly. "I did."

Rosaline took a step closer, the smell of freshly tilled dirt and lilac heavy on the air.

"Do you like my little oasis?" Gretchen opened her arms to the garden, uprooting Artemis the salamander who had been sleeping peacefully on her shoulder.

"It's pretty."

The queen trilled a laugh, giving Artemis' head a tender tap. "Isn't it?" She plucked an orange bloom from a nearby vine, holding it in the palm of her hand, careful as a bird's brittle nest. "It is my private escape. Without it I think I would go mad – all this rock and fire. Earth needs life, don't you agree?"

Rosaline nodded, sensing it had something to do with the task.

"Here." Gretchen held out the flower. "Take it."

The flower was soft and delicate and Rosaline feared she'd crush it in her rough, gypsy hands.

Gretchen's smile widened, turning up like a perfectly tied bow. "It's okay. Take it. It's just a flower. You can't hurt it."

This time Rosaline swallowed and scooped it from the queen's hand, cradling the bloom in her palm.

"Are you ready for your task?" the queen asked in a gentle voice.

Rosaline lifted her head to nod.

"Then close your hand."

Rosaline hesitated. Why would the queen want her to destroy the flower? She wanted to marvel at the color until it withered away and dissolved. The queen waited patiently for Rosaline to abide and eventually she did, closing her fingers around the blossom.

"Now open your palm," Gretchen instructed with her eyes fastened on Rosaline's clenched fist.

Again Rosaline obeyed, releasing one finger at a time until her hand lay flat. Where the flower had been now a single pea-sized seed rested. "Where did it go?" she asked, batting astonished eyes.

"It's right there," answered the queen, inclining her head, "in your hand."

"But," Rosaline stammered, "the flower is gone. There's just a seed."

"Changed," the queen conceded, "but not gone."

Rosaline stared at the seed, frowning. It was fat and brown and useless. "But what am I supposed to do with a seed?"

Gretchen spread her hands wide and lifted them to the sky. "You are to make it grow. Give it life."

Rosaline's mouth twisted into a doubtful grimace. All she had to do was plant a seed and wait for it to grow? That seemed far too simple. She must be missing something. There was almost always a catch when something seemed too easy. "That's all?"

"That's all," the queen replied happily.

"Oh." Rosaline peered at the seed, willing it to sprout, but the fat brown thing just sat, lazy. "That *seems* simple."

"It can be," the queen agreed. "Have you ever grown a flower?"

Rosaline smashed her mouth in a line, thinking. Back in Romania the gypsies had kept gardens, but she'd always been too young to help. Once or twice her mother had let her water the plants with a heavy watering can, but often she spilled on her dress and muddied her shoes and she didn't consider that growing anything but a mess. Eventually, Rosaline met the queen's gaze with a sad shake of her head. There were far too many things in life she had never done – never been given the chance. "No."

Gretchen's smile did not falter. "It's not so difficult."

"I can do it," Rosaline said and closed her fingers around the seed, determined to keep it safe.

"But -" said Gretchen and Rosaline's stomach dropped.

The inevitable *'but'.*

The queen picked up her skirt, heading for the exit in a graceful swish of fabric. When she reached the door she turned back and motioned for Rosaline to join her. After tossing the garden one last longing look, Rosaline crossed the small courtyard and joined the queen in the dark musty entrance hall. The queen removed a brass key in the shape of a wand from around her neck and closed the garden door with a heavy *boom.* "Do you see this?" the queen asked, holding the key.

Rosaline nodded.

Gretchen locked the garden door with a *click*. "For this task, you will not have access to the garden. You must grow the seed without it."

No garden? Rosaline frowned, puzzled. "But how do I get what I need to grow the seed?" she asked, thinking of soil and water and tools.

"You don't." The queen's smile waned, softening her features into a look of pity. "You must grow the seed without the help of the garden. You must grow it from the rock of the Fire Lands, and it must sprout in three days time."

"Three days?" Rosaline nearly choked on surprise, having no idea how long it took for something to grow, but figuring it was longer than three measly days. "What about water?"

Gretchen gave a sad shake of her head, rustling her auburn curls. "No water. This is the task. You must grow the seed from the gifts of the Fire Lands."

Rosaline couldn't think of one gift the Fire Lands offered aside from punishing heat - which would help the seed grow. "But - nothing grows here. It's barren with no living thing for miles. What does it offer?"

"It has much to offer," Gretchen replied, unwavering, "you just have to find it."

Rosaline's spirits sank. She had seen nothing but endless red earth and a river of fire for miles. A plant could not grow without water. She didn't even know if it could grow without dirt.

The queen bid her farewell with a gentle hand on her shoulder, leaving her alone with the miserable, fat seed. At first Rosaline simply stared at it, rolling it around her hand, caressing it into growth. Maybe all it needed was attention? When that yielding no gain she went in search of Nicolai and found him on an upper terrace overlooking the Fire Lands.

"So," he said as she came to stand beside him, "did Gretchen give you your task?"

Rosaline held the seed between her finger and thumb, squinting at it. "I'm supposed to make it grow without earth or water."

"I know," answered Nicolai with a sympathetic smile. "It wasn't easy for me, either. If I could help you, I would."

"You've done this task?" Rosaline was surprised, although maybe she shouldn't have been. The Magician had told her all new recruits must pass the tasks. Only, she'd thought they'd be different for everyone.

He nodded. "I've done all the tasks you will do, except one."

She peered at him, interested. "Which one?"

Nicolai fell silent. He took a step closer, gently touching her arm. "All except the last task. The one for the King and Queen of Cups. For our House."

"Why not that one?"

Nicolai brushed her cheek with the back of his thumb then quickly dropped his hand, looking at her with a longing she didn't understand. "Our roles in the Order are different, Rose." It was the first time he'd used the endearment and it made Rosaline's heart soar and hurt at the same time. His words were filled with so much sadness. It confused her. What was there to be sad about? If she passed the tasks they would be together forever. She would be Queen and he would be her handsome knight. Even in her dreams it had not been so perfect.

"I know that." She pocketed the seed before a gust could tear it from her grip. "But that won't matter. I know the Knight of Cups is free to love and so is the queen."

There was something important unsaid lingering behind Nicolai's blue-fire eyes, but he forced a smile, weak and troubled. "Yes," he agreed. "But love isn't always enough."

LULLABY
ERTA ALE, AFAR DEPRESSION, ETHIOPIA

On the first day of the third task, Rosaline wandered the halls of the Sand Castle with the seed clenched in her hand. Making a seed grow didn't seem like it should be all that hard, but she was stumped, and couldn't stand the thought of Nicolai, Gretchen, or Gustav seeing her fail, so she spent much of the day in the castle catacombs where it was cool and dank and the walls were stone and the floor dirt.

Long ago, when Rosaline was still a child, her mother used to sing her lullabies whenever she was afraid. Rosaline cherished those memories, clinging to them like scraps of her heart. There was one scrap she remembered best. She'd been small, no older than six or seven, huddled in her mother's arms as a storm raged outside their creaking caravan. Tree branches scraped the windows with long gnarled claws and lightening lit the back room as distant thunder rolled across the angry sky.

As Rosaline whimpered, pressing her face into her mother's breast, she'd asked, "Are the giants mad?"

Her mother had laughed. "What giants?"

"In the sky."

"Oh, those giants. No, Sweet Pea, they're not mad."

"But mama, why are they shouting?"

Her mother had smoothed her hair and kissed her head, rocking Rosaline back and forth in her arms. "They're not shouting," she replied. "They're only talking."

"But it's so loud."

"That's because they're so big."

"I wish I was big too," Rosaline had said, clutching a fistful of her mother's shirt.

"And why is that, mon petit?"

"Because then I wouldn't be afraid."

"Ah!" her mother clucked. "Well then, let us make you big, eh?"

Rosaline blinked with big, round eyes. "How?"

"Didn't you know singing will make you grow?" And so her mother sang, a lullaby, sweet and tender.

"Au clair de la lune

Mon ami Pierrot

Prête-moi ta plume

Pour écrire un mot

Ma chandelle est morte

Je n'ai plus de feu

Ouvre-moi ta porte

Pour l'amour de Dieu."

It was silly, her mother had just been trying to make her brave, but as Rosaline wandered the tunnels she remembered and she wondered if maybe, just maybe, her mother's words held a ring of truth. So, she began to sing; timid, quiet, barely a whisper, but she held the seed close to her lips so it could hear. "*Au Clair de la lune…*," she sang the simple melody, "Mon ami Pierrot…"

All day she sang to the seed, louder and louder until her voice filled the catacombs, bounding along corridors and chasing ghosts. Over and over she sang the lullaby until the lyrics had lost all meaning. Hours later, when the day was gone and the seed remained unchanged, Nicolai found her huddled on the floor in the deepest, mustiest corner of the tombs.

"I brought food," he said, handing her a bowl of soup. She looked up, staring into his kind face and sad eyes.

"Thank you." She took the bowl gratefully and slurped it straight, like a child.

Nicolai smiled. "How did it go?"

Rosaline held up the seed, fat and whole and lazy in her hand.

"Ah." Nicolai slid down the wall to sit beside her on the cold stone floor, crossing his legs. "Not well, then?"

Rosaline gave her head a dour shake. "It's stupid. I think it's broken."

A smile twisted Nicolai's tired mouth. "I don't think it's broken. You can try again tomorrow."

Rosaline continued to stare at the seed, wanting to throw it at the wall, though she kept it tight in her protection.

"I think you should come upstairs." Nicolai took the half-empty bowl from her hand. "Come on, I'll help keep your mind off the task."

Rosaline agreed, letting Nicolai pick her off the floor and lead her back to civilization above.

The next day she woke with a brilliant idea and gathered a day's worth of supplies. She spent all morning trekking the desolate Fire Lands, searching for the perfect place to put her plan in motion. It took hours, but finally she found it: a patch of earth, soft with ash and crumbling rock. Eagerly, she used her hands to dig a hole and after burying the seed deep, she sat back on her heels to wait.

After two hours of blistering heat and stifling boredom, Rosaline wiped the sweat from her brow with a sooty hand and dug up the seed. Not a sliver, not a crack. Angry, she threw it, letting it bounce along the hard-packed earth. On sooty hands and knees she crawled after it and picked up a large flat rock, smashing the seed over and over again until it should have been pulp, but the stupid thing remained whole, not even as a scuff.

Defeated and exhausted, Rosaline reclaimed the unbreakable seed and dragged her filthy self back to the castle, head low and covered in black earth. Nicolai waited for her at the gate, arms crossed over his chest, watching as she lumbered up the ramp. "How did it go?" he asked.

"How does it look like it went?" she grumbled, trudging past him.

Later, he brought her a plate of stew and sat quietly while she brooded, helping her wash the ash from her hair. She was grateful he didn't offer to boost her spirits, it wasn't what she needed. What she needed was him, and that's exactly what he gave.

On the final day Rosaline woke to gnawing desperation. There was nothing left to try; there were only so many ways to make something grow – and almost all of them involved water. In a moment of hysteria she shoved the seed in her mouth, thinking the moisture might do it good. It wasn't technically cheating - saliva wasn't water, was it? But all that did was make her thirsty. And hungry.

In the dungeonesque kitchen of the Sand Castle, she smothered the seed in honey from her tea. But all that did was make it sticky. Once sticky, she had the bright idea of creating an outer cast, so she rolled it in flour. Then the seed was just covered in useless goo. Annoyed, and not wanting to look daft when she returned the seed, she decided to wash it. But how without water?

As she sulked, the queen's sadistic black cat slinked into the room, eying her with hollow, yellow eyes. "Get out of here," Rosaline hissed, snapping her fingers at the cat. It ignored her, strutting across the kitchen toward a bowl of milk. Rosaline watched him wearily then perked up when the cat's pink tongue lapped mouthfuls of frothy white milk from the bowl.

Milk! That was it! People drank Milk to grow, why not seeds?

Rosaline scrambled from her chair and gently nudged the cat with her shoe. It hissed and clawed the leather. "Pst, go away," she said with a snarl. Dutifully, the cat paid no mind. After another attempt and a rather unkind yank of the tail, the cat finally took the hint and lurked off, tossing Rosaline a murderous scowl as he went.

Dropping to her knees, Rosaline plunked the seed into the bowl and sat back to wait. Sometime later, long after her feet had gone numb, Nicolai sauntered into the room searching for food – or possibly her. "What are you doing?" he asked, eying her with interest as she looked up at him from where she crouched on the dirty kitchen floor.

"Milk," she explained, pointing to the bowl.

"I see," replied Nicolai in a tone that suggested milk wasn't the answer.

Reading the hint in Nicolai's raised brows, she snatched the seed from the bowl and stormed from the kitchen with him looking after her in bemused silence. She ended up in the watchtower, the Sand Castle's highest point, well above the thick clay walls and stone battlements. It was a quiet place to think, looking over an endless ocean of slowly moving sand. Defeated, Rosaline spent the remainder of the day up there, rolling the seed in her hand and watching the Fire Lands shift from butterscotch to red clay to muddy earth as the sun moved across a cloudless blue sky. It was strange; despite the aridness of the land she realized this place was not dead as she had originally thought. It burned with life of another kind – living in color.

With the day coming to an end, the sun sank lower in the sky, heavy like a drop of blood on the horizon. Rosaline felt her dreams sinking with it. Tears came and she let them fall on the seed, covered in her sorrow, but still it would not open. It would not grow for her.

When the sky darkened to violet-black, Rosaline returned to the queen's garden where she found Gretchen standing under a tall palm, bathed in desert moonlight. She did not turn when Rosaline entered, but spoke softly, almost as if speaking to herself. "You've failed," she said, sounding disappointed and filled with regret.

Rosaline's heart withered and died in her chest. "I couldn't get it to grow," she admitted, ashamed. "I tried everything."

"Hold out your hand," said the queen, her back still turned.

Rosaline did as she was told, letting the seed rest in her open palm. As if on command, it began to sprout. A crack appeared, tiny, just a hairline fracture, widening until the seed split and a tiny green bud emerged. As she watched in awe the bud grew, larger and larger until it was a bulb that broke open, the orange bloom flowering in her hand as if it had never left.

"How did you do it?" Rosaline marveled, staring at the flower with wondering eyes.

"Magic," said Gretchen, turning to face her. Today her hair did not gleam as it had before. It was pinned back; her crown of golden flames dim upon her head, as if the entire House of Wands mourned for Rosaline's loss. "That is what you failed to see, my girl. I know you could feel it. The magic of this place is ancient- it is the well on which the world draws its energy. It comes from the earth itself, from the fires deep within, and all you had to do was call upon it to assist you."

The thought of using magic had not occurred to Rosaline. She had never known what it was – not really – it had always felt like a humming, distant radio static, and she would never have thought to try. "Magic," she breathed. "I didn't know how."

The queen's mouth drew into a tight-lipped smile, her eyes flat and ordinary without the brilliant sun to make them spark. "It's not a skill, Rosaline. If you feel the power calling, it will answer, and as Wands it is our job to create life where no life should exist at all. We must draw upon all sources to make that so, whether it be water, earth, air, fire or even...magic."

Rosaline nodded and held out the flower to return the beautiful gift. Tears burned behind her eyes, but she would not let them fall. "I am sorry I failed you."

Queen Gretchen shook her head, reaching to close Rosaline's hand around the bloom. "You keep it," she said. "It's a lucky flower and with one task left you'll need all the luck you can get."

AFTER THE MUSIC
KRAKOW

A high-pitched whistle rattled the windowpanes. Jude strode across the small kitchen and removed the boiling kettle from the stove while digging around the cupboard until he found an old wood box of teas. He selected a packet from the first row and tore it open, placing the tea bag in an empty mug. Carefully, he filled the mug with boiling water and the kitchen filled with the scent of fruit, spice and herbs, reminding him of a tropical garden somewhere far away – somewhere he wanted to go with Ophelia someday.

As he lifted the mug from the counter, he flicked off the burner and concentrated on not spilling as he carried the tea into the next room where Ophelia sat up expectantly in bed. She was swaddled in every blanket Jude could find, along with his red scarf and a pair of lamb's wool mitts. Hours after falling into the pond she still looked chilled, pale with a blue tinge to her sullen lips.

"Here," he said, handing her the mug. "It's some kind of herb, I think."

Ophelia smiled, taking the cup between mitted hands and blowing away billows of steam. "Thank you."

Jude pulled up a chair and grabbed his guitar from the stand, plucking randomly at the strings.

"Will you play me something?"

Jude looked at her, considering. He had never played for anyone. Certainly he didn't consider himself a musician, but the way Ophelia was looking at him - almost pleading - made his heart thump loudly in his chest. Honestly, he doubted he could deny her anything in that moment. "What would you like to hear?"

"Anything," she whispered, closing her eyes and leaning back against the headboard.

"I don't sing," he said, tuning the pegs with deft fingers.

"You hum. I heard you."

Jude winced. He hadn't realized she'd heard him hum that first night. "Let's save the humming for another day."

She smiled, settling back with a peaceful look upon her face. "Okay, then. Play me something sweet."

"Sweet?" He put one foot on the edge of the bed, leveraging the guitar in his lap.

"You know. Something...easy. Something nice."

Jude wasn't sure what she meant, but he was willing to try. "Okay," he agreed and began to play. It was an old song, one he'd heard the Magician play long ago – a Celtic lullaby that was probably once accompanied by heartbreaking lyrics, now forgotten. The song always resonated with Jude; lingering long after it was over like flowery perfume left by a women in an empty room. If that wasn't sweet, he didn't know what was. The song was sad too, a little tragic, but romantic - or at least, that's how Jude heard it. He wasn't sure if Ophelia agreed, but after the first verse, he thought she did.

Silently, she watched his hands and the way they moved over the strings. He was self-conscious, but tried to hide it, concentrating on the music. Eventually, she closed her eyes as if to cherish every note, a faint smile appearing at the corner of her mouth.

When the song finished, Jude sat back, studying her. She was so beautiful, so imperfectly perfect with unevenly chopped bangs and slightly far-set eyes, yet the way the early morning sun kissed her skin she glowed, candescent.

"Jude," she said.

"Hm?" He went back to his guitar, plucking absent notes.

"I'm ready to talk." She opened her eyes and they almost looked soft, as if the lies and secrets had drained the light from her, making his heart ache. He didn't want her spark to die. Not like his. "About what?"

"About a few things, really."

He waited patiently for her to go on.

Ophelia took a breath, as if to gather courage. "A girl came to your door the morning you went for coffee."

Jude raised a brow, unsure what to say, or better yet how to explain. He knew it had probably been Karazyna – the Polish girl he met up with from time to time - but he didn't think Ophelia would appreciate knowing his past exploits. He certainly didn't want to know hers. How did he respond without hurting her feelings? "Oh," was the best he managed.

"Oh?" Ophelia echoed. "Is that all?" She sat up, eyes widening ever-so-slightly.

He was going to clarify, '*what girl?' b*ut then reconsidered, thinking it might sound tactless. "Thank you for telling me?" he tried instead.

Ophelia jerked her head as if stung, then curled her lip in a way that would have been comical had Jude not been worried she'd slap him if he laughed. "Is she – was she?" she seemed to be at a loss for words, fumbling through her vocabulary.

"No," Jude hurried to reply. "No." He shook his head, firmer this time. "At least not like that. Not how you think. She was just *someone*. We were just...lonely." The look on Ophelia's face was gut-wrenching and he knew he'd crushed her, even if he'd been trying desperately to avoid it. How could he fix something that was the truth? He hadn't known Ophelia then. If he had, or if he'd even known she would come into his life, he wouldn't have looked at Karazyna twice. "Karazyna was someone I spent time with because there was no one else," he tried better to explain, hoping the honesty would come through in his voice. "She just needed company."

"And you?" Ophelia's voice was tense, full of unsaid accusations. "What did you need from her?"

Jude fell silent, sure he would make things worse if he spoke too soon. After a moment, he cleared his throat and replied, "I guess I needed the same. My life has never been easy, Ophelia. It's complicated. More complicated than you could ever possibly understand."

"You could try to explain." Her voice was raw, almost yearning, as if she needed to know.

"I don't know," he said, looking down at his guitar. Could he trust her? He knew she was a liar, but how could he expect her to be honest if he wasn't? "You really want that? You really want to know about my life? It's not pretty. There is no picket fence or loving parents or charming little sisters."

Ophelia nodded, holding his gaze firmly. "I want to know."

Jude was torn. His entire life he'd wanted to share his existence with someone, and there was no one else he could imagine telling his secretes to - but what did it mean if he did? He knew the answer to that – he would have to renounce his vow. He would have to choose. Even now his mark was growing dimmer by the day, and he was sure it was only a matter of time before it faded to black completely. He clenched his fist, hiding the evidence. "Are you sure?" he asked again. "If I tell you – if I let you in...."

"I want to know," Ophelia replied, steadfast. "Jude, I want to know you. I want to know you like no one else does."

You already do, he wanted to say, but instead took a breath and said, "Ophelia, if I tell you my story, you have to promise to listen." He knew she'd hear the deeper meaning: *you have to listen and not judge. You have to listen and try to understand.*

She nodded and leaned forward in a barely perceptible manner, as if being half an inch closer would make it easier to do as he asked.

Jude gripped his guitar nervously, dropping his eyes to the bed where Ophelia's hand rested. He concentrated on her veins, blue and faint, tiny rivers feeding her with life. He thought of his life in the Tarot, struggling under the weight of the world, and then he thought of his time with Ophelia; the two of them, alone in this room sipping tea. He thought of them outside in the snow, holding hands, walking the streets of Krakow, and he knew he had no choice. Maybe he never really did.

Forgive me, Magician, but I choose to be happy.

Jude exhaled a heavy breath, releasing the unwanted weight, and began his story, "I grew up in an ancient society known as the Order of the Tarot." He swallowed, finding the words difficult to speak. He knew he sounded crazy and was terrified she would laugh in his face. "The Tarot believes they uphold a precarious balance of forces and as one of them I must follow a certain set of rules. I swore a vow to them, and part of that vow is that I can never love. It keeps me distant. It keeps me – alone."

For a moment Ophelia only stared, but then she dragged a breath and asked, "Never?" The question was soft and timid, as if she were afraid of the answer.

Jude slowly raised his eyes to meet hers. "Not unless I renounce my vow to the head of the Tarot," he explained, waiting for her to scoff, or blink, of laugh hysterically, but Ophelia did none of those things. She just stared, tracing his face with her dark, pondering eyes.

"Would you?" this time her voice barely formed sound at all, but Jude read her lips, his eyes locked on them, unable to look away.

"I -" he didn't know how to say it. He didn't know how to find the courage. They were inches apart, leaning toward one another as if waiting to break so they could collapse into each other's arms. "I might be willing to give up my vow. If it was right."

Ophelia did not move. She looked past him as her eyes glazed over, lost in thought.

"Ophelia," Jude reached out, touching her knee, terrified she was about to cry. "I'm sorry. I didn't mean to upset you."

Still fixated on the wall, Ophelia shook her head. She blinked, allowing one tear to escape her eyes. Jude considered capturing it with his thumb, but instead watched it roll down her cheek to land on her collarbone.

"You didn't say anything wrong, Jude," she finally said. "I'm the one who's wrong."

He didn't understand and pulled back to get a better look at her face, now crumpled. "Ophelia -"

"Please," she said, meeting his eyes once again, though hers were now red with tears. "Play me something else."

There was more than needed to be said, more he needed to explain, decisions to be made, but looking at her now, devastated by something she refused to share, he did not have the heart to make her speak. And once again he did not have the heart to deny her. "Okay," he said, taking his hand back and replacing it on the guitar. "I'll play for you."

The new song was sweet and sorrowful. She closed her eyes, letting more tears escape. They rolled down her cheeks like waves across the ocean, never-ending and silent. As Jude watched her, beautiful and tragic and needing him, he realized, even if he wasn't ready to say it aloud, he loved her.

The room began to shake; gentle, trembling, then violent.

Jude shot to his feet as Ophelia cried out and dishes crashed to the floor. She reached for his hand and grabbed it tightly. For a second Jude was distracted, wanting to hold her, comfort her, and the tremor worsened, books toppling from the shelves and a potted plant shattering to the floor in a mess of dirt and broken terracotta.

"What's happening?" Ophelia rose to her knees, teacup still clutched in her shaking hand.

"I don't know," Jude admitted, fear tight in his throat. If it really was an earthquake what was he supposed to do? Stop, drop, and roll? No. That didn't sound right. But what if it wasn't an earthquake? What if it was something much worse...?

He closed his eyes, knowing it was a warning. Just because he couldn't say the words *I love you*, didn't make them untrue. Maybe he wasn't in love, he tried to reason. Maybe it wasn't too late. He clung to that thought, to the fact that he hadn't completely made up his mind. He had not forsaken his vow. Not yet.

The shaking subsided.

When the dishes steadied and the room settled back in place, he stepped away from Ophelia, detangling his hand from hers. "I have to go check things out," he said, abandoning his guitar on the bed and grabbing his coat from the bedpost.

"But -" Ophelia put her teacup aside and stood, blankets falling from her shoulders until only his red scarf remained, wrapped snugly around her neck.

A pang of regret twisted Jude's heart and with it he felt the rumble return. *No.* He squeezed his eyes shut. He had to sort this out. He had to think this through before it was too late. "I'll be back," he said, turning away from her. "Just stay here."

Ophelia nodded, hurt in her eyes, and Jude left the apartment before he lost all control. He ran down the stairs and out the door, across the street and did not stop until he reached the corner.

Outside, the street buzzed with the aftermath of the quake. Store vendors and residents loitered around asking questions and pointing to random things. It appeared the shaking had not been isolated to Jude's apartment, though he wasn't sure if that was good or bad.

As he stepped away from the curb someone grabbed him by the arm and he spun, expecting to see Ophelia and surprised to find the Knight of Coins. "Sol," said Jude, "what are you doing here?"

"Some quake." Sol nodded to a nearby car crashed into a street pole.

Jude shoved his hands in his pockets and nodded. He had a feeling he knew where this was going. "Did the Magician send you?"

"No," Sol replied. "He doesn't know I'm here. Come, let's walk."

Jude frowned but followed the older knight down the street, shooting a look over his shoulder to make sure Ophelia did not follow. If there was anything he knew about her – which wasn't a whole hell of a lot - it was that she could pass virtually unseen in a crowd and that she never stayed put.

"I think you know that quake did not happen on its own."

"I had a feeling," Jude admitted, guilt sharp in his tone as he chanced a glance at his hand. His mark was still green, but barely, more like a tinge of moss than the vibrant emerald it shone when his vow was new. "I guess it's a little late to admit I'm at risk of breaking my vow."

"A little."

"What do I do?" he asked, utterly confused. "Being a knight is all I've ever known and apparently I'm not very good at it."

Sol stopped, turning to face him. "That's not true." He looked thoughtful, if a little disappointed. "You're a good Knight, Jude, and this doesn't have to be the end."

Jude's expression tightened. "What do you mean?"

"I know about the girl. She's lying to you, Jude. She's not who she says she is."

That struck Jude in a bad way. How could Sol possibly know Ophelia's secrets? And then he remembered he'd asked the older knight to find out. "What do you know?" Jude asked. He had never pressed Ophelia because he'd wanted her to tell the truth when she was ready, but if Sol knew something that would change how he felt - change the outcome of his vow- he needed to know now.

"I know everything," said Sol, his expression changing drastically, as if troubled by the news he was about to deliver. "I'm not eager to tell you...."

"Just tell me."

Sol looked to a group of men examining a broken window, avoiding Jude's eye. "She's working with some radical scientist. A theoretical physicist."

Jude made a face, confused. "What does Ophelia have to do with a scientist? She told me she's being tracked by criminals."

Sol gave him a look that said enough. Even though Jude had already guessed as much, it was clear Ophelia was not in trouble and she was most definitely not the daughter of a deceased criminal art dealer.

"It has something to do with the Magician," Sol continued. "She wants to destroy the Tarot, Jude. She's been sent by this scientist to follow us and she's been doing so for years. You have to stop what you're doing. You have to stop what you're feeling. She's a liar, and a con artist and she doesn't care for you like you do for her."

Jude shook his head, feeling a stress headache coming on. "I don't understand. Why would she be following us? Why would she want to destroy the Tarot and what does it have to do with me? With *us*?"

"I don't know," Sol reluctantly replied. "All I know is she's deceived you. And she's not what she seems. Everything she's ever said or done has been meant to disarm you; meant to break your vow so her and her uncle could take control of the worlds opposing forces from the Tarot."

"But how?"

Sol shrugged. "I'm not sure. I haven't got that far."

Jude's whole body felt like lead, heavy and immobile, his heart heaviest of all.

Sol placed a hand on his shoulder. "I can't pretend to understand, but I see how much this hurts you. We may not be brothers in blood but we are in oath and I take my vow seriously. It's my duty to protect you. It's my duty to protect the Order."

Jude snapped his eyes to meet Sol's. "You don't think I take my vow seriously? I've been killing myself for weeks trying to fight the way I feel, all to protect the Tarot. All because it says I should be someone I'm not."

Sol's expression hardened to stone. "It's impossible for you to be anything but what you are, Jude. You *are* the Knight of Swords. You were chosen."

"Yeah?" Jude goaded. "Well, I think you're looking at the Magician's one and only mistake." With that, he turned and stalked away. "Don't come after me," he shouted over his shoulder. If Sol was right, he had to confront her. He had to hear the truth from Ophelia's lips.

WATERS OF FATE
THE FAROE ISLANDS, NORWEGIAN SEA

Two hundred miles off the northern coast of mainland Scotland, a small island of jagged grey rock and lowland marshes rose from the rough black waters surrounding the Faroe Islands. Near the island's heart, Nicolai steered a small boat up a wide waterway, under an ancient stone viaduct and between two great trees, standing waist-deep in water.

As a wide, crystal-clear lake spread into view ahead Rosaline moved from the back of the boat for a better look and Nicolai laughed, making room. "Beautiful, isn't it?"

She looked back with a smile. "Yes."

At first, so much water had scared her. Back in Romania, Rosaline had learned to swim in a scummy pond surrounded by reeds, her toes squishing mucky bottom when she needed a break. But this water was different: deep and all-surrounding. In the end, Nicolai had convinced her to get on the boat, and now she was glad. The island was so breathtakingly beautiful she couldn't imagine never seeing it like this.

As the boat slid effortlessly under a canopy of low hanging branches, bowed to create a tunnel of green, Rosaline reached out, grabbing a handful of dry leaves and tossing them to the wind. She watched them scatter across the water as the trees fell away, drowned in the lake, and the House of Cups appeared: a towering castle of glass spires, footholds submerged deep in the water. From the gates, a long dock stretched onto the lake and a tall young man walked slowly along the planks to meet them.

From the boat, Rosaline watched the figure grow larger, and when at last they bumped against the dock the man caught the bow and pulled them in.

"Tristan," Nicolai greeted dourly.

The man smiled and Rosaline recognized him as the King of Cups. The memory seemed long ago now, foggy and distant, but she recalled his snow-white hair and dashing smile, even his eyes – so blue, yet so utterly different from Nicolai's in a way she couldn't quite explain.

"We've been waiting for your arrival." The king smiled as Nicolai tied off the boat, offering Rosaline a hand. Unsteady, she accepted and climbed clumsily onto the dock, glad for the solidity of ground.

"Thank you."

The king bowed his head. "Welcome home, Rosaline."

A smile broke across her face at his words. *Home.* When was the last time she'd had a real home? She bent her head back to stare up at the castle, mesmerized by the way it gleamed against the water. It seemed to float like a yacht, all glass windows and masts, and she wondered how deep the waters below her feet ran. High above, white towers shimmered, pearlescent, linked with stone passes and arched bridges, reminding her of a fairy-tale palace.

"Thank you for accompanying our to-be Queen." Tristan turned his back on Rosaline to face Nicolai, a distinct authority hardening his tone. "The Magician has asked for your return to Order Headquarters as soon as possible."

On the dock, Nicolai worked on the rope and gave a nod.

What did he mean 'return'? Concerned, Rosaline took a step back to her knight. "Leave?" she asked, her brow knit with worry. "But, you can't leave."

"Not yet," agreed Nicolai, but there was something about the way he looked at her that scared her, removed and forgone, as if he'd already said goodbye.

"You'll tell me before you go anywhere, right?"

"Knights are notoriously disappearing, Rosaline." Tristan stepped forward, placing a hand on the small of her back. "We cannot possibly keep him here. That would be selfish. The Magician needs his knight's service"

Before she could respond, Tristan steered her toward the castle doors; giant things carved with leaping trout, seashells and laughing mermaids. Working against him, she twisted around to see Nicolai rise and follow a few paces behind. He kept his distance, eyes fixed ahead, and it was clear by the look stamped on his face something was horribly wrong - he looked as if someone had torn out his heart and fed it to the sea. Rosaline felt her own heart thump in her chest, heavy with dread. There was something Nicolai hadn't told her – something that was killing him. Did he think she would fail the final task and be sent back to Paris? Did he know she could never possibly succeed?

"This way." Tristan regained her attention, leading her into the House of Cups' grand foyer. Momentarily, Rosaline lost her train of thought, dumbstruck with awe. A giant fountain of Poseidon stood center of the lavish marble room, decorated with white flowers and pearls tangled about his golden trident. Above, a glass domed ceiling spilled clear beautiful light onto polished stone floors where white rose pedals were scattered.

"Beautiful," said Rosaline, craning her neck to see a thundering waterfall that seemed to originate from the second story freefall into a stream below. The rushing water cut a path through the stone floor and disappeared through the wall on the far side of the vestibule, pouring into the lake beyond.

"I'm glad you like it." Tristan smiled at her wistfully. "I've had the Court of Cups working hard for your arrival."

She couldn't think of anything to say that would be worthy; no words expressed the sheer emotion of seeing this place – of being home, at last. "Thank you," she offered, knowing it wasn't enough.

"Go on," Tristan flashed a stunning smile, seeming to read her mind, "the fish won't bite."

Rosaline smiled politely and knelt by the river, stretching her fingers and trailing them in the cool water as little multi-colored fish nibbled. It tickled and she laughed, the sound bounding around the airy room.

"Come," said Tristan, "my page will show you your room."

As a young man with dark golden hair approached, she stood to meet him. The page wore a blue tunic, beret, and scarf draped about his shoulders in the fashion of his Tarot card, and the mist of the falls glistened off his skin, making him look fresh as a sea nymph. "Miss Rosaline," he greeted with a perfect bow. "I'm Eli, Page of Cups."

"Nice to meet you." She imitated an awkward curtsy.

Eli extended an arm for her to receive. "If you'll come with me?"

Torn between exploring the castle and staying with Nicolai, she turned to the knight for guidance. He stood apart from the group, leaning against the wall with a distant look upon his face. "It's all right," he said, though his voice remained dull, implying anything but.

"Will you come with me?" Rosaline asked, knowing she'd feel better with him close by. Whatever had him bothered, she hoped she could keep it at bay if he was near.

For a second she thought he would refuse, but then he nodded. "In a moment. I need to speak with Tristan first."

Reluctantly, Rosaline followed Eli from the room, watching as Tristan turned to the knight and began speaking in a low voice. Whatever the king said it was clear Nicolai did not approve, every line of his body rigid with defiance.

"Do you know what's wrong with Nicolai?" Rosaline asked as the page led her up a grand, sweeping staircase. "He seems troubled with Tristan."

Eli glanced back. "The king is kind, but cautious. I do not believe Nicolai has ever appreciated that quality in him. The Knight of Cups is a very open and honest, unlike the King who holds his feelings closer."

"But Nicolai likes Jude, the Knight of Swords, and he expresses himself about as much as a shoe."

Eli fought a smile, leading Rosaline down a long hall studded with beautiful wood doors. "The Knight of Swords is different. He doesn't have a choice. The king does. Here," Eli opened one of the doors and stepped inside, "this is your room for now." It was a small, but well appointed with a four-post bed and large window overlooking the water. "I'll give you a moment to get settled." As he left, a young woman appeared in the doorway, nearly swallowed by layers of crinoline.

"Do you need help?" Rosaline asked, moving toward her.

"Oh, no," the girl shifted her burden, revealing a ball gown sewn with hundreds of pearls and delicate lace trim. "There you are," she greeted with a friendly smile. "I'm Isadore. But please call me Isa, Three of Cups, sworn to the queen in friendship."

Three of Cups. Rosaline thought back to her cards, recalling its purpose. Three maidens with hands upheld in a toast to friendship. Rosaline had never been sworn a friend before, but the idea seemed nice. She smiled as Isadore laid the gown over the bed. "Is that for me?"

"Of course." Isadore trilled a laugh. "It was made especially for you."

For me? How wonderful. Rosaline could not remember owning anything half as beautiful. Breathless, she gathered the fabric in her hands. "It's so soft. Is it for the task?" It seemed strange to require a dress, but then again stranger things had happened.

Isadore looked mildly surprised. "For the task? Well, yes, I suppose it is."

"Oh, good." Rosaline clasped her hands, pleased.

"I'll help you dress." Isadore, a tea-cupped sized woman with white-blond hair and small sapphire eyes, went to work unbuttoning the dozens of tiny pearls along the back.

"Now?" Rosaline asked, wishing she had time to wash the soot off her skin and brush the knots from her hair. The journey from Erta Ale had been difficult and long and she still had sand in places she couldn't reach.

Isadore nodded, smoothing non-existent wrinkles from the silk. "We're in a bit of a hurry, actually. The Magician sent word the current Queen of Cups is dying as we speak...."

Rosaline chewed her lower lip, unsure how to feel. It seemed strange to grieve for the woman she was about to replace, but she was indebted to the dying queen for saving her from the streets.

"Don't fret," Isadore assured, catching the look on Rosaline's face. "The queen has lived a long life and seen her end coming. She was lucky. She had time for goodbyes and hugs and kisses. Not many get the chance." Isadore pulled the dress from the bed while Rosaline nodded and stripped to her underwear, letting her ragged gypsy clothes fall to the floor.

When Isadore finished, Rosaline stood in front of a tall gilded mirror, admiring the swish of silk on her slender frame, pretty as a bell. The neckline was modest, the bodice boned and corseted, the skirt full and underlain with crinoline making her look like a frosted cupcake, ready to be eaten or put on display.

"It's so pretty," she said, running a hand along each perfect pearl decorating the neckline.

Isadore smiled, coming up behind her. "The finishing touch," she said, placing a silver robe around Rosaline's shoulders and tying it with a blue silk ribbon.

The robe shimmered like moonlight and Rosaline wondered if it was the same material as Adalain's blindfold, slipping through her fingers like water. Isadore returned to her side with a gold circlet, placing it on Rosaline's head and ignoring the mess of tussled curls beneath.

Complete, Rosaline found it impossible see beyond the matted hair and dirty fingernails, and the more she stared in the mirror, the more she saw the same scrubby-faced gypsy she'd always seen. Maybe it was impossible for someone like her to become a queen? Maybe it had never been in her cards at all?

"You are stunning," Nicolai said from the door.

She turned and smiled, forgetting the dirt and grime, seeing only him. "Thank you."

"Isa, can give us a minute?" asked Nicolai, leaning against the doorframe with his ankles crossed and arms folded over his chest. The Three of Cups bowed her head and left, flashing Nicolai a blushing look as she went.

"I look silly, don't I?" Rosaline asked, feeling a bit ridiculous in the fancy gown. Nothing about her was fancy; she was all bone, scraped knees, and fly-away hair.

"No," said Nicolai firmly. "You look like a queen." The words were heavy and his eyes glinted with sorrow.

Rosaline took a cautious step forward, one hand partly outstretched, undecided if she should touch him or leave him be. "I can tell something is wrong," she said. "Tell me, please. It's making me sick." She wrapped one arm about her stomach, trying to quell the rising waves of anxiety.

Nicolai stepped into the room, taking her hands in his. "Do you remember that day on the mountain? You said you knew you'd find me?"

Rosaline didn't like his tone. It was frightening. "Nicolai, what's going on?"

"Do you remember?" he asked again, the urgency unmistakable in his voice.

"Yes," she answered, nodding. "I remember."

"What if you had never found me? What if it meant your life would be easier? Would you still have searched?"

"What are you talking about? Nicolai, stop." She tried to back away, but he held on.

"Just answer me, Rose. Please."

A sob lodged in her throat at the desperation in his eyes. "I didn't know what I was looking for until I found you...I couldn't have."

He searched her face for something more, something deeper. "What makes you think it was me you found and not this?" he nodded to the room, the gown, to the whole of the Tarot.

Afraid and confused, her gaze faltered, finding every corner of the room. "I don't understand what you mean."

"Maybe you were never supposed to find me. Maybe you were supposed to find the Tarot and I just tagged along."

"What? No." She gave her head a resolute shake. "I found the Tarot because that's where you were. Not the other way around."

"Rose," Nicolai exhaled her name, gritty, placing a hand on the side of her cheek so she had no choice but to look him in the eyes. "Do you know what your last task is?"

"How would I know?" she scolded. Why was he doing this now? Why would he put her through this right before her final task? It was cruel....

Several heart-pounding seconds passed before he spoke again. "Why do you think you're wearing that dress?"

Rosaline looked down, blinking at the white lace and crinoline. "A party?" she suggested. "For when I become queen?"

"Not a party, Rose...a wedding."

That couldn't be right. She stared at him, accusing, as if he were lying to scare her. "What are you talking about?" she pulled away, confused. "Who's wedding?"

"Rose." Nicolai took a deep breath, as if gathering strength to explain. "You have to marry Tristan, the King of Cups, and you have to do it before the old queen dies. It's the last task."

That was impossible. No one had ever mentioned anything about marriage. "But-" she shook her head, overwrought with denial. "I don't love him. I'm not even sixteen. I can't be old enough to marry."

In Nicolai's eyes she could see his heart break, the pain tearing across his face. "It doesn't matter. It's not about love or age - it's about the union. No king or queen can rule without a counterpart. You don't have to love him, but if you want to be queen, you do have to marry him."

Rosaline's face twisted, horror-stricken. "But I'm supposed to be free to love whoever I want. You said so," she protested, blaming him. "I am supposed to be able to live my life how I choose."

"And you are," said Nicolai, trying to calm her. "You just can't marry whoever you want. If you marry Tristan, if you become queen, you can never be with anyone else."

The world tilted beneath her feet. She dropped to her knees, clutching her sides as the wedding gown pooled around her. "But-?" She looked into Nicolai's pleading eyes. "What do I do?"

"I can't tell you what to do, Rose." Nicolai stood stiff, hands working at his side, balled into fists then flat, then fists. "If you marry him, you'll live in this castle and have everything you've ever wanted. If you refuse him, you will not be queen. The Magician will send you back to your old life in Paris."

"And you?"

"I don't know," he admitted. A frown pulled across his face as if drawn with black coal. "I have my vow... this is all I've ever known. If I leave the Order...."

"No," Rosaline shook her head, clutching at his ankles, blood rushing in her ears, thick and panicked. "You can't leave the Tarot. We'll both be destitute. We'll both be on the streets!"

"We could try -"

"No," she silenced him with a shriek. "You don't understand. I can't go back."

Deafening silence hung in the room, burdened with broken dreams. The dress was choking her now, the corset cutting and silk laced with poison. She wanted it off; she wanted to tear it free. "Do you want me to refuse?" She looked around the room, envisioning everything she'd ever wanted. "Do you want me not to be queen?"

"No." Nicolai stood unmoving, watching her with his own internal horror. "That's why I never said anything. I wanted you to have a chance. I didn't want you to be distracted. You *deserve* this life. I want you to be happy in this life and the next, forever, even if it isn't with me."

"Then why can't I marry him and have you too?" she felt sick for asking, but she had to know.

By the look on his face she could tell the question hurt. "You must respect your marriage to Tristan. If you break your marriage vow, you break your vow to the Order. Your heart is free to love, but you can never act on it. You must remain faithful to the king."

"What about Gretchen and Gustav?" she pleaded, searching for an answer, a way out. "How can they be married if they're brother and sister?"

"They are already blood," Nicolai explained, voice calm but trembling. "They don't need marriage to bind them."

The air was too thin and Rosaline struggled to breathe, clawing at the gown. "So I have to love you from afar? And you'll get married and have children and we'll all live under the same roof?"

"I would never do that." Nicolai knelt in front of her, taking her face in his hands. "Look at me. I would never do that to you, Rose. It's like you said - I have known you my whole life. And I will always know you, in this life and past and many to come. Nothing will change that."

"A lifetime is a long time." She bit her lip, fighting to keep control when all she wanted to do was scream. "Ten years from now you'll be lonely and I can't blame you. Look at Jude. It's destroyed him."

"Loneliness I can survive." Nicolai brushed his hand across her cheek. "Seeing you miserable, I can't."

"Either way, I lose." The irony made her laugh hysterically.

"But you also win." He silenced her with a disarming smile.

She stared at him, lost. "Kiss me, Nicolai."

A look passed between them – deep and knowing and Nicolai cupped her chin, drawing her close to press his lips softly against hers. Together they stood, clumsy as their arms tightened around one another. The kiss lingered sweetly, and in the distance Rosaline swore she heard music: a guitar, lonely and longing. And when at last Nicolai pulled away his cheeks were wet with her tears.

"Rosaline?" said Isadore from the door. "It's time."

PAST LIVES AND OTHER LIES
KRAKOW

Ophelia stood by the bed long after Jude had left, staring longingly at the door. Eventually, she grew tired of waiting for it to open and began tidying the flat to occupy her mind. As she was scrubbing dishes a knock sounded at the door. Surprised, she turned, wondering if Jude had forgotten his keys. And then a thought struck her: *what if it was Karazyna?* Instantly, her heart was in her throat and she dropped the bowl she was scrubbing with a clatter.

By the time she reached the door, a jealous fury had burst into her chest. "Can I help you?" she demanded, before the door was all the way open.

Only the waiting victim was not Karazyna, but Uncle Milo, standing meekly in the poorly lit hall.

"Uncle Milo?" She blinked, thinking it must be a hallucination. It was impossible for him to be here. "What are you doing here?"

"Can I come in?" he asked, darting a glance over her shoulder into the apartment.

It took a moment for the question to process. Eventually, she nodded and stood back, letting him pass. "You can't stay," she hurried to say, peering down the hall to ensure Jude wasn't coming up the stairs. "He'll be back any minute."

"I won't be long."

"I'm sure you won't," Ophelia replied under her breath, shutting the door. When she turned back Milo was already settled in the living room. Annoyed, she followed, shooting him a look that said 'hurry up and explain.'

"I was worried," he said, running a hand through wild, unkempt hair.

Upon closer inspection, Ophelia noticed Milo's clothes were rumpled and stained and that he smelled as if he hadn't washed in weeks. "What happened to you?" she asked, crinkling her nose in disgust.

"Me?" Milo pointed to himself. "What about me?"

"You look like you've been hit by a garbage truck. And then rolled in it. And then threw up in it."

Milo made a face. "Don't be ridiculous."

"I'm never ridiculous," countered Ophelia, gravely serious. "Tell me what you're doing here and be quick about it. Do you want Jude to see you here? Do you want to risk your precious Omniworld?" Her words were clipped with anger, but the fear of Jude discovering Milo was stifling. She was so close to having the life she wanted it terrified her. The thought of going back to London and helping Milo spy on the Tarot made her sick. She wouldn't do it. And she wouldn't let Milo take Jude away from her.

"I was worried about you," Milo repeated, blinking with eyes oddly big and goggling.

Ophelia put a hand on her hip, scrutinizing her uncle with narrowed eyes. "You were worried about me?" she mirrored his earlier action, pointing to herself with an exaggerated finger.

"You never returned my call last night," he explained in a faraway sing-song voice. "I waited and waited and the phone just rang and rang."

Ophelia cleared her throat in discomfort. She had no idea how to explain the incident with Sol without admitting she'd been so careless. "You didn't have to come all this way."

"But I did." His voice was growing more bizarre, now haunted and tense and impossible to dismiss. "I didn't know what happened to you. I thought someone.... I thought it was my fault...."

Ophelia's tilted her head, examining the stranger before her. The uncle she knew was odd, yes, but not twitchy, and he was always hygienically inclined. She crossed the room quickly, concern reflecting in her eyes. Milo flinched when she stopped before him, searching the air above his head for something that wasn't there.

"I'm fine Uncle Milo, but are you?" she asked, talking slowly. Something was definitely wrong, she could see it in his eyes; madness burning bright around the edges.

"Fine," echoed Milo, eyes darting as if tracking a fly. "Good. That's good. It will work."

"What?" Ophelia took a half step closer. In the scummy light from the window she noticed dark circles under his eyes, purple and bruised. Fear blossomed in her stomach and a sticky lump formed in the throat. Milo might not be a candidate for parent of the year, but he was still her family. She still loved him. She grabbed his hand, suddenly terrified, and notice how badly it shook. "You don't seem well," she said, alarm tightening her voice. "We should get you to the hospital. Did you hit your head?"

Milo quirked his head like a bird, listening, ignoring her grip on his wrist. "What was that?"

"What was what?" she asked.

"I'm fine." Milo suddenly lunged forward, pushing her back. "I'm fine. I'm fine. It will work."

Unprepared, Ophelia thumped back on her hands, startled. When she regained her sense, she climbed to her knees, facing Milo. "What will work, Uncle Milo? The Omniworld?"

"What?" He shouted, looking at her, appalled, as if she'd slapped him. "What did you say?"

"Uncle Milo?" Dread snatched her breath and squeezed the air from her lungs. "Please, talk to me. You're scaring me."

Milo blinked several times and his eyes seemed to clear a little. "Sorry, Sweet Pea," he said, his voice flat. "I'm a little confused sometimes. It will pass."

Tears welled in Ophelia's eyes, but she fought them back, not wanting Milo to see. She rested one hand on his leg. "I'm going to get you some help. You'll be fine." She smiled through her tears, needing him to believe it would be okay. This was the only person she'd ever been able to call hers. She couldn't lose him.

"I was just worried about you," he said. "I came to tell you- "

"Tell me what?"

Then he was gone, whirling like a leaf caught in the wind, muttering, "It will work. It will work. It will work...."

"No. No, no. Uncle Milo. Uncle Milo I'm here. Come back." She snapped her fingers in his face, frantic, but it was too late. "Come back," she grabbed his hand, crushing his fingers. "Please!"

Milo ripped his hand away and clutched it to his chest like a broken wing. Confusion clouded his eyes, veiling him from her, just as the necklace had once done for Jude. It was a bizarre moment to miss that necklace, she hadn't thought of it since the day she'd realized it was gone, but now she wished for it. It had been meant to keep her safe. Milo had kept her safe. "You'll get better," she promised him, her words choked with tears. "I'm going to get you help. You wait here, okay?"

Milo continued to stare blankly ahead.

On shaky legs, Ophelia climbed to her feet and stumbled toward kitchen. How had she missed the severity of this? She had wanted so badly for Milo to be proud of her that she'd failed to notice something was wrong with him.

In the kitchen she fumbled for the phone and knocked it off the stand. "Shit," she said, catching it by the cord and yanking it to her ear. At the sound of the dial tone she let out a breath, trying to steady her hand to dial. Just as she hit the number pad, a commotion came from the front hall, startling the receiver from her grasp. Again the phone dropped, clanging against the side of the cupboard as the front door banged open and heavy footsteps thudded into the apartment.

Paralyzed, her empty hand remained by her ear.

Jude.

He was back and he was going to see her half-mad uncle. She would have to explain. And what if Milo started talking?

Oh, god. No. This can't be happening. She whirled on her sneakers, desperate to intercept him in the hall. But it was too late. He was already in the living room, standing before her uncle with a look of horror on his face.

Only, it wasn't Jude.

"You," she breathed, lurching before the Magician. "What are you doing here?"

The Magician's head snapped in her direction. "Who are you?" he demanded, brows bent in furious question.

"Marty?" Milo rose from the chair, glassy eyes fixed on the other man. "Marty, is that you?"

Rosaline choked on a laugh, eyes darting between the two men. Had Milo called the Magician *Marty*?

The Magician spun back to face Milo. "What are you doing here?" he demanded of Milo, his voice layered with confusion. "I thought you were in London. How did you get here? *Why* are you here?"

Milo's face fell, murky with doubt. "I don't know. Where am I?"

"You're in Krakow," the Magician said with a hint of anger.

"I was looking for my niece," Milo replied, as if the thought had suddenly struck him. "The bellman said he'd delivered a message for her here yesterday."

The Magician took a half step forward. "Niece? What niece? What are you talking about?"

"How do you two know each other?" Ophelia put herself in the middle of the conversation, moving to stand between the two men while staring pointedly at her uncle.

"This man is my brother," the Magician explained in a tone that suggested he was both irritated and looking for answers. "I haven't seen him in eighteen years. The better question is how do you know him? And what are you doing here?"

Milo blinked and Ophelia gaped, pulling her gaze from her uncle's weathered face to the Magician's pinched one.

Not possible, she thought, shaking her head. Milo hated the Magician. He'd spent her entire life trying to bring him down. "Is this true?" she demanded, turning her fiery gaze back to Milo. "Is the Magician your brother?"

Milo continued to stare through her as if she weren't there.

Oh no, she thought crossly, *I will not go back to being invisible.*

Color rose in the Magician's face, scalding the tips of his ears. "How do you know me?" he asked, raking Ophelia with stormy grey eyes. "And what, may I ask, are you doing in Jude's apartment?"

How did she explain? The truth would never do. "He's my friend."

For a moment the Magician said nothing, grinding his jaw in silence. Then he inhaled with a sharp gasp. "You're the girl!" He seemed stricken, immobilized by realization. "You're the one that's causing all the trouble."

Ophelia made a face, offended. What right did he have to call her trouble? Sure, she *was* trouble, but he couldn't possibly know that unless Sol had managed to find him, and by the look on his face she didn't think that was the case. "What are you talking about?"

The Magician confronted Milo. "Milo, *who* is this girl?"

"Who? Her?" Milo pointed to Ophelia as if she were a passing waitress.

"Yes, her!"

For a second Ophelia thought Milo was going to shrug, which she might have preferred, but then he bit his lip and answered, "My niece."

Ophelia felt her world collapsing, slipping, sliding away like the contents off a sloped table. Everything she thought she knew exploded before her eyes. "Am I really?" she demanded. "Are you really my uncle? Or is that a lie too? You lied about knowing the Magician! You lied about everything I thought was true!"

Milo paled, dropping his shame-filled eyes to the floor. "I didn't lie. I just failed to mention the entire truth."

"Tell me you're really my uncle!" The anger was unbearable, searing her lungs and closing her throat. "Tell me the truth! Who am I?"

Milo met her fury with a long face. "You *are* my niece, Ophelia. I swear you're my blood."

"That's impossible," the Magician rumbled, tossing Ophelia an accusing glance. "We have no siblings and you were never married."

"I know that," Milo replied. "But she *is* my niece."

The Magician's face turned ghost-white. Slowly, he shifted his eyes to meet Ophelia's, unblinking. "She's -"

"Your daughter," Milo finished.

Daughter? Did he say daughter? Ophelia's stomach roiled and heaved, forcing her to run the kitchen and gag into the sink.

"My daughter?" she heard the Magician ask in the next room. "She's – Melissa's?"

"Yes," replied Milo, sounding remarkably coherent given his earlier state. "After Melissa died and you abandoned the baby, I found her. I took her, hoping you'd change your mind. When you didn't – and when those lunatics found you and talked you into joining their ridiculous cult - I knew I had to free you and fix this. I've spent years searching for a way to destroy the Tarot and set you free. I discovered the ancient Order of Science against Magic and their book of Athios. I built the Omniworld. I trained Ophelia to watch you; to track your Knights. I used formulas from the book to develop a veil so she wouldn't be spotted. I did it for you, Marty. You're my brother. All I ever wanted was to get you back...."

Stinky water and food crumbs stared back at Ophelia from the bottom of the sink. Her stomach continued to churn as her hands clamped around the metal edge so hard it cut. Everything was happening so fast. She couldn't breathe, she couldn't think.

"You used my own daughter to spy on me?" the Magician's voice filled the room like an orchestra, soft, then loud with comprehension, reaching a crescendo. "Milo. What have you done?"

Suddenly full of rage, Ophelia spun, wiping her mouth with the back of her hand. "Is it true?" she shouted, finding her voice through the noise in her head. The question bounced around the small flat, ringing in her ears.

Both the Magician and Milo looked to her from the next room. "Yes. It's true," her uncle finally answered, voice full of shame and regret.

Ophelia clenched her eyes, hoping against hope when she opened them everything would disappear. Everything except Jude. "It can't be."

"You look like her," came the Magician's voice, gentle now, as if he just realized what it meant. He was her biological father - he had abandoned her for the Tarot. "It's remarkable."

Angry tears stung Ophelia's eyes, spilling uncontrollably down her flushed cheeks. All her life she'd wondered who she was and now she knew: she had a mother who died and a father who had given her away. "You abandoned me?" she asked, quiet as breath on wind.

The Magician stared as if she were back from the dead, eyes wide, troubled yet transfixed, hands stiff at his sides. "It's complicated...."

"Complicated?" Ophelia's brow twitched then fell. "I bet."

The Magician winced, finding a crack in the wall to fix his gaze. "I was a mess after your mother died. I didn't know what to do. I couldn't take care of a baby. You reminded me so much of her...it was killing me. After...." He stopped with a shaky breath and tried again, "I went back to the foster home a few months later. I knew I'd made a mistake but it was too late, someone had adopted you and I thought you were gone forever."

That should have been the end of the story, what was there left to tell? But the Magician cleared his throat and continued, "While I was at the orphanage I saw a boy with black hair and blue eyes who'd just lost his family in a house fire. He was small and crying and hugging my leg, begging me not to go. My heart was broken and it was breaking for him, too. So, I took him in. I tried to replace you. It was a mistake. It was all a mistake."

What boy? Ophelia wondered, thinking of the Tarot members she knew. There was no boy of that description. Then the thought struck her, hard as a sack of bricks. *Jude. The little boy had been Jude.* And more importantly, she realized with a start, the Magician had brought him into the Order of the Tarot by *choice.* She was grappling for pieces, trying to put the puzzle together. Did it mean Jude was never meant to be the Knight of Swords? The Queen of Cups had never foreseen him to take the knight's place? Did he know?

"I'm sorry," said the Magician. "You have no idea how sorry I am. I didn't know. If I did...everything would be different."

Different. How long had she wanted things to be different?

The Magician found Milo in the shadows once more. "You should have told me. Why did you do this, Milo?"

Milo flinched, seemingly surprised to be addressed. "You joined the Tarot," he replied defensively. "You became the Magician. You were mad. I had to save you. I had to." He was falling back into madness, slipping away. "I had to make it work. It will work! It will work!"

The Magician took a step back, studying his brother. "What's wrong with him? He seems ill."

Ophelia felt empty all over again, robbed of a past; robbed of a childhood; robbed of a parent. Her world was broken, pieces of it scattered about the room - bits in Milo's hands, others in the Magician's eyes. Her heart was heavy and her chest tight. She needed air. She needed time to grieve and think. "Watch him," she said, striding across the room to the window.

"What are you doing?" asked the Magician, watching her with irritation. "It's cold outside. That won't help."

"I need a minute," she replied, grabbing hold of the frame and forcing the window open. "I'll be back."

"Wait a minute! We need to talk. There's more to say!"

But Ophelia didn't listen and she didn't stop. She climbed out the window and kept climbing until there was nothing left behind.

LOVE LOST
THE FAROE ISLANDS, NORWEGIAN SEA

Why hadn't she seen it; all the white – flowers, and lace and rose pedals? The foyer was set for a wedding, not a welcome, and Rosaline was the unsuspecting bride.

She stood atop the stairs in the shinning gown, a bouquet of white lilies clutched in her trembling hands and the golden circlet weighty upon her head. In the grand foyer, a crowd had gathered, children jumping from riverbank to riverbank, giggling as they made it safely across. Opposite the stairs, Tristan waited at the end of a long aisle, dressed in white with his arm tucked behind his back. He was deep in conversation with Eli, the page, and no one save Nicolai had noticed her arrival.

Her knight lingered at the bottom of the stairs, the only eyes in the room looking at her. A weak smile tugged at the corner of his mouth, but the effort seemed tortured and it broke Rosaline's heart.

Slowly, heads began to turn, eyes finding her. Some of the wedding guests smiled, others glared, one or two wept, and it was the first time since learning of the Order of the Tarot Rosaline realized what it meant. This was not a game. It was not all parties and crowns and fancy dresses. These were real people and this was a real job. It would be hard, just as hard as the streets of Paris, and these people would depend on her to predict succeeding members of the Tarot. Suddenly, it hit her. What if she couldn't do it? What if she'd spent so much time trying to prove she could be the next Queen of Cups she failed to realize she was incapable? She couldn't even remember the last time she'd done a reading without doubting her ability.

At the bottom of the stairs, her future waited, and it was no fairytale.

Rosaline scanned the crowd, searching for faces she knew. Where was Jude? Where was Matilda and Gretchen and Gustav? "Where's the Magician?" she asked aloud.

Isadore stood beside her, fussing over Rosaline's dress. "Hm?" she asked offhand. "Oh. He couldn't make it," she replied, straightening the gown's train with a tug. "Something came up. But he gave his blessing to proceed."

"Shouldn't we wait?" It seemed wrong to take the vow without him. He was the solidifying member of the Tarot. How could they proceed without his presence? Or maybe she was just looking for reasons to stall....

"No," Isadore clucked her tongue and patted Rosaline's hand in comfort. "I'm afraid we cannot wait. The Queen of Cups passed on a few hours ago and the world's balance is in a weakened state. If we wait...well I mustn't say what could happen if we wait. You must take your vow before it's too late."

Maggie. Rosaline had almost forgotten about the old woman– the woman she would replace. An intense feeling of guilt washed over her, but she couldn't say why. "But who will perform the marriage?" asked Rosaline tersely. "Who will make my mark?"

"Madeline, the High Priestess," Isadore explained, nodding to the raven haired woman Rosaline recognized from the Magician's manor. She stood beside Tristan dressed in a long blue robe with the crown of Isis upon her head and a silver amulet in the shape of the moon resting between her defined collar bones. As if sensing her stare, Madeline lifted her eyes, deep and knowing, connecting the distance between them.

"Come," the priestess' voice rang like the clearest bell, powerful and ancient to reach Rosaline at the top of the stairs. "You shall be wed and welcomed into the Tarot as our new Queen of Cups."

A murmur spread through the crowd, some approving, others not. That was a striking revelation. Rosaline had never considered some of the Tarot may not agree with her as Queen. In her head it had always been perfect, easy and effortless, with Nicolai by her side, Jude and the Magician looking on with approval as she stepped into her new life and left the old tattered one behind. But where were those people? And where was Nicolai's smile? Certainly not on his face. She felt vastly alone in a crowd of strangers, about to marry the biggest stranger of all.

Doubt ebbed and flowed. *You don't have to do this*, it hissed in her ear, *you can turn, you can flee, you can go back to Paris.*

"No." Never. She would not return to the streets. She would not welcome a life of poverty. This was her sacrifice. These were the cards she'd been dealt. She squeezed her eyes shut tight, banishing the doubt away.

"Sorry?" Isadore touched her shoulder with feather-light fingers. "Did you say something?"

Rosaline shook her head, rustling her veil as her eyes passed between the priestess, Tristan and lastly, Nicolai, where they rested. He gave her a nod, the slightest gesture with the biggest meaning, and she knew, no matter what, he would forgive her for what she was about to do.

"You must go," Isadore said, giving Rosaline a small push toward the first stair. "You cannot wait."

The sand in the hour glass had finally run out.

Rosaline thought of the dirt under her fingers nails and the deep ache of cold in her bones on the streets and she took the first step, then another, until she was standing level with Nicolai.

He held her gaze, his eyes searching hers for answers she could not give, encouraging the seed of doubt to grow. But then his eyes fell to the floor and the moment passed, vanishing like the sweet orange blossom she'd once held in her hand. A pang of sorrow tightened around her heart, but she stepped through the pain, and she was past him, leaving Nicolai behind.

At the end of the aisle Tristan smiled, perfect teeth gleaming in sunlight. Around his neck a jeweled fish winked obnoxiously, and at his back doors opened to the lake, crystal clear and blinding like the scene from a fairytale ending.

With each step Rosaline's feet became heavier, until they dragged as if weighted at her ankles, pulling her to a watery grave. Even the gown was cumbersome, weighted down with abandoned dreams. But she kept on. She was a gypsy and gypsies did not quit; one step after another until she reached her groom.

At the altar Tristan held out a hand. Rosaline gently placed hers in his, conscious of how wrong it felt, and tried not to look back.

Before them the Priestess stood tall, holding a large leather bound book with a look of grim responsibility etched on her beautifully aged face. "Rosaline," she began in a voice regal and sure, "do you accept this vow, this bond, to your husband, King of Cups, as a member of his House? Do you choose from your own freewill to walk with him as long as you both shall live under the sacred eye of the first High Priestess, honoring your position forever in the Order of the Tarot?"

"I do," she whispered, amazed the words didn't lodge.

The High Priestess nodded and turned her expressive eyes on Tristan. "King of Cups, ruler of the Isle, advisor to the Magician and counsel to your House, do you accept this new bride as your queen, to have and honor for as long as you both shall live under the Order of the Tarot?"

Tristan tightened his hold on Rosaline's hand, almost crushing. "I do."

The High Priestess nodded once more and turned to Eli who stood dutifully behind her. "Eli, the wand please."

Silently, Eli came forward, holding a long branch that looked as if it had been recently torn from a tree. Madeline took it gently, holding it for Rosaline to see. "This is the Sacred Wand, the first wand of the Wands, taken from Earth's first tree. It conducts magic and ties the Tarot to the Earth. Those who bear its mark shall be bound to the Earth and all its forces forever, until their passing or until their oath is broken."

Warily, Rosaline eyed the Sacred Wand. It looked like any other tree branch, stripped of off-shoots and leaves with a slight hook along smooth ash-white bark. Only, upon close inspection the branch was not so mundane. It seemed to be alive, tiny green lines criss-crossing over the surface, faint as iridescent veins on a hand.

Madeline stepped forward, extending the branch. "It you are prepared to accept the mark of your vow, please extend you left hand."

Ignoring the gnawing in her stomach, Rosaline stepped forward and gave Madeline her upturned palm, placing it gently in the older woman's. Delicately, The High Priestess touched the branch to Rosaline's skin. At first she felt nothing but a tingle, then slowly it turned to burning, white hot and painful, causing her to hiss and draw back.

"It stings a little," the High Priestess admitted with a sympathetic look, "but not for long, it the magic working its way into your blood."

The thought struck Rosaline as oddly gruesome, but she had come too far to give up now. This was the last step; the last challenge to win her new life. Determined, she drew herself up and returned her hand to Madeline's. When the High Priestess resumed, Rosaline did not flinch.

It took several minutes for the Priestess to complete the marking - the wistful Queen of Cups in her throne, staring deep into a cup – and it was somewhat crude, but legible, and as promised, the sting quickly faded, leaving a warm sensation snaking through her veins.

"I feel funny," said Rosaline, suddenly dazed and finding it hard to see straight. She stumbled, nearly tripping over the hem of her skirt as she clutched her head, saved by the page Eli who steadied her with a hand.

"Yes," the High Priestess replied kindly. "It's the magic. You'll get used to it. It takes a few hours for your body to adjust." Madeline handed the Sacred Wand back to Eli who took it and replaced it in a beautifully carved wood box. "Are you ready?" the woman whispered and after a moment to gather her churning thoughts Rosaline nodded. "Welcome to the Tarot." The High Priestess took Rosaline by the wrist and turned her to face the crowd, raising their conjoined hands as she announced, "Court of Cups, welcome your new Queen, Rosaline."

A roll of claps spread through the crowd, tentative at first, then louder, until the entire room shook with celebration. Streamers soared from the ceiling and flower petals dusted the room like snow, landing on Rosaline's cheeks, her hair, her dress....

She closed her eyes, feeling as if the world trembled beneath her feet. What had she done? The rising dread boiled in her stomach like bile and she was forced to her knees as her legs gave out.

"Rosaline," said Tristan, dropping beside her. "Are you all right?"

There was a gasp from the crowd and Rosaline opened her eyes to see Tristan rise and take two steps in the opposite direction, staring at something beyond the bobbing heads of onlookers. Through head fog and tear-filled eyes Rosaline tried to see past him. Cheers quickly turned to cries that turned to hysteria as the shaking intensified, so strong Rosaline knew it was no longer in her head. She saw people running, screaming, pushing, trying to get away from the violently shaking walls, but it was no use; the entire castle was shifting, moving, rumbling.

A bloody scream cut from her lungs, but it was swallowed by the sea of other cries. From somewhere she heard Tristan call her name, begging her to come, but they'd been separated in confusion and she had no desire to search for him. There was only one person she wanted to see, and she could not find him in the chaos. As she struggle back to her feet, intoxicated with magic and weighed down by the gown, cracks big as canyons formed across the ceiling as the floor beneath her lurched. Chunks of rock fell, crashing to the floor and covering the crowd in debris and white dust. Rosaline sucked in a scream then coughed, trying to expel the dust from her lungs – but it was thick and choking and refused to budge, coating her throat in plaster and cement.

Tears of regret and terror stung her eyes as she turned round and round, unsure of what to do or where to go. The entire room was in violent upheaval with no clear path for escape. *What have I done?* she thought, seconds before a block of concrete smashed at her feet, throwing fragments of rubble in her direction. She recoiled and fell backward over her dress, flattened against the cold hard floor, waiting for it to end. Had she done this? Had she broke her vow the second she'd taken it? She didn't want to know. She was too frightened to look at her hand, pressed to her racing heart, afraid she would find the mark black.

"Nicolai!" she cried out. "Nicolai!" She could feel the floor beneath her weaken. Across the room mothers desperately tried to save their children while men helped women from the floor. Yet no one stopped to help their new queen. It was as if she didn't exist. It was as if she was invisible. *Just like that girl on the train,* she thought ironically, wondering whatever happened to her. Had Jude found her? Had he discovered the truth?

And then Nicolai was there, rising from the wreckage and using his body as a shield.

"Nicolai," she said his name as a prayer, reaching for him through air thick with grime.

He reached her, gathering her in his arms like a lost child. "Thank god. I thought -"

"I'm sorry!" she begged, kissing his cheek, his mouth, his chin. "I'm so sorry. I made a mistake."

He grabbed her face roughly in his hands, smothering her hair. "Don't be sorry," he whispered soothingly.

"I want to be with you," Rosaline cried, twisting her hand in his shirt. She wanted so bad to take it back. Take it all back. "Only you. Take me home to Paris. Take me away from here."

Nicolai's face fell and around him the castle walls broke apart, allowing sea water to pour in over the trapped wedding guests. "Rosaline, I'm afraid it's too late."

"No." She refused to believe him, shaking her head and trembling uncontrollably. Her beautiful wedding gown was already soaked, her bouquet floating peacefully nearby. "I love you."

Nicolai placed a cold hand on her cheek and kissed her as if it would be the last chance he ever had. "I love you too," he said as the room pitched and the floor sunk in a heart-plunging drop.

"What's happening?" Rosaline clutched him tight, desperate to hold on as long as possible. Above them, the waterfall burst, spewing gallons of crushing water. The torrent hit hard, like a truck load of ice, knocking her back and filling her mouth with salt water. She coughed and kicked and fought her way back to Nicolai once more. In the onslaught she found his hand, locking her fingers around his, refusing to let go.

Nicolai cemented his grip. Water littered with debris and flower petals swam around their feet, rising to their ankles, their knees, followed by the booming echo of three-thousand tons of sinking stone. With his cheek pressed to hers, chest-to-chest, heart-to-heart, Nicolai held Rosaline tight and whispered, "I'm afraid our time is up."

THE VOW
KRAKOW

Of all the lies, of all the heartaches in history, Jude could not believe this one belonged to him.

White noise pounded in the background as he hurried up the stairs.

One floor.

How could she?

Two floors.

How had he'd fallen for it?

Three floors.

How had it come to this?

At the top of the stairs he stopped, hearing shouts rattling down the hall from his apartment. He recognized the Magician's troubled voice, but there was a second, one he didn't know, sounding close to hysteria. Jude hurried to the door and threw it open, filling the tiny front entrance with his wrath. "What the hell is going on?" he demanded before setting eyes on his unwelcome guests.

"Jude." The Magician turned, his face tight with surprise. "You're back."

"Yes, I'm back. This is *my* flat."

The Magician tipped his heady in concession. "I came looking for you."

"Who's this," Jude stabbed a gesture to the old man standing by the window with a vacant, yet pinched, look on his face.

"Ah," the Magician said, sounding incredibly tired, "this is my brother, Milo."

Jude made a face. "Your brother?" He studied the old wiry man, disbelieving. "Since when do you have a brother?"

"Since now," the Magician replied coolly.

"Milo," said the stranger, introducing himself unnecessarily. "You must be Jude."

Jude frowned, wrinkling his nose at the old man's stench. There was no way these two could be brothers. This man looked as if he belonged on the streets begging for loose change. "You've never mentioned a brother," Jude spoke to the Magician, though his gaze was fixed on Milo.

The Magician scrubbed his face with a sigh. "Well, it's been a long time. I wasn't sure I still had one."

Jude, growing more confused by the second, scratched his head and asked, "Is something wrong? What are you doing here?" Then he realized that Ophelia was nowhere to be found. "There was a girl here," he pointed to the spot where he'd last seen her, "where did she go?"

"Ophelia!" said the man at the window, trying climb out.

"Milo, no!" The Magician sprung after him, grabbing the other man by the back of the shirt and yanking him inside.

Jude's head pounded and he placed a hand to his temple. It felt as if someone had driven a nail into his skull and was slowly twisting it deeper, angled toward his right eye. "How do you know Ophelia?"

"Ophelia!" the crazed man parroted, eyes glued out the window, staring up at the sky as if waiting for an angel to appear. "My niece."

"What the hell is he talking about? Where is she? The girl."

The Magician was distracted, doing his best to keep the man from hoisting himself out the window and throwing himself to his death. "He's crazy," said the Magician, tossing the words over his shoulder. "But the girl you're in love with does happen to be related to this charming fellow."

Jude was horror-struck; first that the Magician knew of Ophelia, and second that this lunatic was the man who had sent her after him. "This is the brilliant scientist who had her spying on me?"

The Magician looked back sharply, nearly releasing his grip on his brother. "You *know* she was spying on you?"

"It was a recent discovery," Jude replied dryly.

"Ophelia!" Milo screamed.

The Magician grunted. "A little help here, Jude. Please?"

"Where is she now?" he asked, joining the Magician at the window and grabbing the old man by the belt.

Before he could answer, the Magician hissed, dropping to his knees and releasing Milo to Jude.

"What is it?" Jude asked, torn between Milo, his thoughts of Ophelia and the Magician who was clearly in pain.

The Magician did not reply, though he pulled up his right pant leg to reveal a freshly inked tattoo of the new Queen of Cups. "She took her vow," the Magician said, rubbing a hand of the brightly glowing mark, though as he spoke, it had already began to fade.

"It's fading," Jude said, astonished, nearly releasing Milo to the window.

"This isn't good," the Magician said, the blood draining from his face.

"Where's Ophelia?" Jude barked, jerking Milo inside for the second time.

"She went out," said the Magician, eyes glued on the fading mark as he pointed to the window.

"Out the window?"

"Ophelia!" Milo was still trying desperately to squirm free, slapping at Jude's hand. "Ophelia come back!"

"I'm going after her." Jude angrily yanked Milo back and shoved him to the ground beside his brother, using him as a foot stool to climb out the window.

"You can't." The Magician called after him, ignoring the whimpering Milo who was now drooped against the wall. "Jude, your vow! You've almost broken it! Please. I need to speak with you."

Jude stopped long enough to look back. "She lied to me, Magician. Trust me," he stepped onto the slippery ledge, "I will not break my vow."

"Wait," the Magician pleaded, shooting back to his feet and throwing his upper body through the window. "I must speak with you before you go. There are dire things that need to be said."

"Take care of your brother," Jude demanded, stepping out of the Magician's reach. "I'll be back."

"No! Wait!" the Magician entreated but Jude was already climbing away.

The roof was slick, covered in sleet and ice, and his feet kept sliding off the ledge, saved only by his fierce grip on the gutter. Eventually, he managed to hoist himself onto the roof, one knee then the other, until he was on his hands, clinging to roof tiles packed in snow.

Fingers burning with cold, he climbed to his feet and looked around. "Ophelia!" he called, cupping both hands around his mouth. "Ophelia, are you up here?"

A gust of wind picked up chimes and distant bells, but no Ophelia.

Carefully, Jude edged his way to the peak, hoping to get a better look. He kept low, one hand skimming the roof should he slip and need something to grab in a hurry. Down below Krakow was dizzyingly far, twisting and turning, dark and blanketed with snow. He could see the busy street of Godzka and beyond that the tower of Main Square where he'd first met Ophelia. He called her name again.

Nothing.

The silence was eternal but as he scanned the streets he caught a glimpse of red. "Ophelia!"

She was sitting on the next roof with her knees pulled to her chest, watching him, still wearing his scarf.

There was a wide gap between them, too far to jump, though she had crossed the same steel cable on their first encounter. Jude slowly made his way to the edge of the roof directly across from her. Somehow he managed to wedge his feet in the gutter and face her. "Ophelia, what are you doing?"

"You know, don't you?" she asked, staring at him, head held high, though he could see the glassiness in her eyes.

Jude thought about yelling, calling her a liar, screaming at her for what she'd done. But there was no point. He had known all along she deceived so how could he scold her for it now? It was his fault for letting her in. He'd accepted her without really knowing her, and there was no one else to blame but himself. "Yes," he replied. "I know who you are."

"Then what are you doing here?"

"Looking for you."

Frozen tears left tracks down her flushed cheeks. "Why?"

Jude opened his mouth then snapped it shut, unprepared. He shook his head and gave a small shrug. "I don't know. I guess I needed to know you were okay."

"I lied to you. I tried to destroy you."

"I know."

"And you don't care about that either?" Her voice was accusing, resentful.

Jude scoffed; irritated that she would think so. "Of course I care. What kind of question is that? What I don't understand is why you did it."

Ophelia' mouth twisted into a grimace. She squeezed her eyes tight, banishing more tears. "I did it because my uncle asked me to. That's the only reason. It had nothing to do with you. I didn't even know who you were. Not really. Not by name."

That didn't make Jude feel better. "But why did he ask you? Why does he want to harm the Tarot? We're the good guys." He had to fight from laughing. It felt strange to defend the Order after so many years of cursing them under his breath.

Ophelia stared at him through wet lashes, scrubbing tears away with the back of her mittens. "I don't know," she admitted wearily. "I thought he was doing the right thing. I thought he was trying to keep the world safe. But I think he really did it for his brother- the Magician."

"I see." Jude took a breath, not knowing where to steer the conversation. There were so many questions, so many revelations. "So did he do it? Did he find a way to destroy us?"

"I don't know," she said quietly, "Did he?"

The way she was looking at him pulled his heart in a million directions, none of them pleasant. "Nearly," he admitted, letting the words carry. "He nearly broke me. *You* nearly broke me."

Ophelia's face fell as she closed her eyes. "He didn't really succeed. He's sick. I don't know how long it's been since he's lost his mind, but his machine never worked. The Tarot is safe."

"I'm sorry," said Jude, not really sure why he was apologizing. Was he sorry for her uncle going mad? Or that she'd failed?

"Don't be." Her expression changed, breaking from despair to torture. "Why are you being so nice? I tricked you into liking me. I deceived you. I'm no good, Jude. I'm a con artist. I don't deserve your kindness."

Jude gave her a punishing look, wishing they weren't so far apart. It was only feet but it felt like miles. "You didn't *trick* me into liking you."

"Yes, I did," she snapped. "I lied so you would fall in love with me and break your vow."

"No," he spat, annoyed by her rendition of the truth. "I have never believed anything you said, Ophelia; except maybe your name. And it turns out I like you despite your lies, not because of them."

She looked startled, blinking. "You said like."

"So?"

"Present tense."

That caught him off guard. He took a pointed breath. "I'm angry," he admitted. "I'm really, really angry that you pretended to like me to break my vow. But it doesn't mean I blame you for it."

"You should blame me," she said, wrapping her arms around her knees and fixing her gaze somewhere far below. "I did it because I wanted to. I did it because it's the only thing I've ever known how to do. And I did it because I wanted my uncle to be proud of me."

"Fine," said Jude. If she wanted him to blame her, he would. But it didn't change much.

"But I never pretended to like you," she added after a beat.

What did she mean? He wanted to know – no, he *needed* to know. "No?"

Now it was her turn to be angry, eyes flashing fire. "Of course not," she shouted. "I've always liked you, Jude. Ever since we were kids. I saw you in Paris, did you know that? The first time you went with the Magician. And I knew then you were special. Nothing like the others."

That was news to him. He tried to hide his surprise. "No. I didn't know that."

"It was the first time my uncle ever asked me to follow the Magician and I followed you all the way there on the train. You never saw me."

"But why couldn't I see you? I would have noticed you, Ophelia. I would have noticed you anywhere."

Ophelia eyes bled with pain. "Because you weren't looking."

Jude knew it wasn't the whole story, but it didn't seem like the time to ask for answers. "If you're so angry with me then why are you still sitting on my roof?"

She chewed her lip. "I'm sitting on your neighbor's roof, actually."

Jude scowled. "You know what I mean."

"Yeah," Ophelia agreed dully, "I know what you mean."

"So what do you want from me?"

"You're a knight, aren't you?"

That was a stupid question. "Yes," he hurled the response across the gap, letting it slap her in the face, though she didn't flinch.

"I was hoping you would save me."

He gave her a look, one that said so many things and yet not enough. "You still want me to save you?"

She gave a small, barely perceptible, nod. "Always."

He hurt so badly and he was so damn broken. How could he possibly save her and fix himself too?

"Do you hate me?" she asked, not looking at him.

"No."

"You should."

"Maybe," he agreed. "But I don't." Something sparked in him, reconnecting whatever it was he had monetarily lost. "Come back." He stood. "And I promise I'll try my hardest to save you."

Shadows flickered behind Ophelia's eyes. Wordlessly, she brushed the snow from her pants and stood. As she stepped onto the wire Jude found he wanted to hold her and never let go. Despite everything, despite all the stupid lies and harder truths, he wanted her, and nothing could stop it. Nothing he said or did would change that, because now he knew her light and dark and he loved every part. They would go downstairs, back into his tiny little apartment and confront the Magician, and there he would renounce his vow and she would quit her uncle's work, and they would scrounge a life out of this miserable Earth, together.

Ophelia reached the roof and Jude grabbed her around the waist, pulling her to safety.

"I'm sorry," she said, her arms tight around him.

"I know." Jude wiped a tear from her cheek and kissed her softly.

Just then, as their lips touched, Jude felt his vow snap clean in two. The jolt was tremendous, pushing them apart like the hands of god.

"What's happening?" Ophelia asked, eyes darting for an answer.

"My vow," he breathed, staring at his hand, his mark gone deathly black. "It's broken. It's too late."

The shaking was sudden and violent and unmistakably real. Ophelia screamed and Jude tried to grab her but the roof shifted beneath his feet and he was knocked back. For a moment she teetered on the edge of the world and Jude saw her on an icy mountain in another place, in another time, caught on a wisp of air. Their eyes locked one last time and as his red scarf caught on the wind she fell from the roof. She fell so far he would never find her. She fell so far she would never return to Earth.

In the distance Jude swore he heard someone scream, "I thought it would work. I thought it would work."

A NEW BEGINNING
PARIS

It was a miserable day in the Tuileries Gardens and Rosaline was cranky, cold and tired. Her hands were frozen and her hair hung in limp strands from earlier rain. Business had been slow all day, and at this rate she wouldn't have enough money for dinner, let alone a place to spend the night. She shivered, thinking of the dark underside of the bridge where she often slept. It was times like this she felt most sorry for herself, silently grumbling at her mother for leading a lackadaisical life and her father for being, well - horrible. But her grumblings changed nothing. She was still a homeless gypsy reading Tarot cards on the streets of Paris.

While shuffling the cards to keep her fingers nimble, she had the strangest urge to look up. As she did so, she met the eyes of a young man making his way toward her. Instantly, she knew him: the Knight of Swords. The boy from her visions. He'd come at last.

A twinge of excitement flitted through her. Was this it? Was this the moment her life would change? Her visions had certainly hinted so, and there was no mistaking the young man's face: kind but hard, eyes the color of endless ocean. *Yes*, she thought, *I know it's him.*

Eager, she sat forward. Did she accept his offer? What would happen if she did? Surely nothing could be worse than her life in Paris.

"Are you Rosaline?" the young man asked, one foot on the path as if hesitating in decision.

Rosaline pointed to the sign, rattling the bangles around her wrists. "That's what the sign says, doesn't it?"

"It does," he agreed.

"Do you want a reading or not?" she asked, hurrying him along. If he was going to offer her a new life, she wanted him to do it quickly so she could get out of the drizzle.

"Please," he replied, taking a seat on the edge of the blanket.

Rosaline shuffled the cards, spreading them on the blanket in an arc. "Choose one." She nodded, already knowing which he would choose. The young man selected the card she'd guessed, holding it between two fingers. "The Knight of Swords," she said without needing to verify. "This is you?" The question wasn't really a question, but a hint to another, '*Are you truly the Knight of Swords, come to take me away to a better life?'*

He placed the card on the blanket and inclined his head. "Yes."

Rosaline hmmed then gathered the cards, splitting the deck in three. "Choose one." Again, the young knight chose without hesitation and Rosaline stacked the deck with his selection, flipping the first card. "The Tower," she said, crossing it over the knight.

A smile tilted across face, as if darkly amused. "You think I'm ruined?"

"I only read the cards," answered Rosaline, though truthfully she did see his ruin – great ruin, but that was none of her concern. "They say what they want." She pulled the next card from the deck and laid it horizontally across the Tower. *The Queen of Cups.* "This is your obstacle." *More than he realizes,* thought Rosaline with a knowing spark in her eye.

The young knight looked as if he wanted to say something, but Rosaline continued the reading, laying cards above and below. From there he remained relatively unmoved until she flipped the sixth card, the one representing the future coming into being: *The Lovers;* a card of attraction, love, and beauty – a man and a woman standing side-by-side under a starburst sky.

Rosaline did not know much about this particular young man except that he was her mind's representation of the Knight of Swords come to give her a new life - whatever that meant. Sometimes it was hard to decipher her visions, details foggy at best, and she knew little to nothing of him as a person, but the surprise on his face was enough to tell her she'd hit a chord with this particular card.

Curious, she thought, wondering why the Lovers caused such a stir. She slid the card in his direction, nudging. "Unexpected?"

With a grunt, the knight regained control of his expression, taking a closer look. "It's wrong," he said, matter-of-fact.

Rosaline shrugged again, gathering her cards and shuffling them back in the deck. "Think what you like, but the cards are never wrong."

The knight's expression hardened. "I'm not actually here for the cards. I'm here with an invitation"

Rosaline let his words sink in, savoring every note like candy. Her future had arrived – finally. And all she had to do was reach out and accept. "I know…."

"Do you?"

Just as she was about to reply another of her cloudy visions interrupted, this one fast and furious, seizing her attention and jerking her from reality in a whirr of color and images and faces blurred together to form the future….

A dinner, *a boy with golden hair,* a forest. She gasped as the images kept coming, barraging her with the future. A Coin Box, an ice castle, a land of fire and rock. A wedding. *Destruction*. And not just her own future but the knight's as well, intertwined - a necklace, a girl, a machine, the Magician, a secret, a lie, a stalker, a broken vow and…death.

When at last the vision subsided and Rosaline returned to the present in a breathless state, the gardens were in shambles, chairs overturned, trinkets strewn across pathways and leaves floating in the basin.

The knight, who she now knew as Jude, untangled himself from the windblown blanket, looking at her with deeply troubled eyes. "Are you okay?" he asked.

Rosaline blinked, eyes fixing on a girl standing alone across the square. She stared at the girl as if from the opposite side of a two-way mirror, and without having to ask, she knew it was Ophelia, the girl who would one-day destroy Jude. Or maybe… she would save him. After all, the future was never set in stone. Her mother, not good for much, had taught her that.

Jude turned, searching for whatever had caught Rosaline's eye, but of course, he saw nothing. Ophelia wore her metal charm and it would keep her hidden from the Order of the Tarot until she decided otherwise or until someone snatched the necklace away.

"What are you looking at?" Jude asked, his voice growing impatient.

"Nothing," Rosaline replied. "It's just -" she began, but then stopped, tugging hair from her face while she tried to find the right words in her rather small vocabulary.

"What?" Jude's brow creased, imploring. This boy may be many things, but he was not stupid and he was no fool. "What did you see?"

Rosaline angled her head, considering him. How much did he understand? Did he know what his future held? Part of her wanted to tell him - he deserved to know. Maybe then he'd stop blaming himself and have a real chance at life. But instead Rosaline straightened her blanket and found the Lovers card hidden in the folds. "I saw this," she said, handing it to him.

Jude frowned, tentatively taking the card.

"Tell me," Rosaline pointed to it. "Do you believe in the Tarot? Do you believe that I can see your future?"

Looking rather uncomfortable, Jude adjusted the scarf around his neck. "I would be stupid not to, all things considered."

Rosaline nodded in agreement. "Then it should be no surprise that I already know why you're here." Calmly, she shuffled her cards back into a neat pile. "You don't have to explain. And thank you, but I decline."

Jude jerked his head as though he'd been punched in the face by surprise. "Are you *sure* you understand?"

"Yes," Rosaline insisted and then decided to elaborate for demonstration, "I know about the Order of the Tarot and your Magician, Mr. Knight. But I have just seen my future, and yours, and the price is too high."

"My future?" Jude looked a little frightened, pointing to himself as if there might be another person.

"Of course."

"Forgive me," he began carefully, "but you live in a park. How could the price of what I ask possibly be too high? What do you have to lose?"

"My heart," replied Rosaline in a low voice. "Love is worth more than any life as queen. I understand that now."

A deep line etched across Jude's brow, drawing his face in confusion – they were always confused, Tarot clientele, humming and hawing over a future they couldn't see. But one day it would be clear, and then that person would say, *ah*, as Rosaline's prediction came to fruition. Too bad she was never around to see it.

"You're just a kid," Jude went on. "You can't possibly know what love is."

"No?" she arched her brow as high as it would go. "And you do?"

The knight's cheeks flushed, hot and uncomfortable. "I have a feeling you already know I don't."

"Not yet," she agreed. "But soon."

Jude gave her a look of utter skepticism. "If you're as gifted as you say, you should know that's impossible. I can't love."

"Nothing is impossible."

For nearly a minute, Jude said nothing, continuing to stare in disturbed question. Eventually, he grew tired, or fed up, and gathered himself to leave. "Well, I appreciate the insight, Miss Rosaline, or whatever your name is, but I should be going. I have to find a new replacement now and the Magician won't be happy."

"Wait," said Rosaline, raising a hand. "I have more to tell you."

Jude's expression remained guarded but he settled back. "Go on then. Be quick about it."

Slightly off put by his demanding tone, she took her time replying, "Rescind your vow."

A look sharp as glass cut across Jude's face. "Careful gypsy, you're overstepping."

"Maybe," she agreed, "but you should listen anyway. The Magician has a plan for you, but he is too fretful to share it and he won't – at least not in time – unless you withdraw your vow."

Disquiet flickered behind Jude's stormy eyes, although his body remained still.

It shouldn't have pleased Ophelia to see him this way, but it did - payback for the train ride that would never happen. "Oh," she added with a syrupy smile, "you should also know someone is trying to break your vow."

"Break my vow?" Jude's already puzzled brow drooped even lower. "Why would anyone want to do that?"

"Because they have no choice. They are chained to their life, as you are to yours. That said, you should forgive them."

"Forgive them?" Jude scoffed. "Who? And why would I do that? That makes no sense."

Rosalie smiled. "The future yet unraveled rarely does."

"Of course not," Jude gave her a cynical look, as if he didn't believe her, but was trying to mollify her in case she turned out to be crazy.

Rosaline tucked her cards away, pleased. "Just one more thing."

"Oh. Please share. I'm all ears…."

"Tell Nicolai I'm looking for him."

The shock exploding across Jude's face was plain. "Nicolai?" he echoed, as if trying to comprehend the name.

"Promise me."

For a moment Jude looked as if he were about to refuse, but then his expression relaxed and he laughed, shaking his head. "Yeah, sure. I'll tell him, little gypsy."

"Don't forget."

"No." Jude got to his feet, tugging the scarf around his neck. "I don't think I could forget if I tried."

"Good."

"Goodbye, strange girl." He turned to walk away and then stopped, looking back. "Hey. What's your real name?"

Rosaline glanced at the fallen sign by her blanket, mildly surprised. "How did you know?"

Jude shrugged. "I'm good at seeing through lies."

A smile broke across Rosaline's face, strangely proud. It was funny to feel she knew him. Her visions always seemed to do that; so real it was hard to tell the difference. "Rosaline was my mother. My name is just plain Rose."

"Rose," said Jude, testing the sound. "It's sweet. It suits you."

"Thank you."

With a tip of his head, Jude turned and left. He walked slowly and when he reached the water basin he stopped, staring at the invisible girl, searching as if he sensed her.

The girl, Ophelia, stiffened and stepped back. And for a moment they stood, face-to-face, yet worlds apart. Eventually, Jude moved on, the wind tugging the tail of his scarf as he turned the corner out of sight.

After, Rosaline returned to her job, straightening the blanket and sign, hoping she'd made the right choice. *If he sends Nicolai, which I think he will, it will all be worth it,* she told herself, feeling warm despite the cold. Another future awaited now, one that would be a surprise. As she daydreamed of her knight's face, a shadow fell across her lap. She looked up expectantly. "Oh. Hello."

"I know you know something. Will you tell me?" asked Ophelia, arms crossed over her chest with a scowl ruining her pretty face.

Rosaline stared at her blankly.

"Fine, don't tell me." Ophelia moved like she was going to leave but then changed her mind, turning back. "If you can't tell me, then tell me what you told him. What made him look at me?"

"Well," smiled Rose, "I told him he was going to fall in love."

42601952R00193

Printed in Poland
by Amazon Fulfillment
Poland Sp. z o.o., Wrocław